More praise for Gail Godwin
and *The Finishing School*

"Long before the terms 'role model' and 'mentor' entered common parlance, adolescents sought the company of grown-ups, other than their own parents, whose sympathetic interest and vivid presence represented the best of the adult world. . . . In her fine novel, *The Finishing School*, Gail Godwin charts the exhilaration, the enchantment, the transformation, then the inevitable disillusionment and loss inherent in such a friendship and such self-discovery. . . . Her characterization is one of the most trustworthy portraits of an adolescent in current literature."
—*The New York Times Book Review*

"She never for a second loses the reader's attention."
—*The Wall Street Journal*

"An arresting story . . . The pleasure of reading *The Finishing School* is nearly equaled by the fun of thinking about it afterward."
—*The New York Times*

"Makes an indelible impression . . . Gail Godwin is in top form!"
—*San Diego Tribune*

"An engaging, shapely narrative of cumulative power . . . It helps us to live our lives."
—*The New Republic*

"Marvelous, moving drama . . . Not only the dominant strains of the story keep running through one's head, but all those deeply buried harmonies and variations, too."
—*Mademoiselle*

"Irresistible storytelling . . . Just as immediate and affecting as *A Mother and Two Daughters*."
—*Kirkus Reviews*

Also by Gail Godwin

FICTION

Evenings at Five: A Novel and Five Stories
Evensong
The Good Husband
Father Melancholy's Daughter
A Southern Family
Mr. Bedford and the Muses (short stories)
A Mother and Two Daughters
Violet Clay
Dream Children (short stories)
The Odd Woman
Glass People
The Perfectionists

NONFICTION

Heart: A Natural History of the Heart-Filled Life

The finishing School

Gail Godwin

BALLANTINE BOOKS · NEW YORK

A Ballantine Book
Published by The Random House Publishing Group

www.ballantinebooks.com/BRC

Library of Congress Control Number 99-90162

ISBN 0-345-43190-1

Manufactured in the United States of America

First Ballantine Edition: May 1999
First Ballantine Reader's Circle Edition: April 2004

10   9   8   7

To the Ursulas of this world,

whoever they were—or weren't.

Bang verlangen wir nach einem Halte,
wir zu Jungen manchmal für das Alte
und zu alt für das, was niemals war.

(Anxiously we clamor for a hold,
we, too young sometimes for what is old
and too old for that which never was.)

—Rainer Maria Rilke, *Sonnets to Orpheus*, II, 23
(translated by M. D. Herter Norton)

THE FINISHING SCHOOL

I.

*L*ast night I dreamed of Ursula DeVane. We were sitting on the crumbling threshold of The Finishing School, and she was telling me something in her rich and compelling voice. Then, suddenly, the sky turned an ominous color, the pond shivered like a live thing, the old pines hissed and swayed, and hard rain pelted down.

"Let's make a run for it!" said Ursula, tensing her body for the dash.

"But why?" I asked. "We'll get soaked. Why not sit here and wait it out?"

"Ah, Justin," she said, putting her arm around my shoulders and giving me a shake. "Haven't I taught you anything? Didn't you learn anything from me?"

She leapt up and hurled herself boldly into the storm. Lightning cracked all around her. She was wet to the skin before she had even reached the far side of the pond. I huddled in the shelter of The Finishing School and watched with mounting despair as her figure grew smaller and dimmer in the downpour. I knew if I did not jump up and run after her now that I would lose her forever. But I was powerless to move.

When I woke, I could still feel the pressure of her touch on my shoulders. I could hear the pitch of her tender, teasing voice. All day I have gone around under the spell of that dream.

Is it the dream that has its hold on me, or is it Ursula herself, after all these years? In the dream we were the same age, both young girls; yet when I knew Ursula, that single summer, she was a woman of forty-four and I had just turned fourteen.

All day I have wondered whether I would want to see the real Ursula again, even if I knew where to find her. She would be seventy this year, if she is still alive. How would I feel about her now? Would she be very changed? Or would she, regardless of age and of the hardships she may have suffered since that summer's end, still retain the power to bewitch my imagination? Would her voice still enchant with its melody and its challenge? How would she feel about me? Would she be glad to see me, or would what happened at the end of the summer have eclipsed our friendship and made her bitter and angry? If I were to see her again, what would I say?

(Ursula, which were the true parts and which parts did you make up? Do you know, I am still trying to sort out which was which?

You'll be gratified to hear—at least, I hope you will—that I did choose a life in the arts. "Your soul craves that constant heightening of reality only art can give," you told me one afternoon, down at the old stone hut by the pond, which you called my "Finishing School," where you enthralled me with tales of your past and planted aspirations in me.

I'm sorry for the way I behaved at the end. The older I get, the more cruel that behavior seems. Yet, at the time, I was unable to behave any other way.

If you hadn't materialized that summer, I would have had to invent someone like you. If I hadn't come along, whom would you have invented? A girl like me? Or would just any gullible audience have served your purpose?

For what it's worth, you left your mark on me. Despite everything that happened, I have absorbed you. As long as I live, you live in me. Sometimes I hear myself speak in your voice. And, as you did, I watch its effects on others.)

I am a great respecter of dreams. Many turning points in my life have been heralded by dreams. A few have actually occurred in dreams. I believe that dreams transport us through the undersides of our days, and that if we wish to become acquainted with the dark side of what we are, the signposts are there, waiting for us to translate them. Dreams say what they mean, but they don't say it in daytime language.

A friend tells me she dreams regularly of a girl named Megan, whom she hated in grammar school. But over the years, in these dreams, Megan has grown up along with my friend, and they have become important to each other. My friend says she actually looks forward to her Megan dreams. In these dreams, after an initial animosity, the two get together and reveal how they have always secretly admired each other and wanted to be friends. Each shows striking insights into the other's nature and confides to her what strengths she has been jealous of all these years. The two of them discover they are opposites of the same self.

"But what about the real Megan?" I asked her. "Have you ever tried to get in touch with her again?"

"Good heavens, no." My friend laughed. "I'm sure *she* grew up to be a horrible person."

Which is to say: I won't hire a detective to go in search of a real seventy-year-old woman, who might still be found. (And who, perhaps, would retain her power to shatter or elude all my ideas of the kind of seventy-year-old woman she might have become, just as, during that summer, she was never as I expected her to be, from visit to visit.) But I will attend to what her image, playing its role in last night's dream, came to tell me. This is not the first time I have dreamed of Ursula DeVane. I dreamed of her on the night of the day I met her, and many times since. I will probably be dreaming about her for the rest of my life. She, along with a few others, has claimed a permanent place in the theater of my unconscious, where each figure—based wholly or in part on some real person—has its function.

When Ursula appears in a dream, it is usually to stir things up.

"There are two kinds of people," she once decreed to me emphatically. "One kind, you can tell just by looking at them at what point they congealed into their final selves. It might be a very *nice* self, but you know you can expect no more surprises from it. Whereas, the other kind keep moving, changing. With these people, you can never say, 'X stops here,' or, 'Now I know all there is to know about Y.' That doesn't mean they're unstable. Ah, no, far from it. They are *fluid*. They keep moving forward and making new trysts with life, and the motion of it keeps them young. In my opinion, they are the only people who are still alive. You must be constantly on your guard, Justin, against congealing. Don't be lulled by your youth. Though middle age is the traditional danger point, I suspect that many a fourteen-year-old has congealed during the long history of this world. If you ever feel it coming, you must do something quickly. . . ."

Over the years, her vivid figure of speech has stayed in my mind. "Am I congealing?" I ask myself. "Am I getting stuck in a role, repeating myself?" Or I will think, Poor So-and-So has congealed, gathering his same old themes around him like a shroud and being content to embroider them. I wonder if he knows it.

What would I be like if I congealed? Would I know it? Would I go on doing my work? Would others know?

The Ursulas of the world would.

"It's too bad about Justin," I can hear her say, launching into that *musical* tone she used when taking apart people's characters or summing up their fates. "When I knew Justin, she was just a young girl with large, questing eyes and very brown legs from riding her bicycle away from a house that was boring her to death. She was new to our village; she was disoriented. She had lost all the props that defined her. At the time we met, she saw herself as the victim of Tragedy: in a relatively short period, she had lost the grandparents who raised her, her father, and then her home. That is a lot to lose, of course, but hardly Tragedy to someone like myself, whose family *contretemps* would have kept Sophocles *and* Ibsen scribbling around the clock if they'd lived in our neighborhood. No, there are things much more tragic than the deaths of pleasant, unexceptional people and having to start all over in a new place.

"The girl's situation interested me, however. I have always been drawn to stories in which people have to start over. I saw immediately that, for all her sadness and disorientation, this girl was determined to escape the ordinary and had the intelligence to see that I was her best bet in the village. So you might say I was initially flattered by her recognition—one is taught by experience to put a premium on those few people who can appreciate you for what you are—and then I grew fonder of her as the summer progressed. There was a sweet, old-fashioned gravity about her; unlike most young people, she listened well. I loved to watch her face as she listened, and also when she struggled to articulate her thoughts. She was not as eloquent as she wanted to be, but she was better than she knew. I did what I could for her: fed her mind and stoked her desire for the larger life. If she hadn't burst in on me that summer, who else could have done it for her? Yes, I take my share of the credit for what she has become. Not that she ever thanked me for it. And she was very cruel at the last.

"I'm sorry, all the same, that she is in danger of congealing. She doesn't know where I am, but I've kept up with my old protégée, and I'm sad to say she shows signs of falling into complacency, that alarming early warning signal of congealment. She's done well, of course, but to reach the range and intensity I have seen others capable of, she must tap new sources of feeling. Or old sources which she turned away from at the end of that summer, when she was afraid and confused. Ah, Justin, if you were to come riding over to me again, I would stir up your blood. 'Don't you recall,' I would say, 'how I warned you to be alert for the first signs of jellification? How you must *fight*, the moment you feel its clammy grip. You must hurl yourself into action, take some new risk. Remember my ancestors, the Sires DeVeine; how, every spring, when the snows melted, they roused themselves from the snug stronghold of all their old trophies and triumphs and rode boldly down the Jura Pass looking for trouble?

"'When did you last leave *your* stronghold, Justin? When was the last time you went out alone, forsaking all the props that have come to define you?'"

Fourteen. Be fourteen again. Is that possible? Can I ride back into the country of youth, even on the conveyance of memory, propelled by imagination?

It was a long time ago. I was such a different person. What connection is there between the woman I am now and that lost, diffident girl pedaling up the steepest part of Old Clove Road, silently bargaining with herself, If I can reach the top of the hill without getting off my bike, something will happen, something will change . . . ? Well, right there is a connection. I still make superstitious bargains with myself. Only now I usually bargain for something specific. I have come to know, perhaps too well, what I want. On that May afternoon, I wished only for something interesting enough to rescue me from my present life.

Actually, I was not yet fourteen. My birthday was a month away. We had been living in this rural community—the township of Clove—in upstate New York for one month, my newly widowed mother, my little brother, and I. I still thought of it as enemy territory. Wasn't it part of "the North" that I had been brought up to hate because its interference and brutalities had destroyed our gracious past? By sheer geography, these Clove families with their harsh and peculiar names of Terwiliger and

Hasbrouck and DePuy and Osterhoudt were implicated with the rude general who, my grandfather said, had not had the decency to remove his foul-smelling cigar from his mouth while our noble Lee was in the act of signing away our way of life.

Not only that, but the people here were different. They were deep in themselves and slow to respond, not given to graces or flourishes. They were like their weather. As we had come north, last month, on the train from Virginia, I had watched in dismay as the green on the trees folded back into red buds and then disappeared altogether as we came close to our destination. Why had my mother done this to us? I still could not understand. She had said we could no longer afford to live in the big house on Washington Avenue, the only house I had known in my life. Well, I had accepted that. My grandparents' illnesses had eaten up the family savings and my father's accidental death had robbed us of our only breadwinner. But why could we not have stayed on in the place where people had always known us? We could have moved into a smaller house and cheerfully pinched our pennies the way fatherless families did in books. Everybody would have said, "Look how hard Dr. Frank Justin's poor daughter is trying," and would have helped us, would have encouraged us in our bravery. But my mother had decided instead to throw away everything familiar and move us north, into Aunt Mona's house. Aunt Mona was my father's sister. She and her husband had just separated, and she had the room for us. My mother said she was doing this for our future, for my brother Jem's and my college education. But I couldn't stop believing she had done it out of some perverse love of extremes: if she could no longer go on being the protected wife and daughter, then she would be the martyr. It was as if she were so grieved by all she had lost that she didn't want to leave herself a single thing to be thankful for. Of course, as she kept saying, she still had *us*. But by bringing us away from all we had known, hadn't she hurt us, too?

And as I pumped and puffed up the strenuous hill of Old Clove Road that warm May afternoon, I held myself back from any love of the place, even though the sun made the backs of my legs feel warm and alive, even though the landscape, with its old farmsteads and freshly sown fields, its rural scents and roadside blossoms, was now as lovely and as fragrant as any country road in Virginia.

Every afternoon I rode my bike compulsively on this picturesque and meandering route I had learned from the school bus that took me to and from my new school. I rode to flee my Aunt Mona's house, to emphasize my solitary state, to give myself the illusion of going somewhere.

My turning-around point on Old Clove Road was at the top of the hill, where the land leveled off at the Cristianas' horse farm. On the left side of the road was their gaunt frame house with its peeling gray paint, and, to the side of the house, a well-raked stableyard bracketed by smart, streamlined stalls. The roofs of the stalls were in better shape than the Cristianas' roof, and the stalls had new white paint, with dark green trim around the doors, where the horses stuck their heads out. From the looks of things, horses lived better than people here. A professionally hand-lettered sign hanging from the crossbar of the main gate read:

CRISTIANA PATROON FARM

Abel Cristiana, Prop. Horses Boarded and Bred

On the right side of the road was a training ring and a paddock. In this paddock, for the past few weeks, had been a magnificent stallion, all by himself. After seeing him, there was not much point in going on: I knew I was not likely to see anything more splendid and dramatic than that stallion. But I always did continue on about a hundred yards or so, because Ed Cristiana was in my class at school, and though I'd seen him glance at me more than once with shy appreciation, it just wouldn't have done to turn around right outside his house. He might think I had come looking for him. Besides that, he embarrassed me, with his old blue jeans and bouncy country walk.

Some afternoons the stallion would be measuring the boundaries of his paddock in a continuous self-conscious trot, the tense, arrogant arch of his neck, the backward pricking of his ears showing that he was aware of his solitary importance. On other afternoons, I would reach the crest of the hill only to find him planted stubbornly at the farthest corner of the paddock, pretending to graze like any ordinary farm animal, too far away for me to see the fire in his eye that I knew was there.

But this afternoon, I was met by an unexpected sight. There was a second horse in the paddock, with a bandaged tail. As the two of them cavorted erratically around their confines, I saw that the new horse, a mare, wore some sort of boots tied to her rear hooves. The two horses zigzagged skittishly about, the stallion in pursuit, until, suddenly, just short of overtaking the mare, he reared up and plunged down sideways on her. As he clamped himself to her hindquarters, she responded with a violent kick with her booted hoof. But then, with a quivering of her long legs, she bowed her haunches to his frantic thrusts.

I don't know why this scene should have distressed me. I had known the facts of life since I was nine. My grandmother had explained, in a careful, euphemistic way, what has to happen between a male and a female before offspring can be born; we had been walking on the beach one morning, down at Pawleys Island, when we had seen two golden retrievers scuffling bizarrely in the sand, and I had been afraid the dog on the bottom was going to get hurt.

Perhaps I was upset because I had become possessive of the stallion, identifying him with my own proud aloneness in this place. Maybe it was because I hated to see him lose his dignity like that and join the herd. Or maybe it was the way the mare had capitulated; how she hadn't had much chance anyway, with her tail bandaged to one side and those boots on her hooves. But what made the incident mortifying was that I realized someone had been watching me watch.

Ed Cristiana's father, his thumbs hooked under his belt, was slouched back against the fence in front of their house. A coarse, stocky farmer, he nodded brusquely at me. He was the kind of man I had not known in my life, but I had eyes to see that I was as of little value to his world as he was to mine. In his narrowed blue eyes I saw a country man's contemptuous amusement at a squeamish girl—who nevertheless had gotten down from her bicycle to gawk.

I barely managed a hello, and then, mounting my bike with

what little dignity I could muster, I rode off with a little wobble. I felt his shrewd, amused eyes on my back. It would be impossible for me to turn around at my usual point, a hundred yards down the road, and cycle back past his scornful gaze.

So—for the first time—I went on down the next hill, continuing farther than I'd ever gone. The school bus always went faster here, as there were no children to be picked up.

I rode on, absorbed in my humiliation. The road curved and curled back on itself. Fields planted with some crop I didn't recognize followed on both sides. My bike clattered as it bounced over a wooden bridge, and I wondered how far I would have to ride before I could be certain that the horsebreeder had gone away.

Then came a pine forest on the left side of the road. Tempted by its shade, I parked my bike and sat down under an old tree. I leaned my head against its rough bark and surprised myself by starting to cry. Fredericksburg, Virginia, and the happy existence I had known in the house on Washington Avenue were gone forever. Things would never be the same again. I summoned up pictures of the ways they would never be the same again and sobbed.

Then, oddly revived by this accomplishment of tears, I walked with my bike down a narrow, overgrown road that led alongside the pine forest. For it had seemed to me during my crying that I had heard snatches of music coming from somewhere within the pine forest or on the other side of it. It had been my grandfather's favorite music at the end of an exhausting day at the hospital or when he worked in the evenings on the historical articles on slavery it had been his hobby to write. "J. Sanity Bach," my grandfather liked to call his favorite composer. Bach, he said, was one of the few places in the world where you could still find order. It was as if, the mystical side of me fancied, the ghost of my grandfather had sent me these snatches of music, traveling faintly through the spring air, to console me. And yet the pragmatic side of me was curious to find out just who in this rural village was playing J. Sanity Bach.

By this time I had come to the end of the pine forest, but the music—after several enticing overtures—had abruptly ceased. Ahead of me were acres of open field. The sun was beginning its late-afternoon descent toward a purplish mass of low, undulating mountains in the distance that culminated abruptly at their northern end in a sharp ledge. Atop this ledge was a tower of some kind. There had been mention of a tower and of a famous old hotel on top of a mountain during Aunt Mona's exhaustive briefing on this area that was to be our home; but I hadn't listened very carefully, partly from not wanting to hear anything about landmarks that served to remind me I was no longer in Virginia, and partly from not wanting to be drawn into Aunt Mona's manner of looking at life. She had a way of infecting everything with a deadly practicality. In her telling, the romantic tower up there with its tiny window winking in the sun would turn out to have some utilitarian purpose; the hotel, no matter how old or mysterious, to cater to convention groups at special rates, which Aunt Mona, a travel agent, would know to the penny.

But because I had discovered it, led on by the music, the vista exerted a charm and a release. My chagrin over the stallion and Mr. Cristiana seemed silly. But beyond that, as I faced these acres of fields, moving softly with wind, stretching toward the rise of the mountains with the intriguing tower, my pain for the world I had lost expanded into a wider kind of sorrow, a sorrow that could coexist with future prospects. For the first time since coming here, I felt curiosity about the place. What, since I had to live here, would happen to me in it?

Then, like a tease, the Bach again. Did it come from within the pine forest? Or from somewhere on the other side of it, invisible from where I was? The phrases of the music burst forth, with every promise of going on, then suddenly stopped as they had before.

I laid down my bike at the edge of the field and entered the forest at the point of a stream. All at once, it was quieter. I could hardly hear my own footsteps on the carpet of pine needles. The air was pungent with pine smell, and the sunlight seemed filtered through a light brown glass. A sudden stir of wind through the high branches made the pines hiss softly, and I felt the flutter of fear that comes from trespassing.

The stream fed into a round, dark pond, and beside the pond stood a stone hut—or, rather, the ruin of one. Part of its roof had fallen in, and the windows were blank, open squares in the ancient-looking masonry. It was hardly big enough to hold a piano, even if someone had been foolish enough to put one there. But the structure itself was compelling. There was something primitive and mysterious about the way it just *was there*, so rooted in its setting that it might have grown out of the earth.

The temptation to have a look inside was irresistible. But I went cautiously, anticipating the thing I would least like to see again. Once, my grandfather and I had been foraging around in an old slave cabin in Virginia for one of his articles and I had looked out of the corner of my eye and seen what I had thought was a thick yellow rope suddenly uncoil itself from the sunny seat of a dilapidated chair and plummet through a hole in the floor. "Scared him more than he scared us," said my grandfather, after I had stopped screaming. That was my grandfather's trademark: always to see the other fellow's side.

Forearmed with my prevision of some Northern-hued reptile napping in the corner where the sun would still be streaming through the window, I stepped warily over the crumbling stone threshold. I swiveled my eyes rapidly toward the sunny spot, and was so unprepared to see a human figure lying there that I screamed anyway.

The woman on the Army blanket shot up, flung away her book as though *it* had suddenly become a snake, and with a cry that was more an intake of breath, clasped one hand to her throat.

We confronted each other for a protracted moment, during which her face grew calm again, even though she continued to press the hand dramatically against her throat, as if dutifully finishing off the requirements of a scene. At last she said, in a low voice, thrilling to me for its elegant diction as well as its composure: "Who are you, and why did you scream like that?"

She was my mother's age, or older, but there was some indefinable thing in her style as she sat there, barefoot, in an old wraparound skirt and a man's shirt knotted at her waist, that made me unable to "place" her the way I habitually did adults, either relegating them to their function pertaining to me or judging them with pity or sternness because they had spoiled themselves or been defeated by life in some visible way. This woman seemed—how shall I put it?—not judgeable by my usual standards and categories for older people.

"I was expecting to see a snake," I told her.

"Oh. Well. Sorry to disappoint you. I don't think I've been a snake in any of my incarnations. I'm not the snake type. Where did you come from?"

"You mean, right now?"

"What else should I mean?"

"Well, originally I'm from Fredericksburg, Virginia, but now we live over in Lucas Meadows, here in Clove."

"That's interesting, but"—her wide mouth twitched with amusement—"I meant something more immediate. I mean, did you come from the direction of our house, or from Abel Cristiana's, or what?"

"There was just this overgrown road that ended in the field," I said. "What happened was, I was looking for the music."

Her forehead wrinkled. "You mean you want to *take* music?"

I thought this remark odd. "No, ma'am. I heard some. It seemed to be coming from somewhere in these woods, or maybe on the other side of them. Now it's stopped. But it was Bach."

"Ah!" She looked enlightened. "What you heard was coming from our house, which is on the hill on the other side of these trees. It was *trying* to be Bach, but I cannot go so far as to call it music. Which is why I am down here. These woods keep it at a bearable distance, though I'm afraid the sound carries over the field more than I would like. You see, my brother, Julian, is forced for the time being to supplement our income by giving piano lessons. He is a superb musician. He made his debut at Carnegie Hall—and I don't mean Little Carnegie, either—when he graduated from Juilliard. This particular little girl is my least favorite of his pupils. Do you want to know why? Because she is just like a robot. She can play whole passages by heart without ever once feeling the music."

And, slamming her eyes shut, the woman sitting on the blanket hunched down, making herself very tight and small. A prissy, rather imbecilic smile sealed itself across her face. Right there before my eyes, she *became* the unmusical child, addressing an invisible keyboard, her fingers woodenly calling forth in my imagination the very notes I had heard coming through the trees.

" 'By heart' is certainly a misnomer in her case," she concluded, snapping back into herself again. Her sharp brown eyes drank me in. When she saw that her performance had enthralled me, she smiled. It was a unique smile, breaking away from her large, slightly irregular teeth as if from the force of its own irrepressible mischief, and igniting the fine, thin skin of her mobile face with a blush. A constellation of freckles traveled across the bridge of her imposing hawklike nose. "You must have come down the old haywagon road," she remarked, with a magnificent reversion to the bland topic of how I had gotten there. "You came around the back of our land into Abel Cristiana's fields. Which used to be *our* fields, until sacrifices had to be made. *C'est la vie.* Are *you*, perhaps, a musical child?"

"No, ma'am. It was just that the music reminded me of my grandfather."

"Is he a musician?"

"No, ma'am, a doctor. But he's dead now."

She nodded thoughtfully. "So many people are," she said.

There was a silence then. I stood awkwardly near the door, thinking I should go. It was hard for me to know what to do, because she was like no person I had ever met. With most people you could tell whether you were welcome or not, but her signals were not conventional. She had been quick to respond to having a visitor—even showing off with that remarkable mimicking of the "robot" child—but maybe she was just being polite. On the other hand, she did seem curious about me; she had watched me intently the whole time I had been in the hut. That last remark, however, had been somewhat strange, and for all I knew it might have been meant as a dismissal.

But then she asked me whether I would like to have a swim in the pond. "It's still a bit chilly, but very refreshing, once you take the plunge. I had one around noon today."

I thanked her and said I ought to be getting home. "Besides, I don't have a suit," I added, though that dark pond, with who knew what in its invisible depths, invited me not at all.

"I never let that stop me," she said, laughing, "but I suppose Southern belles are more modest." Then she sprang up lightly and toed two worn brown leather sandals to her and wiggled her feet into them. "Not that I have anything against modesty," she continued, in a somewhat ironic tone. "Modesty and politeness are the staples in your repertoire, I know. Which accounts for that unsettling 'ma'am' of yours. I've never thought of myself as a 'ma'am' any more than I have a snake, though I've been called one before."

"A snake?"

"No, silly. A 'ma'am.' During the war, I taught at a girls' school in New York—really more of a finishing school—and I had some budding belles who always called me that. You're brought up to it, I know, but for the recipient it can be terribly disorienting. There I was, thinking of myself as slightly more than a girl, and then suddenly the drab weight of this 'ma'am' is thrown over my shoulders. I'm older now, but I still can't think of myself as a 'ma'am.' I have nothing against Southerners, however, don't get me wrong. I can appreciate their good points. I can even see the good points in Catholics and I've been bred in my blood to hate them ever since 1685, when Louis the Fourteenth ran my ancestors out of France. I find it all very amusing, the way human beings divide themselves up into all these sub-genres and then run around hating everybody in the other sub-genres. Most people spend their entire lives identifying themselves with their little subgenres. They spend money on them, erect shrines to them, organize clubs around them—I'm in one of the clubs myself: the Huguenot Society, it's called—and often kill for them. That way, they can manage to get through life without having to discover who *they* are. Did you walk here, all the way from Lucas Meadows? Surely not."

"No ..." I omitted the "ma'am" this time, though it felt rude. "I left my bike down by the fields."

"Well, I'll walk you to your bike. My name is Ursula De-Vane. What's yours?"

"Justin Stokes." The name that had clung, close and natural as my own skin, for all these years, sounded suddenly flat and unromantic, compared with hers.

"Ah, an androgynous name!" she said, clamping a firm hand to my back as she steered me out of the hut and past the dark pond, in which I was glad I did not have to swim. "I often thought I would have preferred an androgynous name. It gives you more *room*, somehow. Do you find the name Justin gives you more room?"

"I don't know," I said. "It's my mother's maiden name. But I've always liked it. I couldn't imagine being called anything else. Is that what you meant?"

"Not *exactly*," she replied with a slight smile, "but it will do for now. Tell me, Justin, how long have you lived here? Not very long, because I know most of the young people by sight, as well as who their ancestors were. This is the kind of community where everybody is known as somebody's daughter or grandson or niece until they're ninety. After which they're nothing, but it doesn't matter by then."

"We only moved here last month. My father died in February and I guess my mother felt she couldn't make it alone. So we've moved up here to my aunt's house. She and her husband just recently separated, so she had the extra space."

"And who is your aunt?"

"Mrs. Eric Mott."

"*Oh* God." Ursula DeVane smote her forehead dramatically. "Then your cousin is little Becky Mott. Well, Justin, I'm afraid that jinxes our friendship right from the start."

"Why?"

"Better ask your aunt. I'm not saying my brother, Julian, didn't misbehave, but I do think an artist is entitled to an occasional display of impulsiveness. Especially when forced to waste his talent in a place like this for economic reasons."

"We moved up here for economic reasons, too," I said. I intended, of course, to find out when I got home what Ursula DeVane's brother had done to Becky, just as I intended to look up the word *androgynous*. But right now I was more interested in laying a groundwork of things in common between me and this unusual woman, who had given more of herself and asked more of me than my inscrutable ten-year-old cousin had bothered to do in the whole month I had lived in the same house with her. When Ursula DeVane had said the words *our friendship*, an idea I would not have presumed to have by myself had materialized into an intriguing possibility.

"Money," said Ursula DeVane, still steering me lightly by the backs of my shoulders, "lurks somewhere in the plot of everybody's life. Sometimes more than passion, I think."

We had reached the open field. For a moment I could not see my bike for the tall grass, and I created a scenario in which it had been stolen. Then I would have to go back with Ursula DeVane to her house, which was situated somewhere on the other side of the pine forest, and telephone home. I would meet her brother. . . . But there lay the conveyance back into my other life, exactly as I had left it.

"Oh, a Raleigh," said Ursula, springing forward and lifting the bike. "*I* rode a Raleigh when I lived in London. I was at the Royal Academy of Dramatic Art. But why do you ride a man's bicycle?"

"It was my father's." Now I felt ashamed for having imagined it stolen.

"Ah." She nodded understandingly. "You must miss him. Julie and I lost our mother when we were young. I was ten and he was just six. It was harder on him because he was closer to her. I was my father's favorite and, quite frankly, liked him better than my mother. I hope for your sake that you like your mother."

"Oh yes," I said, but I could not quite meet her gaze. With her unorthodox question, she had hit on a truth that made me ashamed: since we had moved up here, I had not felt as friendly and compassionate toward my mother as a daughter should.

Ursula DeVane was now prancing the bike up and down by its handlebars, looking as though she would like to leap on the seat and be off somewhere. In the sunny light of the field, I could see silver tendrils twirling up from the richness of her red-brown hair. Though her unconventional demeanor made her seem much younger, I realized she must be some years older than my mother. She was not a pretty woman, like my mother, but her features, I thought, went with her personality: sharp, generous, and bold.

She saw me studying her and at once straightened her shoulders and lifted her chin. "Well, Justin," she said with a touch of irony, "your dramatic entry into my day was quite stimulating. I ought to thank you for it. There I was, trying to reread Proust, but he is all wrong for this year. I have reached a time in my life when I need to be refreshed by the unexpected rather than consoled by the stately rhythms of what I know. Of course"—and her face was once again transformed by the unique smile—"your stunning scream certainly helped matters along."

As I stood there thinking of some way I could say good-bye that would keep the possibility of another meeting open, a dazzling cascade of musical notes burst upon the sunny evening air. Only this time there were no fey stoppings and startings. This time the music, a piece I did not know, continued, triumphantly sure of its power.

"Ah," said Ursula, lifting her face toward the sound as though showering in it. "My favorite Chopin scherzo. It's my brother's all-clear signal. The last of the brats has departed, and the good life can recommence."

She handed over my bike, her interest already somewhere else. Then she said, as if it were a polite afterthought, "Next time you drop by, bring your suit."

Without waiting for a reply, she started back toward the woods, taking jubilant, muscular strides in the direction of the music coming from the invisible house somewhere on the other side. I noticed that there were freckles on the backs of her legs.

She must have known she had left a captive audience, however, because when she reached the trees, she turned, smiling, toward the exact spot where she had left me.

She lifted her hand to her mouth, indicating she had something further to impart.

I strained forward to hear.

"Now *that*, my dear," she called, "is music."

II.

Returning to Lucas Meadows constricted my heart. This was my home now, but there was no connective tissue to bind us together. There was nothing of my past here, and, I certainly hoped, nothing of my future. It was just the place my mother, in her panic and grief at losing everyone in life she had depended on, had decided we had to be now; and when you are thirteen years old you have no choice in such decisions, though you may have plenty of feelings about them.

Although I could not feel at home in Lucas Meadows, I did feel sorry for the place. I compared its downfall to mine. As recently as two years ago, we had both existed without a thought that our vistas would ever be altered. There I had been, happily ensconced in that big, rambling house in Virginia whose every object and corner contained my history; and, hundreds of miles away to the north, poor Lucas Meadows had still been meadows, presided over by a dignified old farmhouse. The farmhouse still stood, though it was bereft now of all its furniture, and children could peer to their heart's delight through its curtainless windows. But the beautiful meadows had been plowed up, its hundred-year-old trees cut down to make way for several dozen "split-level" houses, all alike in the treeless sunlight except for their colors. Every third house was light yellow, like ours. The two in between, light blue and light tan. Each "level" was about half the height of a normal story. On the top level were the family bedrooms and a bath; on the middle level were the living room, dining room, and kitchen; on the bottom level were the den, utility room, and half bath. Aunt Mona had explained to us that these houses had been designed to hold what was, statistically, the average modern American family, which numbered, according to my aunt, two adults and two and a half children. When my six-year-old brother, Jem, had boldly asked what a half-child would be like, Aunt Mona had laughed and winked at me and replied to Jem that it was simply the statisticians' way of saying the family would have to move to a larger house when that half-child turned into a whole child.

What bothered me most about these houses, what bothered me even more than their lack of history, was that they seemed designed to make everybody as alike as possible. And the people who lived in them seemed to conspire. In Lucas Meadows, all mothers seemed to be cooking dinner at the same hour, and all the lights in the children's bedrooms went out at night before the lights in the master bedrooms. Even worse, every single living room had a lamp, its shade still covered with cellophane, on a table squarely in the middle of the picture window. That the mother in every one of these houses had gone out, on her own volition, and bought a lamp to fill her window exactly as her neighbors had done, seemed ominous to me. It was as though Lucas Meadows emanated a germ, and if you caught it, you would become just like everyone else. Not only that, but most of the fathers in Lucas Meadows worked for IBM in the town of Kingston, eight miles away. And they all washed their cars and mowed their lawns on Saturday mornings. Even Mr. Mott, who now lived on a rented houseboat in Rondout Creek since he and my aunt had separated, came over faithfully on Saturday mornings to mow our lawn and wash Aunt Mona's car. While there, he talked seriously with the other men—for he, too, worked for IBM—who were mowing the lawns and washing the cars on either side of us. Then he repaired anything in the house that needed repairing, saw whether Aunt Mona's car needed gas, and changed the oil himself before driving my cousin Becky away with him for the weekend in his own car. It was a very friendly separation, Aunt Mona said. It was just that she and Mott had decided they wanted different things out of life. Also, she admitted, Mott got on her nerves and she supposed she got on his when they were together too long. It happened to lots of married couples, she said, only she and Mott (as she always called him) had decided to be sensible about things before "one of us killed the other." Mr. Mott did not look like the killer type to me, even though I knew he had killed Japanese from his submarine during the war. He was a solemn, conscientious man, and what he seemed to like best was doing other people's chores and being nice to children. He would spend hours with Jem, explaining how airplanes get off the ground, showing him how a transistor radio works. He had built Becky a real ballerina's *barre* along one wall of her room, so she could practice her ballet lessons in earnest. He had fixed the chain on my bike. I wished I could like him more, but his presence deadened my spirit. When I was around him, I always wanted to yawn. Also, I could never remember his face.

Mr. Mott and my aunt had both been orphans. It was one of the things that had brought them together, Aunt Mona said. But whereas my father and Aunt Mona had been raised by an aunt in Fredericksburg, Mr. Mott had endured the horrors of an orphanage. If a child wet his bed at Mr. Mott's orphanage, Aunt Mona told us, he was made to come down to breakfast wearing his wet sheet. One reason they were not getting an outright divorce just yet, Aunt Mona said, was that Mott couldn't bear having to tell old Mr. Watson, the founder of IBM, who came frequently to the Kingston site and always asked after Becky and Mona by name. To Mott, my aunt said, IBM was like the family he had never had as a child. Mott had actually cried the first Christmas he was with IBM, Aunt Mona said, when all the employees filed into a big room and sang Christmas carols, because Mott felt he belonged somewhere at last.

I could not imagine my mother ever calling my father "Stokes," as if they had been two buddies or something.

Also, Aunt Mona had admitted, in her practical voice, from which all traces of a Southern accent had been expunged, that if she and Mott got an outright divorce, she would lose the excellent health insurance IBM provided for wives.

I parked my bike in the garage and went inside. On the ground "level," where the den and utility room had been turned into living quarters for my mother and Jem, things were quiet. That meant they were taking a nap. Since we had moved here, my mother took a lot of naps. She would read Jem to sleep in her bed in the afternoon and then doze off beside him.

From two levels up, came the sounds of "Les Sylphides." Becky was practicing her solo number for the upcoming ballet recital.

I found Aunt Mona in her spotless kitchen, which always looked as if she were expecting a photographer from *House Beautiful* any minute. She was indulging in her obsessive pastime, wiping the kitchen counter with a paper towel. "Well," she greeted me, as she did every day, "and what have *you* done with your afternoon?"

"Rode my bike on Old Clove Road," I replied, as I did every day. "Only, I went a little farther today. Something smells delicious in the oven."

"Well, it's your own mother's meat loaf," said my aunt. "Louise has been so good about helping out, after all she's been through. 'Mona, you're the working woman of this household,' she told me. 'The least I can do, after you've offered your home, is to prepare supper.'"

"Would you like me to set the table?"

"You're a doll, Justin. If Becky ever offered to set the table, I think I'd have a heart attack. But, as I was telling Louise the other day, your grandmother brought you up in her image. Honora Justin was just the perfect lady." As she pronounced this eulogy to my late grandmother, her short, feathery haircut trembled on top. With her quick, nervous gestures and her sharp eyes and her preference for colorful clothes, my aunt reminded me of a high-strung bird of paradise. Even in her relatively still moments, you could detect a slight *quiver* about her head and neck.

"Be glad for your early training," she told me, as I laid out the plastic mats at the round Formica table and placed a folded paper napkin beneath each pair of forks. "It sets you up for life. I never had it, you know."

As I aligned the tines of Aunt Mona's stainless-steel salad and dinner forks with the same care as if they had been my grandmother's heavy Georgian silver ones, now packed away in a shoebox in the room where my mother slept, I tried to pretend that the ghost of my grandmother hovered approvingly behind me. But, though I wanted to feel her near, I could not imagine how she would be able to find her way here, even by spiritual means. How much did the spirits of the dead know about what happened *since* they had died? It might be cruel to summon my grandmother, even if my love could give me the power. "But what has happened?" she might wonder. "Why is Justin setting the table with those forks? Whose table is that? Where are our forks? Where is my husband? Where is Louise's husband? What strange house are they living in, and why are they no longer in *our* house?" Trapped in her ghost world, she would be unable to comprehend all that had happened to us since she had gone. No, I would just have to go on living with the good example of her memory. But it was hard. I was not as good as my grandmother, no matter how much Aunt Mona might think I had been raised "in her image." My grandfather had told me once that my grandmother was the only woman he had ever known who would behave exactly the same way if nobody were looking. I knew I could not say that of myself.

"Well," said Aunt Mona, gazing restlessly about her for the sight of some bit of disorder, some small thing out of place in her spotless kitchen, "I went to Chicago twice today, to the Grand Canyon once, and tomorrow I may be off to Yugoslavia." In this whimsical manner she liked to describe her job of sitting behind a desk in a Kingston travel agency, phoning airlines and booking reservations. Her critical eye lit in triumph on a brown-tipped frond of the spider plant hanging in the window above the sink. She reached up and excised the brown tip between painted fingernails.

I said Yugoslavia sounded interesting. Then I asked, "Do you know some people named DeVane?"

Her chin shot up so fast that it set in motion the crest of her feathery haircut. "Where did you hear about *them?*"

"I met her. I met Ursula DeVane." Saying her name made me self-conscious, as if I were pronouncing the name of an esoteric book whose contents were far beyond my years.

"When? Where?" My aunt looked at me sharply.

"Today, when I was riding on Old Clove Road." Instinct told me to keep the meeting in the hut to myself. "She was outside. She seemed very nice."

"Oh, she can be nice enough when it suits her. But why was she nice to you?"

Aunt Mona was often blunt to the point of tactlessness. But I understood what she meant. "I don't know. She liked me, I guess."

"Did you tell her who you are? Did you mention that you are my niece?"

"Yes, ma'am."

My aunt's wavy crest quivered. "And what did she say to *that?*"

"She said that her brother had misbehaved in some way with Becky."

"Oh, she said that, did she? That he had misbehaved? Well, well. Tell me, Justin, did she start being nice to you *after* you told her you were my niece, or before?"

I sensed what she wanted me to say, but I couldn't say it. "Before, I think."

"You think, but you're not sure?"

"No, I'm sure."

"Well . . ." A fresh square of paper towel was tugged from the roll and the spotless kitchen counter wiped again. "Well, I don't know," my aunt said. "I have nothing against her, really, except that she puts on airs, but her crazy brother *killed* music for Becky. Two solid years of piano lessons wasted. At fifteen dollars a lesson—which is an outrage, but he can get away with it—that comes to one thousand five hundred and sixty dollars: Mott figured it up. That's not cheap. And the whole investment goes down the drain because of that crazy man!"

"How was he crazy?"

"Not *was*. *Is.* Always has been, probably. Only, people protect them, you see, because they are the DeVanes. I sure as heck wish I was from one of those creepy old families dating back to God. It sets you up without you ever having to lift a finger. That, plus a little money, and I'd be set. I'd be able to put on a few airs myself."

"But how is he crazy?" I wanted to keep her off her favorite theme: how her life would be so different is she had had "family" and money. It was hard to believe that she was the sister of my father, who had been brought up with the same disadvantages but who had possessed so much charm.

"Well, I'll tell you. But if Beck comes down, I'll have to stop. He just did the craziest thing imaginable in the middle of Becky's recital. They were having it over at the Dutch Reformed Church in Kingston because he has so many students now—thanks to IBM opening its new site here—and just before time for Beck to get up from the pew and play her 'Für Elise' that she had slaved over to get perfect—and it *was* perfect—do you know what this idiot does? He's standing in the doorway to the church to get a breath of air—this was the end of last May and it was stifling in that old church—when suddenly he calls out to some person on the street: 'C-come in! C-come in!' He has this stutter, you know. 'I order you to c-come in!'

"And we all turn around to look, and in comes this young man wearing tennis clothes and carrying a racket. He looked *very* embarrassed, but Julian DeVane just pushed him up the aisle by the elbow. 'No, I insist. I insist,' he says to the young man.

"Well! The next thing everybody knows, this young man in tennis shorts sits down at the Steinway, and Julian DeVane is stammering excitedly that this was his most talented pupil from a few years back and now he will play something for us 'as an inspiration to us all.' I have to give the boy credit, he looked thoroughly ashamed for his teacher, but he adjusts the bench— where poor Becky was scheduled to be sitting—and plays the 'Hungarian Rhapsody.' I mean, can you imagine? This boy is at Juilliard now—DeVane announces it—and that lunatic drags him in, in the midst of a children's recital, to 'play something.' To play the 'Hungarian Rhapsody.' And after *that* was over, he tried to get him to play an encore!

"But he wouldn't. He got up and shook his teacher's hand, and bowed to all of us, and then took his tennis racket and left. And all the parents look at one another, as if to say, 'What the heck . . . ?' and then DeVane says, 'And now, Miss Becky Mott will play "Für Elise."' And Beck gets up, she's pale, but she walks up there like a trouper and sits down and adjusts her bench back to where it *should* have been. Then she takes a deep breath and puts her fingers on the keys. She did fine all the way through the first passage, but then she made a mistake. I saw her hesitate whether to go on or start over. But she just stopped. She put her hands down to the side and just sat there for a minute; then she stood up, smoothed her crinolines down, and walked right out of the church, right past Julian DeVane as if he didn't exist.

"Well, Mott and I followed her, of course, and then Julian DeVane rushes up to us and says, 'That's not like Becky. She *always* sees things through to the end.' It was if he didn't even realize it was his fault! Can you imagine?"

"Poor Becky," I said, really meaning it. My cousin had not exactly won my heart during the five weeks we had shared the same house, but what a humiliating thing. The man did seem crazy. Or very insensitive. Ursula DeVane had called it 'an occasional display of impulsiveness' to which an artist was entitled. But, as much as I had liked her, I couldn't excuse him. It seemed to me that artists, if anything, had more of a duty to behave well, because people looked at them more. I was disappointed: I would have wished for Ursula DeVane's brother to be better.

"We missed the reception, naturally," Aunt Mona went on, still intensely reliving the outrage of that day, "which, I must admit, I had been looking forward to. She always serves May wine with strawberries floating in it, and these Englishy sandwiches to remind everyone she lived over there—it's an elegant affair for this community. Also I wanted to poke around that house of theirs. At a reception you can do that. It's one of those original old stone Huguenot houses—never been out of the family since it was built. Well, you saw it, if you met her on Old Clove, because it's right on the road. The one time we were inside, I couldn't look around. He insists on a personal interview with the parents to make sure they'll enforce his strict practicing regime. Now it makes me sick to my stomach when I think how Mott and I sat in that bare living room—they don't even have any carpeting on the floor—and twisted our hands on our laps *praying* he would accept Becky. Mott had doubts about him then, because, when we were making polite conversation, Mott asked him about his war record, and it turns out he didn't join up until almost the end of the war. He was living in Argentina during most of the war. Mott didn't like that one bit, because Argentina was strongly pro-Nazi. *He* said he was 'concertizing' down there, but, as Mott pointed out later, when your country's at war, you don't hang around in some other country that likes your enemy better. I also wanted to see their bedrooms. You can tell a lot from people's bedrooms. I mean, let's face it, they've got to be peculiar, a middle-aged brother and sister living together. Never been married, either of them. Anyway, now Becky's got her ballet and she adores her teacher. Thank God, Mrs. Roosa is a normal married woman with children. But don't bring up Julian DeVane to Beck in any of your conversations, Justin. No use opening up old wounds. Okay?"

"Okay." So far, Becky and I had not *had* any conversations.

"Though I must say it's gratifying," said Aunt Mona, "that she *admitted* her brother had misbehaved."

"*Whose* brother misbehaved?" asked Jem, coming into the kitchen. A bright-eyed, nervous boy, he was curious about everything. His eyelids were still puffy from his nap.

"Not you, Jimbo," said Aunt Mona. "Somebody else's brother."

My six-year-old brother sighed. "How many times do I have to tell you, my name's not Jimbo. I'm not some circus animal."

"Jem, darling. That's no way to speak to Aunt Mona." My mother followed him into the kitchen, looking not quite awake. She gave me a languid hug and kiss. Her breath was not sweet, and this upset me. In the old days, she would never have come into a room without being perfectly groomed. In the Fredericksburg days, her entrances had been those of the doted-upon star whose affectionate supporting cast has left center stage for her. But since we had lived here, she seemed to be uncertain of her role, and this uncertainty had robbed her of the breezy self-assurance I had admired in her—even though it had sometimes made me jealous. "I think you owe Aunt Mona an apology," she told my brother gently. There was a sad, resigned quality about this act of discipline; I could almost hear her thinking: Well, I'm no longer anybody's cherished wife or beloved daughter, but I must try hard to be a good mother—it's all I've got left.

"I'm sorry," Jem told Aunt Mona. "But my name *is* Jem." He glanced toward me for support. "*Whose* brother was it that misbehaved? I want to know."

"Nobody you know, just a man," said Aunt Mona, not particularly wounded by his rudeness. She was used to much worse from Becky. "Just one of our village eccentrics."

"What's an eccentric?" pursued the inveterately curious Jem.

"Someone in a place who can misbehave and still be accepted by society," said Aunt Mona, seizing a bright green sponge and annihilating a drop of water perched on the rim of her stainless-steel sink, "because he's got family or money."

We all sat around the Formica-topped kitchen table with the gold-painted pine-cone centerpiece Aunt Mona had copied from a magazine, and her Scotty dog salt and pepper shakers, the white dog for salt, the black one for pepper.

"Beck," said my aunt, "you'll have to take more food than that if you want to keep up your strength for the dance recital."

Becky sat with her spine arched conspicuously away from her chair back, as if she denied all possible contact with the family scene. She looked calmly at her mother from under her bangs. "I don't like squash."

"Well, take some of Aunt Louise's meat loaf. It's very tasty. She was nice enough to make it while I was at work today; all I had to do was pop it in the oven when I got home. Here, try it, it's delicious." Aunt Mona pushed the platter at her daughter.

Becky rolled her eyes and compressed her lips, as if to say: You are *forcing* me to be rude. She said slowly and evenly to her mother, "You know I don't like onions mixed in with my meat."

There was an embarrassed silence. Then my mother smiled apologetically and said, "Oh dear, I'm so sorry, Becky. I would have left them out if I had known."

Becky slid her eyes briefly toward my mother but made no reply. I was furious, not only at her blatant rudeness but at my mother's humility. She was acting as if she were some kind of *servant,* or something. This would never have happened, I told myself, if we had stayed in Fredericksburg. Even if we had moved to a smaller house, there would have still been the familiar air of Fredericksburg all around us, to remind my mother who she was.

"When my brother, Rivers, and I were growing up in Fredericksburg," said Aunt Mona, "*we* ate whatever our aunt could put on the table for us, and were glad to get it. If we didn't eat it, we knew, we would go to bed hungry. Orphans can't be finicky."

"Well, I'm not an orphan," replied Becky in her toneless, rather high voice. "And even if I was"—and she gave her mother a peculiar look, as if she were testing in her mind the idea of orphanhood—"I still wouldn't eat onions mixed in with my meat."

My mother lowered her eyes and ate a hearty forkful of her own meat loaf. I knew she thought Becky had gone too far, but she would never say so. That was Aunt Mona's job. But when, presently, Jem got excited over something he was saying and flung a bite of meat from his fork, Aunt Mona bolted from her chair and lunged for the paper towels as if acid had dropped and were eating away the foundations of the house. As she fell to her knees and scoured the shiny kitchen tiles, I tried to catch my mother's eye, to exchange a glance of Our Way of Life against Theirs, but she purposely evaded me, I thought. Becky intercepted my glance. She raised her flat gray eyes at me and smirked. A month ago, I would have put a lot of effort into interpreting *any* communication from Becky—was the smirk meant to show contempt for me, or conspiracy against her mother, whom she took pains, it seemed, to annoy?—but my ten-year-old cousin had repulsed my overtures so many times that my pride finally asserted itself over charity (and loneliness) and I had resolved that any concrete move toward friendship would have to come—unequivocally—from her. It seemed a bitter irony that one of the reasons my mother had given for our moving here was that Becky and I could grow up together. "Like sisters," she had said.

My mother and Aunt Mona then found some topic that took them back to when they had been girls in Fredericksburg. The way my mother talked, you would have thought they had been best friends, or something. But I knew that was not the way it had been, and I had to admire Aunt Mona's tenacious insistence on the truth. "Now, Louise, I'm flattered, but you hardly knew me before you and my brother eloped. Why should you? You were the daughter of Dr. Justin and lived on Washington Avenue, and I was just the baby-sitting orphan girl whose aunt took in sewing. I'll never forget when Auntie got the telegram from Rivers, saying you two had eloped. 'But Louise Justin could have had *anybody*,' she kept repeating. 'Auntie,' I told her, 'Rivers has an ease that makes him anybody's equal. He has a sunny temperament and a gorgeous body. Any girl would be a fool to refuse Rivers, and that includes Louise Justin.' I'm sorry, Louise, but I did say that."

"You were right to say it," replied my mother softly. "And you were right about Rivers's wonderful ease."

I sat eating my meat loaf and thinking about how my mother had eloped with my father instead of going to Sweet Briar. But she had been clever: she had saved her father the first semester's unrefundable tuition by offering to mail the check herself a few days before she was to leave for college. "Oh, I'll mail it at the corner box, I'm going out for a walk anyway," she had said, and as soon as she was out of their sight she tore up the envelope with the check in it and dropped the pieces down the sewer grating. This story became one of my grandmother's favorites because it illustrated both what a devoted daughter and a passionate, headstrong young woman my mother had been.

Toward the end of the meal, when everyone had finished and was waiting for Becky to nibble a few more forkfuls of the ground meat she had painstakingly separated from the onions, Aunt Mona said, "I've got to rush off to the real-estate class. Do you mind holding the fort, Louise?"

She always asked this, even though we all knew very well that one of the agreements of this new joint household was just that: my mother would "hold the fort" whenever Aunt Mona had to go to work or to her real-estate classes.

"Of course I don't mind. What else have I got to do?" The gracious martyr.

"I'm sure Beck won't be any trouble, will you, Beck? She's got to work on her sundress for 4-H."

"I wish I'd never started the stupid thing," said Becky vehemently. "I made a mistake and now I have to rip out the whole top part. Stupid dress."

"Be thankful you're learning to sew, Beck. We didn't have 4-H in our high school, did we, Louise? If I had been able to sew, I wouldn't have had to wear those dowdy numbers my poor aunt whipped up for proms. I would have made myself something really stylish, from a *Vogue* pattern. Who knows, I might have captivated some eligible planter's son with my *haute couture*, and my whole life would have been different."

Although my aunt winked as she said the part about the planter's son, to show that she was getting wise to her own habit of running down her past, Becky scraped back her chair violently and rolled her eyes back in her head. As she was making her disdainful exit from the kitchen, my mother amazed me by saying, "Bring the dress down and let me have a look at it, Becky. I'm not a seamstress, but I've got lots of time and a pair of sharp nail scissors."

My cousin, without deigning to turn and face my mother, stopped long enough to raise her eyebrows. "Okay," she said with a majestic shrug, and left.

"Beck misses her father," said Aunt Mona, clearing her daughter's dishes. "She wasn't always so abrupt."

It was too much. I took my plate and glass and eating utensils to the dishwasher, said, *"Excuse* me, please," very distinctly, to impress upon them the difference between Becky and myself—I had a lot more reason to miss *my* father, whom I would never see again—and, with an aggrieved spirit, mounted the few carpeted stairs that led to the level of "my room."

Aunt Mona had decorated this room to greet me on my arrival, her brother's fatherless child. But I was still trying to figure out what image of me she had in her mind when she chose the paint and the fabric, which assaulted my peace of mind whichever way I looked. The color of my walls was an unsettling purplish-pink. "Raspberry Ice" was its official name. Had my aunt, studying the samples in the paint store, picked the color for its name, thinking her niece would like raspberry ice cream? Nobody, I thought, could pick the color for its looks. And what about the figures of the milkmaids, row after row of them, with their wide skirts and pert, beauty-contest smiles, who adorned my curtains, the flounce around my dressing table, and the dust ruffle of my bed? Had Aunt Mona pictured me as being like that: a false-smiling, full-skirted girl? But how could she have? She had seen me at my father's funeral. I wasn't at all like that. Why had she picked the milkmaid fabric, then? Was there some obscure association in her mind between their accommodating facades and the old-fashioned graciousness of the South she couldn't wait to leave but still retained nostalgia for?

I found this hour of the day a particular trial. The evenings here contrasted so sadly with the "old" evenings in the house in Fredericksburg, before anyone had gotten sick or died. Evenings there had a comforting flow of communal awareness about them: you could feel the flow like a current moving through the rooms of the house, keeping us in touch with one another as we went about our separate pursuits. My grandfather might be closed in his study, with his slavery articles and "J. Sanity Bach"; my grandmother up in her bedroom, already in her nightgown and bed jacket, reading a novel from the library; my mother loafing unashamedly on the sun porch, leafing through a magazine or talking to my father if he was home; Jem already in bed in the room next to mine, where I could hear him going over his day aloud, in strange little phrases, while I did my homework. I luxuriated in being alone, I even loved my homework, because I felt, somehow, that I was everybody else in that house as well as myself, so I was not missing anything.

But now there were new people in that house, strangers who had moved their own furniture in and would never know that we had always kept a vase of flowers by a certain window or pushed our chairs together in a certain way on the sun porch. Some other girl might at this very moment be lying in bed, under the eaves in my room, looking out at the thick foliage of the backyard and listening to the birds I had listened to last spring.

This thought made me so sad I could not stay in the room. There was at least another hour until dark. There was no homework for me to do, because this was a rural school and teachers did not give homework during planting season. We had what were called "study-hour assignments," which could all be done during the afternoon period assigned for them.

I decided that, rather than getting depressed at dusk in "Raspberry Ice," I would walk up to the old farmhouse that overlooked Lucas Meadows and think my thoughts there. I crouched in front of my dressing-table mirror and combed my hair. Was I pretty or not? I couldn't tell.

The piece of furniture that was now my dressing table had been Mr. Mott's desk. This had been his room. He snored, Aunt Mona had explained, and also he *tinkered*. He had to have a place where he could take his transistor radio apart if he wanted to. Mott had a way of tinkering with things, Aunt Mona said, until she thought she would go out of her mind.

Whenever I wanted to open the center drawer of my dressing table, I had to part the milkmaid fabric that Aunt Mona had tacked around it, and I always felt disconcerted when I saw the sturdy legs of Mr. Mott's former desk beneath. It was like having him, hidden behind a skirt, spying on me in my room.

As I went downstairs, I passed Becky coming up. She gave me a quirky raise of her eyebrows, which could have meant "Hi," or "How dare you be on my stairs," or "Isn't life exasperating."

My mother was sitting on the living-room sofa. She already had Becky's sundress and was picking out the seam. My cousin certainly hadn't wasted any time.

My mother was wearing her new, martyr's look as she bent over Becky's sewing. But she was a very pretty martyr, and something about the way she held her head made me think she saw herself now in the role of a person who is determined to make suffering noble and beautiful.

"I'm going up to that old empty farmhouse for a while," I said from the doorway.

She raised her light blue eyes from her work and smiled at me. I thought I glimpsed the ghost of the look she had rewarded me with occasionally in the old days, a flirtatious look that said: Something about you pleases me right now, but I'm not going to tell you what it is.

Maybe it was not too late yet: maybe I could still say or do something to persuade her to pack up our things and take the train south again. I had made no new friends at school yet. There was nothing in this new place that I would be sad to leave behind. Emboldened by this flicker of her old self that I had spotted, I made a wry face at Aunt Mona's clear plastic runners, which led, in three directions, from the doorway to the main places one was expected to sit in the living room. This way, her seafoam-green wall-to-wall carpeting would be protected forever from a dirty footstep.

"What's she waiting for?" I said. "It's like those women you see downtown with their hair in rollers. You wonder what the special event would have to be for them to take them out."

In the old days, my mother would have giggled and said, "Justin, don't be naughty," but in a way that signified that the nonmotherly part of her, the part that was not required to instill respect in me, approved of the truth in my "naughty" observation. But now she only said gravely, "Come and sit by me a minute." She patted a place beside her. "I won't keep you long."

I crossed Aunt Mona's plastic bridge to the sofa and sat down beside my mother. She resumed picking out Becky's errant seam with her nail scissors. The early-evening light was still strong, and, as she bent over her work, I noticed a new little line along the edge of her chin. It was nothing very awful, but it had a strange effect on me: it made me angry with her. I felt, unreasonably perhaps, that, in her present way of life, she was encouraging such lines, that she was purposely trying to transform her whole being as a way of avenging herself on her unhappy fate of losing all her supporters and protectors. But wasn't I still here? Wasn't Jem? And we needed her as she had been. This new image of her made it seem as if our glamorous, carefree mother had died along with everybody else.

"You know, Justin," she began slowly, picking diligently at Becky's seam, "everyone in the world isn't going to have Honey's taste in furniture and rugs." Honey was our name for my late grandmother.

I sat silently, knowing I was in for a reproach.

"But we're going to have to go on living in that world. I'm not saying we'll never have a home of our own again, with our own things, but right now this is the best I can do for you and Jem."

"Is it?" I could not resist replying bitterly.

"Justin. Do you remember, after we buried your father . . . and . . ." She picked out the next few stitches in silence. ". . . and Mr. Fowler at the bank came to the house to explain to me what my choices were, you remember the talk we had afterward, you and I?"

"Yes, ma'am." Of course I remembered it: how could I ever forget it? That was when she had told me we had to sell the house. And, just as I had been able to accept that, just as I had gotten us comfortably and bravely settled into a smaller house I was sure we could find somewhere in town where everybody would still know who we were, who would remember what we had been—she had dropped her bomb: we were to go north, to live with Aunt Mona and Becky, the cousin I had never seen.

"I thought you understood why this was the only sensible choice. Frankly, Justin, I don't know what we would have done if Mona hadn't invited us to share her home."

"If she hadn't invited us, we would have found a way. If she and Mr. Mott hadn't gotten separated, we would still be at home. You know we would."

"Yes, perhaps. And it would have been terrible. I don't think you have imagined just how painful it would have been to have gone on living there with all those reminders. I mean"—and she put her scissors down upon the cloth, and a savage edge came into her voice—"did you imagine us taking *walks* every Sunday from our dinky little house over to Washington Avenue, so we could see how the new people were enjoying living in our old home? And what, exactly, did you imagine me doing to bring in an income, to bring in money so that your future and Jem's could lie safely in the bank collecting interest, so you could have your chance when the time comes?"

"You could have found something. Everyone would have wanted to help you. Granddaddy helped so many people. And I told you I was willing to get a job after school." I had to keep a tight hold on myself; tears of frustration were threatening to spill. We had been through this before.

"Justin, honey. You are *thirteen years old*. You can't even get a real job till you're sixteen."

"I could have baby-sat my way out of poverty and shabbiness, like Aunt Mona."

"Sarcasm doesn't become you, Justin. Mona may not do everything in the style you've been accustomed to, but she is making an effort to become self-sufficient. I admire that." My mother picked up the nail scissors and went back to Becky's seam. "God knows I admire that," she said with a sigh.

"Well, you could do it, too. You could get your realtor's

license, like Aunt Mona is doing. She said, once she had it, she could make money hand over fist."

"Sooner or later I will have to train for something. I'll have to get some practical education. But, don't you see, my hands are tied until Jem's in school next fall. Until then, I just have to do what I can to help Mona out, and . . . and take the consequences for the kind of person I have been."

"What do you mean?" I said. "I don't understand."

"I'm just beginning to understand, myself," she said in a wistful, *humble* tone I had never heard her use before. "You see, all my life, I got to do exactly as I wanted. When I chose to run off and get married rather than go to Sweet Briar, I did it. There was some fuss made, but what could they do? I was their only child and they had raised me to believe I was a law unto myself. And when your father had to go to war three months later, and I was already expecting you, I was welcomed home like the prodigal daughter. After you were born, I got to go off to Mary Washington every day and take what courses I wanted while someone looked after you at home. And I took art, and courses like 'The History of Furniture,' things like that. Nothing so boring as shorthand or typing or anything that would help me get a job later. Who needed a *job?* I had three people to take care of me. And then, when the war was over, and your father wanted to go off to Charlottesville and get his education, I got to go off with him and lead a carefree young college married life, while Honey and Father felt privileged to keep you at home and begin to spoil you as they'd spoiled me. And when we decided it was time to have another child, even though your father hadn't found the career that suited him yet, my loving parents encouraged us to come right home . . . there was plenty of room for everybody in that house . . . and I suppose it could have gone on like that for decades if Honey hadn't got cancer and then, on top of that, Father his stroke.

"And, you know, we still thought we could make it, your father and I, if we mortgaged the house to pay the staggering medical bills, and having those round-the-clock nurses for your grandfather. It wouldn't have been easy, but Rivers was doing real well selling college jewelry for Balfour. I mean, it wasn't the kind of profession I had hoped he'd have, but it suited his personality. Your daddy had more personality and charm than any man I ever met. He was just a marvelous salesman.

"But what I had never counted on—after all, he had come home without a scratch from the *war*—was one little rainy night and his car skidding on a slick road." She put down the scissors and folded her hands tightly on top of Becky's dress. "So there you have the story of the little girl who got her own way for thirty-two years. Recently I have been thinking . . . well . . . that it would have been better if I hadn't had my own way quite so much. And I've been thinking about you, too. I know there are lots of things you don't like about our new life, but . . . pardon me if I sound hard . . . I think you may grow up to be a better . . . certainly a more useful person than I am because of the very things you suffer now. You'll have to develop strengths I never bothered to. Does that make sense?"

"You make it sound like you brought us here so we could suffer." As soon as the words were out of my mouth, I knew they were unfair. I had said them as a defense against the bleak life she seemed to be holding up to me. Who wanted to spend the rest of their youth developing strengths from suffering? But my pride kept me from retracting them. And also something else: something about her whole penitential speech had upset me profoundly.

"Then you have misunderstood everything I have been trying to say," she replied sadly. "Oh well"—she started ripping Becky's wrong seam with renewed vigor—"maybe I didn't say it well enough. I have only just barely thought it out for myself."

Now I knew what it was that hurt so, as I watched her rip the seam. Her renouncement of the way she had been was ripping out some vital thread that had run through my whole childhood. In our other life, my mother had always starred as "The Daughter." I was left with the role of the sturdy little soul, the companion of the grandparents, who colluded with them in allowing Louise to go on being herself. "We must let Louise have the rest of her college," my grandfather would say. "We must let the young couple have the honeymoon that the war interrupted," my grandmother would say. Leaving me feeling, almost as far back as I could remember, like a prematurely aged little parent myself, who must exercise self-restraint and empathy—the two chief virtues of my grandmother and grandfather, respectively—so that my mother could prolong her life as a girl.

And now she was saying she wished we hadn't allowed it, she wished that self had never been. Where did that leave me? In some kind of limbo, with a lost childhood on either side. There was no reason for me to go on being the kind of person I had been in Fredericksburg; in fact, I couldn't be, even if I wanted to, because it had been in my role as granddaughter that I had excelled, and my grandparents were dead. And as for the few years of childhood left to me now, hadn't my mother just implied that those must be devoted to the art of suffering?

I sat on miserably, in uncomfortable silence with my mother. Even now, the old responsible adult-child self was asserting itself in me. I knew I should say something "wise," or at least gracious, in order to take away some of the sting of my previous remark. But what could I say? Then I recalled the words of the woman I had met today, as we had been walking back toward the sunny fields from the hut, when she had her hand on my shoulder.

"Money does lurk in the plot of everybody's life, then," I heard myself saying. "Even more than passion, probably."

My mother stopped what she was doing and gave me a strange look. "What a deep thing to say. When I was your age, I wouldn't have been capable of such a thought." She laughed bitterly. "Up until a *year* or so ago, if someone had said what you just said, I would have tossed my head and retorted, 'Don't be an old fogey, passion is what makes the world go around!' " In the act of saying this, she tossed her head and became the old Louise for a moment: the girl-mother I worshiped and admired and was jealous of, all at the same time, and was so proud to show off to my friends.

It was this mother I allowed to hug me, and whom I hugged back. "You see," she said, as she let me go, "that's what I'm talking about. Already you are becoming a much stronger and smarter woman than I'll ever be."

But I went outside feeling her triumphant words had been more a threat than a compliment.

Jem was riding his small bike with training wheels up and down the sidewalk in front of our house. He was bright for his age, but small, which put him at a double disadvantage with the other "development" children: if he had been larger, he would have fitted in with the older boys because of his intelligence; the children of his size looked upon him cautiously, as a kind of phenomenon, and he quickly tired of their games. He suffered the additional handicap of having been born in October—just after the cutoff date the public schools cruelly enforced—so he could not enter first grade until next fall, when he would be almost seven. He looked up with such hope, when I came out, that I didn't have the heart to tell him I wanted to go up to the empty house alone and meditate.

We climbed the grassy hill together, Jem taking manly strides to keep up. He was breathing fast with exhilaration at my having actually asked him first. "Want to hear the joke Mott told me?"

"Sure." I could not imagine what kind of joke steady, serious Mr. Mott would tell.

"Why did the robber take a bath?"

"I give up. Why?"

"Because he wanted to make a clean getaway!" Jem cackled hilariously, and I laughed, too, though I thought it was a strange joke for a grown person to tell: so simplistic and childlike. But it would be just like Mr. Mott and his sense of responsibility to go around collecting jokes especially to tell to children.

Neither of us spoke as we climbed the front steps of the old farmhouse. There was something awesome as well as mysterious about an old and empty house where people have lived for many generations. We peered into each of its bare front rooms, which were already full of shadows at this time of evening. Jem, breathing audibly, took my hand. Still holding hands, we walked around the porch and looked in the windows of a long room with a big fireplace. "This was probably the dining room," I said, "because the kitchen's right through there." Jem said he was sure a big family had lived there. "Then the grandmother got sick and died and the grandfather was so sad he got sick and died, and then the father died, and the people left had to sell the house and all this land so they could go somewhere else to live and have enough for later." He looked up at me, in the orange light of the setting sun, for confirmation. "Remember the magician?"

"I sure do," I said.

"You know," he said, "I still think of that magician almost every day."

The last year we had lived in Fredericksburg, during the time that my grandfather had been so ill, a magician and his family had moved into a house on our block. During the week, he went on the road, just like my father, but on the weekends he practiced tricks in his garage and let the neighborhood children watch. After we had buried my father and sold the house, and Mother was packing our boxes and labeling which furniture was to go to storage and which to be sold, Jem had walked back and forth through the empty rooms, saying in a surprised voice: "You know who I'm really going to miss? I'm going to miss that magician."

After we had finished looking through all the windows, I sat on the back steps of the house while Jem climbed a tree. This side of the house faced away from our development, which had spoiled its meadows. From here you saw a thick line of trees and the western sky, which was an orange-pink, with the cirrus clouds that my grandfather had called "mare's tails" scudding across its surface.

If I had been alone, I might have given myself up to the twilight mood and pretended to be some other person, from another time, sitting on this porch. Sometimes I would meditate aloud up here, pretending I was thinking another person's thoughts. Strange phrases would come, fully formed, with a sort of predestined ease, from my mouth, as if I were simply repeating what had actually been thought or said at some other time. And then I'd feel refreshed, a little bit magic, and could take a deep breath and go down the hill feeling impervious to the ordinary life that had begun blinking below, from the lamps in the picture windows. This feeling of imperviousness would sometimes last me all the way to the "Raspberry Ice" walls of my room.

That night I dreamed I was riding my bike home from somewhere. Home was, of course, the house in Fredericksburg. It was night and there were no lights in our house. The only light on the street came from the magician's garage. He was in there practicing his magic, and I could see his figure, with arms outstretched, fingers moving, as he performed some sleight of hand. When I reached our house, the front door was swinging open. I went inside, knowing something was wrong. It was all dark, and I couldn't find a light switch, but I could see from the magician's light down the block that our rooms were completely empty and that there was grass growing abundantly all over the floors.

I sobbed out in panic and distress, and then, suddenly, a firm hand pressed my shoulder, and a low, amused voice told me not to grieve, that this was a good sign, that all our ancestors had lived in houses with grassy floors. I was calmed by the authority of the voice, and, in the dream, I didn't even need to turn around to know whose it was. It was the voice of Ursula DeVane.

III.

*L*ater, in college, I played Nina in *The Sea Gull*. I was having trouble with the scene in which Trigorin is about to leave the Sorin estate and Nina rushes in to tell him she has decided to run away to Moscow and become an actress and she will meet him there. The director told me I acted more thrilled by the prospect of going on stage than I was by Trigorin. "Be enchanted!" he ordered. "Don't you know what it's like to be enchanted?" I knew he was right. Part of the problem was that the actor playing Trigorin was too young. I could not imagine him as the seasoned literary man, the ironic, pleasure-seeking Trigorin; I could not imagine myself being enchanted by him. But I knew that if I were going to do the part well, I would have to find a way to feel enchanted by *Trigorin*, by the essence of enchantment a character named Trigorin personifies. I remember walking slowly back to my dormitory room, determined to evoke in myself the necessary state of enchantment. I waited until dusk, until my roommate had gone to the library; then I opened the windows to the raw spring air. "This is summer air on a country estate in Russia," I told myself, "and I am an ambitious, impressionable young girl whose dreams and feelings are getting too large for her quiet environment. She craves change, she craves romance, she craves danger—the kind of danger that leads to transformation. Then, enter suddenly this magnificent older man who has not only seen and done the things she longs to do, but who seems bored and sarcastic and even sad about it. She is enchanted by him not only for the great world he represents, a world she wants to be a part of, but because, when he looks at her and talks to her, he appears to know something about her that she longs to know about herself. She feels somehow that if she can know and possess him . . . if she allows him to know and possess her . . . that the longed-for, mysterious world will be revealed and she will finally possess herself."

Having reasoned this out, speaking it aloud in my room, I felt closer to Nina. Now, to imagine the scene.

But here my imagination balked. Perversely, it flashed images of the face of the too-young actor playing Trigorin in our production; not the face of the enchanter.

"Be *enchanted*," I ordered myself. "Imagine a convincing enchanter and the rest will follow."

I tried turning my back on the enchanter. I closed my eyes and inhaled the chilly spring air. Let the enchanter approach me from behind. I would not try to picture his features, any features at all. I would simply permit the essence of enchantment—what it would mean to me, how it would make me feel—to enter this room.

After I had stood there for a while, breathing deeply and getting very cold, I did feel in the presence of something. I kept my eyes tightly closed. What was approaching? I was slightly afraid. What if I had invoked something?

It seemed I had.

Purposely breaking the spell I had invoked, I spun around and faced an empty room.

But I knew, with a coward's knowledge, that by turning around when I had, I had limited the Nina a braver me could have portrayed. Yet, I couldn't do it. I was afraid to confront whatever had been in the room with me.

Now I know who it probably was. I think I knew then, but couldn't acknowledge it. Of *course* I knew what it was like to be enchanted. I had been enchanted the summer I was fourteen and living in that quiet rural village that, after we had left it, seemed a passing dream. I had felt enchantment that summer: the constant, straining alertness toward one person and one person only. All I needed to do in my college room was to remember those feelings and put them into my Nina. I would have been a stunning example of the enchanted girl.

But I didn't want to acknowledge, didn't want to remember. Only six years had passed. Six years had not put enough time and healing distance between the fourteen-year-old who had felt shocked and sick and guilty over what had happened, and the twenty-year-old apprentice actress who might have been able to use those memories for an inspired performance.

Perhaps I was wise. If I had remembered her, I might still have felt revulsion for all that happened, and, consequently, all she had made me feel. And I might have decided that I was trying to be an actress because of her influence, because she had wanted to be one.

At twenty, I might have given it up to spite her. To spite her memory.

Now, ironically, I can allow myself to feel again exactly what it was like. With no trouble at all (I don't have to close my eyes or turn my back or stand in a chilly room), I can summon back my obsession to know everything about her life, everything she thought and felt . . . even her memories. And the sense that whatever she was doing at a given time was bound to be more compelling than anything anybody else was doing: at least, anybody in my world. And the continual charged consciousness I had of her, as I went about my day, of the marvelous fact that we shared the same village and that I might see her at any time: that, if I chose to come riding over to her, she always seemed glad to see me. And how, on the days when I didn't want to push my luck by making her tired of me, I could absorb myself completely by going off by myself and imagining her routine—she would be in the garden now; she would be preparing their lunch; she would be down by the pond, reading or swimming (and maybe having a thought or two about me); she would be leaning her head back against the sofa, in that abandoned way she had, while he played her favorite scherzo.

And wanting, somehow, to *be* her; to wake up one morning and find myself waked inside her body, with her memories, and her duties, and even her disappointments. To find out how it felt to be her. To find out what she knew that I didn't know.

And the curious tenderness I felt toward her, as the summer matured, when I realized I would *not* want to be her; when I realized it was far better to be me imagining what it was like to be her. Because my life was still unfolding, and, in many ways, hers—by her own proud admittance—had been foreclosed.

I say it's ironic that I can let myself feel these old feelings again, because of course it's too late for me to play enchanted young girls. And yet I became what she wanted to be. I did that. In that sense, I am her creature. But I couldn't have admitted it, back there in the chilly dormitory room when I was struggling with the part of Nina. I couldn't have admitted it without being engulfed by too much confusion and pain. And in turning away from the pain, I might have turned away from the thing I wanted to become, the thing I most wanted to be.

However, if someone were to write a play with a character like Ursula DeVane, I think I could do justice to that part now.

After Julian DeVane had accepted me as one of them that summer, he sometimes played for me. Once, just before time for me to rush home to supper on my bike, he played one of Rilke's *Sonnets to Orpheus*, which, he told me, stuttering shyly, he had set to music for an old teacher and friend who was a singer. I thought the music was very strange—discordant, even—but compelling, especially the way he played it, with his eyes almost closed, his fingers touching the keys with restraint, as if he feared he might evoke more than he could bear.

Then Ursula made him play it a second time, and she went over and stood beside him at the piano and laid her hand lightly on his shoulder as she sang the words. I could see that she was pleased with herself for singing the German so well: she knew she was impressing me; she knew I was completely in her power. She sang in a deeper voice than her own because she said that this man, a lieder singer, had been a bass baritone and Julian had written the music to accommodate his low range. I remember watching her and thinking she had the ability to transform herself into anything she pleased. Right now she had *become* the man, the lieder singer. Her performance dazzled me, but I was also distraught: she was too much for me and she knew it. I was afraid I would lose her completely, during one of these transformations, and yet her power over me made me miserable at times. What am I to *do* with all these feelings? I remember thinking.

She must have read my mind, because afterward, when Julian had left us, she sat down beside me on the sofa and explained to me that the song she had just sung had been about a special kind of love. "It's a love that can never be satisfied," she said. "That is its property. It's more like"—and she leaned her head back against the sofa and contemplated the low ceiling with its old beams—"it's more like a *yearning*. The person in the song is really addressing a powerful and constant state of yearning more than he is any real lover. It's the state of yearning that torments him, yet he also loves his torment. He *needs* it. Because he understands that being able to feel this yearning so exquisitely is his secret strength." She reached over casually and put her hand on top of mine. "Do you understand that?"

I could barely nod. I was so full of the things she was describing.

"That is one of the best compositions Julian ever wrote," she said, removing her hand as easily as she had bestowed it. "That is the power of the artist, you see. If you are an artist, you learn how to trap the yearning and put it where you want it, put it where it goes. That's the secret all true artists come to know."

Now, enough time has passed for me to repossess—and be repossessed by—that late-summer evening, twenty-six years

ago. I can revisit that room, which then seemed a kind of taber-
nacle devoted to the life I wanted: music, art, travel, sensibility,
drama; conversations that moved easily into the realms of the
imagination. And the amazing thing is, I am possessed now by
the same emotions as I was then, through the act of intensely remembering. I remember how I looked through the window, as
Julian played and Ursula sang, and saw the mountain and the old
hotel's lookout tower, to which Ursula had, just that afternoon,
promised to take me the following week, the tower to which Ursula and I would climb after she had told me the strangest of all
her stories about her life. I remember sitting on that sofa, surrounded by so many feelings that I didn't know whether I was
miserable or ecstatic. I remember being afraid that it would rain
the day we planned to go to the tower. Now, after all this time, I
can almost reach out and touch that girl I was, as well as the
woman who sat beside me, in that room still filled with echoes of
Julian's music, written as a gift of love to his own fateful mentor.
At last, I can feel what my mentor felt, think the thoughts she
must have thought, as she spoke to me of unrequited yearnings
and shaped my demands on the future. And, having gone
through the stages of adoring her, despising her, and forgiving
her, maybe I am finally ready to forgive myself. That's why I am
now able to appreciate her even more than I did when dazzled by
her. She was a unique woman. And a tragic one.

But the rebirth of all these long-suppressed feelings has
made me anticipate my story. We are not in the middle of the
summer yet. We are still at the beginning, and I have met Ursula
DeVane only that one time, in the broken-down hut by the pond
in the woods. And dreamed that curious dream about her on the
night of that day.

Which two events had given me an interest in riding the
school bus. I no longer dreaded being trapped twice every school
day in its fume-filled interior with several dozen kids whose
voices, as they rose in pitch as the bus grew more crowded in the
morning, and fell into murmurs between friends as it emptied in

the afternoon, seemed almost foreign in their rough consonants and different cadences. Because this bus now took me, twice a day, five days a week, past a house that grew more and more interesting to me.

In the mornings I would take a window seat on the left side of the bus and wait for those few seconds when, after Ed Cristiana and his sister climbed aboard and the bus gathered speed for the childless stretch of Old Clove Road, the DeVane house came into sight.

I would stare intensely, trying to memorize details. Then, in the afternoons, I would take a window seat on the right side of the bus and concentrate all my attention toward those few seconds when the bus rumbled past the house.

I should mention that, the day after I had met Ursula in the hut, I shortened my afternoon bike rides on Old Clove Road. Now I went only as far as the hill *before* the Cristianas' horse farm came into view. This was because I did not care to face the horsebreeder with his knowing eyes again, after he had seen me watching the horses. But even if that event had not occurred, I would have stopped short of the DeVane house, which was half a mile farther along the winding road. And I certainly would not have returned to the hut where I had burst in on Ursula reading, even though she had said, at the last, "Next time you drop by, bring your suit." Anyone who suffers from shyness will understand me. I had decided that our next meeting would have to occur by chance, and then if she had really meant it she would let me know. The dream I had had about her had given her an added, a mystical dimension, and I felt we were fated to know each other because I had dreamed about her in such a way. Even then, I took my dreams seriously, and I knew the difference between ordinary dreams, which mixed together all sorts of leavings from the day before, and important dreams, which, in some wonderfully economical way, seemed to be able to solve a problem, or at least illuminate that problem, by combining a simple, often strange and symbolic scenario with powerful feelings. The powerful feelings that remained with me after one of these dreams were the proof that it had been an important dream.

And after I had dreamed of the house with grassy floors and Ursula's hand on my shoulder and her voice telling me this was good, not bad, I knew that she belonged to me. I never doubted that a subsequent meeting would soon come, and I almost enjoyed delaying it because of the added significance it would now take on.

Of course, if Mr. Cristiana hadn't seen me watching the horses, I would have turned around at my usual spot that day and gone home, leaving Ursula bored by Proust and wishing vainly for something unexpected. But, as I interpreted it—and my lonely, undemanding life allowed me pleanty of time to fantasize and interpret—fate had intervened once and would surely do so again. Meanwhile, I could study the house.

When I first saw it, I was disappointed. Something Aunt Mona had said had put different pictures in my head. Yet all she had said was that it was one of the original stone houses built by the Huguenots, and that it was right on the road. But the "old houses" I had been taken to see—the grand, ruined plantations I had visited with my grandfather when he went out on his field trips to research the family life of slaves, the famous Revolutionary house across the street from ours that my grandmother's club had helped restore—did not prepare me to be impressed by the plain, lonely-looking house with yellowed mortar holding together the crude, uneven gray stones. There was an austere dignity about its old, plain facade, but it was in no way beautiful or grand. It had two stories, though the upper one, with its narrow dormers, looked like an afterthought. The east side of the house, which looked even older, was sunk lower on its foundations and gave the whole structure an asymmetrical effect. The shutters on the downstairs windows were painted the same glossy black as the front door, and the shrubbery and lawn were cared for, though not with the meticulous care given by the IBM fathers to the lawns in Lucas Meadows: from the window of the bus, I could see unchecked spurts of onion grass and several bare patches that should have been reseeded. A towering lilac bush that was just now blooming at the old, left corner of the house did a lot to soften the harsh and solitary aspect of the place.

At first I had thought, Surely Aunt Mona meant some other

house, but it was the only stone house that came anywhere after the Cristianas' house, and it was the first house following the pine forest and a field between. Finally my desire to know for sure overcame my shyness, and I tapped Ed Cristiana's sister Ann on the shoulder one morning when she sat just in front of me. "Whose interesting old stone house was that, that we just passed?" I asked. She looked surprised that I had spoken to her, but then she said, "Oh, that's the DeVane place," and smiled at me and stayed turned around for a minute, as if she hoped I might ask her something else.

Then, a couple of mornings later, I saw Ursula in the yard. She wore the same clothes as she had in the hut, only her hair was tied back with a bright kerchief. She was cutting lilacs. As the school bus hurtled past with its noisy load, she looked up, straight at my window, where I was already ducking my head in embarrassment. I rode the rest of the way to school feeling foolish for being so curious about a woman I hardly knew. But I also went on imagining her: how she had looked different in the kerchief than with her hair curling loose around her head that day in the hut (the kerchief made her look more like a housewife, one of the mothers in Lucas Meadows); and how, after she had cut some more blossoms, she would have gone into the house and found a vase, or maybe an old silver bowl, and arranged the lilacs in it to enhance some room. She had looked so sure of herself in the yard, as if the best thing you could do on a morning like this was tie a housewifely kerchief around your curls and go cut blossoms for "the good life," as she had described the life she led with her brother. "I mean, let's face it, they've got to be peculiar, a middle-aged brother and sister living together," Aunt Mona had said. But, somehow, that made it more interesting to me than if Ursula DeVane had been living with a husband. There was more mystery, this way; there was some hidden story to be brought to light. And also—I understand this now, too—it isolated Ursula more from the ordinary world and made her more accessible to me.

Ann Cristiana stopped me in the hall and asked me if I rode. I said "a little," which stretched the boundaries of truth, though it allowed me to keep my pride. Her gentle smile widened. "I thought so," she said. "My dad's seen you admiring our horses. Well, I mean, they're not *all* ours, but we take care of them as though they were."

I looked closely at her face, to see if she was making fun of me about my "admiring" the horses, but she seemed completely in earnest. She asked me to ride with her and her brother the next afternoon. "Bring your riding things to school and get off with us at our stop, and somebody will drive you home afterward."

I said yes; I couldn't think how to say no. I was flattered because she was a year older and had her own crowd. I guessed that, in my sadness and preoccupation with my lost world, I had seemed aloof to my schoolmates, and that my speaking first to her on the bus had released her sense of hospitality. And then it occurred to me that going riding at the Cristianas' might give fate the very opportunity it had been waiting for: wasn't their land right next to the DeVane land? I saw myself, looking splendid on horseback, somehow running into *her*.

My mother got animated when I told her about the invitation. She dragged out her trunk and unpacked the riding clothes her parents had bought for Sweet Briar, unaware that she was planning to elope with my father instead. "I've hardly even worn these," she said, "but now they might fit you." She seemed so pleased about Ann Cristiana's asking me that I felt selfish for not having come home with an invitation sooner.

The jodhpur boots were a little roomy, but they stayed on when we strapped them tight. The jacket was way too big in the chest, even though it was the right length. But the brown twill jodhpurs fit perfectly, as if they had been made for me. "Thank goodness it's so warm," my mother said. "You can wear your yellow oxford cloth shirt without a jacket." Then she suddenly frowned.

"Oh Lord, Justin, haven't we forgotten something?"

"What?"

"You can't ride very well, honey. Remember those few times when I took you out to Mr. Eames's stable? And how your horse was always stopping on the trail and Mr. Eames finally said to you, 'Let him know who's boss, Justin,' and *you* said, 'Oh, he already knows, sir.'"

I didn't remember saying that, I barely remembered those trail rides, but it was wonderful to see my mother laugh.

"I expect I ought to have taken you there every weekend while you were still so young," she mused, frowning again. "But that's when Rivers and I were commuting back and forth from Charlottesville so he could go to school, and our weekends with you and Honey and Daddy were just so short."

"It's okay," I said. "I'll keep my heels down and watch my posture and try to fool him about who's boss."

"If it was me going over there," said Jem, who had been overseeing my costuming with interest, "you know what I'd do?"

"I hope you'd ask for a gentle horse," said my mother, looking at me.

"Well, I might do that," said Jem. "But if it was me going over there in those jodhpurs, I'd just act like they were mine and I'd been riding since I was a *baby*."

Aunt Mona, coming home from work, heard our voices and poked her head around the door. "Why, if it isn't Miz Scarlett," she said when she saw me in the riding clothes.

"Scarlett never wore jodhpurs," said I.

"Well, the effect is the same," said my aunt. "You look like one of the privileged few, getting ready to ride off on your horse."

"That's what I told her!" shouted Jem, for once agreeing with Aunt Mona. "She looks like she's *always* ridden."

"Come in, Mona," said my mother. "Justin's been asked to go riding over at the Cristianas'. Do you know who they are?"

"Oh, they're fine. Mott was on the Volunteer Fire Squad with Abel Cristiana. He liked him. The Cristianas have been here forever, just like the DeVanes. Only they don't put on airs like the DeVanes; they're just simple farming types."

"Who are the DeVanes?" asked my mother.

"All that's *left* of them are a brother and sister who live in the old family house over on Old Clove. The brother is an awful man who used to teach Becky piano; *she* puts on a show of having been greater places and done greater things. But get your daughter to tell you about her: they're great friends."

"That's not so, Aunt Mona," I said, feeling my face go hot, "I only met her that once."

"You never mentioned it to me, Justin," said my mother.

"I didn't think you'd be interested." Then, sensing that I had hurt her feelings, I added somewhat coldly, "It just wasn't very important. She was just this woman I happened to meet when I was out riding my bike."

"Why is the man awful?" Jem wanted to know. "Has he done something bad?"

"Well, he killed music for your cousin Becky," said Aunt Mona, her feather cut starting to quiver a little. "But get Justin to tell you about it. We don't talk about it in front of Beck, because it's not productive to bring up old setbacks. But, Louise, the Cristianas are perfectly okay for Justin to know. They're good, hardworking types. He built up that horse business himself, after the war. Before that it was just a rundown farm he'd inherited from his father. Mott liked him when they were on the Fire Squad together. Mott said he'd had a good war. That's Mott's measuring stick for a man. Now, Mr. Julian DeVane had a very *questionable* war. But"—she gestured toward me—"get the Equestrian Lady there to tell you about it. I told her the other day, and I haven't got the time to dwell on people like that."

And I might have had to, had Aunt Mona not suddenly got another bee in her bonnet. She cocked her head and looked disapprovingly at the former den, which was now my mother's bedroom. "Louise, why don't we redo this room? You can't be happy with those old plaid curtains."

"Oh, they're fine," said my mother.

"But they're so plain," said my aunt. "They're so unlike what you've been used to."

"Maybe that's why I like them," said my mother.

"I was thinking maybe organdy," said Aunt Mona. "Of

course we'd have to iron them. But no, they might look a little out of place against the pine paneling. I wonder if we could wallpaper over pine paneling. One of those soft English country scenes would just suit you, Louise."

"Honestly, Mona, I'm just fine as I am down here. I mean, there's nothing here that *reminds* me of anything." And then I saw my mother look embarrassed, because this statement might be conceived by Aunt Mona as a slur on her taste. "I mean I really do *like* those plaid curtains," she added quickly.

"Well," said Aunt Mona, not seeming to notice any slur, "I really should have done it over before you came, to be a little more like the style you are accustomed to, but I thought it was more important to get the kids' rooms fixed up first. I was so tickled with that circus wallpaper I found for Jimbo . . . excuse me, *Jem*"—and she made a mock bow to my brother—"and with that nice screen we found to put in front of the washing machine and dryer—nobody would know it was a utility room. But I was really happy with the way Justin's room turned out. Exactly the kind of room I might have wanted for myself when I was Justin's age—that is, if we could have afforded luxuries like new curtains and flounces and two cans of paint. I wanted to do Beck's room over, but she wouldn't let me near it with a ten-foot pole. Beck is going through a moody phase."

"Well, I really am very comfortable, just as I am," insisted my mother, careful not to catch my eye. I had informed her, in no uncertain language, how I felt about my room.

After Mona had gone upstairs, I posed some more in my jodhpurs and boots. I liked the way I looked in the full-length mirror affixed to the door. My mother must have liked it, too, because she sat looking at me in a wistfully admiring way, as if she were thinking, Ah yes, my daughter is becoming an attractive young woman, even if life is over for me.

"You certainly do look the part, Justin," she finally said. "But you must promise me one thing, before I let you go."

"What?" I said.

"That you'll tell those Cristianas you haven't ridden very much, and to give you a gentle horse."

I made this promise to my mother, and my dilemma grew acute as I changed into the riding clothes in Ann's bedroom the next afternoon. It was a warm day and the windows were open, and the sounds and smells of horses were all around us. As I buckled the straps of the jodhpur boots into their tightest holes, I knew Ann, who had simply put on old jeans and a pair of heavy brown oxfords, was impressed by the clothes and assumed I wore them all the time. Then, to make things worse, her little sister Jenny, who was in grammar school with Becky, stuck her pigtailed head in the door, looked me over with awe, and said, "Boy, Annie, do we have anything good enough for her to ride?"

"I'm sure we'll find the right horse for her," said Ann, with the calm I already admired. There was a sweet, motherly quality about Ann, who was the oldest child in the family. "If not, I'm sure Ed will let her have Mercury."

Mercury! Wasn't he the god of speed? Now, I thought, was the perfect time to speak out, to explain about my riding experience. Hadn't I promised my mother?

We went downstairs. My boots sounded loud and pretentious on the bare boards, compared to the soft, placid scuffle of Ann's oxfords. I felt like a pretender hiding behind a costume from these simple, friendly people who were so willing to accept me at face value. Their house was rather bare and shabby— everywhere you could see signs of patching up and making do— but it made me homesick for the house in Fredericksburg to hear the stairs squeak. Ann introduced me to her mother in the kitchen. Mrs. Cristiana was a thin, older version of Ann. There was the same calm, accepting manner about her, only she looked rather tired and was expecting a baby.

Out in the stableyard Ed was saddling the horses, assisted by his young brother. They had already saddled a restless mahogany one, who backstepped when we approached: was that Mercury? Across the road Mr. Cristiana was in the training ring with the stallion. He was walking the animal testily around the circle, holding him by a lead attached to the halter. The stallion was tense and wary, and the horsebreeder carried a stick, which he nudged threateningly against the stallion's muzzle whenever the animal started shaking his head. Even from where I was standing I could see that there was a war of wills being played out between the tough man and the excited horse. For one panicked moment I thought that maybe the *stallion* was Mercury, and that Mr. Cristiana was getting him ready for me to ride, someone having sent down the news about my elegant jodhpurs. Maybe Mr. Cristiana thought it would be poetic justice to put the pretentious girl in her citified finery up on the beast she had gaped at while he mated.

Then Ed came over to me with that bouncy, country walk that kept me from taking him seriously. He began explaining at once the plans for our afternoon ride, as impersonally as if I were just some stranger who was hiring one of the horses for the afternoon. But as he talked about the route we would take around the fields, he never once met my eyes, and a pink glow spread up his neck and over his entire face. I remembered the way he had looked at me at school, and put two and two together: Ann Cristiana had asked me here because her brother liked me. I was annoyed because I had no intention of being "fixed up" with Ed, but at the same time I felt more sure of myself.

"We won't be able to warm up in the ring," Ed was apologizing, "because my Dad's stallion, Turk, has this bad swollen tendon and has to be walked there so he can get his exercise. I know you're probably used to warming up in a ring." He cast a shy glance at my riding outfit.

"Turk has to keep in shape," explained the little brother, "so he'll stay fertile. Turk will serve more than twenty mares before the summer's over, and *that's* strenuous work!"

"And that's enough, Petey," said Ann, blushing. "Who's Justin going to ride, Ed?"

This was the time for me to speak. "I think I'd better explain something," I said. "It's been a little while since I last rode a horse. In fact, the last time I did ride—I was *thrown*. It was a . . . a stallion. I really shouldn't have been allowed to ride him at all, but I wanted to. Since then, I've been a little nervous. So maybe you'd better start me off on a ... you know ... gentle horse."

I was amazed at how fluently this story sprang to my lips. While I was telling it, I actually *saw* myself, wearing these very clothes, toppling through the bright air like a stunt girl in the movies. I was equally amazed at how readily they accepted it.

"Gee, it's lucky you weren't hurt," said Ed, venturing to meet my eyes for the first time.

"Our father would never let anybody ride Turk except himself," murmured Ann.

"And even *he's* scared of Turk when he's in one of his moods," put in Petey.

And then I was being mounted on a horse called Gentleman Johnny, who, they explained to me, was to have been my horse all along. "Johnny's dependable," said Ed, "and as we didn't know how much you had ridden ... how would you like your stirrups? Southerners like them long, don't they?"

"Geldings," explained Petey from the ground, "are better mannered than stallions. That's because—"

"That's enough, now, Petey," said Ann, mounting her palomino; then she gave her little brother some instructions about mucking out the stalls.

Ed gave his horse, Mercury, some slight signal that set all three mounts moving slowly toward the pasture, where we were "just going to hack around," Ed said protectively, until I got accustomed to riding again.

It was a beautiful afternoon, with a bright golden light on the pasture that made you have to squint your eyes. Ed and Ann made brother-and-sister horse talk, tactfully letting me get the feel of my horse. Gentleman Johnny was unusually smooth and agreeable and responded to my lightest touch; sometimes it even seemed that he responded *before* my touch, as though he had taken this same ride many times before and knew exactly what was expected of him. I was almost sorry I had told my fib. With this diplomatic horse I could have passed easily as an intermediate-class rider.

"Annie and I thought we'd ride over and show you our new land," said Ed, coming alongside of me. "Our dad just bought it. It's great land; we were lucky to get it. Our neighbors had to sell because they needed the money. But I've got my work cut out this summer because of it. I have to put up post-and-rail fences all around the new acreage."

I was so intent upon keeping my heels down and my hands relaxed and my spine straight and my face casual that it took me a minute to realize Ed must be talking about the DeVanes. Hadn't *she* said, that day in the hut, that Mr. Cristiana's land had been their land until sacrifices had to be made?

"Oh, which neighbors are those?" I asked.

"The DeVanes," said Ed.

"They live in that stone house. You know, the one you asked me about on the bus," said Ann. "Only they had to take a mortgage on it. Our father says that's the beginning of the end when you have to borrow money on your own house."

"Well, we borrowed money to buy their fields," said Ed to his sister.

"That's different," she said in her motherly tone. "That was just getting a straight-out loan from the bank, because the bank knows our credit is good and we can pay it back. But we didn't mortgage our own house that has never been out of the family, like the DeVanes did."

"I guess you're right," said Ed, deferring to his older sister. "Anyway, it's fine land, with a stream and everything. Only she refused to sell us the pond. There's this great little freshwater pond in the middle of the woods. Dad was going to stock it with fish, but she told him she couldn't give up her refuge. There's this old stone hut in there, too. It would have been great. We begged Dad to insist on that hut and the pond as part of the bargain. But Dad said she was entitled to the few pleasures she had left and he wasn't going to push her."

"Are they so *poor*, then?" I asked.

"Pretty poor. They don't have any income, except from his

teaching. He teaches piano. But my dad told us she wants him to make a comeback and that costs money. He was going to be a concert pianist before the war. So what she's trying to do is invest everything in this comeback. Dad says it's a big gamble. The reason they had to sell the land was so he could buy a really good Steinway to practice on. He's kind of a strange guy. He and Dad don't get along at all. He didn't want to sell the land when he found out we wanted to buy, but she talked him into it. My dad says she's sacrificing herself for him, when she could have done great things herself."

"Like what?" I asked.

"I'm not really sure," said Ed. "How do you like Gentleman Johnny?"

"He's *very* smooth."

"He's a Tennessee walker. We bought him for my little sister Jenny, but you shouldn't feel insulted or anything. My dad rides Johnny sometimes, when he's inspecting the land. You know, these horses were bred for Southern planters, so they could ride them all day long without getting tired. That's because of their gait. It's this soft rocking motion where you don't have to post. Want to trot him now? Just give him the slightest pressure with your legs and he'll do the rest."

The next thing I knew, I was gliding along on the affable Johnny, who was certainly doing everything he could to let me pretend I was boss. I didn't even have to post. Ed posted on Mercury, showing off a bit, but I had to admit he looked much more commanding on a horse than down on the ground, bobbing up and down with his bouncy walk. I would have liked to ask more questions about the DeVanes, but I couldn't trot and talk at the same time. Ann had dropped some distance behind us, and I was certain that my being there was at her brother's instigation. Well, I would do the same thing for Jem, when the time came, so I really couldn't blame her.

"You're doing great!" Ed called to me, riding a little ahead. There might as well have been a lead tied between his horse and mine, so dutifully did Gentleman Johnny follow in Mercury's steps.

We descended into a lower field and I looked to the right and realized that this was the spot at which I had entered, the day I found Ursula. There was the haywagon road that stopped abruptly at the beginning of the field. And there was the pine forest. She might even be reading in the hut right now. I strained to listen for music coming from the house somewhere on the other side, but all I heard was my own creaking saddle and Gentleman Johnny's rhythmic footfalls in the grass.

We rode a little farther; then Ed abruptly turned Mercury around, as if stopped at a border. "That's as far as we'll go now," he said.

"But where is the DeVane house?" I asked. "I don't see it." Gentleman Johnny was obediently turning around, to follow Mercury.

"Well, it's just around the corner from those pines," said Ed. "It sits up on a hill. I'd be glad to point it out to you, but our father told us to stay out of sight of it whenever we could. You see, it makes DeVane mad to see us, and then he takes it out on his sister. Of course, we're going to have to be in sight when we start putting up the fences, but for now Dad said play it cool."

"He sounds like an ogre. Why does he hate you all so much?"

"I don't think he hates *us*, except that we're my father's children. He and Dad had this fight about something a long time ago, when they were both a lot younger. It wasn't a real *fight*, because Dad says DeVane never could fight with his hands on account of his talent, but they had a terrible argument about something and he's hated Dad ever since."

"Does your father hate *him?*"

"Not really. He just thinks he's kind of strange. And he thinks he's a drag on his sister."

"What was the fight about?"

"I'm not sure. I think it was something about their mother. She was in an insane asylum. I think Dad said he had mentioned it once, and then DeVane got mad and said some pretty unkind things about our family. The DeVanes are terrible snobs, my mom says. Anyway, Dad doesn't talk about it much, except to tell us to avoid him as much as we can."

"I guess that's best," I said. An insane asylum! I thought she said her mother had *died*.

We rode together in silence for a few minutes. I was so deeply engrossed in all this new information I had learned about the DeVanes that I was borne along on my horse in complete unselfconsciousness. Gone were all fears of making myself ridiculous.

Then Ed looked over at me and swallowed hard and blushed again. "Justin, you're doing just great," he said.

"I'm having a wonderful time," I told him.

"Well, you'll have to come back and we'll . . . do it again. I mean, if I have any free time between putting up those fences. Of course . . . of course, you and *Ann* can always ride . . ." He stopped, looking thoroughly confused at all he was trying to say and trying not to say.

"Of course," I said graciously. All I felt was a sort of wonderment that I could have power over someone without having tried for it, without even wanting it.

We trotted our horses back to where Ann, that cupid, was actually allowing her horse to graze, so as to let us keep to ourselves. I was sorry not to have been spotted in my equestrian glory by Ursula DeVane, but, because of this ride, I knew more about her than I had before. A mother in the insane asylum! And Mr. Cristiana thought she was sacrificing herself for her brother, when she could have done great things herself. It had all the makings of a drama, and with quite a bit of mystery attached, as well.

As the three of us made our way back to the stableyard across the bright fields, I felt happy and at the same time pensive. The happiness was because I had comported myself well on my horse, however much that horse had contributed to the effect. I had not disgraced myself with these new friends, and Ed Cristiana admired me. It was not that I wanted a boyfriend—or that I wanted Ed Cristiana as a boyfriend—but I knew that the time was coming when it would be desirable for me to have boyfriends, and I was relieved to know that my charms were sufficient to attract one without even trying. My pensiveness came from what I felt to be a new and profound truth I had discovered during this outing: that the same things can be important to people for entirely different reasons. Ed Cristiana had been satisfied with this afternoon because I had been in it; whereas my greatest interest in the afternoon had come out of the additional things I had been able to learn about his fascinating neighbors. Poor Ed would never in a million years suspect this divergence, and if someone told him, I knew he would not be happy to know it.

Mrs. Cristiana was busy preparing supper for her large family, and, as neither Ed nor Ann was old enough to drive, it fell to Mr. Cristiana to take me home. To my embarrassment, I overheard Ed and his father speaking outside in the stableyard while I was upstairs in the bathroom.

"Isn't she riding her bike?" the father asked gruffly.

"No, Dad. She came on the bus with us."

"Where does she live?"

"Over in Lucas Meadows. You know, those new houses?"

A silence. "Who's going to hose down Turk's tendon? It's got to be done now."

"I guess I will."

"You guessed right. Well, tell her to come on. I haven't got all day."

The horsebreeder removed some tools from the passenger side of the truck, and I climbed in.

"Lucas Meadows, right?" He started the engine with a roar.

"Yes sir." Sitting beside him in my jodhpurs, a department store shopping bag containing my school clothes on my lap, I felt how superfluous I must seem to his concerns.

We started down Old Clove Road. He kept his eyes straight ahead and might as well have forgotten me. He smelled strongly of sweat and horse and some pungent liniment, probably something he had been rubbing on the stallion's sore tendon. It would be at least eight minutes, I calculated, before we would be in Lucas Meadows, and I wished I could just blank out until that time: it would certainly make no difference to him. But I had been brought up to make polite conversation with my elders so as not to seem "sullen." "Speak to them about what they know, and what it is appropriate for *you* to know," my grandmother had instructed me once, when our rector and his wife arrived too early for a visit and I had to go down and entertain them while my grandmother finished dressing. "And steer clear of topics that are too familiar, or original," she had added, as I left her bedroom.

I told Mr. Cristiana that I was very sorry to hear about Turk's tendon. Would it be all right, did he think?

Then I had to repeat myself because I had apparently startled him out of some deep thought. I spoke louder, this time, to be heard over the noise of the truck.

"Oh, he'll be okay," said the horsebreeder.

"Did he *stumble?*" I asked.

"Nope. A mare kicked him. It's what you might call an occupational injury." He gave a short, dry laugh.

"Oh, *I* see," I said enthusiastically, not seeing at all.

He turned then and looked at me. "That's right. You were there, weren't you? You did see. She kicked hell out of him. Thank God she was booted. Did your people keep horses down south?"

"No sir." So he had actually mentioned it: how he had caught me watching the horses. But it had not been as awkward as it could have been.

We rode for a minute without saying anything. Then he declared, "But I still hold out for corral breeding."

"Oh, do you? Why?"

"Well, *because* . . ." He narrowed his eyes at the road in front, and his face and neck grew ruddier. It must have occurred to him that it might not be quite the thing to discuss breeding methods with a strange young girl he was driving home. But his passion got the better of him. "My father did it that way, and his father before him. They didn't tie a mare up with all these hobbles and twitches. They would have laughed at me for putting on the *boots.* And the most unnatural thing of all is this new 'colt-by-mail-order' business. Who's to say what kind of material you're going to get through the damn mail."

"The *mail?*" I squeaked. What was he talking about?

"Artificial insemination," he replied brusquely.

I thought my grandmother would have given me about a "C-minus" for that conversation.

We rode on for what seemed another *eighty* minutes, and we still hadn't left Old Clove Road. I knew I should leave well enough (or not so well enough) alone, but I was more than ever determined to have a successful conversation with him.

"My uncle, Mr. Mott, said—"

"Oh, Eric Mott's your uncle? How is he?"

"He's just fine. He lives on a houseboat now. He and my aunt separated."

"I think I heard something about it. He still with IBM?"

"Oh yes. It's a very friendly separation," I went on. "He comes over every Saturday and mows the lawn and sees to things around the house."

"That's nice of him," said the horsebreeder dryly.

"He said you had a very good war."

This took Mr. Cristiana aback for a minute. Then he said, "I made the most of what I got. If you want to call that good." But I caught a pride in his tone that made me think it was safe to go on.

"What did you . . . get?"

"Well, first I got shot down. But I flew eleven missions first. After they shot me down, they put me in a German prison camp. That was no fun. But horses got me out." He looked at me in that provocative way people do when they want you to ask them to go on. I had found the right subject, I decided.

"*Horses?*"

"The Germans found out I was good with horses. This was in the winter of 'forty-four, when the Russians were on their way into Germany. Roosevelt had made this deal with the Russians, see, that they could go in and take the east part of Germany and we'd wait and take the west part—but don't get me started on Roosevelt. Anyway, the Germans wanted to get their Trakehner horses out. The Trakehners were the best German breed of horse there was . . . beautiful, powerful horses . . . a unique breed of horses . . . and the big Trakehner stud farm lay right in the path of the Russians, in a part of Germany that later became Poland. Well, they asked me to help out, and I did. A German officer who'd lost an arm in the war and myself got a hundred mares and stallions to what's now West Germany. Altogether, about nine hundred horses were saved. I might go back there one day and visit the descendants of those horses. I might even look up that German officer. We had a lot in common. We both grew up on farms where horses were raised. If he's still alive, I'd like to thank him. You know what he did?"

"No sir, what?"

"After we got the horses to the farms where they were going, he looked the other way and let me escape to the Allied front."

I thought it was a very exciting story. I especially liked the part about the one-armed German officer looking the other way. It expressed a kind of camaraderie I wanted to believe existed in the larger world. But one point bothered me, a point having to do with patriotism. My grandmother would no doubt have advised me to leave well enough alone (for we had now *had* a successful conversation), but I wanted to clear up something. Why was it considered all right, by such people as Mr. Mott, that Abel Cristiana had helped the enemy save their horses, when Julian DeVane was criticized simply for staying too long in a country that sympathized with the enemy? Mr. Mott had said Mr. Cristiana had had a good war, whereas, according to Aunt Mona, he considered Julian DeVane practically a traitor. I decided it must have something to do with bravery. Mr. Cristiana had proved his bravery by getting shot down, whereas Julian DeVane hadn't joined up until the war was almost over. But to Julian DeVane, music came before fighting; hadn't Ed said that, even when he was young, Julian DeVane would not fight with his hands because of his talent? Julian DeVane had been pursuing his talent in Argentina, and Mr. Cristiana had been true to his love for horses in enemy territory. But Mr. Cristiana had been brave, and Julian DeVane hadn't. I wondered how Ursula DeVane would defend her brother on this question.

"Did you ever feel you were being disloyal," I asked Mr. Cristiana, "when you were helping the Germans?"

"I wasn't helping the Germans, I was helping the horses. *They* didn't cause the war. The *horses* didn't vote for Adolf Hitler. If we'd left them there for the Russians, the breed would probably be extinct by now. Those Bolsheviks would have made horsemeat out of them."

"Oh," I said.

"On a scale between Russian and German," pursued the horsebreeder more heatedly, "give me German any day. We've got more in common with the Germans. And while we're on the subject of loyalty, I'll tell you something else: I had a lot more respect for that German officer riding all that distance when he'd just had an arm amputated, in order to save those lovely Trakehners, than I have for some of my close neighbors."

And he scowled so angrily at the houses, as we turned into Lucas Meadows, that I thought he would have gladly sold us all—especially one talkative young girl—down the river for the sake of that German officer. But after I had thanked him for the ride, and he had looked at me as though I hadn't turned out to be quite as silly as he had expected, and had said, "You come back and ride again," and I was starting up the front walk of our yellow house with its lamp in the window, I knew he had probably been thinking of one particular neighbor over on Old Clove Road.

IV.

On Saturday morning of Memorial Day weekend it rained, so Mr. Mott could not cut the grass. He telephoned to say it was supposed to clear up by early afternoon; meanwhile, if it was all right with us, he would spend the morning making some repairs on the houseboat and collect Becky in the afternoon.

This change of plans, along with the rain, upset the household. Becky pouted because her father always took her out to lunch on Saturday. Jem was grumpy because he could not play outside. Aunt Mona worked half-days on Saturdays at the travel agency in Kingston, and after that she always had her hair done, so my mother was pretty much stuck with the job of amusing us. She suggested we all help her go through some boxes from Fredericksburg she hadn't yet unpacked, and see what we could find.

As the things came out of the boxes, I could remember my mother hastily packing them in, almost vengeful in her grief. Supposedly I had been helping, but even at that zero hour, with our reservations already booked on the train to Aunt Mona's, I had been trying to talk her out of going. Now, as each thing was withdrawn from the boxes, I could remember arguments I had been making as it had been put in. There was my old paint set, my father's shoeshine kit, the Ink Spots album they had loved to dance to, and the little enamel-topped card box in which my grandmother had kept her solitaire deck: that had been when we were packing up things we had used on the sun porch. I had been standing by the open windows (for it was already quite warm) and gazing out on my grandmother's garden, where, from the middle of March to the middle of October, there was a succession of flowers. I had been advancing my arguments for that small house, somewhere in town, where we could live in cheerful frugality and still have all our old friends and landmarks. Finally, having heard all she could stand, my mother told me I was "too young" to have thought out all the complications of staying in a place when your supports were gone. Rather than being reminded constantly of how much better things used to be, she said, it was far better to start over again where nobody knew you. And just as I was going to protest that there was no reason to go to such extremes, she silenced me with the adult's ultimate ploy: she had made the decision, she said, and, since I was still a child, I would have to abide by it.

So, when my mother, beginning on another box, to divert Jem and Becky on this rainy Saturday, pulled out a yellow taffeta evening dress that she had worn as a girl, and said she had saved it for me, and asked me to try it on, I was still smarting from our argument on the sun porch back in Fredericksburg. I said I didn't "feel like it, right now," even though I had been the one who had begged her to save that dress when she was about to put it in the Salvation Army box with my father's and grandparents' clothes.

"I'll try it. Let me try it on," said Becky, who had been eyeing the dress with a grudging respect ever since my mother had unfolded it and shaken out its creases. She disappeared into the utility room (now Jem's bedroom), and we heard the rustling of the taffeta and fast breathing from her exertions. Then she called out to my mother, "Can you come and help me zip this up?" Becky never used anyone's name when she was addressing them, but she had perfected her omission to such an art that everybody always knew whom she meant. My mother, with her new humble manner, went at once to zip up Becky.

"I'll never forget the first time I wore that dress," my mother told Becky, as my cousin stalked back and forth in front of the mirror, holding the dress to her nonexistent bosoms to keep it from falling down. "I was sixteen and my mother had taken me down to South Carolina to visit some of her people. A cousin gave a dance in my honor, and there was this perfectly gorgeous boy at that dance, his name was Craven Ravenel. In those days, we had cards at dances and the boys would come up to you and write their names beside the dances they wanted. I was almost all filled up—I was the guest of honor, after all—and still Craven Ravenel had not asked me for one of the dances. We hadn't even been introduced yet, and I was getting worried. So you know what I did? When nobody was looking, I wrote his name in for the last dance."

"But what if he'd asked some other girl for the last dance?" asked Becky, swishing back and forth in front of the mirror with one of her ballerina poses. I knew this story well, but this was Becky's first time hearing it.

"I'm coming to that," said my mother, smiling at Becky. "What happened was, when other boys came to ask me for the last dance, I would look down at my card and say, 'Oh, I believe I've already given that dance to someone called Craven Ravenel.' And the news got back to him, because, when the last dance came, suddenly there he was. 'Miss Louise Justin,' he said formally, 'I hear you have given me the honor of the last dance.' And so I danced the last dance with Craven Ravenel."

"But what would you have done if he *had* already asked some other girl for the last dance?" persisted Becky, who had listened intently to the story.

"Oh, I had prepared for that, too," said my mother. "If he hadn't shown up before the band started playing, I was going to tell my cousin I had a headache and had to go upstairs and lie down. The dance was being held at her house. And then everybody would have assumed that poor Craven Ravenel had had to find another dance partner at the last minute."

As Mr. Mott had predicted, the rain stopped. Shortly before lunchtime, the sun came out, and my mother said, "Well, Ladies and Gentlemen, what is your pleasure for lunch?" Telling the old story had restored some of her former jauntiness. Jem said he'd like a tuna casserole, and after my mother, with just a touch of humor in her solicitation, had ascertained that Becky had nothing against tuna, cream of mushroom soup, potato chips, or a combination of those ingredients, I volunteered to ride down to Terwiliger's to pick up the needed can of soup. After my refusal to try on the dress, I thought it would become me to make this small peace offering.

Terwiliger's was a country store, run by an old farmer. It smelled of animal feeds and fertilizers and catered to people who grew things; but it suffered consumers like ourselves when we ran out of eggs or forgot some staple from the big Kingston supermarket.

I had just located the only can of cream of mushroom soup on the depleted shelf and was blowing the dust off it, when Ursula DeVane came sauntering toward me. She was wearing Army fatigue clothes (my father had brought home some like that) and her hair was quite damp and curled all around her face. She balanced a little box of green-leafed plants on the tips of her forefingers, as if she were a waiter about to serve them.

"You know, I've been thinking about you." she began, as if we were simply continuing our conversation from several weeks before. "I've been thinking about why you never came back for that swim." She brandished the little box close to my nose. The leaves emanated a smell like licorice. "Isn't it a wonderful smell, basil? I planted our vegetable garden this morning. Just put on my slicker and planted everything in the rain. It's the ideal way, in a soft rain. You don't have to water afterward. Then I went in and was running my hot bath and was just about to pour the bubbles in, when I remembered I'd forgotten the basil! Do you know what I concluded when you didn't come back?"

"What?"

"I concluded"—and the smile that was hers alone made its irrepressible way over her features—"that you were afraid of snakes."

I must have answered something. I had forgotten how compelling her voice could be, with its low, rich timbre that was both intimate and ironic. Then we were walking together to the cash register, where the dour old farmer, Mr. Terwiliger, waited.

"Would you believe it, Twiggy," said Ursula, going first. "I forgot to plant basil flats." She took a wallet from her pants pocket and fished out a wrinkled dollar bill.

The old farmer pushed it away. "No charge for the basil," he said.

"Now, Twiggy." She pushed the bill forward again. "I insist. Otherwise I'll have to start shopping all the way over in Kingston, where they'll be glad to take my money."

He folded his arms across the bib of his overalls. "An old man can't give a gift?"

Ursula gave him a look of affectionate exasperation and put the dollar back in the wallet. "Every time Julian and I sprinkle basil on our tomatoes, we will think of you, Twiggy," she said.

"Did you put your cutworm collars around your tomatoes yet?" he asked gruffly, meanwhile showing no hesitation at accepting *my* money.

"No, but I'll go and do it," said Ursula obediently.

"Better not wait," cautioned the old man.

We went out into the parking lot. The wet green trees sparkled in the sunshine and the birds were singing loudly.

"So tell me," she asked in that low voice, managing to sound both confidential and amused. "I'm curious. Why did you never come back? Did your aunt warn you off?"

"Oh, it wasn't that."

"Well, what was it?" We were the same height, but she seemed to be looking down on me indulgently.

"Well, a lot of times people say to come and see them, but they're just being polite, they don't really mean it."

"I never ask people if I don't mean it. However, I'm glad it was your Southern scruples that kept you away. I was afraid your aunt might have warned you off. Didn't you tell her we met?"

"Yes, ma'—I mean, yes. I did."

She smiled at my truncated "ma'am." "And did she tell you all about my brother?"

"She told me about . . . the recital."

"Ah, yes, that ill-fated recital. I *told* Julie he was making a mistake to give in to the parents and have it there. That Dutch Reformed Church has vivid personal associations for my brother. But nobody knew that, you see. All the parents were clamoring for the church because there was more room, but what they didn't know was the powerful influence of my brother's memories. This year we had the recital at our house again, and everything went beautifully: no passionate music or untoward interruptions. The parents got their money's worth, and no one was inconvenienced by the threat of real Art. Poor Julie didn't even realize what he'd done to Becky. I had to explain it to him afterward. He had simply been caught up in all those old associations—artists are more sensitive to the atmospheres around them—and then his favorite former student happened to pass by, and he thought he would be doing something charming and spontaneous by inviting him to come in and play. Julie thought it would be an inspiration to the children and the parents: 'See what can happen if you practice?'—that sort of thing. He had no idea he was doing any harm, or that Becky would take it personally. My brother is so tenderhearted, he wouldn't hurt a fly. I mean that literally. The other night, during dinner, a gnat fell into his wine, and he went to great trouble to rescue it and let it dry on his fingernail until it could fly off again. That's how tenderhearted he is."

"Well," I said, "Becky has her ballet now, and she's doing well with that, so I guess no real harm was done."

"Ah, yes, Imogene Roosa," said Ursula wryly. "A *much* safer mentor for little girls who want to express themselves and be rewarded for it. I went to school with Imogene. In those days we all went to a one-room schoolhouse, there were that few of us. There were Imogene and Abel Cristiana, and myself and Julie, and a few others. Well, look. If your aunt didn't go so far as to tell you to *eschew* the DeVanes, why don't you ride over and have tea with us tomorrow? We always have it at four on Sundays. Just continue on Old Clove past that haywagon road you turned into before, and you'll come to our house. It's the ancient stone job, with black shutters. If it's as nice as it is now, we'll have it down on the terrace. Is that specific enough to convince you I'm not just being polite?"

"I'd like to very much." I had to stop myself from adding, "If you're sure you really want me." The invitation, coming so suddenly, had startled me. I had hoped to see her again, hoped she might ask me to come back to the hut, but somehow I had not expected an invitation to tea.

"Good! I want you to meet my brother. We'll have a nice high tea and amuse one another." She patted me on the shoulder and strode off to an old green station wagon with wooden sides. The wagon door groaned on its hinges when she opened it, and she laughed and called back, "Neither of us is as young as we used to be! *À tout à l'heure*, then."

When I got back to Lucas Meadows, they wanted to know what had taken me so long, but I said nothing about meeting anyone. I simply said I hadn't meant to take so long. I was not a secretive person, and I would have told my mother about the invitation later, when we were alone. The reason I didn't tell at once—or so I reasoned—was that I didn't want to bring up the DeVanes in front of Becky. And maybe also I wanted to keep the meeting with Ursula—which had happened, as such things inevitably do, just when I had stopped anticipating it—to myself for a few hours. Perhaps I felt I needed to go over it in my mind, relishing its details, before sharing it with someone else. At any rate, I said nothing, and my silence was to cause difficulties later in the day.

At lunch, Becky was still immersed in the Craven Ravenel story (as I was immersed in my recent meeting with Ursula De-Vane), and, for once, she was the most talkative person at the table. She wanted to know what Craven Ravenel had said to my mother during the last dance; had he been angry or pleased to have been "signed up" like that? And had she ever seen him again?

"I don't remember a single thing he said," my mother replied, laughing. "You've got to realize, I was beside myself. I felt I had made magic happen. No, he wasn't angry, I think he admired my little maneuver. It was an enterprising thing to have done. Next to the way I arranged for my elopement with your uncle Rivers, it was probably the most enterprising thing I have ever done. I was just determined to have that boy dance with me, and I made it happen. But you know, my mother and I went back home to Virginia a few days later and I didn't think about him anymore. That may sound strange, after all the fuss I made, but it was as if . . . well, as if his magic never crossed the state line of South Carolina. He was the best-looking boy at the dance, and I wanted to crown the evening with him. I suppose I thought it was my *due*, or something. I'm afraid, Becky, that I was a very spoiled girl, in many ways. I mean, I always had excellent manners, that was a point of pride with me, but I did expect the sun and the moon on a silver platter—and usually got it in those days! As a matter of fact, I did see Craven Ravenel again. It was during the war, and I was already married and a mother. Honey and I and Justin, who was only a baby, had gone down to Pawleys Island to spend the first two weeks of June, as we always did. Those were the only two weeks of the year that my mother and father agreed to separate. He went up to The Greenbrier, in West Virginia, and played golf. My father liked his golf, and he liked the company of other men, and my mother respected this. And she liked to be with her relatives and the friends she had grown up with in South Carolina, and my father, who was a taciturn man, found their 'effusions,' as he called them, a little wearing on his nerves. So they went their own ways, those two weeks every year, and I believe that's why they had such a good marriage the other fifty weeks of the year.

"Anyway, it so happened that Craven Ravenel was stationed at Myrtle Beach at that time, and he drove over to Pawleys to see some friends—and we met again. He shook my hand and smiled and said, 'I have never forgotten that last dance.' You see, there were other people around, and, as he was a gentleman, he didn't want to embarrass me by saying any more. And then we talked a little and he learned I was married and had a baby. He looked just a *shade* disappointed, but not long afterward I heard that he had married a rich girl from his hometown."

"Were you sorry you were married when you saw him again?" asked Becky, who had listened respectfully, with (for Becky) something like awe, to my mother's story.

"Sorry? Gracious no, honey. I had what *I* wanted. I wish you could have known your uncle Rivers, Becky. He was the most charming man in the world. Everyone who met him said so."

Becky looked dubious. "How was he charming? In what way?"

"Well . . . in just every way." My mother, not used to being contradicted on this subject, cast about for an example. "I can't think of anything specific, but . . . well, his face, for one thing, the expression on his face. It was the expression of someone with a happy, slightly mischievous secret, and you felt it included you. And even in the midst of a setback, Rivers had this wonderful way of making you feel that the very next day was going to be great."

Then she paused and looked around and seemed surprised to find herself in Aunt Mona's kitchen, sitting around with a bunch of children over the remains of a tunafish casserole. A moment of pain and amazement passed over her face. "Oh no," she said in a softer voice, "I didn't regret being married when I saw Craven Ravenel again. I mean, he was still very handsome, and there was a certain sad, romantic quality to our meeting again, but what I had felt for him had less to do with love than with . . . satisfying my pride. There's a whole world of difference between the two feelings, Becky."

For the first time since we had come to live at Aunt Mona's, Becky took her own plate and glass and fork to the dishwasher. She did it with much ceremony, looking at my mother once or twice to make sure she was watching. I attributed this change in my cousin's behavior to my mother's remark about having always had pride in her own manners, even though she (too) had been a spoiled child.

I spent the early afternoon on the back porch of the empty farmhouse on the hill. I had my newfound box of paints, a water-color block, some rags, and a jar of water. Facing away from the hivelike drone of the fathers' lawnmowers in our development below, I lost myself in the production of an imaginary scene that appealed to my mood: a woman in a long dress stood at a shore-line, looking out to sea. As I evoked the whitecaps by painting the darker waters around their tips, I went over my dialogue with Ursula DeVane: first from my side, to recall how each of her re-marks had affected me, and then from her side, to imagine how my remarks had impressed her. Then I worried about tomorrow: "We'll have a nice high tea and amuse one another," she had said. I was not very confident of my powers to amuse on de-mand. During our two meetings so far, I had not been very inter-esting or eloquent. I tried to think of things I could say tomorrow that might or might not be amusing but that would reveal my life to have some interesting aspects.

Then, as I brushed in the shadows in the folds of my figure's long skirt—it was supposed to be blowing a little in the wind—I fell to wondering why someone as interesting as Ursula DeVane would invite someone like me to tea. Had she done it to prove a point, to prove that she had meant it when she had invited me to come back to the pond? Or had it been a spontaneous, queenly gesture on her part, because she could see it would mean a lot to me? Or had she wanted me to meet her brother, this peculiar man about whom I had heard no good words, except from her? Maybe she wanted me to come so that I could judge Julian De-Vane for myself. (I imagined possible ways a young girl might irritate his sensitive artistic nature, and resolved to commit none of them tomorrow. I was not at all sure that I would like him, but I wanted him to like me, for her sake.)

Then my attention was drawn back to the figure I had created on the watercolor block. Her back was to me, and, judg-ing from the long dress, she was from another time. But who was she, and what was she waiting for? Was she someone to whose story I was attracted because of its uncertainty and pathos, or was she someone I wanted to be? I painted in some storm clouds, not because I wished her trouble, but because they made the scene more charged with potential drama. Then I decided to "enter into a trance" and let her speak aloud. What would she say if she were to speak aloud at just this moment in the picture?

"Oh, when, if ever, is he coming back to me?" I intoned in a solemn voice. The words had come easily to me, as things were supposed to do in a trance, but I didn't like the hopeless, self-pitying sound of them. I wondered if it would be okay to start over. Surely, if the words made me feel so dissatisfied, they couldn't have been the right ones. I studied the woman's figure, and the horizon which she faced, and the clouds. They might be storm clouds, or they might just be dark, heavy clouds that would make her life more interesting but weren't necessarily deadly. "What is out there?" I decided she might say. As soon as I had decided that, I "heard" the next words; they came exactly as they were supposed to, as if dictated by an inevitable force.

"What is out there?" I asked, in a low, level voice. And then I answered my question with the new words, in a voice that thrilled me with its timbre and control. "Soon I shall know." The effect was so great that I felt almost as if I had turned into someone else. I was filled with a strange elation.

"What is out there? Soon I shall know," I repeated, wiping off my brushes and emptying the jar of cloudy water on the ground beneath the farmhouse stairs.

As I descended the hill toward the lookalike houses of Lucas Meadows, I saw Mr. Mott, his lawn mowing completed, and all of the members of our household gathered in our driveway. I was still so much under the spell I had cast on myself through art and daydreaming that I was afraid my transformation would be visible to them. I made an effort to redisguise myself as the adolescent they believed me to be. As Jem came running toward me, I turned the picture on the watercolor block inward, hoping that no one would ask to see what I'd been doing.

"Guess what!" Jem cried, racing up to me and seizing me by one of the pockets in my jeans. "Mott has invited you and me to the houseboat tomorrow! We're going to charcoal hamburgers on deck."

"Tomorrow? What time tomorrow?" As my little brother tugged me possessively toward our family group, I realized they were waiting for me to show some excitement about Mr. Mott's benevolent offer.

"If it's all right, I'll come and pick you kids up around four," said steady Mr. Mott, running his palm across his short, prickly crew cut. His voice was full of complacency. Here he had mowed the lawn of a house in which he didn't even live anymore, and now, on top of that, he was inviting his daughter's fatherless cousins to charcoal hamburgers on his deck. Becky, standing ready with her little overnight suitcase, looked complacent, too: wasn't her father wonderful to do this for us?

"But I can't go tomorrow at four," I said, wishing IBM had transferred Mr. Mott to some distant site, so he could not be such a dutiful uncle. I also wished now that I had said something to my mother about the other invitation: she could have stopped all this.

"You *can't?*" screamed Jem incredulously. "Why can't you?"

"Because ..." I sought my mother's eyes. "I've already promised to go somewhere else. I've been invited to tea tomorrow at four."

"*Tea?*" chimed in Aunt Mona, whose freshly sprayed coiffure made a feeble attempt to quiver. "Who in this place has *tea?* Oh, oh, wait a minute, I'll bet I know." And she gave me a hideous, knowing wink. "Your grand friend over on Old Clove Road."

"Ann Cristiana?" my mother asked uncertainly.

"No, ma'am." The serious Mott and his impatient daughter stood waiting for me to explain myself. I couldn't utter the incriminating name of Becky's former music teacher before *them.* "It's just that woman I met, you know, a few weeks ago, when I was riding my bike on Old Clove Road. I saw her at Terwiliger's when I went for our mushroom soup, and she asked me for tomorrow at four, and ... I've already *said* I would." To my dismay, tears started to well up in my eyes. "I'm really sorry, Mr. Mott," I managed to say before anyone saw them, "I'd like to come another time, if that's okay." And then I wheeled around and started for the house as fast as I could.

"Does that mean I can't go either?" I heard Jem wail. Followed by the solemn assurance of the good Mr. Mott that he would come and pick Jem up just as planned.

"Oh damn, oh hell," I cursed tearfully, slamming the door of my room. How had one simple, independent act of accepting an invitation to tea compromised me so? After all, I wasn't a baby anymore. I wasn't even a child. I was a person struggling to stay free of all the fetters trying to bind me to a boring, ordinary, mediocre life in which I was obliged to exist for a few more years until I could have my own life, my own place, free from petty restraints and clinging baby brothers and hurt looks from mothers and hideous winks from know-it-all aunts.

I paced the confines of "Raspberry Ice," growing more agitated and aggrieved. If only I could be eighteen—no, better twenty-one, for safety! Then I could come and go as I liked, I could have a job and earn my own money and paint and furnish my room as I pleased. I could see the people who attracted me and stimulated me and brought me closer to the life that I was determined to have for myself. I could not, as yet, imagine this life I wanted, but I could recognize very well the one I didn't want: it was all around me! It was threatening to suck me in.

To console myself, I took a look at the watercolor I had done, hoping it would bring back to me the rapturous feeling I'd had on the hill: that self-transformation did lie in my powers. But here in the confines of "Raspberry Ice" the painting had suffered a sea change. The figure was no longer mysterious or potent or even lifelike. What was worse, I saw now that her outline bore a very close resemblance to the figures of the milkmaids who adorned my curtains, flounces, and dust ruffle. She had the same wasp waist, and her skirt fell in similar folds. I felt that if she should suddenly turn around, she would smile at me with their same shallow smile. I remembered a radio drama my grandmother and I had listened to once, in her bed. We had snuggled up close, one winter evening, and let ourselves be scared silly by a program. It was the story of a little girl whose mother loses her in a huge department store. The little girl is left in the store all night, and the mannequins come to life and take her back to live with them, make her one of them. The next day, the mother comes back to the store to continue her search with the police for her little girl. They do not find her, of course, because the little girl has been turned into a mannequin. At the end of the program, the mother passes the mannequin that is her own frozen child. The mother remarks tearfully that the mannequin looks just like her lost daughter. The policemen tell her that she is exhausted to the point of imagining things, and they lead her away.

Oh God, I thought, what if "Raspberry Ice" and Lucas Meadows get me, after all? Even now, they were closing in on my soul.

What if my mother wouldn't let me go tomorrow? I would fight for the right to go, if it came to that.

As it turned out, no battle was necessary. After Mr. Mott and Becky had driven off, my mother came up to my room and told me not to worry any more about tomorrow, but that she hoped in future I would tell her my plans ahead of time and prevent this sort of confusion. Then, seating herself on the edge of my bed, she inquired gently about Ursula DeVane. How, exactly, had we met? What had we talked about? Wasn't she much *older*? What did I know about her history?

I don't know why, but I felt instinctively that my preoccupation with Ursula should not be revealed to my mother. I wasn't sure I understood the full extent of it myself. But I *was* sure my mother would think it odd if she knew how present this woman was in my mind, and she might also feel threatened by another woman's competition for her daughter's affections. A story that wasn't really a falsehood, but more like the outer shell of the truth, came to my aid. I told my mother that what had made me like this woman—in addition to the fact that she seemed so warmly interested in me—was that she lived the kind of life that reminded me a lot of the one we had lost.

(Here I could not help noticing the sad, almost *wincing* look that appeared on my mother's face, but I told myself, with a hard

heart, that she deserved a little punishment for having deliberately removed us from all traces of that life.)

"You know," I elaborated, "the kind of life where people
stay in the same place all their lives, maybe even in the same
house, and where you know who everybody's grandparents were
in town . . . and listening to classical music, and arranging flowers in vases, and talking about history . . . that kind of thing."

I told my mother that Ursula DeVane had said her family
was descended from the Huguenots that Louis (I forgot which
one) had chased out of France, but that I didn't know much
about *her* history except that she had studied drama at the Royal
Academy in London and had taught at some girls' school in New
York—some finishing school—but that now her life seemed to
be dedicated to her brother's career and helping him make a
comeback. "Mr. Cristiana says she is sacrificing herself for her
brother," I added, thinking my mother, in her present state of
mind, would approve of sacrifice. I did not say anything about
the mother in the insane asylum, however, or about Julian De-
Vane's old fight with Mr. Cristiana.

My mother had listened to all this in a pensive reverie of her
own, and, at last, she said: "I keep forgetting that you spent so
much of your childhood with older people. I hope I didn't do
wrong, letting you stay with Honey and Father when I went off
with Rivers to college in Charlottesville. Maybe I was trying to
have my cake and eat it too. But they did want you so much, they
would have been heartbroken if I had taken you away, and you
seemed so happy there, you wanted to stay. But I hope"—and
she passed her hand gently over my hair—"I hope I haven't gone
and made you into an old person before your time." Then she
told me to go and enjoy myself tomorrow. "This Miss DeVane
must think you are good company, otherwise she wouldn't have
invited you. Poor woman, she probably gets lonely all by herself
in the country with just her brother. And from what Mona implied, he's a bit of a problem."

After these generous words, I felt a pang of shame at having
decoyed my mother. But it had to be this way. There were other
loyalties here, loyalties I didn't completely understand. I only felt

the force of them. It was like Mr. Cristiana choosing between patriotism and the horses in some way, I decided. Though I got confused when I tried to trace out the analogy.

At three twenty-seven on Sunday afternoon, I wheeled my bike out of the garage and set off from Lucas Meadows, glimpsing, in the lookalike picture windows of the houses I sped past, the reflection of a girl in white blouse and white Bermuda shorts flashing along in a series of moving frames.

At a quarter to four, I reached the Cristianas' farm. No humans stirred about the place. I was glad, because I would have had to stop and be polite. The only creature in sight was the active Turk, tensely trotting around his paddock. He hugged the fence and lifted his head over it at a self-conscious angle, as if he were playing to an audience of fillies.

I dawdled on the next winding stretch of road, afraid I would arrive too early. And then, afraid I might be late, I raced around the final curves. I was out of breath when I knocked shyly on the front door of the house.

No sounds came from inside. I knocked louder. I put my ear to the door and strained to hear sounds of approaching footsteps from within. Nothing. Only the sound of a truck approaching on Old Clove Road. A man and a woman riding in the truck stared out at me curiously as they passed the house. I saw myself through their eyes: a lanky, anxious girl all in white, petitioning for entrance to the aloof stone house. I tried to peer in the nearest ground-floor window, but it was at too steep an angle from the doorstep. Could she have forgotten? Could they have gone away for the afternoon? There was no old green station wagon in sight, but maybe the timbered outbuilding on the other side of the driveway served as a garage. Its doors were closed.

Then I remembered she had said they would be down on the terrace if the day was nice. I went around the side of the house, by the lilac bush where, from the bus, I had seen her cutting blossoms that day, and then I came upon a whole new aspect of the place I would never have guessed at from the road. A steep lawn sloped down to a semicircular stone terrace. All around the terrace bloomed masses of red poppies. Beyond the poppies lay the fields, and beyond the fields rose the soft, undulating mountains, with the suddenly sheared-off ledge at the northern end and the mysterious tower atop it. From where I stood now, I could look down to the left and see, across the fields, the shape of the pine forest, jutting out like a wedge of pie pointing toward the mountains. From up here, you would not guess the presence of the pond or the hut, hidden within the trees. I thought I could pinpoint exactly where Ed Cristiana had made us turn our horses around, so we would still be hidden by the pines from this house's view—and "he" would not see us and take it out on her.

And there "he" was, down on the stone terrace, sitting next to her. They had their backs to me and were facing the fields. There was something haughty and majestic about their posture as they reclined in the old-fashioned lawn chairs. Waiting for the curtain to go up on their afternoon's "amusement"? On a low table before them were spread the tea things. A third chair, which I assumed had been placed for me, was turned sideways from the view and facing them.

Feeling very unsure of my capacity to provide amusement, I started down the hill, turning my toes in a little to keep my balance. Shouldn't I call out to them, rather than creep up from behind?

Then, as if she had known I was there all along but had wanted to give me an opportunity to appreciate the picture they made first, Ursula DeVane turned in her chair and waved me down with a grand sweep of her hand. And then he turned, too, to watch me approach. My first impression was shock: from here he looked younger and handsomer than anyone had led me to expect.

But then, when I reached them, and he stood up to be introduced, I saw that Julian DeVane was not young. In an eerie way, the outlines of youth had frozen themselves on the features of an older man. He was still handsome—beautiful might have been an apter word—but the beauty had something desiccated about it, like a dried flower that has been preserved in shape and color but not freshness.

"How do you do?" he said quietly, shaking my hand. He

was a slim, proud-looking man, more delicately built than his sister. He should have been the girl and she the boy; he would have been strong, then, and she would have been the beautiful one. He had wavy, sandy-silver hair, which he wore much too long for the fashion of those times, when men considered it suspicious if their hair was long enough to move. But I expected he was a bit vain of the way it lifted in waves over the crown of his head and flowed softly back to the nape of his neck. His eyes were the same deep brown as hers, but they did not flash and penetrate as hers did: they had a somber, rather weary, in-turned cast. He had on sandals and khaki trousers and a kind of shirt I had never seen before: it was worn outside the trousers and had colored embroidery on it.

"I was just telling my brother what a picture of youth and spring you were as you came down that slope," said Ursula. "You are a walking metaphor of spring. Isn't she, Julie?"

The brother nodded in a pleasant, world-weary way, and they both stood gazing indulgently at me as if I were some puppy Ursula had brought home. Ursula was wearing a light green two-piece dress that nipped in at the waist and flared out in a peplum over the hips: a fashion that had been in style when I was a little girl. It was still a pretty dress, but too formal for the occasion, I thought, especially when worn with those old brown thong sandals. She had also put on lipstick, which made her look older. Had they dressed up for me, or did they do this every Sunday?

"Ah, we're embarrassing her," said Ursula. "Do sit down, Justin, and be tolerant of two old siblings envying you your youth. The tea ought to be steeped by now."

We all sat down, and while Ursula was pouring the tea from a pretty blue-and-white china teapot, Julian DeVane asked me how long it had taken me to ride my bike here from Lucas Meadows. For the first time, I was aware of his stutter. It was the kind of stutter in which the speaker has learned to press hard on the reluctant letter and wait until the word comes. His slight handicap made me feel easier in his presence. He passed me a platter of open-faced sandwiches (very nicely arranged combinations of cream cheese, cucumber, and watercress, and egg salad with chopped onions and a curl of anchovy on top) and I noticed his graceful, long fingers with their nails clipped very short.

After I had taken a sip of tea and complimented Ursula on the sandwiches, I felt less of a child. It was grown-up, as well as safe, to tell a hostess that her food was good. I could see they approved of my manners, so, seizing on a good thing, I looked around the terrace for a minute and said what lovely poppies those were and how nice it was down here.

"Father built this terrace himself," said Ursula. "He designed it and had the bluestones cut from a quarry up in Woodstock and put in every one of them himself. It was his present to our mother, right after they married. She liked to sit down here and look out at the mountains. Sometimes she would sit for hours. When I was a little girl, I used to watch her and wonder how anybody could sit still for that long."

I stole a look at the faces of brother and sister as Ursula was describing their mother. But I saw nothing in the expression of either to give away that she had been in an insane asylum.

"Did . . . did she plant all these poppies?" I asked.

"No, Father planted those," said Ursula, helping herself to another sandwich. "He was the gardener. This used to be a showplace in summer. Well, who knows, maybe it will be again, when our ship comes in, eh, Julie? I have something of a green thumb myself. Father loved red flowers in particular. Red tulips, poppies . . . later in the summer, that whole area to the left of the terrace will be a blaze of red bee balm: the 'Cambridge Scarlet' variety. But Father hated yellow flowers. I remember when he was so sick, in his last days, if anybody sent yellow flowers to the house, he made me get rid of them immediately. He wouldn't have a yellow flower in his garden. One time"—she laughed mischievously—"he got into an awful rage because, overnight, some kind of yellow flower had sprung up all over his garden. Julie and I were sent out to pull up every single one by the roots. Do you remember, Julie?"

Julian DeVane nodded. "F-father was a man of very strong likes and dislikes," he explained to me.

"Ah, yes," agreed his sister fervently. "Father had certain

ideas about the way life should be, and if life dared to contradict
. . . why, he pulled out the contradiction like an offending weed."

Julian DeVane uttered a harsh laugh. There was a silence.
The two of them sat there, obviously remembering the father,
who did not sound to me like a very sympathetic person.

"What is *your* favorite color?" Ursula asked me, leaning
forward in her chair and clasping her hands as people sometimes
do when they are "encouraging" a young person to talk. I found
her changed slightly in attitude toward me, in the presence of her
brother; when we had been alone we had been more like equals.

"Well, I used to like red myself," I said. "But lately, I think, I
prefer blue. Or sometimes"—I sighed, thinking gloomily of my
room—"just a clear, pure white."

"Lately? Why lately?"

I hesitated. "Well, because of the room I have now, at my
aunt's house. It's this terrible color. The thing is, my aunt painted
the room just to please me, so I can't say anything. But it's driving me crazy."

"Wh-what color is it?" asked Julian DeVane. He, too, sat
forward in his chair, and the delicate, world-weary face perked
up with a sudden interest. I caught the quick, amused glance between brother and sister, and decided to sacrifice Aunt Mona in
order to be "amusing."

"Its *official* name is 'Raspberry Ice.' But no raspberry was
ever that color and there's nothing the least cool or icy about it.
It's this sickening color, sort of between muddy pink and laven-
der. And, to make things worse, there are the *curtains*."

"Oh, do tell us about the curtains!" said Ursula, wriggling in
her chair. She looked triumphantly toward Julian as if to say:
See? I told you she wouldn't be a bore.

"Well," I began, relishing my role as a successful performer,
"they have these milkmaids all over them. Everywhere I look, I
see milkmaids, because not only are they on my curtains but
they're on the dust ruffle around my bed and they're all around
my dressing table . . . which is really my uncle Mr. Mott's former
desk. Sometimes . . . sometimes when I have to open the center
drawer, you know? And I part the skirt of my dressing table and

see those thick wooden legs of Mr. Mott's old desk? Well, it's like having a man spying on me in my room."

Ursula burst out laughing. Julian DeVane had a delighted, superior smirk on his face, as though this was exactly the sort of story he liked to hear.

"But the *worst* part about the milkmaids," I went on, resolving to go all the way in order to win their approval, even if it meant making light of one of my most serious thoughts and abiding fears of late, "is, I'm afraid they're going to do me in. I mean, everywhere I look, there they are, with their full skirts and their little milk pails and their shallow, beauty-contest smiles. What if I wake up one morning and look into my mirror and discover I am like them? I don't mean I'd have a milk pail or anything, but that . . . well . . . I'd suddenly be just like everybody else. I'd no longer remember what it felt like to be me . . . before I lived in that room."

Although I had meant to keep it light, my voice faltered and I could not hide the anxiety I felt about the subject.

"I don't s-see that happening to you, somehow," said Julian DeVane. He said it quite gently, with no ironic or superior overtones. I saw I had made him like me, made him take me seriously, and I couldn't help liking him in return.

Looking thoughtful, Ursula poured everyone more tea. "The influence of a place is no light matter," she said. "Some places threaten your very essence. While others reinforce your sense of who you are. There's a threat there, too, of course. I sometimes wonder if this place doesn't encourage me to be *too much* myself."

"Wh-what do you mean by that, Sissie?" asked her brother, turning to her with respectful attention. In the eager look he gave her, I felt I could read many moments of their childhood together: "Baby Brother" pricking up his ears when Big Sister started to lecture about some aspect of life that she had discovered first.

"Oh, you know, Julie. Everybody around here has formed their opinions of us. They formed them years ago. Because they've always known us—or think they have—they take it for granted we will behave in a certain way. And so we do. It becomes a self-fulfilling prophecy. That's why I envy Justin here in no small way. Despite her unfortunate room, and all those milk-maids threatening to swallow her with their smiles"—and Ursula gave me her warm and singular smile—"she can start her life over and be anything she chooses to be. Nobody knows what she was like back in Fredericksburg. She has lost all the props that defined her. Nobody knows all the peculiarities and character traits of her forebears so they can pretend to recognize those traits in her. She's a clean slate. When she meets new people, or new challenges, she is free to respond to the unique demands of the moment. Whereas *I* often feel I have been playing the same part in a show that's been running too long. I have a starring role, of course: I'm the sophisticated woman who's gone away to far places and come back again; who can be counted on to provide a bit of mystery and speculation for the provincials to chew on, as cows chew their cud."

This last comparison struck me as funny and I laughed.

"What part have I, then?" asked Julian DeVane.

"Ah, you know quite well what your part is," his sister scolded him playfully. "You are the natural genius to whom I have devoted my considerable energies. If we want to be symbolic about it, you are pure, inspired art and I am the practicality and the ambition and the driving force that art needs if it is to impose itself on the world."

"The dear old world," said her brother sarcastically, shaking his head so that the silvery-sandy hair rippled in the light. "That's where my sister and I differ," he explained to me. "I could be perfectly happy p-playing my music to the birds and the trees—and my memories. She believes it will be all wasted unless I perform before crowds of coughing idiots."

"Oh, Julie, how can you say that! You know you are capable of electrifying an audience. If you've forgotten, I have all those reviews from South America to remind you. It's wrong to want to hide your light under a bushel. You used to tell me you wouldn't be satisfied until you had performed on the concert stage of every major city in the world."

"That was in the old days, when I was still looking for something," he replied, giving her a meaningful look. "Now I'm not looking for it anymore, so why c-can't I stay home and play for the birds—and my sister?"

There was something teasing in his manner, yet something serious at the same time. I had the feeling they had had this conversation many times before, that it had become almost a game with them—a game they could even play in front of a third person—but that, underneath, there was a subtler battle going on. I was reinforced in this belief when Ursula went suddenly deflated in her chair. But then she rallied and said casually, "You can play for me anytime you like. I'm your captive audience and you know it. So, for that matter, are the birds. I've heard them sing with you."

"I hope you'll play for me sometime, too," I said. "I mean, when you know me better, of course."

He regarded me with his somber brown eyes. "She has a nice voice, hasn't she, Sissie? Most young girls are so shrill and edgy."

" 'Her voice was ever soft, gentle, and low, an excellent thing in woman,' " intoned Ursula, in a deep, caressing voice. "We did *King Lear* when I was at the Royal Academy of Dramatic Art, in London. Only I wasn't Cordelia, I was Goneril. I was always being cast in those tough roles for women. I've been Hedda, and Medea, and if I hadn't had to rush back to America I was going to be Saint Joan. Now you, Justin, would make a perfect Cordelia. Wouldn't she, Julie?"

"P-possibly," said Julian DeVane. "If it's in her nature to want to perform before coughing crowds."

"You are incorrigible, Julie, but I love you anyway."

"That's lucky for me, isn't it?" replied the brother, sending her a rueful little smile. Then he crumbled a bit of bread between his long, delicate fingers and, crouching low in his chair, sprinkled it carefully in the pathway of an ant.

"Tell me, Justin," said Ursula, "how do you find living here? I mean, how does Clove compare with your hometown?"

"Well, the two places are very different."

"Yes, I know that," she said impatiently, "but *how?*" I

couldn't help feeling this was some sort of test of my mental acuity.

I cast about for some out-of-the-ordinary thing to say. All I could come up with was that the people up here seemed more deep down in themselves that the people back home. She liked this remark; it interested her. She fixed the flashing brown eyes on me and told me to pursue the subject further: *How*, "deep down"? Be more specific. Could I think of examples? Comparisons?

But then my mind blanked, the way it still does when someone asks me who were the major influences on my life, or what good plays I've seen during the past year. I knew I had an answer somewhere in myself, but I couldn't perform the necessary function of translating it into speech on demand. I stumbled around the question, taking shameless detours into the deaths in our family—the one subject I had come prepared to talk about—and sounding more and more stupid and scatterbrained and inconclusive. And yet I could see, from the motions of her expressive face, that her agile, grasping mind was darting here and there, seizing on my incoherent morsels and forming them into impressions of what kind of person I was and how my mind worked. I could somehow tell that she, in her imperious way, had already decided that I was going to be "worthwhile." I think I already knew she was the kind of woman who, once she had made up her mind to like somebody, even if it had been an impulsive decision, would invest that person with all sorts of interesting and romantic aspects rather than admit she had been wrong.

"How do you get on with your cousin Becky?" she asked, with an impish twitch at the corner of her mouth.

I glanced over at Julian, who seemed engrossed in the gathering conclave of ants he had enticed forth with his bread crumbs. "Well, we're not very close," I said. "I mean, I tried to be friends at first, but she keeps to herself most of the time. If you try to make conversation, she can be very abrupt. She gives me odd looks I can never figure out. They might mean anything."

"From her point of view, you must seem a terrible threat," said Ursula.

"A threat?" This was something I had never considered. "*How?*"

"You've got a sweetness she doesn't have. I don't mean a cloying, goody-goody sweetness, God preserve us from that, but a certain subtle sympathy that makes people trust you, seek you out. If I had been her age and you had moved into my house, I would have felt . . . perhaps not *threatened*, because I could always stand up for myself, but I would have felt competitive. I would have taken a good look at your ways, and then I would have examined my ways, and . . . well!" She gave a sharp, harsh laugh. "If it had been I, I might have found some way to depose you or drive you away. However, if I weren't so sure of myself, I would probably pout . . . or go underground until I had assessed the situation more carefully. And then, don't forget, you're older. At that age, two or three years can seem a hopeless gulf for the younger person. Exactly how old *are* you, anyway?"

"I'll be fourteen in two weeks," I said.

"Two weeks! What day is your birthday?"

"June fourteenth," I said shyly, wondering if she would feel she had to send me a card.

"June fourteenth, June fourteenth, why does that date ring a bell, I wonder?"

Julian DeVane looked up from his ants. "Don't you remember, Sissie?"

"No! What happened on June fourteenth?"

"That's the day you sailed for France on the *Normandie*."

"Oh God, so it was. June fourteenth, 1939. Getting away at last! Oh, it will be good to have you around, Julie, when I become senile. I can simply say"—and she affected the querulous voice of an old lady— " 'Now let me see, what happened on June fourteenth?' And you'll snap right back with '*Normandie*, dear Sissie, pier—' Do you remember the pier number? I don't."

"No, but I remember the sailing time. Three p.m. I felt dreadful. I was sure I was never going to s-see you again."

"Well, I can recall worrying I was never going to see *you* again a couple of times, with a *lot* more reason," she retorted, her tone thick with innuendo, "so we can call it even."

A look so full of private associations passed between sister and brother that I felt left out, almost jealous of their closeness. Then, with a weary smile, Julian returned his attention to the ants. After a moment, he said musingly, "You know, I've watched them carry their dead away. They're a highly organized society—they have a great love of home, I read somewhere—and they're always helping one another out. I like w-watching them."

"We know you do," said Ursula wryly. "You made poor Jill Van Kleek postpone her lesson for almost half an hour so you wouldn't miss the baby cardinals." To me she explained, "We had a nest of cardinals in the shrubbery outside our living room, and Julie made that little girl I told you about—the one who plays like a robot—stand at the window and watch with him until all three fledglings took off one morning."

"It was a once-in-a-lifetime spectacle," he replied, leaning down to watch the ants carrying away the crumbs in a militaristic little procession. "Jill's playing will remain pretty much the same after all the b-birds have flown."

Ursula and I continued talking. She was still being the demanding inquisitor, trying to make me formulate my thoughts. "That was hard," she said, "to have all those people you loved die within such a short time. Three family members dead within less than two years, wasn't it?"

"Yes, it was a real tragedy," I replied, somewhat self-importantly.

"No, dear, it was not a tragedy," she surprised me by saying. "It was unfortunate, it must have been extremely sad and painful, but you mustn't call it tragedy."

I didn't know what to say.

"Tragedy is something different from misfortune or catastrophe," said Ursula. "When something terrible happens and it can be traced back directly to the inevitable process of someone's living out his destiny, *that* is called tragedy. There is a foredoomed quality about tragedy. There is nothing random or accidental about it, when you look closely and examine the causes that led up to it. Tragedy is when you can look back and say: 'Given who that person was, and how he, or she, habitually confronted life, *this was bound to happen.*' Tragedy has the shape of a beautiful, inescapable pattern. Look at Lear. Or at Oedipus. Or Hamlet. Every time we watch their stories being reenacted, we suffer them afresh, no matter how many times we've seen them before. Oh *no!* we think, each time we watch, here they go *again!* But the paradox is that their suffering purges us as we suffer with them vicariously. It sometimes allows us to take warning and escape our own destruction."

Interlacing her fingers on her lap, she lifted her head and gazed raptly at the skies, looking quite satisfied with her eloquent discourse.

There was a silence. Then, abruptly, Julian DeVane rose. "I'm going up to the house," he said.

Ursula snapped out of her raptness at once. "But why?" she asked, looking almost afraid of him. "I thought we were all getting on so well."

"We were. But now there is a b-blot on the view."

Ursula looked out at the fields, where the afternoon shadows were deepening. I looked, too, and saw a man riding slowly and deliberately along. He reined in his horse, appeared to be studying the ground, then rode slowly on again.

"Oh God," murmured Ursula.

Julian DeVane stood above me. "It was nice to meet you," he said, offering me his hand. His face had twisted petulantly, but his eyes absolved me from the cause of his annoyance. "Happy b-birthday, if I don't see you b-before."

He climbed the hill rapidly to the house, and we heard the screen door slam.

"Oh God," repeated Ursula in a dull voice. "That's our neighbor, Abel Cristiana, out inspecting his new boundaries. He's the farmer I sold our meadows to. I expect they'll start fencing soon. Julie detests even the sight of him from a distance. It's an old family feud, too complicated for me to explain. Damn it, Abel," she addressed the distant figure on horseback, "why couldn't you have waited until our tea hour was over?" I noticed, however, that a touch of humor had crept into her tone. "I'm sorry it's ruined the mood," she said then, returning her attention to me. "Julie liked you. I could tell."

"It's okay. I ought to be going soon anyway," I said. She

didn't reply to this. "I think that's Gentleman Johnny, their Tennessee walker, that he's riding," I added after a minute.

"How do you know that?" she demanded, looking at me sharply.

"Because of the way he picks up his legs, and stops and starts so nicely. I rode him myself last week," I added casually, trying to keep the pride out of my voice. "Ann Cristiana invited me over there to ride after school. But what I really think is, her brother Ed got her to invite me over."

I expected her to tease me for "making a conquest," the way most older women would, but she studied me for a moment and then said thoughtfully, "Funny, you gave me the impression that you were just a lonely waif, all by yourself in an alien land. But of course you must make friends your own age. I don't know the Cristiana children well. This feud we've been having for decades precludes any social intercourse between our families."

I was embarrassed when she used the word *intercourse*. I also felt I had betrayed her in some way by having gone out riding with people my own age, like an ordinary young person. As if I cared about Ed and his sister! Whom had I been hoping to meet for almost the entire ride? I sat there miserably, wondering how to reinstate myself with her. She was staring fixedly at the man down in the fields that had once belonged to her family. I thought there was a masochistic intensity about the way she watched him ride slowly along, as if every deliberate tread of his horse's hooves on her lost land were felt upon herself and she were determined to have it so.

A deep rumbling of chords, like thunder, came from the house. They thickened into a series of sinister runs up and down the keyboard, and then burst into explosions of fiendish energy. I had never heard such violent music coming through the open windows of a country house; I had never heard such music, period.

"He's playing the 'Mephisto,' " said Ursula. "That means he's really in a temper."

But she sounded proud, and, even to me, who knew little about music, except for nostalgic memories of my grandfather's

Bach, the sounds coming from the house were impressive. The music dominated everything with its passages of almost threatening intensity. Even I knew that not just anybody who "played the piano well" could make so many notes come out sounding at once so hard and separate and clear and yet all blended together in this stunningly ominous manner.

"I've never heard anybody play the piano like that," I said.

"Of course you haven't," she replied triumphantly. "Not unless you had heard Paderewski . . . or Liszt. Even Rubinstein doesn't have that clean sharpness. My brother has been blessed by the gods with a rare combination of clarity and passion when he sits down to that instrument—even if he can be a stubborn fool at other times. That's why that piano was worth every one of those damn acres, and all this . . . strife. That's why it's all worthwhile. One day, not too far away, I hope, I won't be the only one to think so."

"Will he play before crowds again?" I asked. I had started to say "coughing crowds," as he had done, but decided not to risk humor at the moment.

"If I have my way, he will be doing it in two years. Otherwise, what has this all been for?"

There came an eerie hiatus in the music, a sort of metaphysical calm during which the notes seemed to be asking sad questions they already knew the answers to. Down in the field, the man on the horse continued the pacing of his recently purchased boundaries, but the effect of the music was so dominating that it relegated him to a small, picturesque element in a summer landscape over which some eternal power loomed.

"What is that tower up there on those mountains?" I asked, when the metaphysical passage had given way to another furious burst of stormy notes.

"It's a lookout tower," said Ursula. "It belongs to the hotel up there. If we had binoculars, we could see it, nestled beneath that ledge. It's a magnificent old hotel, on a lake. The whole thing might have been transported from Europe. One night last winter when I couldn't sleep, I was prowling around the house in the dark, and I happened to look out of the living-room window, and there were all these sparkling lights *hanging* there in the clear black night. At first I thought I might be having a vision—or that a whole cluster of stars had suddenly moved closer to earth. Then I realized it was simply the lights from the hotel rooms. The atmosphere that night was so cold and clear that everything looked closer."

"I wish I had seen it," I said. I wished I could have been there, like a ghost hovering behind her, and seen her prowling around her dark rooms, then looking out and seeing the lights. I wondered what had kept her from being able to sleep.

"It's not that far away, you know. Only in New Paltz. I'll take you up there one day. There are miles of mountain trails where one can walk. I'll make a picnic lunch and we'll eat it by the lake. I think you would like it up there." She gave me a fond, possessive look. "But promise me you won't go with any of your other friends, because I want to show it to you first."

"Oh, I won't," I vowed so solemnly that she burst out laughing.

Then, becoming serious again, she said, "You know, Justin, I am thirty years older than you, but I have a feeling we are fated to be good friends."

"I feel it, too," I said.

"Of course you do. When people are sensitive, they can tell when they meet someone who is going to influence their lives."

V.

"What did you think of the house? Did you see the up-stairs?"

"No, ma'am. We had tea down on the terrace."

"You mean you didn't go inside at *all?*"

"No, ma'am. I offered to help her carry the tea things in before I left, but she said she wanted to sit a while longer before going up to the house. He was inside, playing the piano, and I guess she didn't want to disturb him."

"You mean he didn't even have tea with you? How antisocial!"

"No, he had tea. Then later he went up to the house."

"Well, I'm disappointed. Here I was, waiting for a report on those upstairs rooms. If it had been me, I would have asked to use the bathroom. That's perfectly acceptable, you know. Then you could have had a quick look around at the rooms."

I had been trying to sneak upstairs to our bathroom when Aunt Mona had waylaid me. "Come back and tell me all about it," she had called from the living-room sofa, where she was watching some late Sunday afternoon show on TV. I had wanted to escape the house without speaking a word. My mother was taking a nap and Jem was over on the houseboat, grilling hamburgers with Becky and her father. I had hoped to make myself a peanut-butter-and-mayonnaise sandwich and go up to the abandoned farmhouse on the hill and absorb my visit with the De-Vanes. So much had occurred that I needed to go over it while it was still fresh, before all the special looks and words had become diluted by the commonplace affairs of our household. But Aunt Mona wanted a "report" on the tea, and I had reluctantly crossed the plastic bridge over her prize carpet and sat down beside her. She had even turned off the sound of her program, she was so interested in what I might say.

"What did you talk about?" she wanted to know, curling her toes.

"Oh, about flowers," I said, "and the influences of different places, and ants. . . ." I was trying to pick off the superficial elements to satisfy her curiosity, while guarding the big topics from being drained of their charge until I could sort them out and file them away safely in privacy, up on the hill.

"*Aunts?* You mean like me?"

"No, the insects," I said, to her disappointment. I gazed at the two black-and-white figures on the television screen: a woman in a low-cut dress was turning away in anger from a man in a tuxedo who was imploring her about something. "Aren't you missing your program?" I said. "I could come back later."

"No, no, it wasn't very good. Sometimes I think I prefer the old radio plays. You could see so much more in your mind. What did you think of *him?*" From the sour face she made and the way her feathery crest quivered, I knew whom she meant.

"Well, he was okay. I mean he was nice to me." I hesitated, torn between loyalty to him for Ursula's sake and reluctance to offend my aunt. "He seemed kind of moody, but he's probably a very talented musician. Maybe he's even great. She thinks he may be a great artist." The more I said, the more I could feel the magic drain out of the afternoon.

"Talented musician, maybe, but great he's not," pronounced my aunt, folding her arms combatively over her bony chest. "If he were great, he'd be flying around the world giving concerts and playing with big orchestras."

"Well, that's her plan. She hopes he'll be playing in public again in two years. She has big ambitions for him; he got wonderful reviews in Argentina, but now he's withdrawn from the world for some reason. He seems kind of . . . haunted."

"Haunted-schmaunted," said my aunt, with a vigorous shake of her plumage. "Acting like some sort of superior hermit is just a good way to hide failure. Besides, there was no competition to speak of in Argentina during the war. Only Nazis and Nazi sympathizers would go there and perform. And even if he *was* the best thing in Argentina, that was almost fifteen years ago. Great artists aren't suddenly 'discovered' when they're already middle-aged."

My heart felt heavy for Ursula. Surely she had considered this: this *practical* side of things that my aunt was always reminding you of.

"And whatever kind of 'artist' he is," Aunt Mona went on, "doesn't excuse him for being rude and thoughtless. Or for showing contempt for pupils he's being paid good money to teach." She pinned me with her quick, nervous eyes, and her gold hoop earrings swung faintly with her indignation. "*You* don't think it excuses him, do you?"

"No, ma'am," I said honestly, "I don't."

My aunt relaxed. "That's good. I told your mother you were a sensible girl. We had a talk about your going over there today. She said you were so set on going that she didn't like to say no, but she asked me if I thought these people were okay for you to know; I hadn't spoken too kindly of them. I said, 'Louise, I've known Justin going on two months now, I'm a close observer of people, and in my opinion she's a smart, sensible girl. She's been brought up to tell right from wrong. Now, for some reason, she's taken a shine to Ursula DeVane, and Ursula DeVane seems to have taken a shine to *her*. I think we can trust Justin to get what she can out of knowing this woman, who *is* a cultured person, whatever airs she puts on—and leave the rest alone. I don't have any use for the *brother*,' I said to your mother, 'but since Justin isn't going to be taking piano from him, he can't do her much harm, he can't ruin music for her the way he did for Beck. You've

got to remember,' I told your mother, 'that *you* grew up surrounded by cultured, educated, well-bred people who knew how
to behave and had been places. Who knows what I might have
made of myself by this time if I had had a few of those people
take an interest in me and want to polish me up? Now, there's
not a whole lot of *polish* in Clove, so I say let's give Justin her
chance to pick up what she can.' And Louise agreed. 'That's why
I'm here, Mona,' your mother told me, 'so that Justin and Jem can
have their chance.' ''

I left the house feeling compromised. I went up to the empty
farmhouse with my peanut butter sandwich and sat glumly on
the back steps, trying to figure out what had been saved and what
had been lost during the exchange with my aunt. So much of my
life in those days seemed to be occupied with trying to keep
track of my soul's progress (or lack of it) upon a confusing map
where adults had already charted their conflicting ideas of reality. Gone forever were the earlier times when I had been con-
veyed securely along by the cherished traditions of authorities I
loved and never thought to question. Those authorities were
mostly dead now, and though I could still rely on their advice to
guide me through small social crises (such as how to begin a
conversation with a brusque farmer who was driving me home in
his truck), I found them less useful when it came to choosing
how I would (how had Ursula put it?) "respond to the unique
demands of the moment."

My talk with Aunt Mona had muddied things. I had a horror of getting muddied, because I was afraid I would lose sight of
myself. And, once that happened, I might turn into just anybody.
It was all part of the same fear that made me uncomfortable
about living in Lucas Meadows with the lookalike lamps in the
picture windows and the milkmaids surrounding me with their
insinuating smiles that seemed to say: "Come on, now, stop resisting and just be one of us!"

So before I could allow myself the luxury of going over the
hour I had spent with the DeVanes and committing to memory

all the gratifying moments as well as the tense and mysterious ones, I had to sit on the old farmhouse steps and determine how clear I was to myself after my encounter with my aunt.

My skin prickled when I recalled her horrible phrase "taken a shine to." It cheapened what I felt toward Ursula, and what I believed she reciprocated. It reduced our affinity to some kind of showy, whimsical fondness between a young girl and an older woman. But what really disgusted me was Aunt Mona's assumption that because I was "smart" and "sensible" I would be able to "get what I could" out of knowing Ursula and "leave the rest alone"—as one might skim the cream off a bottle of milk that had already turned sour below. (Not that I thought Ursula had turned sour below; I had no idea what my aunt meant by "the rest.")

Was this what "smart, sensible" people did in the world, then: use parts of people and throw away the rest, the parts they didn't need? That would mean you saw other people as if they were those pull-apart building toys Jem loved: take the pieces you need to build what you want, and throw the rest back in the box.

That meant human beings weren't necessarily seen by others as whole persons, but only as negotiable parts.

If Aunt Mona saw Ursula as just her "culture," which could be used to "polish me up" so I could get ahead in the world, then what might someone see me as? I tried to think what part, or parts, Ursula might want from me.

The trouble with the "parts" theory was that it reduced things. It took away the vibrant, undefinable connection and left you with just . . . parts. Those things Ursula had said to me, about how she felt we were fated to be good friends despite the great difference in our ages; and about how we would influence each other's lives (or did she only mean that she saw herself as influencing mine? I couldn't be sure from the way she had said it, I was too timid to ask): where did you fit such words, and the vibrations they set going in your imagination, into the "parts" scheme of things? I didn't want to fit them, didn't want to mix the rarefied air of the DeVanes with my aunt's down-to-earth atmosphere. But how to keep them apart, when I lived with my aunt, when I felt myself even now being infected by her sensible skepticism. (*Was* it too late for Julian DeVane to realize his sister's dreams of glory for him? Was she throwing her life away, *avoiding* her own life somehow, by dedicating her ambition and driving force to the service of his art?)

Divisions, divisions.

For most of that summer I would be divided, commuting between prosaic Lucas Meadows and seductive Old Clove Road, making an effort—which got harder as the summer progressed—to render unto the Stokes-Mott world, with its practicalities and family duties, what it required of me, while secretly preserving my highest loyalties for the DeVane kingdom, with its long-standing prides and alienations, its private fantasies, and its obsessive dreams.

After my tea with the DeVanes, there were two more weeks of school, filled with those kinds of end-of-term activities that keep you busy without really involving you very much. Class periods were constantly being preempted by a glee club concert, a 4-H fashion show. There were a few exams, which I thought were insultingly easy, though I did not make top scores on any of them. In those two weeks, a sort of golden, dusty boredom descended on me as soon as I entered the school each morning, and it stayed with me until I got on the bus to go home. The windows of the classrooms were open, and one or another of the meadows surrounding the school was constantly being mowed; a girl with hay fever sneezed and sneezed until the tears rolled down her cheeks.

Although Ann Cristiana was always friendly when we met in the halls, and though Ed found a pretext almost every day to stop and talk, I could not shake the feeling that this part of my life did not really matter; I would form no friendships here that would carry through the years. Even though this was supposed to be our home now, I couldn't imagine myself ever feeling connected to it in the permanent way I would always be connected to Fredericksburg, to the house on Washington Avenue, to the schools I had attended there, to the friends I had made, even though it had not been heartbreaking to leave these friends behind. During my last two years in Fredericksburg, my friendships had been under certain restraints, owing to the slow dying first of my grandmother and then of my grandfather. Though I continued to see my friends at school and go to their parties, it would not have been seemly for me to offer hospitality at our house or to get too involved in any particular friendship when the grandparents who had raised me, and who were so loved and respected in town, were living out their final days. Yet I could imagine myself meeting these friends at some later time in my life, taking up with them where we had left off; whereas something in me knew that the Cristianas, or any other young person I might get to know in the village of Clove, would not last any longer than this period of my life lasted: it was just an interim to be survived between the past that I loved and the future that would surely compensate me for my endurance of present miseries and boredoms.

I say "something in me knew," but I may be attributing to myself more prescience than I had. Maybe I'm confusing psychic knowledge with retrospective knowledge; it's a mistake frequently made. But I remember believing firmly that Clove would be temporary for us, that *something* would step in and save us from living out our lives here. Whether I believed this because I wanted so badly to believe it or because I "felt something," I can't honestly say. As I review these memories in painstaking detail, trying to see what was true and not flinch from those truths, I've even speculated whether my "possessed" behavior toward Ursula was a semiconsciously contrived ploy on my part to make my mother see that she ought to take me away from Clove. But no, that's going too far; that would make me a monster, like little Mary Tilford in *The Children's Hour*, who wrecks a school and the lives of two women in order to keep from being sent back to the school. I was not a monster—not that kind of monster, anyway. I told no lies; I even kept from my mother the extent of my preoccupation with Ursula. I loved Ursula more than I loved my mother that summer, and I didn't want my mother to know it. Yet she did give much thought to the older woman with whom I spent so much time. She worried, I know she did; I could tell Ursula DeVane was often in her thoughts just by the kinds of "casual" questions she would ask me when I came home.

But children trying to protect themselves from real or imagined assaults on their integrity *have* been capable of monstrous things. I remember how shocked I was when Ursula told me, later in the summer, how, at the age of ten, she had betrayed her own mother. I thought *she* had been something of a monster, even though I could see her side of it, how it had seemed to her as a child.

Now I am struck by the appalling similarities between what Ursula did to her mother and how I contributed to Ursula's tragedy. Not that I planned anything ahead of time, as she had done; I was as unconscious of what I was bringing about as the young Ursula had been resolutely conscious. Yet I did bring it about. Without me, it wouldn't have happened. But I couldn't have been the agent of destruction if the props for that destruction had not been set into place, some of them years before. And who more than Ursula had set them up? It was almost as if she needed me, recognized me from the first, as the perfect, daughterly agent of her retribution. In many ways, didn't she groom me for that role during most of the summer? Or is that going too far?

In following the natural flow of my memories as they leap forward, then draw back, then leap forward again, I am digressing from what I want to do most. I want to go back and claim the girl I was—the girl Ursula DeVane chose for her special friend, that summer in Clove. I want to take myself through the summer as it unfolded, allowing myself no conscious lies or glossings-over, but only the wisdom of retrospect. Recently I read a passage in a memoir by the actress Florida Scott-Maxwell, who became a playwright and, after that, a Jungian analyst. "You need only claim the events of your life to make yourself yours," she writes. "When you truly possess all you have been and done, which may take some time, you are fierce with reality." I want to be fierce with reality.

One of the end-of-school events was my cousin Becky's ballet recital, held at the Grange Hall, which had the biggest stage in Clove. It was this event that Becky had been working toward during all those hours of practice in her room, and I was frankly curious as to how good a show she would put on. Despite her chilly reception of me into their house, I did not wish her to fail. In fact, I had made up my mind that if she was good, I would be the first to tell her so. Maybe then she would relent toward me a little.

It rained steadily all the day of the recital, and yet a large, cheerful crowd showed up at the Grange Hall, shaking out their umbrellas at the door and acting as though they couldn't have asked for anything better. Mr. Mott explained to us that many of these families had just put in their summer crops and to them this soft, constant, all-day rain had been a godsend.

I remember watching Mr. Mott as he escorted us, one at a time, from the car to the Hall under his large black umbrella. He took Becky in first, so she could warm up backstage; then he came back for Aunt Mona, who consented to hold on to his arm in an arch way; then he took my mother in, and then me, and, last of all, Jem. I remember how my uncle looked as he scrunched his tall, awkward body low so as to cover Jem better with the umbrella. And I saw that, far from considering all these trips a chore, Mr. Mott was in his element. His bland, unmemorable face grew brighter with each plodding trip he made from car to porch, sheltering the current dependent from the rain. I understood then that Mr. Mott's happiness and self-esteem were measured in terms of how useful he could make himself to others. Were there many people like that in the world, people who, instead of just assuming they would be appreciated for themselves, knew that they must barter for love with the services they performed? Once Aunt Mona had told me, in her frank style, that she had married Mott because she knew he was the kind of man she could trust to take care of her, no matter what.

Obviously, then, Mr. Mott was one of those people other people valued only for some "parts." And he looked as though he knew this. He looked as though he woke up every morning and asked himself: "What valuable service can I perform at the

IBM site today, so my co-workers will say: 'What would we ever do without Mott?'" Or, "I wonder what I can do for the folks over in Lucas Meadows, so they'll be grateful, so maybe even Mona will miss me a little." At what point in his life had Mr. Mott decided he wouldn't be lovable enough just as himself? Did it happen back at that orphanage, where they made him come down to breakfast wearing his wet sheet?

I felt sorry for Mr. Mott. He was the first adult I can remember pitying. Yet I couldn't like him. There was something intrusive about his helpfulness. Could it have been that I sensed—and sensed rightly—that his helpfulness might one day come at exactly the wrong time?

Becky did dance better than the other girls. She was not one of those born dancers whose movements serenely mock the clumsier world, but she performed her number with a learned, determined grace. Her face wore a secure expression, as if while dancing she inhabited a place free of the daily irritations that exasperated her: she did not raise her eyebrows or smirk or grimace in the usual Becky fashion. I could not wait for the recital to be over, so I could go backstage and congratulate her. I am not sure that I didn't make myself see her dancing as better than it was in order to justify doing this. My cousin had at first intrigued me, then hurt my pride; but what Ursula had said—about Becky's feeling I was a threat to her—had made me magnanimously ready to try again.

As soon as the recital was over, I pushed my way backstage with the crush of parents and siblings and told Becky I thought she was wonderful. I went further than I had meant to and added: "Watching you made me feel *jealous*. I wish *I* had something I could do so well."

But as I told her this, Becky's eyebrows shot up and her small mouth twisted in an incredulous smirk, as if to say: "What on earth do you want from me *now*?" Yet when my mother came up and hugged Becky and said quietly in her ear, "You were the best one, by far," my cousin got a fixed and earnest look on her face and asked worshipfully, "Did you really think so?"

I turned away, disgusted with myself for having let Becky

snub me once again, and wandered about the Hall. The dancing teacher, Mrs. Roosa, whom Ursula had called "Imogene," from the old one-room-school days, was surrounded by gratified parents. I thought then of Ursula, with that lift of spirit one feels when remembering something pleasant. She was the only person whom it inspired me to think about. She was the most interesting person in the village, and *she* found my company worthwhile. What a shame she was not here tonight, but why would she attend a recital where, as she would put it, little girls expressed themselves and got rewarded for it? She would be at home, in the old stone house where DeVanes had always lived; she would be doing something interesting—perhaps with her brother's music in the background, whatever music matched his mood of the evening—in one of the rooms I had never seen.

I pretended Ursula strolled beside me, making ironic comments on the people, pointing out things I might not have noticed by myself. "*Imogene* certainly seems pleased with herself," she would say, "but why shouldn't she be? Everything went beautifully. The record player was always on cue backstage, and the parents got their money's worth. Oh look, there are your young Cristianas, and here was I thinking you all alone like a waif in a strange land. Did you see how Ed saw you, then pretended not to, so he'll have time to prepare what he'll say when he 'officially' sees you? Ah, the whole family's here tonight, even the pregnant mother. Abel and I went to the one-room school, you know, with Imogene and my brother. Did you notice how little Jenny Cristiana was counting under her breath in that number she shared with your cousin? Listen to how those IBM parents are chiming in with their comments about 'this much-needed rain': that's to show that they are not just interlopers who draw better salaries than everyone else in the county, but that they have entered into the spirit of the community. Ah, yes, Justin, a nice, safe evening. Now the little girls can go home under their parents' umbrellas, their ballet shoes clutched in a paper bag, and not once has anybody been inconvenienced by the threat of real Art."

I had succeeded so well in creating her by my side that I had almost *become* Ursula. It seemed to me that not only could I speak as she would speak, observe as she might observe, but also feel as she would feel. I was so much into my strange little game that when Mr. Cristiana passed me and said, "How are you?" I hesitated. Was I supposed to speak to him? What could I say that would not make a certain brother furious? But my manners recalled me to myself, and I smiled at the red-faced farmer, who looked uncomfortable in his suit and tie, and answered, "Fine, thank you."

Then Ed came over, with his bouncy country walk. He pretended he had just seen me. I wasn't sorry to have some real person to stand talking with me in front of all these people, even though he was blushing and shifting his feet. He said that once they got ahead on those fences they were going to put up all around their new land, maybe we could go to the movies some night. That would be fun, I replied graciously, thinking how odd it was that he should seem so young. I felt as if I were someone decades older, hiding inside the body of a young girl. This feeling was accompanied by an agreeable surge of power. It was as if I had given myself an immunity from self-consciousness, through my exercise of impersonating Ursula DeVane.

On the morning of my fourteenth birthday, I woke up with a disturbing image of my grandfather. One year ago today, on the afternoon of my thirteenth birthday, I had gone in to see him. Following his stroke, he had been moved downstairs to his study. The rented hospital bed was like a sinister intruder standing among his familiar furniture and the shelves filled with his medical books and bound monographs on the daily lives of Negro slaves.

My grandfather was sitting up in the bed. Since his illness, he had grown too small for his pajamas. His day nurse, Thad, a jovial black giant of a man, bustled about the room on crepe soles. I sat down by the bed and asked my grandfather how he was feeling that day. He did not answer, of course, but his eyes grew bright and intense with that look which had substituted for speech since his stroke. Thad, who was replacing some records in their cardboard jackets, told me they had been playing some music. "He love that Bach. Ain't that right, Doctor Frank?"

My grandfather's eyes shone at Thad.

I began the difficult task of making conversation with someone who had helped teach me the art but who now could not utter a word. I believed that he understood everything because he watched my face closely as I spoke. I attempted to keep up a lively account of what was going on in the rest of the house, what my parents and Jem had given me for my birthday, how there would be a cake this evening, and how I planned to blow out the candles in this room before Thad went off duty. As I told him these things, I had to work hard to keep any sign of strain or pity out of my face. My grandfather was famous for his "face-reading." It was said that he could look at a patient's face and diagnose the state of health at once. My grandmother told a story about how, when they were newly married and on a visit to her people in South Carolina, they had walked into a party. After speaking to the hostess for a few minutes, my grandfather took my grandmother aside and said, "Honora, that woman is going to die soon. I wonder if she knows." My grandmother told him that this woman had been red-faced and bug-eyed for years. "Besides, Frank, you can't very well go up to her and say, 'Pardon me, but I think you are going to die soon.' It would ruin her party." "You're right," agreed my grandfather. But the woman did die soon after that party.

The afternoon of my thirteenth birthday, I knew that my grandfather was never going to get any better than he was then. We would never go off together on our excursions again, never wander around some old plantation draped in Spanish moss and then go purposefully to the slave cabins, whose dirt floors and meager proportions always excited my grandfather far more than the grand designs of the big houses the tourists came to see. He would let me measure the dimensions of a floor or a narrow window, while he wrote down my figures in his notebook. We would speculate about what it had been like to be a slave living with a large family in these cramped quarters. Once he led me into imagining it so well that I stamped my foot and exclaimed furiously, "I think if I had been them I would have *killed* somebody!" "No," he said, "nine times out of ten you wouldn't have. You probably wouldn't even have run away. You would have stayed on and done your work, maybe steaming with resentment if you had one kind of temperament, maybe dreaming of a life in which things would be better, if you had another kind. You see, what interests me about these folks, Justin, and why it pays me to study them, is, well, two things: they seem, on the whole, to have been a wonderfully resilient people; and they had an enviable capacity for apprehending the world of the spirit. The more I study the ways they managed to survive as families and keep their hopes up, even in their captivity, the more I admire them."

He talked to me that way, like an equal, like a fellow researcher. He encouraged me to imagine the lives of others. Most of the cruelty and neglect that went on in the world, he said, boiled down to the simple fact that someone just wasn't imagining how the other fellow felt.

That my companion of so many hours, this wise, compassionate man who had helped form my mind, had been reduced to the helpless figure in the bed, with his shining gaze fixed dependently on my flow of words, which he could neither direct nor answer, seemed a very cruel thing. "God works in strange and mysterious ways," I had been taught, but I remember wondering that afternoon if *God* had been imagining how the other fellow felt when he inflicted this stroke on my grandfather.

When the visit was over, I kissed the top of his head, which was pink and warm under his thin hair, and started upstairs to my room. But I was stopped halfway up by the sounds coming from behind the closed door of my parents' room. They were sounds I had heard before, the usual accompaniment to adult passion. But when my mother uttered a high, sharp cry, I knew I could not just continue up the remaining stairs and walk past their door to my room. Even if I tiptoed, the floor would creak and they would know I had heard. So I went quietly back downstairs and outside. I walked to the corner mailbox, past the famous sewer grating where my mother had deposited my grandfather's check to Sweet Briar. I crossed over to the shady side of the street and waved to some ladies kneeling in the dirt, planting flowers in the new beds around the famous historic home where George Washington's only sister had lived after her marriage. The ladies gave one another knowing looks as I passed. They were members of my late grandmother's garden club, and they knew there was more dying going on in our house, the slow kind of dying in which someone you loved who was no longer even himself anymore might live on for years, depleting the family savings. I crossed back into the sun again so I would not overhear anything they were saying.

When I got back to the house, I found Jem, still in pajamas from his nap, peeking through the keyhole of my grandfather's study. Thad had put on some more Bach, which came soothingly to my ears after the hot walk.

"There's something strange going on in there!" whispered Jem, excitedly motioning me over.

"What do you mean?" My heart started beating faster: was my grandfather *dying* this very minute? How horrible my parents would feel if they learned that he had died while they had been enjoying themselves in bed!

"Look! Look in there!" urged Jem, pointing to the keyhole.

I knelt down and put my eye to the keyhole. At first I didn't see anything, though I felt the floor under me vibrating rhythmically. Then my vision adjusted to the tiny focus and I saw Thad's white clothes drifting past. It was Thad dancing to Bach. I was just about to ask Jem what was so strange about that—Thad dancing, to amuse and soothe my grandfather—when I noticed a foot in a bedroom slipper dangling close to Thad's hip. Then I realized Thad was dancing with my grandfather in his arms. I caught a glimpse of his frail pink head resting against the big Negro's starched white bosom. My grandfather's eyes were closed and on his lips was the smile of an innocent child.

It was this image I woke to, on the morning of my fourteenth birthday, surrounded by "Raspberry Ice" and the clubby smiles of the milkmaids. Was I better off or worse off, this time last year? I asked myself, going up and down the stairs on Washington Avenue in memory, hearing the sounds of my parents' lovemaking (but why was my father home that day? It was a weekday. Had he come home for my birthday?) and the scratching of the ladies' trowels in the flowerbeds of Kenmore, and then the sweet, stately strains of "Sheep May Safely Graze," which led to that disconcerting vision through the keyhole. "Oh, it's all right," I had said to Jem. "Thad is just dancing with Grandfather. It's something they like to do." But the sight had bewildered me. It was as if my grandfather had abdicated from us all, escaping to the bosom of Abraham via the bosom of Thad. That day, I knew I had lost the best man in my life. I had started off my life thinking he was my father. And then, when I was three, and they started telling me how my daddy would be coming home from the war soon, I could not comprehend: wasn't the daddy in our house the man my mother called Daddy? Why should there be another one? When they tried to explain that, no, the person they called Daddy was my *grand*daddy, I had screamed and cried, "No! No! No!" With their cruel insistence on nomenclature, it was as though they were trying to take him away from me.

I had never loved my father as a father. It was not his fault that I had found the father who suited me best before I ever met him. The man who came home from the war seemed too young, too easygoing, too mercurial to be a father. He sat around strumming a banjo and singing. He could not keep his hands off my mother. The two of them slept late every morning. "Poor things haven't had their honeymoon," my grandmother told me matter-of-factly, as though I had been a contemporary of hers and we were indulging the two younger people. With my father, existence was uncertain. You never knew when he would breeze in—or out. Or when he would take my mother with him. When they left for Charlottesville "so he could have his college," as my grandmother put it, I felt relieved. The house was peaceful again. I found I could romanticize my father *in absentia*. "My father is charm personified," I told my school friends, quoting my grandmother, even down to her little sigh at the end, suggesting she was a bit overwhelmed by all that charm. Maybe I would have grown to admire him for his own merits if he had not skidded fatally on a wet road coming home to us that weekend, his company car filled with watches, bracelets, and class rings. He had been so cheerful, so sure it was all going to work out, after my grandfather's death. We had one another, didn't we? We had a roof over our heads—and a mighty fine roof, at that: my father loved the house on Washington Avenue; all his life, he had wanted to live in such a house, he told Jem and me. In those few months between my grandfather's burial and my father's accident, he gave us little pep talks about the wonderful life we were all going to have after he'd made some money. He played his banjo in the evenings and taught us funny songs, some of which were a little risqué. They were songs he had learned in the Army, he said, as if that made them all right.

> *Oh those dirty drawers that Maggie Murphy wore;*
> *They were baggy at the knees,*
> *They were size forty-threes . . .*

That was Jem's favorite. When we sang it, he cackled and howled and held his stomach. Then our father laughed. Once he laughed so hard, he fell off his chair and hit his head on the radiator and was out cold for a few minutes. My mother rushed in and bathed his bleeding head with a washcloth. She seemed angry. "Oh Rivers, not again!" she said.

This phrase came back to me as I lay steeped in memories on the morning of my fourteenth birthday. Was that why he stayed home from work on the morning of my thirteenth birthday? Because the evening before had been another of those "Oh Rivers, not again" evenings?

And what about the night on which he had been killed? Had it been the rain's fault? Or had it been one of those "Oh Rivers, not again" nights?

It seemed to me that I had known from the beginning that my father was not to be trusted. He was the man who had charmed my mother into marrying him, and without whom I would not have existed. But beneath his charm lay the weakness that would kill him and uproot us from our home. Why had he been weak? When had it started? When had his drinking started? The first time I remember kissing him, he had had bourbon on his breath.

I was shocked at the waves of resentment that rolled over me now. Why did he have to come back from the war and spoil our lives? I thought. But even if he hadn't come back, if he had died a heroic death, could that have stopped my grandmother's cancer from growing silently in her until it was too late to save her? Could it have prevented my grandfather's stroke? And if my father had died in the war, we wouldn't have had Jem, of course. It would have been just my mother and me, alone in the house on Washington Avenue: my mother unable to earn a living, and all those bills to pay. Wasn't it possible that she and I would still have ended up here, in the house of Aunt Mona? How awful to think that even forked destinies could end up at the same place.

And then I was struck by a blasphemous thought that shocked me even more than my resentment against my father: Why, if my grandfather had been such a superb diagnostician, able to walk into a party and see that a strange woman was going to die . . . why had he not been able to spot the illness growing in my grandmother, whom he slept beside every night and looked at countless times every day?

It was just after this low moment, in which my own thoughts had set me at odds with cherished illusions in my past, that my mother knocked softly on the door and entered my bedroom.

"You aren't feeling ill, are you?" She must have seen the remnants of my struggles on my face.

"No, ma'am. I'm just lazy, I guess. What time is it?"

"After ten. The postman's already been here." She bent down and gave me a kiss. "Happy birthday. This came for you." She placed a small, brown-wrapped parcel on top of my covers, and I glimpsed my name in a bold, loopy script. In the upper-left-hand corner was a number on Old Clove Road.

"It's from your friend, I think," my mother said, rather shyly, as if she were afraid of trespassing. "Did you tell her it was your birthday?"

"No, she asked me when it was. I guess it's easy for her to remember because June fourteenth was the day she sailed for France." I said all this in a slightly bored voice, to keep my mother from seeing how interested I was in the package. But I didn't want to open it in her presence: I had no idea what it might be.

"Well, come on down when you're ready, and I'll make you some breakfast," said my mother. "It's just the Stokeses at home today. Mona dropped Becky off at her father's boat on the way to work."

"But it's a weekday. Becky goes to her father on Saturday." How unfriendly of Becky, not to stay home on my birthday. I would have stayed home for hers out of politeness.

My mother read my look. "Perhaps she has things to do. We've all been invited for a cookout on Eric Mott's houseboat this evening. Something a little special. I know you take after your grandmother in some ways, and Honey always liked to have a hint of warning when people were planning surprises for her."

"Oh," I said.

"But please act surprised this evening. Only, I didn't want you to go around all day thinking we'd forgotten you." She gave a sidelong glance at my package. "Well, I'll be downstairs, awaiting my breakfast orders," she said.

As soon as she had closed the door, I slipped the string off the package, admiring the way my name looked in the bold, slanty script. One dramatic stroke crossed the *t*'s in both names. The capital *J* and *S* were extravagant productions that I made up my mind to imitate in future, when signing my name. I would also copy her Greek *e*, which made *Stokes* look more exotic.

Then I tore off the brown paper, being careful not to damage any of the writing. Inside a cardboard box stuffed with tissue paper was a small, squarish bottle made of thick blue glass. A strange gift, I thought, but then she was an unconventional person. Folded beneath the bottle in its little cradle of tissue paper was a sheet of white stationery with a whole page of writing in the bold, upslanting hand.

While over in New Paltz for a Huguenot Society Meeting, I spotted this in the window of an antiques shop. It reminded me of our entertaining discussion of favorite (and unfavorite) colors, and I could see this stalwart little bottle perched on your window ledge asserting its blueness. We loved having you for tea. You are quite one of us! Julie also has something for you, he found it the other day while looking for his childhood volume of Beethoven sonatas. It was too unwieldy to send through the post, so we'll give it to you when you come again, which we hope will be soon. Happy Birthday!

Ursula

P.S. The chill is off the pond now and it's very agreeable.

She had been out somewhere, but had thought of me. Even he, in search of some old music, had thought of me. They really did like me; they felt I was "one of them."

And the letter was perfect, especially the way she had phrased that part about the favorite and unfavorite colors. It was a letter that even Aunt Mona could read without suspecting she had been betrayed by me in that diatribe about my room.

I got up at once and placed the little bottle in my window, where it caught the morning light and began to "assert" itself. It drained power from the muddy hues of my walls and flattened the smiles of the milkmaids with its clear, twinkling blue. I kept looking at it as I got dressed. Now it did not seem a strange present to me at all, but a magically appropriate gift. She had sent me a talisman to ward off ordinariness and compromise and despondency. It was just what I needed, this bottle, and I liked it all the better because its significance would be known only to her and to me.

VI.

"Ursula DeVane sent me a bottle," I told my mother at breakfast.

"A bottle?" repeated my mother, puzzled. "What kind of bottle?"

"Just a little blue bottle she saw in an antiques shop," I said, purposely nonchalant. "It reminded her of me because I think I said I liked the color blue. But it was nice of her to remember my birthday. It's the thought that counts, after all."

"Of course it is," agreed my mother. "It's very kind of her to take an interest in you." Did I detect a relief in her voice that the gift had not made a great hit with me? "I know you'll be sure and thank her for it," she added.

After I had finished a leisurely breakfast of buckwheat cakes and bacon, my mother said, "I've got something for you, too. It's down in my room. I'd rather give it to you here than carry it over to the houseboat."

"Is it something *huge?*"

"No, not huge," she said, smiling. "But I'd sure hate to see them drop over the side of the houseboat into the water. Besides, it's something that belongs just to the family; I don't want to give it to you in front of all the others."

"First you said 'it,' and then you said 'them.' How can it be both?"

"Well," she said, "come on downstairs to my room and I'll show you how."

In the last few weeks, she had made a corner of her room into a little office. Mr. Mott had lent her a fairly new IBM electric, with typing stand and chair, and my mother was now teaching herself to touch-type from a boring manual Aunt Mona had found for her. She was determined that, come September, when Jem started school, she would be proficient enough to get a job as somebody's secretary. "Though no one will hire me, probably, without shorthand, too," she had said to Aunt Mona. "Nonsense," my aunt had retorted, "they'll take one look at you and see you'll be an asset to their office. With your looks and your luck, you probably won't even have to *type*." "My *luck*, Mona? I hardly see how you can call me *lucky*, after all that has happened." "Now don't be offended, Louise. I know you've had an awful time. First your parents and then poor Rivers, after he'd got through the war without a scratch on him. No, what I meant was, you have this quality—I have always noticed it in you, even way back when we were kids and I could only gaze at you from the other side of the tracks—" "Oh, Mona, I do wish you wouldn't speak in that way. You make out as if you and Rivers were some kind of slum children and I was this awful snob. . . ." "No, let me finish, Louise. I always noticed this quality in you, this attitude. It was the attitude of someone who had been brought up to expect the best. And when you expect the best, you get the best, that's my theory. People see something in you and respond to it. Some lawyer or businessman in Kingston is going to take one look at you when you walk in his office, and say, 'That lady has an air about her, and I want it for my office; it will reflect well on *me*.'" "Well, for the sake of my children, I hope you are right, Mona," my mother had said good-humoredly.

Jem was now seated at the typewriter, pecking out lines of gibberish. "You know what?" he said. "If I keep on practicing every day, I'll be able to type just as good as anybody by the time school starts."

"Darling, they won't have typewriters at your school," said my mother. "But I'll bet you'll be able to *read* as well as anybody else in your grade. At least we've managed that, these last few months. I'm going to give Justin her present."

"Aren't you going to wait for the party?" Then he clapped his hands over his mouth, fearing he'd given the surprise away.

"It's all right. She knows there's going to be a little celebration. But I wanted this to be just among us." My mother opened the top drawer of her bureau and handed me a long, slim box, wrapped in festive paper.

They sat down on the bed beside me while I slipped off the ribbon and undid the Scotch-taped edges without tearing the paper. Inside a brown velvet case I found a pearl necklace that I had known all my life: my grandmother's. Many thoughts rushed through my head as I sat there simulating the awe I knew I was expected to feel. Since I had been a little girl, I had been told that this necklace would one day be mine. Often, as my grandmother fastened it around her neck, she would tell me how this had been a wedding present from my grandfather, and that, since my mother had received a pearl necklace all her own for her high-school graduation, this one would be mine. "And, just between you and me," my grandmother would say, "these are far better pearls." I had always admired the necklace, but was quite willing to wait for it. I had known that it would not be mine until my grandmother died, and she was more important to me than any pearls. But I also connected it with becoming a woman, and I had had ambivalent feelings about this inevitable transformation ever since, as a little girl, I had believed that when you became a woman you grew long fleshy appendages on the bottoms of your feet so you could wear high heels. The high heels looked nice and sounded authoritative as they clacked over wooden floors, but to wear them, I thought, I would have to forfeit my comfortable flat soles on which it was easy to run and play. Though I no longer believed in these sprouting appendages, I still felt unready to inherit these pearls, to look in the mirror and face the young woman fastening them around her neck. I knew I must turn into that young woman within a few years, but something in me held back: there was a lonely, mysterious side of myself I was just beginning to know, a side neither masculine nor feminine but quivering with intimations of mental and spiritual things. I had to save a place for these things. If I let myself be rushed into womanhood with all its distracting appurtenances, I might miss their quiet revelations and be a less interesting person for the rest of my life.

"Of course, you won't want to wear them just yet," my mother said, "but I thought you ought to have them. She always meant for you to have them, you know."

"I know."

"Would you like to try them on?" my mother urged.

"I thought you said I shouldn't wear them yet."

"I only meant you wouldn't want to wear them to *school* or anything. But you can try them on now." She took them from the box and held them out to me.

"Oh, then I'd love to," I said, with convincing enthusiasm. I bowed my head and let her fasten them around my neck.

"And remember," Jem told her, "I get my grandfather's gold watch when I'm older. And his stethoscope."

I couldn't wait for them to have their nap that afternoon. I wrote a note ("Gone for a bike ride. I may stop by Ursula De-Vane's and thank her. Love, Justin") and anchored it to the kitchen table with Aunt Mona's Scotty dog salt and pepper shakers. I liked the way my handwriting looked with the new Greek *e*'s, and the bold crossing of the *t* in "Justin." It would have looked even more dramatic if I had been able to slash on through the *t* in "Stokes," as well, but I could hardly sign a note to my mother "Justin Stokes."

As soon as I rode away from our house, I felt larger, freer. I was almost certain she would be expecting me today. Why hadn't I gone back sooner? More than two weeks had passed since the tea. Part of the reason was shyness, but there was a calculated frugality in it: I didn't want to use up my welcome; I wanted her to miss me a little. But she had been real and present to me every day. I had taken her with me to various places and thought her thoughts while there. Her personality had already penetrated mine.

I rode down the haywagon road and left my bike at the edge of the forest, just out of sight, so nobody would be tempted to steal it. Then I went softly through the woods toward the hut; I whistled a few tuneless bars of something so she would not feel I had crept up on her again.

She was not in the hut, though her clothes lay in a heap on the blanket. Her thong sandals were there, too, the toe of one stepping on the toe of the other, as though she had slipped them off in haste.

To go for a swim? Then why was there nobody in the pond? "Ursula?" I called timidly. The sound of my voice calling her name sounded presumptuous; it reminded me emphatically of the vast difference in our ages. But where was she? The sunlight pouring down through the shafts of the pines seemed suddenly sinister, the way it sparkled on the slight agitations of that pond with nobody in it. In the space of a second, I imagined her drowned or in the process of drowning somewhere on the bottom of the pond. In my imagination I had already torn off my tennis shoes and plunged straight down, overcoming my horror of all the things below that dark surface; I felt my way through the muddy depths for the crumpled form I must somehow, quickly, every breath counting, pull to the top. I would have to give her artificial respiration the way we had been taught in Girl Scouts. But the people we had practiced on had always been clothed. Hadn't she said she swam naked? How would she feel when she revived and found me kneeling over her naked body, blowing air into her mouth? But what if she didn't revive?

I was still paralyzed by embarrassment and indecision when she shot up out of the water, laughing and sputtering.

"I haven't done that in years!" she cried exultantly. She flung herself backward into the water with a splash and floated, regarding me with a wet grin. She was wearing a bathing suit. "I must have been under a whole minute, at least!" She looked extremely pleased with herself.

"I was imagining you'd drowned," I said, resentful of her childish mirth.

"That's the whole point." She raised her head out of the water and squinted at me, then laughed. "Oh, Justin, if you could see your face. You must be careful with that face. *Everything* shows on it. I'm sorry I teased you, but I couldn't resist. I heard you coming through the trees and I thought: I wonder if my breath's as good as it once was. And it *was!* Once, Abel Cristiana and I got so good at this, we staged a double drowning. We had poor Julie in tears when we finally came up. Oh God, we were all so young then. Now look at us: feuding and looking the other way when we meet. I hope you brought your suit today. I brought mine specifically to protect your sense of modesty."

"No," I said. "I really can't stay very long. I only came to thank you for the bottle." I sounded stiff and ungracious. "I really did like it," I added.

"I'm glad," she replied, breaststroking around the pond with her head held up in a formal way. "It was nothing very much, but I wanted you to have it." She seemed offended. It occurred to me then that she had hoped I would come, had looked forward to a long visit. The idea that I could wound her gave me a little thrill of superiority, and at the same time made me relent.

"I guess I can stay a while," I said, "as long as I'm not disturbing you."

"Not at all. Julie is interviewing two prospective pupils. Two brothers. I preferred to amuse myself down here rather than making chitchat with the mother. But it will be much nicer if you will stay and amuse me." She smiled at me from the water, and I thought: She knows everything that has been passing through my head; she knows I know she was waiting for me, but she's still in command. Her humor gives her a command I don't have. Even if someone did hurt her, she would probably smile that funny smile that always starts with the twitching of her lips, as if she's trying to keep it back, and then she would say something that would keep her in control.

"Well," she said, "if you won't come in, I'm coming out. My fingertips have shriveled." She did a show-offy backward somersault and came up with her hair streaming behind her like a mermaid. With several brisk strokes she reached the edge and hauled herself up the muddy bank. She wore an old woolen tank suit, one of those shapeless garments that remind you of school swimming classes, and I could see her stiff nipples sticking up beneath the wool. She had a lean, long-waisted body with broad shoulders and not very much bosom. Her legs were shapely, but I saw with the cruel eye of the young that the tops of her thighs were flabby.

Aware I was giving her the once-over, she immediately turned the tables on me, as she would always do when I was harboring criticisms. "Is it that you can't swim?" she asked, tossing back her head and wringing her wet hair with both hands. "Because I would be happy to teach you. It would give us a worthwhile project for the summer."

"I've been swimming since I was three years old," I said (which was an exaggeration; it was nearer to six); "I went to the beach every summer with my grandmother and she taught me to swim."

"Ah, then it must be that you just don't like country ponds," she said, stepping inside the hut. "You imagine all the creepy-crawly things in a pond, whereas"—I could hear her stripping off her wet suit—"an ocean has its own collection of sting-y, prickly things: jellyfish, crabs, sea urchins . . ." She laughed softly as she reeled them off. "I'd just as soon take my chances with the inhabitants of this pond; I've swum with the great-great-grandparents of every frog and turtle and water snake in it. . . ." She popped her head around the door and winked at me. "Just joking about the snakes, of course. Oh hell, I forgot my towel. Well, I'll have to make do with this old blanket." Sounds of energetic rubbing came from behind the door. "I was in a rush to get out of the house before those boys arrived with their mother. She would have expected me to give her a tour of the house. They all want a tour of the house."

She emerged from the hut with the exuberant superiority of an athlete joining a sedentary friend. "If you can stay a while, we'll go up to the house and get your other present as soon as Julie's finished. The first time, he only does little tests, to find out how musical they are—or aren't. It's a bit dog-eared and faded,

but we thought it might inspire you, under the circumstances."
She strode over to a tree and slung the wet suit across a low
branch.

"I guess I can," I said. "I just have to be back for this surprise supper or something they're giving me on my uncle's
houseboat. I'm not supposed to know about it, but my mother
told me. She gave me my present earlier because it was just a
family thing. I got my grandmother's pearls." I thought this
sounded impressive.

"Oh my," said Ursula, sitting down on the cracked stone
threshold of the hut. She motioned me to sit down, too. "That
must have been quite an occasion. You admired your grandmother, didn't you?"

"Everyone admired her. My grandfather used to say she was
the only woman he knew who would behave exactly the same
way when nobody was looking."

"My God, what a thought!" said Ursula. "Does that mean
she was so sure of who she was that she never had to pretend, or
was it a way of saying she had no private life?"

"I think he meant she was just *good*," I said uncertainly. Nobody before had ever questioned my grandfather's encomium.
That Ursula seemed to find something questionable about it put
me on the defensive.

With her characteristic quickness she saw that she had come
close to profaning a family paragon and made amends by saying
she had never known her grandparents on either side. "Father
didn't marry until he was almost fifty. His parents were already
dead, and, as he couldn't stand my mother's people, we never
saw them. Our mother's family was from Albany. Father met her
when he was serving his one term in the state senate. It was his
first and last foray into government: he couldn't wait to come
home, where he could run things his own way without having to
have a majority. He had known my mother for only a short time
when he asked her to come back to Clove with him as his bride.
She was barely twenty. I've often imagined how it must have
been with them: he taken in by her youth and shyness and
beauty, and she dazzled by his greater authority and position in

the world. Of course, when they got back to Clove it was a disaster. She didn't fit in here, she realized she could never be her husband's equal, and she pined away in loneliness and boredom. Father really shouldn't have married at all; he was too critical of people. I'm the same way, I'm not marriage material either."

I had never heard anyone speak so dispassionately of their own parents. "But if your father hadn't married, you wouldn't be here."

She narrowed her eyes, paler than usual from the swim in the cold pond; her freckles stood out. It was fascinating and disconcerting that she could look like different people from minute to minute. With her wet, curly, uncombed hair and the sharp nose and the freckles, she looked like an urchin just now; in the water, her hair streaming back, her face tip-tilted to the sky, she had been a mermaid; at tea, with the dark lipstick and the green dress, she had been a formal older woman.

"I'm not so sure," she said mysteriously. "I'm not so sure I wouldn't be here, in some form or other, even if Father had never met our mother. I sometimes fancy that I am the living spirit of this family, reincarnated generation after generation since the ancient days of our ancestors, the Sires DeVeine, whose ruined fortress I visited in France. In those days, the name was spelled v-e-i-n-e. *Veine* means luck in French. *Coup de veine*: stroke of good luck. *Pas de veine*: rotten luck. *C'est bien ma veine*: just my luck. Sometimes in these incarnations I'm a man; sometimes a woman. Sometimes I'm rich, other times poor—like now. Sometimes I die quietly and happily in bed, a large and loving family gathered around me; other times I come to a violent end alone." She said all this in an amused chant; I couldn't tell for sure whether she was teasing or not.

"But if your father and mother hadn't had you, how could you have gotten reincarnated in this life?" I asked.

"There are multitudes of DeVane families into which I could have been born. There are over a thousand in this country, according to my father's survey. There are letters from many of these people in his files. His hobby was our family history. He wrote to DeVanes all over the world. If he hadn't married, I

would have found my way back here through one family or another, somewhere in the world. When I went to France to visit
our ancestors' old stronghold, I stayed with a family of DeVanes
in the nearby village of Pontarlier. Father had corresponded with
them before he died. I came very close to marrying the son of
that family. It was the only time in my life I have been that
tempted to marry. Marius was his name, Marius DeVane. He
was killed at the very beginning of the war, in the French Army.
His mother wrote to me in London. She never forgave me for not
marrying him."

"Did you love him?" We were on solider ground with this
Frenchman with the same surname, I thought, than with Ursula's
other possible reincarnations.

"He was my first love." She stretched her arms above her
head and gazed up at her outspread fingers. "I felt . . . we both
felt . . . that we were parts of the same past. He had strong feelings about destiny, too; the way the past reincarnates itself in the
present. We even discussed whether I might not have been his
sister—or brother—or wife, in a previous existence. I see that
polite little mask on your face, Justin, but if you are going to live
a full life, you must understand that there must be ways of
speaking about things we don't completely understand. It never
gets you further to rule things out just because they can't be
proved. Oh yes, I loved Marius, and the erotic aspect was just . . .
well!" A flush spread over her face and neck. "But I couldn't do
it. You see, I had come to Europe to study acting, and I felt that if
I married without ever trying for what I had wanted, I would be
cheating myself. So we left it that I would go on to London, as
planned, and then if we still felt the same, we might marry later.
But there was to be no later; the war saw to that. Yet, somehow I
knew, even before I left Pontarlier, that it would never happen. I
felt it. When I got Mère DeVane's letter in London the following
spring, I knew what was in it before I opened it. It was fate. Do
you know what the DeVane motto is, the motto that was on our
crest in the days of the Crusades? It was in Old French, of course,
but the free English translation is 'Luck is our ruler—and our
weapon!' The tricky part of it is that you must bow to your luck
when it comes, even if it is bad, and yet never give up trying to

turn it to your own ends. It's tantamount to having a double destiny." She scrutinized me with her penetrating eyes. "Can you understand that?"

"Is it like they teach you in religion sometimes? That God gives you free will, but He knows ahead of time how you're going to use it?"

"Not *quite*," replied Ursula, frowning. My answer had not come up to the mark. "Only, you see, in the spirit of our motto, you really can turn things around if you keep your courage and your wits."

"But then . . ." I hesitated, uncertain whether or not to ask this.

"Yes?" she encouraged.

"Well, I mean . . . if it was your destiny to be an actress—"

"Ah, but I didn't say it was my destiny to be an actress," she interrupted quickly. "I only sensed it was *not* my destiny to marry Marius. I had planned to go to the Royal Academy of Dramatic Art in London, and I was determined to go. I had waited for years, postponing it again and again because of my father's long illness. I was twenty-six when I finally sailed for Europe on the *Normandie*, having buried my father and completely organized Julie's recital at Carnegie Hall after his graduation from Juilliard. When I got on that ship, I said to myself, 'Ursula, now it's your turn.' First I wanted to see where my ancestors had come from, and then I wanted to study acting: those were my goals. One must never confuse goals with destiny, although one often leads to the other. In my case, I *was* an actress—when I took the entrance exam at the Royal Academy, the principal, Sir Kenneth Barnes himself, told me I had an innate instinct for acting— but, as it turned out, my destiny was not to make my living by acting. And yet I have the comfort of knowing I was good, the one year I was in London. You've heard of George Bernard Shaw, I hope?"

I vaguely recalled a witty exchange between the playwright and Winston Churchill that my grandfather liked to quote. "Oh, sure," I said, although I could not have named a single play Shaw had written.

"Well, he would sometimes sit in on rehearsals, when the

students were performing something of his. He was very old then, but he looked like a lean, cantankerous prophet, and he said the most wonderful things. One day, when I had been rehearsing for *Saint Joan*—the part I had to abandon in order to rush back to America—he came up to me afterward stroking his long white beard, and said, 'You'll make a very good Joan, Ursula, if you can remember that in the third scene you do not know you are going to be burned to death in the sixth.'"

As she imitated the clipped British voice of an old man, her face took on an excited, rapturous glow. Then she turned to me, looking somewhat arrogant, and put her hand on my shoulder. "Although my destiny has pointed me in another direction than acting, it gives me pleasure to remember that day: Shaw himself telling me I was going to make a good Joan. How many living actresses have a memory to compare to that?"

"Not many, I guess. But why did you have to rush back to America and abandon your play?"

"The war, my dear, the war," she said imperiously. "The Germans began to bomb London—you've heard of the Blitz, haven't you?—and no one knew how long it would last. I had to get out while there were still ships to get out on. You see, Julie was in a turmoil over his career at the time. I was afraid he was going to make a terrible mistake and I wanted to stop him."

"Did you?"

"Ah, no," she said wryly. "He had already left the country by the time I docked in New York. I didn't see him again until after the war. When he got out of the Army, he was very ill for a while, and I had to take care of him. That's when we came back here. Our family history is as convoluted as a Greek drama, Justin. Certain things happened that shouldn't have happened, which led to other mistakes being made, which in turn doubled back and bred fresh mistakes. But, you see, I believe there is still a chance to set things right. And I believe I'm the only one who can do it. Just as in our motto, I may be able to take all the fate that's happened and use it to make possible what still must happen. Come on." She rose lightly to her feet by balancing her hand on my knee. "Let's go up to the house and get your other

present. I haven't heard a sound, have you? Julie must have finished with them early."

As we crossed the field to the house on a path of beaten-
down grasses, she added, as if it were an afterthought: "A bomb
fell on our theater a few months after I had left the Royal Academy. Nobody was killed, but I've often thought that, had I
stayed, I might have been rehearsing there, perhaps even alone,
and that would have been the end of me. It would have meant
the end of Julie, too, I'm fairly sure of that."

We entered through the back door in the old part of the
house, where we found Julian DeVane sitting at a scuffed round
table in the dim kitchen, peeling an apple.

"Why, h-hello," he said, looking pleased to see me.

"We didn't hear a sound, so we assumed they were gone,"
said his sister.

"Oh, they're g-gone, all right." His mouth twisted in a disdainful sneer.

"What is that supposed to mean?" asked Ursula.

"One was hopeless. The other was little b-beast." He did
not look at his sister, but kept his attention on the loop of unbroken apple peel he was making fall in a graceful length onto a
small plate.

Uttering a heavy sigh, Ursula sank into a chair on the other
side of the table. "Are you telling me that you didn't take them?"
She seemed to have forgotten I was there.

"D-do you know what he did? While I was giving his
brother the c-coin test, he t-tore the wings off a moth he f-found
in the corner of the window."

"So you didn't take them?" repeated Ursula.

Julian looked up at me. I was lingering uncertainly beside
the sink. The linoleum was cracked all around the edges. Everything in the kitchen looked old and worn; Aunt Mona would
have been shocked by the ancient appliances and the jumble of
things that had collected on the deep sills of two narrow windows set in the thick wall. "D-did you ever take the c-coin test?"
he asked me.

"I never took piano," I told him.

"Well, you p-put your hands like this on the keys," he said, laying down his knife and apple and spreading his fingers on the table, "and then the t-teacher puts a c-coin on the back of each hand, and you try to p-play without the coins falling off. It t-tests the independence of the fingers."

Ursula propped an elbow on the table and rested her head on her hand. She looked at neither of us as he explained the coin test. I knew he was using me to forestall her displeasure. When he had finished, she asked in a deadly even voice, "What exactly did you tell the mother?"

"I told her I was c-cutting down on beginning students," he said, picking up the knife again. He sliced the apple into neat, even wedges. "I suggested she try Mrs. K-kirk, in Kingston. I t-told her I had to st-start practicing for my New York recital."

Ursula raised her eyes skeptically at him. "You really told her that?"

"I really did," he replied, smiling. He offered her the plate of apple wedges. She shook her head impatiently, still watching him. He held out the plate to me, but I thought I should refuse, too. I felt I shouldn't be there at all, but what was I to do?

Julian took a piece of apple, popped it in his mouth, and chewed it thoughtfully. All during this time, a strange little exchange had been going on between them. It was almost as if he were flirting with her, to win her over, and she was melting despite her annoyance with him. "Don't worry, Sissie," he said at last, "we'll manage without them. It was c-cruel, the way he destroyed that moth. And the other one had weak fingers and a tin ear."

A brief battle went on at the corners of Ursula's mouth. The irrepressible smile won. "If they would have been a drain on you, you were right not to accept them," she said affectionately. "Especially"—and she fixed him sternly with her sharp brown eyes—"since you have finally come around to agreeing it's time to start preparing for the recital. Of course, we're losing Jill Van Kleek to boarding school in the fall, but we'll just have to tighten our belts, as the English loved saying during the war."

Looking reprieved, Julian got up from the table and offered

the apple around again. Ursula, standing up, too, took a slice, and so did I.

"Isn't today your b-birthday?" asked Julian.

"I brought her up here to give her her other present," said Ursula.

They regarded me fondly, like parents who have finished quarreling and have time for their child again.

"Why don't I give her a sm-small birthday concert first," said Julian.

"Now that *is* an honor," exclaimed Ursula, with a proud look at her brother.

We went through the dining room, which was rather gloomy, with its low, beamed ceiling and heavy brown furniture, then into a larger, brighter room, also with a beamed ceiling. This room had windows on three sides, and a stone fireplace tall enough for a child to stand in. The floorboards were at least a foot wide, and looked very old. The dominating focus of the room was a nine-foot Steinway grand. Julian DeVane propped up the lid with an air of ceremony.

Ursula motioned me to sit beside her on a sofa of faded flowered chintz. In front of the sofa was a low table containing books from the Clove Library and a bowl with an unusual arrangement of peonies and rhododendron leaves. She folded her arms across her breasts and leaned against the sofa back with a rapt air of expectation.

At first, I thought it was some kind of joke when Julian DeVane began playing "Happy Birthday" with one hand. But then his other hand joined in, the tune became more complex, and the next thing I knew, he had turned it into a fugue that sounded just like Bach. From there he went on to imitations of Mozart, Liszt, Chopin, Beethoven, Rachmaninoff, and Debussy, all improvised around "Happy Birthday," Ursula of course making certain I knew which composer was being imitated as he went along.

It was an impressive performance, both for its novelty and for the showmanlike manner in which he carried it off. He was engaging to watch, with his desiccated boyish handsomeness, and the way he caressed the keys when doing the romantic passages and looked intense and haunted during the wild ones. I began to doubt my aunt's dire pronouncement that it was too late for him to have a successful career, because he looked and sounded to me like the embodiment of what people would want in a concert artist: that delicate profile with its shadings of a secret, melancholy history, combined with his skillful and feeling touch. Of course I was a novice in judgment. I had never seen a professional musician play before. I wonder what my judgment would be if I could hear him play now. Would I find him affected? Would I be able to detect, behind the trained precision and the emotion, a fatal absence of the spark of genius? I will never know.

After my "concert," they took me upstairs to a room with old-fashioned wallpaper and a sewing machine in it, and presented me with something rolled up like a large scroll that had been lying on top of some boxes. They stood by, like pleased conspirators, as I unfurled it. It was a poster, crumbly and yellow at the edges, of the *Normandie*, the ship Ursula had sailed to France on, the day of my birthday. Only I hadn't been born then. At the bottom of the poster were the words

NEW YORK   SOUTHAMPTON   LE HAVRE

"We thought you could use it to cover up some of that 'R-raspberry Ice,' " Julian said.

"A little window of freedom for you," said Ursula, smiling, "to remind you that one day you, too, shall sail off, all on your own. I had this on the wall of my room when I was teaching at that girls' school in New York. French was my subject, and the day after the *Normandie* burned in New York harbor, I took my class down to see where it had sunk. There was a crowd at the pier; some of the people were weeping. 'An era of history went down with that ship,' I told the girls, 'and, for that matter, an era of my own life, as well.' "

"It's great," I said, gazing down at the shabby poster with what I hoped looked like respect. But I was touched that they had thought about what I had said concerning my room, and that Ursula wanted me to have something on my wall that had once been on hers, something that represented an era of her life. I would put it up as soon as I got home.

"We thought you'd appreciate it," said Ursula, pleased. "I'll find you a bit of string and we'll tie it so you can carry it on your bike. But first, would you like to see the rest of the house? I don't often offer people tours, any more than my brother offers people concerts."

"I'll leave you two, now," Julian said. "I think I'll p-play a while. F-for the birds." He gave his sister a teasing look and, wishing me happy birthday again, went downstairs.

"This is a pretty room," I said, when Ursula and I were alone. As soon as I had said it—mostly to be saying something—I realized it wasn't true. There were large, discolored spots on the wallpaper, and boxes and extra furniture were piled everywhere. It was more that the room *should* have been pretty, with the summer afternoon light pouring through the west window, which looked out to the terrace below, and over the fields to the mountains in the distance and the tower.

"It was nicer once," said Ursula. "It was our mother's. It's got the best view of all the upstairs rooms. Now we only use it for storage, which is a pity."

Was it because the mother had gone to an insane asylum that no one wanted to live in her room now?

Downstairs, Julian began to play the brilliant music that had summoned Ursula home the day I met her. Now she smiled knowingly and lifted her head. "He's playing my scherzo to make amends," she said. "For throwing away thirty dollars a week in lessons. But today will have been worth it if he means it about not procrastinating about his recital any longer. Over here is his room."

She led me across the hall to a much dimmer room, with a narrow dormer that faced the road. It was a room filled with memorials to the past. Many old pictures in frames covered the dresser and most of the wall. Ursula hovered behind me while I inspected some of the photographs. There were quite a few on the wall of Julian with a portly, arrogant-looking man. In several, they were both wearing the sort of odd, ruffly shirt Julian had worn on the day of the tea. In one picture, the man was singing and Julian was accompanying him at the piano.

"That is the lieder singer Julie concertized with in South America," said Ursula, "and this, of course, is myself and Julie when we were children. And here we are with our mother."

I recognized Ursula at once, standing beside her mother's chair, staring defiantly into the camera with bold, dark eyes. Her face hadn't changed much, which made it all the more touching to see it connected to the body of a little girl in a white dress, her sturdy, in-turned knees buckled with baby fat. Cuddled close against the mother was a sleepy baby wearing a lacy christening gown. The mother, in an elaborate, stiff-sleeved dress, held herself haughtily, her long neck arched tensely back, as though she was aware of her beauty but didn't want to entrust it to the camera. Her mouth was serious, she made no attempt to smile, and in the large, light irises of the almond-shaped eyes there was a slightly startled look. I thought there was something altogether uncertain about her, something lacking in confidence. Or was it just that Ursula had told me she had been unhappy and unsure of herself?

"She's very beautiful," I thought I should say. When Ursula's mother married Mr. DeVane, I realized with a shock, she had been only six years older than I was now; and he was almost twenty years older than my father had been at his death. No wonder Ursula's mother had felt she could never be his equal. He must have seemed like her own father and a rather old one, at that.

"Oh yes, she was beautiful," remarked Ursula dryly. "It frankly disappointed her that I *wasn't,* and she let me know it. I didn't please her much in *any* aspect. I was too rough, too curious, too talkative—you name it. She used to say I should have been the boy, and Julie the girl. Julie got her looks, plus a certain aristocratic finish of feature she didn't have. Now, here I am with Father." She hurried me on to another photograph. "I took after his side completely, in personality as well as looks. See? Same nose, same chin, same forehead . . . though you can't see his for his hat in that picture."

I studied the picture closely. His hat shadowed his face. But I could tell from his outline and the way he stood that he thought well of himself. The girl next to him was about ten, gawky as a stringbean. They were arm-in-arm, looking very pleased with their DeVane-ness, I decided. I wondered where the mother had been? Holding the camera? Or already inside the insane asylum?

Then Ursula showed me her father's old room. "It's the official guest room now, only"—she laughed sharply—"we have yet to have a guest." This room also faced the road and had a single narrow dormer window. The wallpaper was faded red, embossed with a pattern. Everything was neat and forbidding: you could somehow tell there had been no sheets under the bedspread for a long time. "Father died in this room," Ursula said matter-of-factly. "It was his wish to die at home, so I took care of him myself. Except for the last few months, when it was necessary to have nurses."

"My grandfather died at home, too," I said. "It's more expensive with the nurses, but my mother felt the same as you did."

"That's right, child, you've had some experience of these things." She put her arm around me and briefly hugged me to her. I felt glad for this new thing we had in common, even though it involved death.

"And now, before I take you to my room, which is still in what Father called the 'brand-new' part of the house, because it wasn't built until 1770, I'll take you to the old quarters."

At the end of the hall was a thick door. Ursula opened it, and we stepped down a stone stair into a room with a fireplace and walls of whitewashed stone. There were a lot of bookshelves with law books, and metal file cabinets, and a massive old rolltop desk and swivel chair.

"Father always called this 'the office,' because he worked in here at night. All those file cabinets you see are filled with his correspondence with DeVanes. After Julie's career is launched, I may go through all that stuff and compile a sort of history. Make it into a book. Several members of the Huguenot Society are working on their family histories. It will give me a project for my old age." She winked at me. "I use this room as *my* office now. I keep all the accounts, bill the parents of Julie's pupils—he's hopeless with finances, artists usually are. When it gets chilly, I build myself a fire in the fireplace and sometimes in the evenings turn off the light and imagine what it must have been like, back in the late sixteen hundreds. You see, when our ancestor Chrétien DeVane built this house, it was just the kitchen and this room above, which was a storage loft. The family lived and slept downstairs. There used to be a connecting stairway, but some later ancestor bricked it up. Do you see that door in the south wall there? It's what they call a mow door. In the old days, the farmers would load the grain from the fields right from their wagons into this loft. And see the two iron hooks in those ceiling beams? We think they must have hung their meat on those hooks. When we were children, we played in here on rainy days, and I made Julie a swing and hung it from the hooks. Sometimes we would pretend to be our ancestors and sleep in here and toast our supper in the fireplace. That was after we lost our mother, of course. She would never have let us spend the night in here. She thought it was a horrible damp place and begged Father to demolish this whole side of the house and build a nice 'modern' wing. My poor mother had absolutely no sense of history. Of course, it wasn't *her* history. That probably made the difference."

She continued to talk of her ancestors when we went to her room, about how she sometimes dreamed about floating through this house at night and being able to see it as it had been at different times in the past. Her room was the brightest and most cheerful to me, especially after "the office," which seemed overrated. Maybe if Chrétien DeVane had been my ancestor, I would have felt different. But I cared more about the living members of this household, especially the one whose room I was now in. I had been fantasizing for weeks about the room she would have, though I had pictured something more formal, with lots of heirlooms. The simplicity came as a surprise, but an appealing one. Except for a big, bowlegged old dresser with a tilting mirror, the room had none of the heavy brown furniture of the other bedrooms. It hadn't as much light as the mother's old room, because it didn't have the wide corner window of that one, only the dormer window facing the fields. But the walls were a warm ivory color and the wide, uneven floorboards had been varnished with a glossy enamel. The high single bed was like a girl's bed—or a nun's: neat and narrow and self-sufficient. Except a nun would not have piled all those colored pillows on it. There were a little table and shelves full of books beside the bed. A whole shelf was in French. I got an impression that this room was her place for keeping herself free, even though she was still living at home, in the house where her family had always lived. Keeping herself open . . . for future turns of "luck." On one wall was a small pencil drawing, elaborately framed; it was of some crumbling fortifications. On another wall was a poster of Sarah Bernhardt as Hamlet.

She saw me notice the drawing. "That's my poor handiwork. Those crumbling ruins are all that's left of the DeVeines' medieval stronghold in Burgundy. I drew it from memory, in London. It was after I had heard that Marius had been killed. I sat for hours, one night, sketching that little picture as a sort of memorial. I was remembering all the nights we had climbed up to those ruins in the moonlight and made passionate love."

I stood respectfully before the drawing, having visions of them making passionate love. I was glad my back was to her.

Then, in that expert way she had, she turned the mood completely. She picked up a hairbrush and ripped it through her hair, which had dried exactly as she had left it after the pond. "Why didn't you tell me I looked like a fright?" she demanded.

"Because you don't. I think you look . . . charming." I sat down on the edge of her bed and watched her. Her nostrils flared as she brushed; she was charged with a fierce energy. "I wish I had thick, curly hair. I'd have it cut just like yours."

I saw her pleased reflection. She said casually, "Oh, Julie and I play barbershop once a month. It takes him a minute and a half to do mine. I simply wet it and part it down the middle and he goes snip, snip, snip in a straight line. It's the cut that suits me best. His hair takes much longer. I have to *sculpt* it back from his face, in layers. I'm the only one who can do justice to his fine, silky hair. But you wouldn't be you, with my unruly mop. It wouldn't go with your looks."

"Why not?" I wanted to find out what she thought I looked like.

She laid down her brush and turned from the mirror to study me. "You have an intensity in your face . . . an ardent quality. Too much *furl* would distract from it. Yes, *ardent* is a good word for you, though it isn't a word people use much anymore. Our language has shrunk sadly since Shakespeare's day. But *ardent* suits you perfectly."

"I'm not a beauty," I said. "My mother is much prettier than I am." I was torn between wanting her to like me better for having one more thing in common with her, and wanting her to disagree with me and tell me I was beautiful.

She put her head to one side, considering me.

"You aren't beauty-contest material, no," she finally pronounced. "But I can tell you this, Justin. You're nice to look at. You've got a face that is definite and expressive and sometimes deep. To know you is to love the way you look. If you should ever distinguish yourself in this world, yours will be the kind of face that your admirers couldn't imagine looking any other way. I hope we'll remain friends. I'm genuinely curious to see what you will make of your life. Now, let's go down and see if we can find some string for your poster."

Julian was still playing when Ursula accompanied me to the back door of the kitchen. He had been going from one piece straight into another, the whole time we had been upstairs. The constant presence of the music had made everything I had seen and heard more vivid and dramatic. I was sorry to be leaving it.

"Thank you for the poster," I said, as we stood just outside the house. "Thank you for the afternoon."

Ursula was gazing down the slope of lawn to the fields. In the far field, the one that now belonged to the Cristianas, two men were unloading posts from a truck.

"I may as well walk you to your bike," she said.

As we walked toward the pine forest, we saw that the two men were Abel Cristiana and his son Ed.

"To speak or not to speak," Ursula said. "That is always the question. But, as Julie is safely indoors, I think we will go over and say hello. Your friend might be hurt if you snubbed him. They've seen us, now."

"Why does Julian hate him so?"

"For many reasons. *Cumulative* reasons. It all started a long time ago, when Julie was a boy and had this pet raccoon named Daisy. Daisy would come to our terrace every evening and Julie would feed her by hand. After she had eaten, she would put her front paw with its long black toenails on his hand. She was really quite tame, and Julie loved her. Then one night she didn't come, and, well . . . what had happened was, Abel trapped raccoons and sold their pelts, and when Julie went over and confronted him, Abel admitted he might have gotten Daisy. He offered to show Julie the pelts drying in the barn, and Julie came home in tears. He said he had recognized Daisy and that Abel was a stupid yokel and a brute. Later, there were more things to fuel his hatred, but I can't go into them now. I was furious with Abel, too, because Julie was so crushed, but now I understand that there are certain cruelties that are part of living in the country—especially when you are hard up. Country people, especially when they are poor—and the Cristianas used to be poor—will kill deer in order to eat venison and will trap animals to sell their pelts. It's a matter of their survival over the animal's—that's the way they see it. Abel didn't go stalking Daisy *personally*, but Julie never forgave him and looked for reasons to hate him after that. Also, their values are very different: Julie is an artist; Abel is a farmer." She lifted her hand in a casual greeting as we approached the Cristianas, and father and son stopped what they were doing. Ursula, acting like a benevolent queen come to inquire into the conditions of the serfs, professed great interest in the progress of the fence-building. She wanted to know which horses would be grazing in the new field. I thought she was showing off, a little. Was it for my benefit? Mr. Cristiana answered her questions gruffly and did not look at her much. Ed said hardly a word. He gave me a funny look when Ursula referred to me as her friend. After a few minutes of awkward exchange, during which Ursula did most of the talking, all four of us parted with relief.

I was still living so strongly in the events of the afternoon with Ursula and Julian that my party that evening on Mott's houseboat was insubstantial to me. It almost seemed it was being held for another girl, and I had to pretend to be that girl so they would not be disappointed. There were presents and a cake and we roasted hot dogs over a charcoal grill on deck. Becky and a little girl named Floreen, who lived in one of the shanty houses above the creek, had blown up balloons and tied them to the railings of the houseboat. Becky seemed charmed by this untidy little girl, and kept reminding us in her high, expressionless voice, "Floreen and I were down here all afternoon blowing up these balloons while the rest of you were at home primping for the party." She cast frequent fond and protective glances at her little protégée. When I was opening my presents, someone made the mistake of asking Floreen where she had found the cute little pincushion shaped like a Chinaman. She bared sadly neglected little teeth, and said flippantly, "I nicked it from Woolworth's." There was an agitated silence. "Does that mean she *stole* it?" I heard Jem ask our mother. "I'm sure she was just joking," murmured my mother. But later in the summer, Becky invited Floreen to our house, and when she left, Aunt Mona announced she was missing some costume jewelry from her bedroom, and from now on, Becky had better just play with her new friend down at Mott's houseboat. On the evening of my party, I suspected that Becky had invited the shabby little girl to annoy me, but now I don't think so, at all. Becky's attentive patronage of Floreen may have been the first signs of the inclination that would lead her to her career. Even today I am mystified by Becky's continued indifference to me, but she certainly isn't indifferent to the youthful offenders she works with. She must care, to get the results that she does, and to win their confidence.

"Were there carpets in any of the upstairs rooms?" Aunt Mona asked me, as we sat eating our hot dogs on the houseboat.

"I think there was one in the father's room," I said. "But the most interesting room was this real old one they call 'the office.' Their ancestors used to store grain up there, and there are still these two huge iron hooks on the rafters where they used to hang their meat. Ursula told me that when her brother was little she made a swing for him and hung it from those two hooks."

"What about *their* rooms?" Aunt Mona wanted to know, not at all decoyed by what I had hoped would satisfy her curiosity about the upstairs. She was no more taken with "the office" than I had been. She was after news of the living inhabitants.

"Oh, they were just dormer bedrooms," I said. "His had a lot of old pictures in it, and hers was just . . . a nice, neat bedroom, with some colored pillows on the bed."

I didn't want to share Ursula's room with my aunt, didn't want to give her a mental picture of the place where Ursula had told me, "To know you is to love the way you look." With the little drawing of the ruins on the wall. And the passionate music downstairs. "But the really interesting room, from a historical standpoint, was that old 'office' with the hooks in the rafters. She says she sometimes sits in there and imagines what it was like, back in the sixteen hundreds, when that room and the kitchen below were Chrétien DeVane's entire house."

Aunt Mona wiped the corners of her mouth with her paper napkin. "I suppose it's natural that you should be drawn to the one with all the history," she said, with obvious disappointment. "Why, when you think of it, that old meat room, or whatever it was, is older than all your celebrated *Southern* historical homes by over a century. I wonder what it is like to know who your ancestors were as far back as she does. Not that it seems to have made her or her brother any great shakes, but it undoubtedly gives you a certain arrogance. I wonder what my life would have been like if I had grown up with that arrogance."

Later in the evening, when we were roasting marshmallows on sticks, Mott hovering protectively by in case some child got too close to the flame, another guest showed up: a Mr. Elmendorf, with a booming voice and a cigar, whom Mott introduced as "Wilbur." He was an older engineer at IBM and recently widowed. He was also the owner of the houseboat Mott had rented. When Mrs. Elmendorf was alive, they had spent their weekends on the houseboat and sometimes taken it on trips as far as West Point. Wilbur Elmendorf spoke of the houseboat, which looked like a floating box, as though it were a trim clipper ship on the high seas. He used lots of nautical terms and always referred to his late wife as "The Skipper." He said he couldn't be more pleased that a former Navy man like Mott was looking after things aboard. I remember he and Mott talked about Mott's adventures on the submarine that torpedoed all the Japs, and Mr. Elmendorf explained to us that he would have given anything to be in the Navy, but that he was practically blind in one eye as a result of a childhood injury. Jem wanted to know why the bad eye didn't look blind, and Mr. Elmendorf told him jovially that in bright daylight you could see a slight difference between the eyes. Then he asked Mott if he'd heard the story about the time Mr. Watson, Sr., had dropped into the men's room at IBM's Poughkeepsie site and discovered an employee disregarding the sign over the sink.

"Mr. Watson said, 'Excuse me, young man, can you read?' The man said, yes sir, of course he could read. 'Well, will you read that sign to me?' the founder of IBM asked. 'Yes sir. It says "Please Wash Hands Before Returning to Work." ' 'Well, why don't you obey it, then?' asked Mr. Watson. 'Oh sir,' said the employee, relieved, 'I'm not going back to work, I'm going to lunch!' "

Mr. Mott laughed so hard that he looked as if he were in pain. He laughed the way people laugh when a story is told about someone who means a lot to them: they go out of control sometimes. I remembered Mott's laughter a few days later, when Mr. Watson, Sr., died and IBM closed all its sites and Aunt Mona took a day off from the travel agency so she could be with Mott. He was completely broken up by the death of the old man, she said. "That man was like a father to Mott." She said Mott had wept and talked about the orphanage again. She said that even when people couldn't live as man and wife anymore, they could share each other's pain. A few days later, Mr. Mott was back in Lucas Meadows, mowing our lawn, his stolid figure guiding the machine with concentration, as if it were the most important thing in the world to cut even swaths that merged with one another. It was hard to imagine him lying face down on his bunk bed in the houseboat, sobbing into his pillow, but not as hard as it had been before I had seen him laugh like that. After the death of Mr. Watson, Mott became more solicitous of our family than ever, as if by doing double duty as a father he could console himself for being so hopelessly fatherless.

I still have two of the presents from that birthday. One of them is, of course, my grandmother's pearl necklace. When fastening the clasp around my neck, I almost always think of her. And sometimes I ask myself the unwelcome question that Ursula planted in my mind on my fourteenth birthday: Was she so sure of who she was that she never had to pretend, or did she have no private life? And I find myself defending my grandmother to Ursula. "Don't you understand," I tell her, "that his saying she would behave exactly the same way when nobody was looking was his way of saying *he trusted her*? Why can't we leave it at that? Why can't we leave her private life alone?" But, nevertheless, Ursula has left her mark there, as she has on so many other places.

The other present I had completely forgotten about until, several years ago, on a visit, my mother brought it to me, wrapped in tissue paper, in a corner of her suitcase. "I found this little book of yours," she said. "It's kind of sweet, the way you faithfully put down everything." It had a pink cover, a pink very similar to the color of those old "Raspberry Ice" walls in Lucas Meadows. "My Personal Life" was embossed in fancy letters on the front. Inside the cover I found birthday greetings from Aunt Mona and Becky in my aunt's handwriting. It was a pert sort of teen record, with illustrations and printed headings for the teenager to write under. There were pages reserved for "This Year's Movie Record," for "My Wardrobe," "That's My Family," "Friends, Classmates, Chums," and "Heart Thermometer" ("Rate your love life for the year! Which boyfriend rings the bell?").

I didn't remember being given this book on the houseboat, though it surely must have been among the gifts I unwrapped along with Floreen McEvoy's pincushion stolen from Woolworth's. I must have thanked my aunt and cousin for it, even if I secretly scorned those insidious, regimental headings that took away your freedom for organizing your own thoughts and feelings. (" 'Peeves and Problems': Every year brings its own special little [and big] problems. Write here in this space, in private and in detail, just what those problems are.")

How Aunt Mona must have loved discovering that book in some store. I can see her now, turning to the first page, where there is a decorated, heart-shaped "frame," all ready for a photograph of the "teen" in question to paste in of herself over the caption "Me, Myself, and I." I can see Aunt Mona, her earrings quivering slightly, scanning the "Message to *You*" on the facing page (". . . Before you can be a woman, you must grow up in *four* ways: *physically* [your body]; *emotionally* [your feelings]; *intellectually* [your mind]; *socially* [your dealings with others]. These are the *Big Four*. They are a large order, and that is why so much has been written about you. You are now in the greatest growing period of your life . . .").

I can hear Aunt Mona thinking to herself, maybe even muttering under her breath, "Now, if *I* had had a cute book like this to help me organize my feelings when I was growing up, what mightn't I have made of myself by now?"

But whatever I secretly thought of "My Personal Life" on the night Aunt Mona gave it to me, I was to write on most of its pages. For a period of five years, starting sometime during my fourteenth summer, I was to document my wardrobe, accomplishments and goals, height and weight, peeves and problems, friends and movies. I was earnestly to answer the questionnaires ("Rate Your Personality Quotient," "How Much Do I Cost?") scattered strategically through the little pink book. As I turn its pages as a grown-up, I am amazed at how many of the specific, everyday details of those years I have forgotten: yet, even as the book recalls them to me, they seem to have happened to another young person, a quite ordinary girl who uses expressions like

"Nuts!" and "Heck," and whose entries too often take on a shallow, insincere tone that makes me wince. From the evidence of this record, I must have been claimed by the world of "Raspberry Ice" and the milkmaids before we left the village of Clove. How did this happen? When did they actually get me? Surely not until the end of that summer, after I had buried the crumpled poster of the *Normandie,* along with the little blue bottle, deep in the garbage can one afternoon, turning my mind away, in the act of doing so, from all that was too volatile and hurtful and strange in "the greatest growing period of my life."

Now, in the light of all I am trying to recover, I take out "My Personal Life" from its tissue paper and search thoroughly, under all the headings of the year concerned, for clues to Ursula. There is only a single mention of her, located, fittingly enough, in the "Notes" section, the one place in the book where the teenager's thoughts are allowed to roam free from any preorganized compartments. The sentence, written in my acquired Ursuline handwriting of that summer, says: "I have made a new friend this summer who I admire a lot because she is sweet, interesting, and funny."

I stare at that commonplace sentence written by yesterday's teenager. I will it to render up all the passions and fears I know lie waiting for me in the silt of the reclaimed past.

VII.

What do I want from Ursula now? Why does she again, after twenty-six years, dominate my thoughts?

I could say: It's because I'm between plays. Actors between plays are like ghosts looking for bodies to inhabit. During a play, you are somebody else as well as yourself. Often this character becomes more definite and real to you than the quotidian self you face every morning in the mirror. You are possessed by your role. It is a form of possession you encourage to happen, because it heightens ordinary life; it makes you feel larger than just yourself. And it does wonders for your stage performance. However, when the play is over, you are in limbo. With no one for you to inhabit, with no one to inhabit *you*, you may get depressed, or go looking for action, any kind of action to keep you from feeling ordinary again. Actors between plays are notorious trouble-seekers. Acting addicts you to dramatic intensity, to a need for everyday life to have a *shape*. When you don't have a play to stimulate you and satisfy these requirements, you go out and stir up reality, trick your life into patterns of drama. Once— and not so long ago, either—I married someone after playing Ann Whitefield to his Jack Tanner in a Shaw summer festival. When the marriage ended six months later, we both admitted that we had chosen to confuse each other with our stage roles, because it had been a time in both our lives when we could not bear to go back to being just ourselves again.

Of course, dwelling on Ursula . . . becoming infatuated with her memory . . . is a lot less destructive than marrying an illusive Superman. But why *now?* It interests me to puzzle it out while I mark time between roles. Why, ever since I had that powerful dream about her, have I become obsessed with recalling her, summoning back the way she was then, and the girl I was, the girl with all those feelings she didn't know what to do with? Why have those old scenes I avoided thinking about for years become my most alluring task?

Is it because I am reaching that dangerous age, the "traditional danger point" that Ursula spoke of so warily, when people must either take some new risk or congeal?

If so, what is the risk involved here? What is "Ursula" trying to teach me or make me do?

And why should I feel so close to her, so strongly in touch with her, after all the years of recalling her with reluctance, discomfort, shame? God knows I don't want to be her, and yet in some way I do. She had an arrogance, a precipitance, a flair for improvisation I wish I had. It seems strange to me that I, not she, became the actress. Of course she *was* an actress, to the very marrow of her bones, but she made her own life into her role.

A dangerous proposition.

It's as if I were preparing myself for two roles in the same play, two roles I couldn't possibly fill at one time: the role of the enchanted young girl with all those seething erotic and spiritual energies not yet channeled, and of the older woman who, thwarted by a too-narrow existence, was nevertheless able to enchant.

No, it's something more. It's as if, in allowing myself full recall of the power she had over the girl Justin, I am trying to *take on* that power, to beam it back onto myself as an adult and as an actress, until it infuses me and I become bright with it.

✄   ✄

Yesterday I rented a car and drove upstate to the village of Clove. There is a thruway now, and the trip took a little more than two hours. It seemed wrong to get there so quickly. I felt I had cheated by returning to the past on a modern route. I got off at the Kingston exit and drove the old road for the eight-mile stretch into Clove. Things began to look less modern and I felt better. There were still extensive tracts of farmland, many already plowed and awaiting their crops. There were the same old stone houses along the road, some now bearing prominent New York Historical Landmark signs, but at least they hadn't been torn down—or painted white. Then I had to remind myself that Ursula's house would no longer look as it had when I had last seen it: for Aunt Mona, several years after we had moved away from Clove, had written that a department store executive had bought the DeVane house and whitewashed the stones and put a cathedral ceiling with skylights above the old, dark kitchen. Which meant, of course, tearing out that ancient upper room where the family of Chrétien DeVane had stored their grain and hung their meat and where Ursula had hung the rope to make her little brother a swing. The department store executive must have heard some part of the DeVanes' story: ". . . you can't keep people from gossiping in a small, rural place like this," Aunt Mona had written, "but we real-estate people sure kept mum about the whereabouts of that last awful episode. So it's six of one and half a dozen of the other whether he heard it from someone else and wanted to do away with that room, or that his wife took one look at that crummy kitchen and said she wouldn't so much as fry a piece of bacon till she had her cathedral ceiling. I know, it's a shame to destroy the lines of an old historical home like that, but when you pay the price *he* paid (my commission alone was over $5,000), I guess you feel you've got the right to put your own convenience and comfort above some snobbish family's past that came to nothing but ruin and sorrow."

The main street of Clove had changed much less than it might have in twenty-six years. There was the library, itself an old stone house, where I had spent several rainy afternoons reading about Huguenots in order to be closer to Ursula DeVane. There was the old movie theater—now remodeled into offices shared by a lawyer and a veterinarian—where Ed Cristiana and I had gone to the movies that one time, at the end of the summer. Terwiliger's market was gone—a branch bank stood in its place. The post office, formerly a prefabricated structure with a tin roof, now made its respectable headquarters in a solid brick building. But, just as in the old days, "town" was only a couple of blocks in a road leading to and from bigger places; and before and after those blocks, farmland still stretched on both sides.

I drove on to Lucas Meadows. Nature and individuality have reasserted themselves there, and it is no longer the prairie of uniformity I remember. Trees have grown up around the houses. Different homeowners have declared their personal tastes by adding wrought-iron trellises, toolsheds, and birdbaths, or little plaster gnomes that sit cross-legged on the grass. The houses themselves no longer adhere to the old consecutive color scheme, and I had some trouble locating our old house: it is now a shiny coral-pink. When I lived in Lucas Meadows, I dreaded being engulfed by sameness. Now, having escaped to return as an onlooker in a rented car, I missed its neatness; I missed, perversely, a certain purity expressed in all those bandbox-trim houses and lawns seeking to blend themselves into an anonymous little enclave of upscale democracy. I counted only two lamps in all of the picture windows I passed, but would I, at fourteen, have felt less threatened by this new, cheerful heterogeneity of houses every color of the rainbow, and trellises and gnomes?

Then on to Old Clove Road. Farmlands still, but a new element in the landscape that wasn't there before: mobile homes. It had seemed longer, the twisting, hilly road, when I traveled it on my bike. Some important trees are gone; others have grown up in different spots, and the light falls differently. Even the contours of the land are altered in places.

I am up on the Cristianas' place before it seems possible. Well, they have certainly endured. Evidences of prosperity everywhere. Two new horse barns down in the field below the house. An elaborate system of fences cordoning off different groups of horses. New paint and a new roof on the main house. Another ranch-type frame house across the road, where Turk's paddock used to be. A sign as large as a movie screen in the front yard of this house reads:

CRISTIANA THOROUGHBRED FARM

I can see a small group of men gathered around a van from which a horse is being unloaded, down by one of the new barns in the field. They are too far away for me to tell whether there is anyone I knew among them. And, if there were, what would I say? If I were to park my car and walk down to them and introduce myself as Justin Stokes, the adult version of the girl who frequented this road quite a lot during one summer in the fifties, how could they possibly be glad to see me? How could they be anything but resentful and embarrassed, considering the reminders I would bring with me?

I go on. Down the hill. Around the curves. Across the little wooden bridge. I am beginning to think: This stretch is uncannily as it was, except it is too early for leaves on the trees . . . , but then I come to the haywagon road, which has a chain across it and a No Trespassing sign hanging from the chain, and I see that the road-front part of the pine forest that led to Ursula's pond has been cut away to make room for a long, tan mobile home with brown trim. A family is very much in evidence: several small children playing in the dirt yard beneath a clothesline, and a young, overweight woman watching them sullenly as she sits slumped on the steps of the trailer.

And so, on, around that final curve, and, oh God, there it is. I pull into the driveway and sit in the car with the ignition still on and gaze on the inglorious sight: the old rough stones mere lumps beneath the whitewash that has been painted over the entire house. And the incongruous cathedral ceiling with its skylights rising out of the old part of the house, that first simple farm cottage built in the late sixteen hundreds. And—the final badge of betrayal—the For Sale by Century 21 sign jammed into the derelict lawn.

I switch off the engine and get out of the car, determined to honor to the dregs this rendezvous with the past for which I have driven a hundred miles. Should I lock the car, or take my purse? I am annoyed with myself for having such petty thoughts. A heroine in a film, having been moved by the changes in an old, beloved landscape, would eschew thoughts of personal property and stride off into the past without breaking the mood.

But today the past is more elusive than I had expected. The sun is under clouds and a helicopter flies low overhead. Its metallic, chopping sound agitates the birds. Some of the old trees around the house look as if they might come down with the next storm. I remember this place best all in green. The lilacs were out when, in the beginnings of my obsession with Ursula, I researched the house twice each weekday from the bus. Oh, that's another change: the lilacs are gone. Now, who in his right mind would cut down *lilacs*? Or did the department store executive's wife take a dislike to them because they had grown too tall and shaded her cathedral ceiling? What has become of the department store executive and his wife? Did the house reproach them in some way for violating its integrity? Or did they become disenchanted with it, or with each other, or both?

I walk slowly down the slope, my purse slung over my shoulder by its strap. It is an expensive purse. Julian DeVane would have had to teach twenty piano lessons for the price of this purse. If Ursula were watching me now from an upstairs window, she would laugh. "Dear Justin, you are certainly more *encumbered* than you were the first time you came down that slope. Do you remember yourself, all in white, the way you poked out your elbows and turned in your toes? You've got more assurance now, of course, but do tell me: who do you think is going to steal your purse in the middle of the country?" But Ursula is not here, not even in spirit. In fact, I can feel her absence from this place as strongly as though she were making a statement.

The terrace is all coming to pieces. Bluestones upended or missing; Father DeVane's painstaking symmetry destroyed. There's no trace left of any garden, only brambles, weeds, and last year's leaves. Someone has left a large tree stump on the terrace. At first I think maybe a tree has grown up through the stones, but no, I can move it with my foot. Now, why would anyone want to leave a loose tree stump in the middle of a crumbling terrace? Vandals? Someone out to do a little wood sculpture, then abandoning the effort before he'd even cut into the wood? There are too many changes here, too many incongruences that have nothing to do with what I came to find. What I came to find is not here. Did I have to drive one hundred miles, and another hundred back, to discover that memory does not reside in places? Places have their own continuing lives. Memory lives in the brain of the rememberer. What had I expected, anyway? To drive up in my rented car and see, as through a mist, the house as it had been when I rode by on the school bus all those years ago? Ursula DeVane and her brother sitting down here like royalty in their two lawn chairs, then slowly turning toward me the faces of twenty-six years ago? In an Ingmar Bergman film it might have happened; but not here, not today.

Yet there, beyond the Cristianas' prosperous fields and fences, are the mountains. The same as they were. Give them another few hundred years, perhaps, and they'll be altered, too. But, for now, they are just the same as they were the afternoon Ursula and I looked at them from this terrace and she promised she would take me up to the old hotel and to the tower. And then that day, in late August, we went. It was our last good day together but we didn't know it. We walked along the woodland trail, and she told me about Julian's broken career. And about how, when she was only ten, she had betrayed her mother. And then we arrived at the old hotel. We went in, and for some silly reason I said I didn't need to go to the bathroom, although I did. When she came back, she teased me into relenting, and while I was gone she saw some old man and called him a *memento mori*, and, as we ate our lunch in a little thatched hut overlooking the lake, she gave her famous speech about congealment.

Then we climbed the steep path to the tower and looked down on the surrounding valleys. She pointed out the Cristianas' shiny roof, and the dark wedge of pines ("The pond is in there, and our 'Finishing School' "), and the clump of trees that hid

what she called "our house," as if it were my house, too, and I
lived in it with them.

And then, going down, I played that strange little game with
myself, decreeing that if I let her out of sight on the path, I would
lose her forever. She was walking ahead of me. I stood still and
let her disappear.

And afterward, when I cried, and she comforted me, and
then that old couple passed us, wearing their funny, baggy walking shorts and matching brown shoes with tassels that flapped.
And Ursula said, "They thought we were mother and daughter. . . . It was a nice feeling, having them think you belonged
to me."

The sun flashed on the spinning mountains. We had drunk
red wine with lunch, and I went into a kind of swoon. "I do belong to you," I said, nestling close to her. "Oh, child, child," she
murmured, resting her chin on the top of my head.

The outline of the tower is particularly sharp today in the
harsh spring light. I know for a fact that the old hotel is still
flourishing. Recently I saw pictures and a big write-up about it in
a magazine while I was waiting in my ophthalmologist's office. It
has become a favorite retreat, the article said, for nostalgic week-
enders harassed by the cruel tempo of modern life. Its Victorian-
Gothic atmosphere is soothing, suggestive. The Mystery Writers
of America, the article said, now hold their annual conventions
there.

I turned my back on the mountains and the tower and left
the ruined terrace. I climbed the discolored, grassy hill and got
back in my rented car and drove back to the haywagon road,
where, resolved to follow through in full the requirements of this
scene, I pulled off on the shoulder of Old Clove Road, locked the
car *and* took my purse, and—under the accusing glance of the fat
woman on the trailer steps and the curious stares of her brood of
children—boldly lifted my skirt and stepped over the chain with
its No Trespassing sign. Slinging my purse jauntily over my
shoulder, I walked down the haywagon road with the assurance

of an absentee landlady come to inspect her property. The Cristianas' name was on the No Trespassing sign, and if any or all of them should suddenly materialize and block my path, I would simply say, "Remember me? Justin Stokes? Well, you see, I've been haunted quite a bit over the years, as I'm sure you must have been, and so I decided to come back and see if I could lay some ghosts . . . if you'll excuse the unfortunate pun." I was angry as I walked down the haywagon road, angry at the Cristianas for prospering, angry at myself for prospering, angry at all the changes I saw around me, from the fat woman and her trailer to the blight that had struck many of the remaining pines, causing them to turn brown. As I entered the pine forest, or what was left of it, I became even angrier when I realized that, once again, I was hearing music. But this time it was not Bach; it was nasal country and western, following me from the direction of the trailer.

The pond was still there, but smaller and full of woodland debris. I could not imagine Ursula, even at her boldest, swimming in it now.

The hut was a heap of stones. But there lay the oblong slab that had once been the doorstoop, the threshold—as if it had preserved itself as the one necessary piece of scenery for this act—and I picked my way through the rubble and sat down on it, first casting a wary glance all around, though I knew it was still too cold for snakes. Who owned the pond now? If it was still "DeVane" land, then it had been sold to the department store executive and was now in the hands of Century 21. I remembered how, that sunny spring day when I had gone horseback riding with Ed and his sister Ann, he had told me that his father had wanted to buy the hut and the pond and stock the pond with fish. But Ursula had needed the pond as a retreat, and Mr. Cristiana had told his children that she was a brave woman and was entitled to the few pleasures she had left.

I could see why, even if the Cristianas now owned the pond, they would be glad to see it fill up with silt and natural debris. Let one more generation grow up, perhaps; let the older generation of gossips die; and then rebuild. A playhouse, a guest cottage. Dredge the pond and let fresh water fill up again. Or fill it in and level the whole dying forest and make a profitable little "estate" of half-acre lots—maybe even a trailer park. Plenty of useful things can be built on the ruins of other people's lives. Look how I have profited from Ursula's influence; look how I have been profiting lately, in spirit and energy, from the memories and dreams she inhabits.

"For you, Justin, I'm convinced nothing but a life of art will do," she told me down here one afternoon, as we sat hip-to-hip on this crumbly slab of stone. Often she would have been in for a swim, sporting around in the pond while I watched her, teasing me for my cowardice, telling me how refreshing the water felt. Afterward, she would dress in the hut and then come out and sit beside me, toweling her curly hair, or rubbing it briskly with her fingertips when she forgot the towel. I loved the way she told stories about her life. As I watched her face, it was as if I saw the stories happening. I would think about them between visits. I would imagine them from her side, pretending I was she. I had bought a bottle of the lotion I had seen on her dresser and I would rub it on my body before I went to bed at night. I would turn off the light in my room at Lucas Meadows and "become" Ursula DeVane, lying in her independent white room in the house on Old Clove Road. I would pretend I was Ursula remembering her past. Remembering her young lover in France, how they had climbed up the precipitous ledge to the ancestors' stronghold and lain down in the moonlit ruins of the Château DeVeine and whispered that they had been united already in past incarnations. And sometimes I would imagine everything so well that I would feel strange stirrings and almost cease to be myself.

I also loved it when she talked about me. She created me as she talked. She examined the substance of me and then prophesied, in grand, sweeping strokes, the uses to which I could be put. "For some people, a life in art is the only way they can survive," she had said. "I know what I'm talking about. I *knew*, I knew that Sunday tea when you described your room to Julie and me that you could not bear the ordinary life. Your soul craves that constant heightening of reality only art can give. So does mine. So does Julie's. Oh, you're one of us, all right. We need our definite, dramatic shapes. I'm not sure what your art will *be* yet. Are you? Well, never mind. You've got lots of time. Even the *times* are on your side. There's no depression, as there was when Julie and I were growing up and Father didn't even have the money to send him to Juilliard. I don't know what would have become of Julie's talent if he hadn't won that scholarship. As for me, I was my own college. I knew Father needed me, and after that, I was going to be an actress. Actresses don't need college. But your mother has put away money for your college, and you must go and soak up every opportunity, keep that absorbing mind of yours busy until your chosen art makes itself clear. Meanwhile, during your so-journ in the provinces with us"—and she laughed in her arch, throaty way—"it will be my pleasure, mademoiselle, to teach you what I can at our little Finishing School here among the pines."

I looked across the pond and saw a dirty little boy watching me from behind a tree. He was about four, or maybe five, or even six. It's hard for me to tell the ages of young children, never having had any of my own. I recognized him as one of the trailer children and said hello. He didn't answer, but continued to watch me with his flat brown disks of eyes. The lids were curiously shaped, almost Oriental. I must have been an odd vision to him: a woman in "city clothes" sitting all by herself among a heap of stones in the woods, her purse beside her.

"Do you ever swim in this pond?" I asked, projecting what I hoped would come across as a cheerful, matey image: for some reason, it was important to me that he think me normal. "I knew a woman who used to swim here."

He narrowed his eyes at me across the pond. I could see from his expression that I was becoming more inauthentic to him by the second. Then he filled his lungs—I could see his ribs rise beneath his soiled T-shirt like a pair of small bellows—and shouted, "No she didn't! They's snapping turtles in there. They'd kill her to pieces." And he ran away as fast as he could through the pines, back to the safety of his trailer home.

When I returned to the car, there was nobody outside the trailer. Had the mother herded them all inside to watch the crazy woman from behind a curtain? Perhaps the mother was telephoning the Cristianas right now. "Sir, I don't like to bother you, but there's this strange woman down by your pond. . . ."

It was not yet two in the afternoon when I left Old Clove Road. I could be on the thruway in fifteen minutes, back in the city by four-thirty, beating the rush hour. Then a hot bath, soaking and meditating on this journey, and supper and a glass of wine. The rest of the evening I would work some more on Lady Macbeth. "Come, you spirits that tend on mortal thoughts, unsex me here . . ." On that soliloquy hangs so much: I become Macbeth's Evil Genius, but I remain also a woman determined to help her husband. If that dual nature of the role is not preserved, something brilliant is lost.

But when I was almost to the thruway in Kingston, hunger overcame me and I stopped for a hamburger at Howard Johnson's. What I did next is hard to explain. I think I did it partly because of that inveterate desire to stir life up when it has not, of its own initiative, met my needs for drama; but also because I had not found the one I wanted to find, and her absence in spirit from her old homestead provoked me into seeking out a long-avoided source.

I called Mott. I went to the pay phone in Howard Johnson's and looked up "IBM Corp Neighbrhd Rd" and dialed the number and asked for Eric Mott. I knew from Becky that he was still there. Steady old Mott. In a corporation whose employees have made its name an acronym for "I've Been Moved," steady Mott has managed to stay put at one location for twenty-eight years.

He was on the phone before I was ready for him. What have I done? I thought, panicking. But I had given my name to the secretary and it was too late. He was so pleased. He had not heard from me in years: he had thought I had forgotten him, he said. He had meant, he had *really* meant, to get down to New York to see me in that last play—Becky had told him about it—but, what with one thing and another, he hadn't been down to New York City in almost five years. Where was I calling from? Kingston! Howard Johnson's?

"Why, you're only minutes away," he said, and proceeded to give painstaking directions, directions even a child could follow, to Neighborhood Road. After he had finished, he made me repeat them back to him.

And so I got back in the rented car and drove, of my own instigation, to meet a person who had bored me as a child; a person whose face I could never remember, even when I saw it several times a week; a person I had never really liked because I sensed—rightly—that he might one day try to "help out" more than you wanted him to. I drove to meet the man whose dutiful protectiveness of me had combined so lethally that long-ago August evening with my obstinate pursuit of Ursula DeVane's attentions.

Neighborhood Road looked like a movie set, though whether for a euphemistic documentary about a friendly corporation or a surrealist's sinister satire on corporate life it was hard to say. I tended to the latter impression as I drove slowly down the neat, straight road (lanes carefully marked for left turns) with smooth grounds and modern office buildings on both sides. I made a left turn into the parking lot beside the big white building with the American flag in front (Mott's headquarters), and a mechanical arm swung up to admit my car after I had pressed a button. A sign directly above the button informed me that the only way I could get out of the parking lot was by depositing a special "gold coin" (available only from the receptionist at the main desk) into the slot at the exit gate. Employees with earnest, abstracted faces walked briskly from one building to another, tiny replicas of these faces flapping with the identification tags on their lapels. After I had identified myself to the stylish middle-aged receptionist at the main desk, and had explained my purpose, and she had confirmed this by a phone call to Mott's secretary, I was given a visitor's badge, with a picture of the building I was now in, but with azaleas blooming all around it. The receptionist, who looked as if she had just come from the hairdresser, wrote out my name in an even, legible hand, and watched me while I pinned it on my sweater. I could tell she was having trouble "placing" me, and I tried to soothe her cautious imagination by chatting briefly about the weather. I was glad I had worn a skirt for this outing. By the time she had issued me my "gold coin" for getting out of the parking lot later, the atmosphere of the place had begun to make me feel like an outlaw disguised as a kind niece, come by to pay dutiful respects to an old uncle at his place of work. I sat down next to a window behind which two uniformed guards kept surveillance over a bank of closed-circuit monitors. On the monitors, you could watch the movements of employees a they went from room to room in the inner recesses of this building. While waiting for Mott, I followed the progress of a stoop-shouldered man with dark hair and a small mustache. Down one hall he went, coattails flopping behind him on the black-and-white monitor. Then through a door and down another hall. He reminded me a little of Charlie Chaplin. Then the door to the reception room opened and there stood the same man in living color. He stared at me, trying to decide something.

"Justin, honey?"

"Good God, Mott, it's you!" I blurted. When had he grown that ludicrous mustache? Surely he had never had such *black* hair. He must dye it. He looked completely changed in externals from the old Mott, with his colorless crew cut and forgettable face. And yet the face *was* his, I now saw. It was just that the mustache and the black hair and the dry creases down the cheeks and around the mouth gave him a definite outline he hadn't had before. "I was watching this man on the monitor," I said, "but I didn't realize I was watching *you* until you came through the door."

"Well," he said, self-consciously lifting a hand to the silky black hair that I had decided must certainly be dyed, "it's been a long time for both of us, hasn't it?"

He proudly escorted me back through the labyrinth of doors

and halls to his office. I was aware that the guards were now following my image on their screens. Such a surprise, Mott was saying, my suddenly phoning like that. What was I doing in the area, anyway? I told him I was between plays and had decided to take a sentimental journey and look at the old places. "Lucas Meadows has changed," I said.

"Oh, it's gone down, there's no doubt about it," said Mott. "No IBMer has lived there in years. The zoning laws have changed over there. A new element has moved in."

"Yes, I noticed a lot of trailers on Old Clove Road." I couldn't look at him while I pronounced the name of the road. "There weren't trailers before, were there?"

"I don't think so," said Mott absently, not appearing to pick up any significance in my mention of the road he had driven me, stunned and shivering, away from, on that night twenty-six years ago. "Here's my office. This is Karen, my secretary. Karen, I'd like you to meet my niece—my ex-wife's niece, actually, but I'm proud to claim her. She's an actress, Justin Stokes—you may have seen her in something. I'm ashamed to say she was in a Broadway hit for over a year, and I never made it down to see her."

"I haven't seen a play since I was in high school," said Karen, a young, neat, sexless person with straight white teeth. "Have you been in any movies?"

"I've done some work in television. Some O'Neill plays. It was a few years back."

"No," said Karen, shaking her head seriously, "I don't think I . . . but I'm *very* glad to meet you." She smiled, showing her white teeth, and then recrossed her legs chastely behind her word processor. I was sure she was the kind of girl who wore white cotton panties under her pantyhose.

We went into Mott's inner sanctum. He motioned me to a comfortable chair and sat down at his own desk and peered at me in a shy-friendly way over his black mustache: did he dye that, too?

"How is your mother?" he asked.

"Oh, prospering."

"And Jem?"

"He's prospering, too," I said. The word seemed to be stuck in my mind today.

"I always liked that little fellow. Made me real sad when he moved away. And now he's married. He sent me an invitation, which I appreciated. I got a nice note from the bride, thanking me for my present." He blinked at me and looked hesitant. "You got married, too, didn't you? But it was a while back."

"I'm afraid it didn't last." Mott was referring to my first marriage, to which, I now realized, I had neglected to send him an invitation. I saw no reason to enlighten him about the second failed marriage, to "Jack Tanner"; it would just confuse him.

"That's too bad," said Mott gravely. "I'm sorry to hear it."

"Oh, neither of us was damaged irreparably," I said airily. It all seemed such a long time ago, a sort of sociable mistake made by two young people trying to honor the conventions.

Mott cast his eyes down to his clean desk. I had worried him with my flip remark. On the shelf behind his desk and stacked on the low round table beside my chair were multiple copies of two books: *The Lengthening Shadow: The Life of Thomas J. Watson*, and *A Business and Its Beliefs: The Ideas That Helped Build IBM*, by Thomas J. Watson, Jr.

"You know, Mott," I said, trying to project an "upbeat, normal" image, "I just realized, I don't know what your job is. I don't think I ever knew. Or was I just too wrapped up in my adolescent traumas ever to ask?"

"If you *had* asked, I couldn't have told you," he said, with a little sparkle in his eye. "I couldn't even tell Mona what I did. We were working on a top-secret project. As a matter of fact, I just got through giving a slide show to some of our new employees. That's part of my job now. I'm the resident historian of this site. If you have a few minutes, I can show you what I did. I can even show you a picture of myself at work, back in those days."

The next thing I knew, I was in a conference room with an elated Mott, who projected his slide show on a screen while I drank a cup of Karen's coffee out of a paper mug and ate a piece of lemon sponge cake left over from the reception for new employees that had taken place that morning. It was very good cake. I sat in the dark and looked at black-and-white pictures of the two-hundred-acre farm this place had been before IBM bought it and turned it into a site. I watched the buildings being built. I saw an early "IBM Family Day" on the site, which Mott told me we had all attended, though I had no memory of going. Mott's steady, measured tone accelerated as he began to show slides of the top-secret project in which he had been involved. What Mott had been doing, that summer when he mowed our lawn every Saturday, and checked Aunt Mona's car under the hood, and played dutiful uncle to his fatherless niece and nephew, was maintaining the vacuum tubes of an enormous secret computer being readied for the military. "It was a top-secret job . . . top secret," he repeated, pausing at the black-and-white slide of himself, the old "colorless" Mott with a crew cut so extreme it looked as if his head had been shaved. His face looked so *young* to me now, in the slide. He wore overalls over his clothes and was kneeling raptly—that is the only word for it—beside a console of vacuum tubes. "See, we had two identical systems trading off every twenty-four hours. Every day it was my job to go over those tubes. If one gave out, I had to find it and replace it. We had to replace about five hundred tubes every month. When we shipped the first system down to McGuire Air Force Base in New Jersey, I was sent down with it to show the Air Force how to do the maintenance process. I don't suppose you remember that week when I was away. It was the last week in June. I'll never forget it, because it was the week after old Mr. Watson died."

Of course I didn't remember it. It must have been one of the highlights of his life: Eric Mott, orphan boy, sent to help install the first computerized air-defense system. On his deathbed, he would probably be remembering that important week in his life. A week in which I had been thinking of myself as the center of the world, and that the most important place to be, in that world, was at the pond, at our "Finishing School," with Ursula DeVane.

God, how *needed* Mott must have felt as he instructed the Air Force how to check and recheck that maze of crucial vacuum tubes! He must have seen himself as an angel of surveillance: watching over those tubes that would maintain the computer's ability to survey the free summer skies of North America and sound an instant alert at the first darkening threat of the Russian menace.

Maintenance and watchfulness. Protect what you have. Watch out for your nearest and dearest. Mott's religion had served him well at work and had spilled over, that summer, into off-work hours. Children must be protected from rotting farmhouses that sat empty, useless, too near to their development. If a niece did not come home at dusk, and she had no light on her bicycle, then Eric Mott was naturally the one to go after her. . . .

"It's still a fine system," Mott was saying. "The SAGE system is still ninety-nine percent reliable. It's used now to catch drug traffickers, mainly. We still have a SAGE depot, for spare parts, right here on the site. I'm in charge of that, too. If anybody with a SAGE needs spare parts, we've got 'em."

He switched on the lights in the conference room and began putting away his slides.

I said, "Mott, I went over to the DeVane house today. It looked terrible. That department store executive seems to have robbed it of its soul."

Mott continued organizing his slides carefully into a round container with slots. "Yep, Mona thought they made a mess of it, too. They didn't stay more than a couple of years. Did all that work and tearing up, and then only came weekends. After that, Mona resold it to a New York dermatologist. He only used it as a weekend home as well. But he sold it after a year, himself. Said it was too dark . . . those little dormer rooms upstairs. Said the place gave his girlfriend bad dreams. It was an IBM listing for a while, but IBM families never took to it. Not enough closets and only one bathroom. And now that area has come down. All those mobile homes, like you said."

"The Cristianas seem to be doing very well."

Something in the tone of my voice made Mott look up. "Abel Cristiana died several years back," he said. "Heart attack. I went to the funeral. He'd been out feeding the horses; then he came in for dinner, helped himself to some string beans, and just fell over in his chair. Went just like that, with his family all around him. Not the worst way to go. They made a good thing out of that horse farm. Everybody in the family worked hard, and it paid off."

My head was starting to ache with the unsaid. Had I come here to listen to tales of SAGE and the Cristianas' family solidarity and success?

"I wish I knew what happened to *her*," I said.

He knew whom I meant.

"I've often wondered myself," he said. "I never liked the brother much, but who would have wished that on her? If it hadn't been for . . . well, her other unfortunate attachment, she could probably have stayed on, made a go of it somehow. But she felt the community was against her. And when *he* wouldn't see her again, not even to speak, I guess that hurt bad. She said to me once, when I went over to help her out with something, she said, 'Eric, I've become a—' What was the word she used? I wish I could remember that word. Anyway, she said she felt betrayed all around."

It was an effort to pretend not to be surprised. "You saw her, then? After it was all over?"

"Oh, yes. I felt kind of responsible. After all, if I hadn't come after you that night, things might have been different. I'm not saying the whole thing wouldn't have blown sky-high sooner or later, but I wouldn't have felt responsible then. So, that winter, when she was so down on her luck, I would make it my business to drop by sometimes, after work. Just to . . . you know. Once I found her sitting there in the freezing house wrapped in blankets. She'd made a fire for herself, but it was smoking, the wood was wet. The furnace had gone off, and she wouldn't call anybody. Said she didn't like to call people after work hours because that's what lonely old women did to get attention. It was just a short circuit in the thermostat—I was able to fix it—but she would have sat there all night in the cold if I hadn't come by."

"Oh God," I said, imagining her in the freezing house. Worrying about her image.

"Yes," Mott said. "I don't know how she lasted there as long as she did. But, the way things were, she had to sell out sooner or later. I was sorry to see her go. She was very nice to me, grateful when I'd stop by. We had interesting talks. She was a fascinating woman." He studied his fingernails.

"Aunt Mona never wrote that you saw her," I said.

He gave me a sheepish look over the little black mustache. Sheepish, but at the same time rather proud. "I never told Mona. She might not have understood. You've got to remember, I was still hoping to get back with Mona. I kept hoping, you know, for years. But . . . hell, Justin, I was a man. I was a human being, with human needs." Now he was soliciting me with his eyes. What was he trying to tell me? I could not meet his eyes; I looked past his left cheek, at a blackboard set up behind his chair. "She was a damned interesting woman," he concluded, with emotion.

Oh *God*, Ursula, would just *anybody* do? Any admirer? Any comfort? Any audience?

I forced myself to look at Mott, taking him in as the comforter of a fascinating woman. That was twenty-six years ago. He had been in his thirties. Maybe he hadn't been as boring as I had thought. The dyed hair and the little mustache had not yet come into being. He was a youngish engineer, quietly self-satisfied by the knowledge of his secret, nationally important function. He was manly, reliable, and kind, stopping in regularly to ask her if he could be of use. And she? What was she, really? A brilliant woman, thwarted by family and fate—and self? Or a colorful failure who was able to fascinate a young girl, as well as some married and lonely men in the neighborhood?

"Did she ever tell you where she planned to go after she left Clove?" I asked.

"She was pretty mysterious about it." He laughed nervously. "Maybe she was afraid I might pick up and follow her, or something." He gave me a coy look, to see if I had read his meaning: so poor Mott had been smitten, too. "She talked a lot about Europe. She said her values were more European than American. She had a whole lot of names of other DeVanes—her father had kept up some kind of correspondence with DeVanes all over the world, she said—and she told me she might go and look some of them up. You know, she may have done all right for herself, Justin. When she left Clove, she had enough capital to last her several years, what with the sale of the house, and the land, and the furniture, even after she'd paid off that second mortgage at the bank. I happen to know that grand piano went for several thousand, by itself. Now just think: an interesting woman like that calls you up one day, or comes to your door, and you find out she's your distant cousin, or you have the same name. Wouldn't you want to help her out? You'd want to help out a woman like her even if her name was Jones and yours was Smith."

"Yes," I said, "you're probably right." I felt strangely cheated. Mott was probably closer on her trail, in his speculations, than I had been, all these years, in imagination. I had created only variations of defeat for her. But, according to Mott, she might have managed to turn her luck, DeVane-style, as in the motto, from her ruler to her weapon. If she could have been Mott's lover, why couldn't she have had other lovers after him as well? Maybe she had discovered a rich European DeVane and married him. Or found other finishing schools to teach in, entertaining fresh young audiences with tales of her interesting history, making whatever adjustments to it that suited her at the time. Who was to know what was true? (Hadn't I, years after she had told me what George Bernard Shaw had said to her about her portrayal of Joan, come across the identical words in Sir Kenneth Barnes's autobiography? Only Shaw had been describing Sybil Thorndike, not Ursula DeVane. "Sybil will be all right," Shaw had told the principal of the Royal Academy, "if she remembers that in the third scene Joan does not know she is going to be burned to death in the sixth." When I came across that passage, I felt betrayed at first. Then I looked for ways to exculpate Ursula. When she had been at the Royal Academy, she had probably heard the story. Or, when it came time for *her* to play Joan, maybe Shaw *had* come to watch her—he was still around in those days—and maybe he had said, "You know, Ursula, I once told Sybil . . . ," and Ursula, in later tellings, had simply left out Sybil and made the story her own. But then a whole new abyss of doubt had opened up: how could I be sure Ursula had *gone* to the Royal Academy? How could I be sure any story she had ever told me had been true? And yet, what did it matter now? What would be changed? She had left her imprint on my life.)

". . . but you took it hard," Mott was saying. "We were all pretty worried about you for a while, you know."

"Well, you see I survived," I said dryly. "In fact, I've reached the point in life when I can see it from everybody's side. I can understand why every one of us behaved the way we did, and probably couldn't have behaved any other way. In acting, we call it playing true to character."

"I could still kick myself for not getting down there to see you in that play. I promise to come to the next one. When will it be?"

"Well, I can't promise another Broadway hit—those don't happen very often. I'm doing Lady Macbeth in June. It's outdoors. Have you ever heard of Shakespeare in the Park?"

"No, but it sounds nice. Maybe—"

"And then I'll be spending the summer in Williamstown. I'll be doing several plays. A Pinter—but you might enjoy the Shakespeare in the Park better." I couldn't quite see Mott watching me play Ruth in *The Homecoming*. He would shake his head afterward and say, "What a strange play. This professor brings his wife back to England to meet his father and brothers, and before you've even got everybody's name straight, she's lying on the couch with one of the brothers and agreeing to be a prostitute to help the family out with expenses. Now, surely that isn't realistic. I wonder why Justin agreed to play such a strange part."

"I'll try to get down. Maybe Becky and I . . . have you seen Becky lately?"

"We had lunch a couple of months ago. I always have to phone *her*, but she always comes. She is very involved in her work."

"Yes. But, do you know, Justin, some of those kids have killed people. One or two of them have killed *a parent*."

"I know, but she seems to feel perfectly at ease with them. She's very respected in her field, as I'm sure you know."

"Yes." Mott looked briefly bewildered. "But she doesn't have a family of her own."

"Well, look at me. I don't, either. It just doesn't work out for some people."

Mott looked as though he would like to ask me something, then obviously changed his mind. "Would you like another piece of cake?" he asked instead. "There's such a lot left over. All the new employees seem to be watching their weight."

I told him I had to be heading back to the city.

"It's been good to see you, Justin." We stood up. "I thought for a long time you hated me."

"Oh, Mott." If I ever hated him, I didn't anymore. Hate this bland little man with dyed hair and a mustache? I couldn't even remember when I hated somebody last. Maybe it would be a good thing to feel such a violent, astringent emotion again. "I don't hate you. I don't hate anyone."

As he walked me back through the closed-circuit-monitored halls, he confided shyly to me that he planned to be married again. "I'm going to retire next year and then we'll tie the knot. She's a fine gal. Her late husband worked on SAGE, too. We're going to buy us an RV and hit the road. See something of the world before we get too old."

"That's wonderful," I said. "Congratulations. What's her name?"

"Dorothy," he said proudly, making a minute adjustment to his tie.

I wished him and Dorothy every happiness. He walked me all the way to my car and then stood and watched until I had deposited the "gold coin" that let me out of the parking lot.

As I drove south on the thruway, I thought about hate and other intense emotions. It worried me that the sheer force of all those youthful passions and furies seemed to belong to some-body else's youth. Had I become too socialized, too modulated, somewhere along the way? Or was it simply that I had been able, increasingly, to put those feelings into my acting? Would I, if I hadn't made it as an actress, have become a dangerous person, dangerous not only to myself but to others? What would I be doing if I hadn't become an actress? Making up tales of my past to impress whoever would listen? Looking for ways to dramatize my environment—and whoever happened to be living in it—to keep myself from going dead?

But why was it that Ursula was still more vivid to me as a person than I was to myself? She shimmered before me in all her elusive mystery, making my life, even with its steady devotion to craft, its dedication to what she called "a life of art," seem unexciting by comparison.

I am the failure and she is the success, I thought. I liked the sound of the phrase. It had that nice, rich, hyperbolic ring. But did I really believe it? Wasn't I overdramatizing to give myself a maudlin interlude on the thruway, to force a shapely, tragic-ironic conclusion on a day that had been disappointingly incon-clusive in its parts?

I turned on the car radio and fiddled with the dial. I was close enough to the city to get my favorite classical music station.

Then one of those things occurred that make me wonder where coincidence really ends and fate begins. The Chopin "Scherzo in B-Flat Minor" invaded the car. I had turned in at the place where the pianist begins to build those rapturous se-quences that ascend in scale and volume toward the stunning fi-nale. That this music which Ursula had loved best in her brother's repertoire should come to me now, at the end of this particular journey when I had been tramping around their terri-tory, trying and failing to summon their ghosts, was uncanny. It moved me to tears. It was the piece she had planned for him to play last on the program on the night of his triumphant come-back. As things turned out, it was the last piece he ever played, and only one other person heard it.

VIII.

What was the source of her witchery? Did all of it emanate from her? Or did I invest her with part of it?

"I have made a new friend this summer who I admire a lot because she is sweet, interesting, and funny." That was the best I could describe it with my adolescent vocabulary. As I wrote that sentence in the "Notes" section of "My Personal Life," what was I trying to capture with those everyday words? I know acuter ways of describing people now. My perceptions of human beings are more complex, I like to think. But can I now, through mere words, get any closer to the essence of her charm?

It had something to do with her elusiveness, her mercurial, protean qualities. I was never sure of her, but I was never bored by her, either. She was never, from one visit to the next, quite the same. I could not pin her down even visually. Sometimes she would look extraordinarily young; sometimes old. She could appear as a sprite or a tomboy or an aging spinster. In a single afternoon she could be amused and benevolent, severe, abstracted, imperious, childish or snobbish, funny, sarcastic or downright spiteful. She could also be poignant and vulnerable. One minute I was her confidante: she would be relating to me her latest schemes for Julian's comeback, which she and a manager in New

York were going to arrange for the winter season one year away. She could be discussing with me, as though my ideas and opinions really counted, what ways "we" might employ to fill up the hall, and which pieces Julian should play, and in what order, to show his versatility and keep the audience so attentive that not a single person would dare to cough. And then, suddenly, in the midst of our dialogue, she would administer a corrective *thwack* with the side of her hand between my shoulder blades and say in a reproving tone, "Don't slump, Justin. Your posture tells others your opinion of yourself." And I would be reduced from an equal to a child.

One afternoon when I was helping her weed her vegetable garden, I started telling her about the flowers my grandmother had grown, and Ursula got very inspired at my description of the delphiniums and launched into grandiose plans for the kind of garden she was going to put in around the terrace after she had gotten Julian launched and some money was coming in. "Of course, I'll have to be away a good deal—Julie'll need someone to pack for him and organize him on his tours—but when I'm home I'm going to make this into such a showplace that all the family buried for miles around will float up out of their graves at night and come over here and gape at what I have made of their old homestead." Infected by her excitement, pleased to have been the agent of it, I elaborated further on my grandmother's gardening prowess. Feeling I had something to teach *her*, for a change, I grew bolder than usual in the repeated use of her name as I dispensed the horticultural advice I remembered my grandmother sharing with fellow gardeners—such as the lifelong investment to your garden of double-digging, even though you'd have a backache for a week after. As I rattled along happily, Ursula-ing her lavishly, I saw amusement spread wider and wider across her face until at last she burst out laughing. "Dear child," she said, "you pronounce my name as if it were some kind of sweet wine. It's not 'Er-*salla*,' it's 'Ur-*seula*.' Eu . . . eu. . . ." She puckered her lips. "Can you say *eu?*"

I was so distressed by her unexpected rebuke that I could not even look at her: for all these weeks, I had been pronouncing her name wrong and she had simply listened to me compounding my mistake, the silent laughter building in her. What was I to her, then: some pet buffoon whose mistakes could be counted on to provide amusement during the dull summer hours when she could not be with her brother? I vowed to myself not to use her name again until she noticed its absence in our conversations and repented of her ridicule. But she read my mind at once and turned the tables on me. "Now, don't pout," she said in a gently teasing voice. She reached over from where she knelt in the dirt to pluck a ladybug from my shirt and blow it into the air. "It's just that I want you to be perfect in all things. If I loved you less, I wouldn't always be harping at you like a schoolmistress." She had actually used the word *love.* Frowning in order to hide my pleasure, I uprooted a large hunk of grass from between the leaves of a squash plant. "Okay?" she said. She was waiting for me to look up and meet her gaze. "Yes," I said, giving in. "Yes, what?" she coaxed. "Yes . . . Ur*seu*la," I said. Satisfied, she went on with her own weeding. We were silent for a few minutes. From the house came sporadic phrases of a third-year student's attempt at the "Moonlight Sonata."

Then she surprised me by saying, "You know, one reason for our great affinity, I think, is that we are both at crucial turning points in our lives. In a strange way, the adolescent and the middle-aged person are neither one thing nor the other: they are both in the process of molting, of turning into something else. That is why we can have this friendship, despite the huge age difference. It's as though we were meeting as spirits, and with spirits, age doesn't matter."

I wanted to know what the something else was that we were turning into.

"Oh," she said lightly, "you are turning into a woman, and I . . . I am turning into an old woman."

"You're not!" I protested.

"Oh, but I am. When you are twenty, I'll be fifty. You've got to agree that fifty qualifies as old age."

After a moment's hesitation, I said, "*You* won't be old at fifty."

"Ah, Justin, it's such an experience just to watch your face. You should see the look on it right now. It's a mixture of . . . let's see . . . oh, so many things. All for my benefit, too. But you mustn't fret or be outraged; it's the law of the world: as one generation comes up, the other goes down. Children bury their parents"—balancing herself with a hand on my shoulder, she got slowly to her feet—"and protégées grow wings and take off blithely from the nests of their aging mentors." She stood with her hands on her hips, looking down at me rather triumphantly. I looked up and saw that, from this angle, she *did* look old. It was as though she had transformed herself deliberately into the way she was going to look as an old woman just to prove her point.

I remember how I rode home full of a delicious combination of sadness and power. All around me the ripe countryside swelled, at the peak of its growing season. I gloried in being young. The future awaited me, whereas she was already becoming old. She had told me and then she had shown me it was so. I felt a magnanimous pity for her. I fantasized how, one day, when I had become a grown woman, happy and accomplished, successful (at something that had yet to be defined), I would come and visit a gray-haired woman in the country with sparks in her brown eyes and a humor and enthusiasm that age had failed to dampen. I think I actually worked up some tears at this tender, clichéd image of the two of us sitting down on the stone terrace, maybe surrounded by the fine garden that would have come into being by then, and my telling her of my exploits in the world. She would nod encouragingly from time to time and remark proudly, "I knew you would do it! I knew from the first that you weren't ordinary."

As the summer progressed and my afternoon visits to her gathered cumulative impact, I was actually relieved to return to the average, less demanding environment of Lucas Meadows, where children shouted and rode their bicycles, and fathers mowed their lawns and washed their cars on Saturdays, and my mother, looking lovely and lost, bowed her head over her typing exercises, and Aunt Mona invariably asked, "Well, and what have *you* done with the afternoon?" I don't think I ever, even at the height of my devotion, visited Ursula more than twice a week (I gave much thought to the spacing of my visits and the "reasons" for each, so she would not grow tired of my company), but, even so, I found that my brain, my emotions, my imagination needed a rest after being with her. She *played* me: until I met her, I never knew I had so many tones and vibrations. It was nice to know I had them, but until I grew more accustomed to having them, it was necessary for me to come back to the ordinary world and play back to myself, in a more restful atmosphere, the responses she had evoked for me.

I often spent the hour or so after supper up at the empty farmhouse on the hill. I would take my appointed place on the top back step, facing away from our development, and go over my latest visit with Ursula. Or I would cull favorite scenes from the succession of visits and make a gratifying montage of proofs that she liked me. I would also fashion and refashion *her* story, taking the information she had given me during different visits, and stage in my imagination various incidents and turning points in her life. Frequently I became so involved in my productions that the lines of my own individuality became blurred: it seemed as though I were remembering my own past. Sometimes these mental fabrications would carry over into sleep, and I would dream strange concoctions of her life and mine.

Even the mysterious blanks in her stories provided me with many absorbing hours as I sat on the steps of the abandoned farmhouse in Lucas Meadows or lay in bed at night. I would embroider around the blanks, imagining what I had not been told. She had said so little about her mother, and nothing about that mother's going to the insane asylum, as the Cristianas said she had. I made up "mad scenes" between the mother and Ursula. Wild-eyed and furious, she berated Ursula for being a disappointing daughter, for not being beautiful. Ursula, the young Ursula, would bravely stand her ground, a glimmer of contempt in her bold brown eyes. Sometimes she would say such things as "There are more interesting things in this world than beauty,

Mother." Once she muttered under her breath, "Fate will rescue me from this if I can only hold out." I remember this mother-daughter scene in particular, because it gave me pleasure to act it out in my head. Though I did not know it then, I was doing what actors do: calling up unacknowledged and potentially dangerous feelings hidden in the depths of my psyche and projecting them onto other characters safely removed from my personal circumstances. Every time "Ursula" muttered with stoic strength, "Fate will rescue me from this if I can only hold out," I was able to avenge myself for certain helpless moments in my own history: the time, for instance, when I had been standing on our sun porch back in Fredericksburg, watching my mother pack up our life there, and I had made one last, desperate effort to make her change her mind, only to have her quash me with the adult's ultimate ploy: that I was still a child and would have to abide by her decision.

The last week in July of that summer, fate really did make a propitious little bow into our lives, and as I am attempting, in these recollections, to acknowledge my fair share of blame for the unhappiness I caused, I think it is only sane for me to accept my share of credit for bringing about something that would eventually lead to some happiness.

It happened in a roundabout way, and in several stages, but it would not have happened if I had not behaved as I had. As Ursula had said, that day she had been explaining fate in terms of her family's motto, you take all the fate that has happened to you and use it to make possible what still may happen. Not that I was trying to cause anything momentous when I befriended Joan Dibble. The friendship came about simply because I was trying to behave compassionately on a day when there was nothing more exciting to do.

It began like this: Mott had a new boss, a manager named Mr. Dibble, who recently had been transferred from another IBM location. As soon as Mr. Dibble learned that Mott had a daughter and a niece, both close to his own daughter's age (Joan was twelve), he had Mrs. Dibble telephone Aunt Mona and invite us all (Jem included) to come over one afternoon and swim in their pool. As it was a weekday afternoon and Aunt Mona was working at the travel agency, my mother took us.

The Dibbles lived on a higher scale of income than the Motts, and they had bought a spacious ranch-style brick house on the outskirts of Kingston. It had elaborate landscaping and central air-conditioning, and, of course, the pool, glowing like a large blue jewel, in the midst of a walled-in patio where Mrs. Dibble, tanned already to the color of burnt sugar, took her sunbaths. Mrs. Dibble was an open, friendly, brassy-voiced woman who was wearing the first real bikini I had ever seen; she chewed a spearmint-scented gum energetically as she talked. She fell, I decided, into that category my grandmother had called "nice, but not quite a lady." She lay baking herself by the side of the pool and chatted, in her ringing voice, with my mother, who, to our delight, swam for a while with us. "I like to swim nude," said Mrs. Dibble. "I do it all the time when it's just Joanie and me here at home. I've tried to get Joanie to do it, but she's too modest."

Even Jem, splashing around happily in his yellow life preserver, had the decency not to laugh. Becky tried to meet my eyes and exchange a cousinly smirk of contempt, but I wouldn't look at her. "Joanie" herself sat placidly on the steps at the pool's shallow end, her lower half mercifully submerged in water, a serene half-smile on her round face. She wore a jumbo-size woman's bathing suit with bright, flashy flowers printed all over its considerable expanse and ruffly skirt. She must have weighed more than two hundred pounds. Yet she showed no shame about her appearance. When she greeted each of her young guests, shaking hands with my little brother, her demeanor had been that of a kindly, regal deity—a sort of pubescent female Buddha—trying to put three embarrassed children at their ease. Now she sat, supremely motionless, watching us benevolently as we splashed and swam in her pool. She had not batted an eyelid at her mother's mention of her modesty, nor did she seem aware of the ludicrous images of the less modest Joanie that her mother's words had sent going inevitably in our imaginations: all those mounds of pale flesh, let loose on their own in the water, without the restricting garment. How could Mrs. Dibble be so cruel? I wondered. But before the afternoon was over, I saw that Mrs. Dibble was blithely unaware—or behaved as if she were—of her daughter's size. When refreshments were served at the round, glass-topped table by the pool, Mrs. Dibble kept passing the cupcakes around to Joan, who always murmured, "Oh, thanks, Mom," with a little air of surprise—as though her thoughts had been on higher matters—before delicately choosing a cake from the plate and transferring it dreamily to her mouth. Yet whenever my mother passed the sandwiches or cakes to "Babs" (they were already on a first-name basis), Mrs. Dibble looked down at the plate as if it contained a mass of writhing little snakes, and clutched at her skinny, dark-brown midriff, and declared, "Oh no, Louise, I never eat *anything* between meals. I have to watch my figure." Did Mrs. Dibble, then, have one set of standards for her body and another set for her daughter's? Could she really be as unaware of Joan's appearance as she seemed to be?

"She ate seven cupcakes, I counted them," said Jem, as we were going home in the car.

"I've never seen anyone so fat," said Becky, narrowing her eyes with malicious glee. "It's *disgusting*. She's very stupid, too."

"I don't think she's really stupid," I said. "She's just very quiet."

"Well, I think she's *very* stupid," said Becky. "Maybe even retarded."

"Oh no, dear," my mother corrected Becky. "She had very intelligent eyes. I felt terribly sorry for her. It must be a thyroid condition or something. Surely no mother would allow a child to get like that if it could be avoided. On the other hand—she *did* eat an awful lot of cupcakes. Oh well, it was kind of them to ask us and it's unkind of us to criticize." She reached over and patted Becky, who sat next to her in the car. "Just be thankful you are so pretty and slim," she said. Becky preened herself and looked smug. She adored getting compliments and caresses from my mother.

Then Jem began singing a song our father had taught us: *"I don't want her, you can have her, she's too fat for me . . ."* and all of us started laughing. My mother looked as though she might cry, as well. She was probably remembering the last time we all sang that song, accompanied by my father's banjo, on the porch in Fredericksburg.

We had to detour by the travel agency to pick up Aunt Mona, who had ridden to work with a neighbor that morning so that we could have her car for the Dibble outing.

"What was the house like?" was the first thing Aunt Mona wanted to know.

"It was very . . . affluent," said my mother. "But the pool was lovely."

"What kind of carpeting did she have? Wall-to-wall or just rugs?"

"Wall-to-wall," replied my mother. "It was a . . . let me think . . . a kind of beigey color, rather shaggy, and the same carpeting went all through the house, except for where the tile floors were."

"Hmm," said Aunt Mona neutrally. I could not tell whether she was expressing jealousy or disapproval. "And what were *they* like?"

"Oh, she's very hospitable," said my mother. "She wore a bikini the whole time. The daughter is sweet, but quiet and extremely fat."

"Disgustingly fat," Becky put in. "You wouldn't get me to go back there for anything. Pool or no pool."

"Well, however fat she may be, Beck old girl, you've got to remember that Mr. Dibble is your father's boss," said Aunt Mona.

"I don't care. She's fat and stupid and I'm not going to be friends with her," countered Becky firmly.

"You know," said my mother, "today was the first time I've been swimming since Rivers's death. The water felt so wonderful, but it made me sad. Rivers loved a nice pool."

"Oh yes, Rivers loved the water. He won the diving contest every summer at the municipal pool," recalled Aunt Mona proudly. "Of course, you went to the country club pool, so you wouldn't have been there."

"He was good at any sport he tried," my mother agreed with a small sigh, overlooking, or choosing to ignore, Aunt Mona's pet theme of their social differences back in the days of their youth.

A few mornings later, the phone rang and I answered.

"Is that Justin?" It sounded like a grown-up trying to imitate a child's voice. For a moment, I thought it might be Ursula, playing a joke.

"Yes," I said, my heart starting to beat fast, "who is this?"

"Joan Dibble."

"Oh. Hello." I tried not to show my disappointment.

"I was wondering if you and Becky would like to come over and swim in the pool."

I grabbed for an excuse and found one. "Gosh, Joan, that's nice of you, but we can't. Aunt Mona has the car."

"My mother could come and pick you up."

"Oh! Oh, well . . . wait just a minute. I'll run upstairs and ask Becky."

Becky was in her room, pasting cutouts from magazines all over her lampshade. "Are you crazy? Waste another day with that fatty?"

"It's hot. We could swim. I could do the socializing."

I was not eager to go myself, but I thought it would be better to go and get it over with and not hurt Joan's feelings. "We don't have anything better to do," I reasoned with Becky. I had been to Ursula's once already that week, and it was too soon to go again.

"*I* have lots to do," said Becky with disdain. "And even if I didn't, even if it was *boiling*, I wouldn't go over there again. *You* go, if you're so desperate for something to do." She turned a page of a magazine and plunged her scissors into a picture she wanted for her lampshade.

I went back downstairs to the phone. "If you're going to do a thing, do it graciously" had been one of my grandmother's maxims. I told Joan Dibble that Becky was otherwise engaged, but that I would "love to come." I had a brief relapse from graciousness when Mrs. Dibble's horn blew a half hour later, and I walked toward the car, Joan's placid moonface watching me possessively from the back seat, where she had spread herself out in comfort, like an indolent pasha. *What have I done?* I thought. But then Mrs. Dibble, a beach robe tied loosely around her bikini, called cheerfully in her gum-smacking voice that I would "ride up front with the chauffeur," and I climbed in beside her, a bit depressed but proudly determined to make the best of what I had gotten myself into.

This had taken place in late June. Everyone was surprised when, after that, Mrs. Dibble's horn sounded regularly outside our house on two or three mornings a week. Becky's reaction was incredulity mixed with contempt. Aunt Mona's way of explaining it was that I was a sensible child and knew the value of a good pool on the hot summer days. My mother, who frequently accompanied me out to the car to say a friendly hello to "Babs," would give me tender, puzzled looks as she watched our strange trio drive off. Finally she asked me if I really enjoyed going over there; I wasn't doing it, she asked, out of any mistaken idea that somebody at our house had to oblige Joan Dibble because she was the daughter of Mott's boss?

"No, really, I *like* Joan."

"Well," she said, kissing the top of my head, "that's all right, then. You go and have fun." Perhaps she was relieved that I spent more days of the week with Joan than I did riding over to see Miss DeVane on Old Clove Road.

I did like Joan, and I did like going over to her house. The first day, when I had gone there by myself intent on "doing good," I had found it wasn't difficult at all to be in Joan's company. Far from being the poor fat girl I had to cheer up, she was the serene and benevolent hostess who put me so at ease I forgot all about my "duty."

"You just swim all you want," she said in her mild, uninflected voice, "and I'll sit up here under the umbrella and watch you." For half an hour I swam obediently back and forth in the sparkling pool, enjoying the streamlined sensation of my limbs coordinating in an efficient crawl, pleased and slightly vain about having an audience watching me with such approval. "You're a good swimmer," murmured Joan in her jumbo-size suit beneath the umbrella. There was no wistfulness or envy in her tone. If anything, there was the gratified note of the indulged pasha, who had sent out for an elegant young swimmer to watch and was complimenting the performance.

Joan was not stupid. And she had a self-possession whose source I couldn't fathom. Where did it come from? Was it something she had developed in order to compensate for her appearance, or did she actually draw some kind of mythical charge from her size? I never found out. We never discussed her fatness. We discussed many other topics—gradually I confided to her some of my admiration for Ursula DeVane, after she had shown me her scrapbook of cards and letters and signed photos of famous people to whom she constantly wrote—but never, never her weight. She never once alluded to it or even appeared to notice it, except that, when getting out of a chair or settling into one, she often emitted a half-humorous and resigned groan. Of course I never said anything. Some other girl, even a well-meaning friend, might have broached the subject after three or four visits. ("Hey, listen, Joan. Does it ever . . . I mean . . . bother you about your weight? Have you ever . . . you know . . . thought about dieting?") What would Joan have answered? But I had been brought up *not* to ask: had been brought up, moreover, to feel superior because I knew better than to ask.

She had, in her red-leather scrapbook, letters from Pearl Buck, Edna Ferber, Dale Carnegie, A. J. Cronin, and Danny Kaye, as well as a postcard from Mary Hemingway (answering for Ernest) and signed photographs from Piper Laurie and Douglas Fairbanks, Jr. Before she wrote to celebrities, she told me, she looked up everything she could find on them, and read their interviews in magazines. If they had special pets, she was sure to mention them in her letters, just as she always made sure to refer to a star's latest picture or an author's latest book. She made an extra handwritten copy of every letter she sent, and when the reply came, she would paste it on the page facing her letter. She wrote in a small, round, extremely legible hand, always mentioned that she was twelve years old, and did not stint in her extravagant praise of her intended correspondent's achievements. Once she repeated herself, but how, for instance, was A. J. Cronin to know she had also written to Dale Carnegie and Pearl Buck that "you have influenced many people's lives for the better"? I am not sure whether she had read their books or even seen their movies. But her letters must have made them think she had, because she had some warm replies in her collection. If I were to receive such a fan letter today from a twelve-year-old girl who told me my last performance was stunning and that I had influenced many people's lives for the better, I would sit right down and pen a friendly, glowing reply. There would be no doubt in my mind that she knew my work. From the small, shapely handwriting, I would probably deduce a small and shapely young person invested with all the mental and physical attributes deserved by such a perspicacious acknowledger of talent.

As I mentioned, I told Joan about my friendship with Ursula after I had been admitted to the red-leather sanctuary of her collection of heroes. I began by saying I didn't really have any friends my own age here yet, but there *was* this older woman I had met who had taken an interest in me and whom I admired a lot. I had to explain to Joan who George Bernard Shaw was, and then I told her how Ursula had acted for him in one of his plays and he had said she was going to make a good Joan of Arc, but then the war had broken out. I shared with Joan various selections from my afternoons with Ursula, always tailoring my narratives to make Ursula appear as unusual as possible. Joan's small, bright eyes gazed on me possessively as I told these stories. She often wore an inscrutable little smile that made it seem she knew what I was going to say next. Then, some other times, I wondered whether she was really listening to what I was saying about Ursula, or whether she was watching me in the same way she liked to watch me swim: as though I were a friendly young storyteller she had sent for, to while away her afternoon, and it didn't matter much what the storyteller told as long as she went on talking in an engaging and animated way. However, Joan's silent attention encouraged me to talk. Her huge, quiet, self-contained presence seemed a safe repository for those things I had told no one else. Joan was so different that it was as if she didn't count as a confidante. She was more like a large, semi-smiling Buddha some lonely traveler pours his thoughts out to in some faraway temple just to keep track of himself.

And so, going to Joan's was far from being a chore to me. Being there had many advantages: I could talk about the person who interested me most, and Joan would listen for hours; I could plunge, whenever I liked, into that inviting blue pool (such a contrast to Ursula's country pond, where I never swam, with its invisible generations of swimming and crawling inhabitants she loved to tease me about); I could take an unselfish pleasure in knowing it pleased Joan that I always wanted to come when she called; I could take a perverse pleasure in baffling Becky and making them all wonder at home why I liked coming here so much; I could enjoy Mrs. Dibble's tasty poolside snacks, which she urged on Joan and me but never touched herself—she disappeared into the house or out on one of her numerous shopping expeditions as soon as she had watched Joan and me heap our plates.

Oh, sometimes when they were driving me home, Joan sprawling serenely in the back, I making polite conversation with the "chauffeur" in the front seat, I felt weary in that way you do when you have been on your good behavior too long. But then I would look down at the deepening tan on my arms and legs and imagine Ursula saying, the next time she saw me, "Just look at you, Justin! You're so dark I hardly recognized you. You must *live* outdoors." A tan was the nearest thing to a transformation I could effect in myself in order to show her I, too, changed from visit to visit. Maybe that's one reason people value a tan: it makes others look at them afresh and say, "Oh, you've been *away* somewhere. You've *changed*." Often, as the Dibbles were driving me home, I would realize, with sudden elation, that I had made one more day pass and it was that much nearer the time when I could allow myself to ride over to Ursula's again.

And so, when Mr. Dibble at IBM, due to some foreign executive's canceled trip, found himself in possession of four tickets to the most popular show in New York, it was only natural that he would think of the girl who had befriended his daughter; and of this girl's deserving mother, the sad, pretty widow. And that's how Joan Dibble and I (Joan this time making space for me in the back seat) and "Babs" and my mother set off early one Saturday morning at the end of July for the matinee on Broadway—stopping for a sumptuous lunch, prepared by Mrs. Dibble, at a roadside picnic table along the way.

The show was *My Fair Lady*, with Rex Harrison and Julie Andrews, and I was impressed without reservation. It was the first time in my life I had seen a professional stage production with fine actors at the top of their form and all those masterful accoutrements of stagecraft that can create an unbroken illusion for the audience. As a child of the movies, I had been impatient with and critical of the few instances of local "little theater" I had been exposed to. Invariably there would come some intrusion of reality in the form of a wobbly cardboard set, or an actor's bungled lines, or a wrong lighting cue, or a shabby costume you had already seen in a little theater production the year before. I had concluded that it was impossible to lose yourself at the theater as you could at the movies. But with *My Fair Lady* came a new experience. I did lose myself, but in a less self-enclosed way. There was a rapport between me and the human beings on the stage: they were really up there *now*, in the same room with me and all the other people in this particular audience. The performance as it happened today would never happen quite the same way again. On this occasion we were all participating together in a human drama, an uplifting one, suitable for songs, about how people could learn from one another and be transformed. And that these actors, flesh-and-blood people like ourselves, not distant celluloid images whose bad scenes could be reshot and edited out, were able to command our emotions with such superb skill was both mysterious and moving. I loved Rex Harrison especially. It would be nice to have a man like that waiting for you when you grew up. But then I thought of the age difference between Ursula's mother and father and how that marriage had turned out, and I wasn't so sure.

The final curtain came down and the lights went on. Joan rolled herself out of her aisle seat with a little groan, and the four of us streamed slowly up the aisle. People were humming snatches of "I've Grown Accustomed to Her Face" and "The Rain in Spain" and smiling at one another.

We had reached the foyer when a man in a cotton cord suit pushed his way hurriedly through the crowd and caught my mother's arm. "Louise, it *is* you," he declared excitedly when my mother turned, startled at the touch. She gave the stranger a searching look, then let out a little cry. "Craven Ravenel, I don't believe it! But what are you doing *up here?*"

"Same thing you are, I expect. We flew up especially just to see this show." He motioned to a tall woman in a red dress who was flowing toward us with the crowd but making no effort to get ahead of anybody. She stuck up five fingers and gave us a languid wave.

"Is that . . . your wife?" my mother asked.

"Yes, that's Charlotte. She was Charlotte Emory before we married. I'm sure you met the Emorys when you came to Columbia with your mother." The way he pronounced it— "mothah"—made me realize with a homesick jolt that I had grown up with people who talked like this. He seemed a nice, gentlemanly man, but he was not at all as I had pictured the Craven Ravenel in my mother's story. That Craven had been young and dashing, with flaring nostrils and ripply hair and a tall, willowy figure and a Greek profile. This was a stocky man who was losing his hair on top; the best thing about his face was the expression of delight and wonder on it as he kept looking at my mother.

My mother introduced the Dibbles and me. As she presented me to Craven Ravenel, she took me by the shoulders and drew me slightly in front of her, like a shield.

"I believe I met you once when you were a little bitty thing," he told me. "It was at Pawleys Island during the war. I was stationed over at Myrtle Beach for a while." Then he turned back to my mother. "Is your husband with you, Louise?"

"My husband is dead, Craven." She said it apologetically, as though she wished she could spare him from having asked. "We live up here now, with his sister. I also have a little boy of six."

Craven Ravenel looked stricken. "I don't know what to say. All this time, I've been thinking of you living happily in Fredericksburg. And your mother? Is she—?"

"They're both gone, too," she told him softly. I felt her fingertips press into my shoulders. "All I've got in the world are Justin and Jem, but they are a great comfort to me."

"I'm sure," he said. "I'm sure they must be." He took his handkerchief out of his breast pocket and dabbed at his brow, anxiously scanning the crowd. "I can't understand what happened to Charlotte," he said helplessly. "One minute she was there and now I don't see her. But that's like Charlotte."

"I expect she may have stepped into the powder room," suggested my mother.

"That's not a bad idea." Mrs. Dibble spoke up brightly. "Come on, Joanie. Remember, it's a long drive home. We don't want to be stopping a lot. How about you, Justin?"

"No, thank you." I felt my mother needed me right where I was.

Craven Ravenel gave the retreating Dibbles a perplexed frown, looked as if he might say something, but didn't. After a moment, he asked my mother if my father had been ill a long time, and she said no, Rivers had never been sick a day in his life, it had been a car accident.

"Well, I'm just as sorry as I can be. Look, can you and your . . . friends . . . come back to the Waldorf and have drinks and supper with us . . . if Charlotte ever does reappear?"

My mother thanked him, but explained we had a hundred miles to drive and that she had left her little boy in the care of a nice man on his houseboat. "He likes Jem, but I don't want to take advantage," she said.

"No, of course not," said Craven Ravenel, who looked

somewhat crestfallen at the mention of this nice man. Then he took out his wallet and showed us a snapshot of two preadolescent girls. "That's our daughter Annabel . . . she's almost twelve . . . and that's Amy . . . she just turned eight." He reached in another flap of the wallet and pulled out a card, which he handed to my mother. "If you all are ever in Columbia, please get in touch with me," he said. "Or if there's ever anything I can do for you or your family, Louise, I hope you'll write. Maybe you'll write anyway and fill me in on what happened to you all these years. I've thought about you many times. . . ."

Then the tall woman in red was suddenly upon us. "Here I go hide in the ladies' room so he can have a reunion with his childhood sweetheart," she bantered in a merry contralto drawl, "and when I come out, I find him showing pictures of our children. I don't call that very romantic!"

"Charlotte, this is Louise Justin," Craven Ravenel began formally, but then he stopped, looked at my mother in consternation, and said, "This is unforgivable, but I can't seem to recall—"

"Stokes," replied my mother, offering her hand to the woman in red. "And this is my daughter, Justin."

"Oh, I feel I know you," said the other woman to my mother. "The beautiful girl from out of town who wrote Craven's name on her dance card because she knew he was too bashful to ask. He tells that story every time he can find a new audience. I think"—and she linked her arm through my mother's as though they were two conspirators against the man—"it may be the most exciting thing that ever happened to him. Why, after he saw you at intermission, he could hardly watch the show. He kept saying, 'I'm sure that's Louise Justin. . . . I'm just sure that's Louise Justin.' Finally I said, because I wanted to shut him up so I could concentrate on Rex Harrison, 'Well, why *shouldn't* it be Louise Justin? She has the right to fly up and see this play, too. Only you *aren't* Louise Justin anymore. You're married now. Where is your—?"

"Charlotte"—Craven Ravenel sent his wife a warning look—"Louise has just told me some sad news. She has lost her husband in an automobile crash."

"Oh Lord," moaned Charlotte Ravenel, immediately shedding her jovial, bullying tone. "Oh honey"—she put her arm around my mother—"I'm as sorry as I can be. Craven, why don't you stop me from jabbering so much?"

"Well, darling, you know it's hard sometimes." As he said this, he smiled helplessly at my mother and me, but there was also in the air a visible relief between husband and wife: It's okay now, we have covered Charlotte's awkward question by our "long-suffering old married couple" exchange.

"I was just telling Craven," said my mother, who was now casting anxious looks toward the ladies' room, hoping for the Dibbles' return, "that we live up here in Yankeeland now. After my husband's death, in February, we moved up here to live with his sister. Justin and my son, Jem, and I share a house with Mona and her little girl."

"Oh!" exclaimed Charlotte. "Then that's who the woman and the . . . um . . . plump little girl were . . . that you all were sitting with. They were going into the ladies' just as I came out."

"No, those are just friends," my mother corrected her. "Kind friends who had extra tickets to the show. Justin and Joan—that's the girl—have been spending some time together this summer."

"Oh, *I* see," said Charlotte transferring her attention finally to me. "Well, *she* is certainly an attractive child. Going to be tall. When I was your age," she told me, "I was already taller than all the boys. You must favor your father, though. You don't have your mother's features, at all. Except maybe around the eyes."

"I think she favors my mother a lot," my mother said.

The Dibbles returned, and all the introductions had to be gone through once more. My mother looked strained. Craven Ravenel repeated his offer for all of us to join them for drinks, at least, at the Waldorf, and Mrs. Dibble seemed intrigued by the idea until my mother firmly declined, reminding "Babs" that Eric Mott had been so good about keeping Jem and she didn't want to take advantage. At the mention of the other man's name, Craven Ravenel backed off at once, saying, "Then we mustn't keep you, maybe another time." He gave my mother a wistful look and added, "It's been wonderful seeing you again, Louise." To his wife he said, "I've given Louise my card and told her if there's ever anything she needs, she must get in touch."

"Of course you must!" declared Charlotte to my mother in her jovial contralto, linking her arm through her husband's. "Craven would like nothing better." She gave us all a broad wink and led him away.

We left the cool, dark theater and went out into the bright, hot, late-afternoon sun of Broadway, passing more species of humanity than I had ever thought possible on the way to our parking garage.

"Was he an old boyfriend of yours?" Mrs. Dibble asked my mother.

"Goodness, no. I only danced with him one time. It's just a silly story about how I wrote his name on my card because I wanted him to ask."

"Oh," said Mrs. Dibble. "From the way everybody greeted everybody, I thought it must have been a lot more."

"It wasn't," said my mother. "It was practically nothing." Then she looked at the card crumpled in her hand. "Craven Ravenel, A.I.A. Oh, he's become an architect. I had always imagined him becoming a lawyer."

"Southerners are more . . ." Mrs. Dibble searched for the right word but couldn't find it. "Bart and I lived in Kentucky for a time when we were first married, and I never could tell when people were inviting me somewhere and when they were just being polite."

"It's hard to tell sometimes." And my mother laughed dryly, putting the little white card in her purse.

She slept for most of the drive home, pillowing her head on her folded white jacket. She explained to "Babs" that the whole day had been so exciting, and confessed that she was in the habit of taking an afternoon nap. Joan and I sat in the back, thinking our own thoughts companionably; except that Joan did tell me she planned to write a letter to Rex Harrison the next day.

In "My Personal Life," *My Fair Lady* is the only play listed for that year on the page entitled "Legitimate Drama and Concerts I Attended." Why didn't I record the production of *Hedda Gabler* that Ursula and Julian took me to in early August? The only explanation I can think of now is that I wasn't sure it qualified as "legitimate drama," being held as it was in that hot, barn-like structure on top of a mountain in a nearby village called Woodstock.

One afternoon not long after our trip to New York, I had been telling Ursula about Rex Harrison and *My Fair Lady*, which she rather archly informed me had been based on a play called *Pygmalion*, by George Bernard Shaw, and she asked me if I would like to go with them the following week to a marvelous play by Norway's greatest playwright. "Every actress wants to play Hedda," she told me. "I played her once myself, while I was at RADA. Though I was complimented highly on my performance, I wasn't completely satisfied. There were certain subtle aspects of her personality I didn't truly understand, which I understand all too well today. That's why I'm very interested in seeing the play again. Mind you, Woodstock isn't Broadway, but it's an interesting place. A Colony of the Arts was founded there early in the century by some English people. There's a whole mountainside full of little brown cottages where artists live and work and paint and act and dance and so forth. Though something in me recoils at the idea of artists in colonies. The artist is by nature a separate beast. But you ought to see the place. And you certainly should see the play. You'll come and have dinner with us and then we'll drive up there. *Now* what? Why have you got such a worried look on your face?"

"I was wondering about my bike," I said. "Mother doesn't like me to ride it after dark."

"Silly child! Of course I plan to pick you up and take you home afterward."

"Oh," I said.

But her picking me up presented another problem, which worried me all the way home that afternoon. If she picked me up, she would have to meet my mother. Maybe I could just wait for her on the front steps of our house. No, that might make her think I was ashamed for her to meet my mother. Also, I knew my mother would never sanction such rudeness. Even when "Babs" honked her horn, Mother would stop whatever she was doing and go outside and say hello. No, Ursula would have to come to our door and ask for me, and my mother would be there to greet her. I knew my mother would not pass up the opportunity to meet this Miss DeVane she had heard so much about and was—I thought—a little jealous of. I was thrilled at the prospect of having dinner with them, spending an entire evening with the De-Vanes, but as the day approached, I became increasingly nervous about the meeting between Ursula and my mother. I had strange and conflicting sensations when I pictured the two women meeting each other. I was afraid each might see in the other the faults I sometimes found: that Ursula would dismiss my mother as being merely one more pretty, passive woman (reminiscent of her mother?); that my mother might find Ursula a bit too colorful or eccentric. I felt particularly protective of my mother, and found myself wishing Ursula could have known her in the old days, before everybody started dying and before she became a widow, when she had that air of entering a room so you knew she was the star. That person would have been sure to attract someone like Ursula DeVane.

Yet I didn't want my mother to impress Ursula *too* much. What if they should, in Aunt Mona's awful phrase, "take a shine" to each other? What if they should become friends? It was not impossible. Ursula was older than my mother, but they had, I now realized, important things in common. Both of them had the aura of deposed stars who, because of family fates and adversities, must now devote the remainder of their lives to promoting the interests of their nearest and dearest. Each, in her own style, was cultivating the role of the glamorous martyr. I could just see my mother and Ursula sipping tea on Ursula's terrace. They would have dressed up for each other, as women do, and Ursula would be confiding her hopes for Julian's comeback recital, asking my mother whether, in her opinion, it would be too "heavy" to start the program with the Beethoven sonata, or should they warm up the audience with something lighter, some Mozart, perhaps? And my mother, in turn, consulting Ursula about the right college for me, when the time came. There were some gratifying aspects of my imagined scene—they would both talk lovingly of me, of course—but where would I be in it? Relegated to the sidelines of their more interesting friendship. This position was not a new one for me: I remembered it all too well from my childhood, when my mother was always going off somewhere in a pretty dress to be with friends her own age who, my grandmother said, would take her mind off my father's being so far away; and then later, when he suddenly entered our lives, going off with him, so they could have the young married times the war had cheated them of.

Before the day came, I had gone through the whole spectrum of possibilities arising out of this brief meeting, when Ursula would come by to pick me up: but, by late afternoon, when I was dressed and waiting in my room, I had narrowed my fears down to fears for Ursula. I hoped she wouldn't wear those old, discolored brown thong sandals, though they were the only shoes I'd ever seen her in. I hoped her hair wouldn't be flying about in one of its wilder manifestations. I hoped she wouldn't be too mocking or outspoken or call into question some cherished belief—as she had done that time when she speculated that my grandmother might not have had a private life and that was why it was easy for her to behave the same way when nobody was looking. I hoped that she would suck in her originality a little, as people suck in their stomachs when trying to make a good impression. It would still be visible, of course, but not threateningly so. I wanted my mother to approve of Ursula as a stimulating friend for her daughter—but not *too* stimulating.

She was extremely prompt. She had said five-thirty; our front doorbell chimed at five thirty-two. I had been sitting on my bed for the last ten minutes. I heard the door open and the exchange of greetings: my mother's and hers. My mother called up to me that "Miss DeVane" was here.

As I came downstairs, I heard Ursula's bold, musical voice. "Yes, it's a favorite play of mine—I even starred in it once in London, though God knows what they'll do to it tonight. Still, Ibsen is like Shaw, don't you think? You can't ever *completely* ruin him: the thoughts are too good. Anyway, it's going to be so interesting for me to see it afresh through your daughter's eyes. She has such a wonderful capacity for taking things in, though I'm sure I don't have to tell *you* that."

"You've been very kind to Justin," replied my mother. "It's a lonely time for her, and I know she's grateful for your interest." My mother spoke with an unusual quietness and formality, I thought, or was it just the contrast with Ursula's more assertive voice?

Then I entered the little hallway where they were standing, between the living room and the dining room, and everything went blank for a minute because I was so self-conscious. Here it was, happening, the real meeting, not all the ways I had imagined it, and yet I couldn't take it in. I *was* able to note that Ursula had on real shoes, high heels, though with the higher vamps and thicker heels that had been fashionable right after the war. And she had done her hair in a nonwild way, parting it in the middle and then sweeping it back from her forehead in two wings: also a style from about ten years before. She wore a dark cotton skirt that flared at the bottom, and a white blouse that just stopped short of being off-the-shoulder, and she had on the dark red lipstick. My first impression was one of relief: she *had* dressed up. But then, as I was able to look at her more steadily, while she and my mother exchanged a few more pleasantries, and Aunt Mona, unable to contain her curiosity, came in from the kitchen and, motioning proudly to her living room, asked Ursula if she couldn't sit down for a moment, I began to perceive an air of costumery in Ursula's appearance. This evening she resembled one of those flamenco dancers with haughty heads and arched spines who clatter their high heels brazenly on the floor, knowing their audience expects them to stand out in an aggressive and colorful way.

"Ah, thank you, but I really can't," she was saying to Aunt

Mona, "I'm baking a chicken in honor of this child and I wouldn't want it to get too done." Then she turned her flashing eyes full force on Mona's living room, with its prize seafoam-green carpet protected by the plastic runners leading to all the places she might sit. A slight smile tugged dangerously at the corners of her mouth. "But what a nice house you have. Everything so new and clean and *light.* Let's face it, two-hundred-and-fifty-year-old houses are darker. In more ways than one. It must be lovely to move into a brand-new house and furnish it exactly according to the dictates of one's taste. And no bumping into one's ancestors every time you turn around at night!"

"Well, how'd I do?" she asked playfully as we drove away in the station wagon.

"You don't really care."

"Of course I care. I care about *you,* so why shouldn't I want to pass muster with your mother and your aunt?"

That seemed logical. Maybe she did care. Maybe that mirthful twitch at the corners of her mouth was to cover up how much she had wanted to make a good impression. Had she? I couldn't tell. Aunt Mona had been gratified when she had praised the house; my mother had been harder to read: she had seemed to be reserving her opinion.

"You didn't really like the house," I said. "You couldn't have liked that carpet and those plastic runners. You're not the only one who can read faces."

"Did I mention the carpet or the plastic runners?"

"No, but you gave the impression you liked the house."

"Well, I did like it, in its way. People who live in houses like that have a *starting-out* quality about them that I envy. I *meant* that about always stumbling over the clutter of the past. I love our house, I will probably die in it, but that's part of what I'm saying. Living in it, I sometimes feel I'm a ghost in the making."

Her words set the mood for the whole evening. The idea of "ghostliness" pervaded me all during dinner in the low-beamed dining room, with its heavy, dark pieces of furniture that looked as though they had not been moved in many generations. The late-afternoon sun poured down on the road outside the windows, reflecting an oblique orange light onto our faces as the three of us sat at one end of a long table that could have accommodated a dozen people. Julian had also dressed up for the play; he wore a dark blue jacket and a royal-blue ascot knotted inside the neck of his white shirt. Both of them looked like personages of note, from another time and place. The air of the past was all around us as they talked entertainingly of things they had done and people they had known. Julian related some anecdotes, in his gentle stutter, about his time in the Army. How he had come back from South America and joined up ("h-hoping to be sent to the front lines and die a n-noble death for my country"), but as soon as they found out he was a pianist, they sent him to Hawaii, where he spent the remainder of the war playing the organ for the chaplain's Sunday services, and earning extra money the rest of the week at the Officers' Club, playing requests. That was when he had worked up his "birthday" number, playing "Happy Birthday" in the styles of many composers: it became such a success that almost every night some officer would claim it was his birthday.

Ursula served ratatouille, made from the products of her own garden, and when I said how tasty it was, she told how her "almost" mother-in-law in France, the mother of the doomed Marius DeVane, had given her cooking lessons during the month she had spent with them in the Burgundy village. "The secret of good ratatouille, Mère DeVane told me, was the secret of most good French cooking: you have to take the time to do it right. With this particular dish, you have to fry the pieces of each vegetable separately and mix them all together afterward in a bowl with freshly chopped basil. Whereas the lazy cook, *le cuisinier fainéant*, fries all the vegetables together and then commits the unforgivable sin of steaming them with the lid on so the odors will mix! Ah, I can still see the way Mère DeVane's whole face wrinkled in disgust when she pronounced those words: *'C'est un péché impardonnable, ma chère.'* " And Ursula bunched up her face and did something to her voice as she spoke the French words, and she became the Frenchwoman jealously protecting her beloved son's palate from any culinary laziness on the part of her future American daughter-in-law.

I felt as though I were floating with them, there in the reflected orange light that played mysteriously on their faces, floating along on the stream of their histories: being invited to stop to examine a highlight, a quirk of fate, a poignant ruin of something they might have done. The floating sensation was heightened by the wine we drank. I was not used to it, but pretended I had often drunk it "back in Fredericksburg" at my grandparents' table, and, taking me at my word, Ursula or Julian refilled my glass whenever they filled their own.

And, as they drew me into their world, I did have an eerie sensation of being abducted into a community of ghosts. Was I really a member of that other life outside, a life with a mother and a little brother and an aunt who put down plastic runners so her new green carpet would not be spoiled? Were not *these* two, in some deeper and compelling sense, my true family? Bemused by the wine, I gave myself up to the notion of being possessed by them. It was obviously a thing they wanted, too. Were they not wooing me with these tales of their pasts, showing me how they had been this and this and this, but that perhaps the most glamorous thing of all was to preside attractively over all those old experiences in the seductive orange light of this room? And, because of whatever it was in them that isolated them from present-day reality, I felt I was also in possession of *them*. As long as they preferred to be here, together, in splendid renunciation of the ordinary life that went on outside, I knew where to find them. And the more I learned about them, I told myself, the more I would be able to summon them at will through imagination when I was not with them, when I was going about my business in the other world. They would remain safely as they were, for me, in this house. Of course, there were Ursula's plans— plans that she said gave her life its meaning now—for Julian's brilliant comeback. But this evening, somehow, in the nostalgic aura of this room, all that seemed beside the point. Julian's future was not once mentioned, even indirectly, and if it had been, I think it would have marred the happiness I experienced in their company that evening. Oh God, what am I saying? Is it true, then, that I wanted them to remain has-beens so that I could be sure of them, so that *I* would be the only bright young ray of future in their lives?

I rode between them in the station wagon to Woodstock. Ursula drove, giving me a schoolmarmish little lecture about what I should "look for" in *Hedda Gabler*, even though I had heard her tell my mother she wanted my fresh impressions. But I loved her; tonight she could do no wrong. I loved him, too, that gentle, melancholy man, fastidiously tucking in the loose ends of his ascot when the breeze from the open windows of the station wagon blew them out. I was drunk with love for both of them, drunk with nostalgia for the moment we were living in: infected by the mood of "ghostliness," I already saw it as part of a summer dream on which I would someday look back. I let my arm brush against Ursula's arm as she drove: I needed to touch her. I think I must have been pretty drunk with wine, as well.

I did not lose myself in *Hedda* in the big brown barn on the mountain as I had lost myself in *My Fair Lady*. It was not just that it was hot and mosquitoes nibbled my legs and I kept being distracted by moths fluttering toward the spotlights; or that the audience sat so close to the stage that you could see the sweat running down the actors' necks, and that the actress who played Hedda was not as young as she should have been; or that the aristocratic Judge Brack's morning suit was too short in the trousers and cuffs; or that the set looked as if it had come straight off the Salvation Army truck.

One problem was that I found it hard to follow Hedda's motivation. Ursula had told me in the station wagon that Hedda had made a loveless marriage because she came from a stratum of society where it would never have done for her to marry the man who really attracted her, Lövberg, and also she needed someone to support her. But I found her behavior more erratic than the circumstances called for, and I grew impatient with her.

All she really wanted—unless I was missing something—was to destroy everyone around her, including herself. But then, I missed many significant lines of the play. One reason was the wine I had drunk at dinner; the other, and more important one, was that I was paying more attention to Ursula than to Hedda. I didn't dare turn and look at her directly, but with a hero-worshiper's second set of eyes, I knew when she grimaced, grew intent, lost herself, then became annoyed with something. And I knew she was also aware of me, watching me out of *her* second set of eyes, taking note of my impressions even while she watched the action on the stage. When Hedda fired the pistol at Judge Brack, at the beginning of Act Two, I shied violently, and Ursula, looking amused, reached over and took my hand and stroked it a few times. Following that, my mind went ecstatically blank, and when I came to my senses, Hedda and Judge Brack were halfway through their scene and I had missed more valuable information.

On the way home, Ursula launched into a stunningly vituperative monologue. She tore apart, in a gloating rage, each of the performers in turn, sparing only the lady who had played the small part of the old aunt, whose hat Hedda makes fun of in the first act. She reserved her greatest scorn for the actress who had played Hedda. "First of all, she is at least fifty if she's a day, and even *I*, at my present time of life, would know better than to accept such a role, even if some backwoods theater company came to my door and begged me. Second of all, her performance reeked of everything that is detestable about this vile new Method Acting. Method Acting, Justin, is a so-called technique developed by an old Russian that the Americans have gone gaga over; Americans will go gaga over anything foreign, because they love to be intimidated. You don't find the *English* falling for such drivel. 'Get in touch with your emotions.' 'Open up your own personality and spill your guts all over the role you are playing.' Of course, this dried-up 'thespian' tonight had no guts to spill. My God, she played most of the performance in a monotone, did you note that, Julie? With your ear, of course you would have. Poor bitch, she probably commuted down to the city for three or four Method classes and is tickled pink with all she's learned about 'getting into herself.' But as for getting into Hedda, the real Hedda Gabler was as far away as Norway is from Woodstock, Justin, and I want you to promise me you won't judge this play from what you saw tonight. It's a shattering play when it's done right. Hedda, if she's played well, is one of the most haunting women in the world."

"You would still be splendid in it, Sissie," said Julian loyally as we drove through the night. Ursula was driving fast, in her heated state, and the tires squealed every time we took another curve.

"Well, I would have been better than *that* colorless hag with her snippets of Method Acting. Sir Kenneth used to tell us at RADA that the actor is the link between the individual and the universal. The point is to play Hedda not so she reflects the *actress's* emotions and shortcomings, but so that every member of the audience becomes aware of the universal potential of the Hedda in herself. Or *him*self. There's a Hedda in all of us: that's why she's one of the great dramatic characters. Just as there's an Oedipus in all of us . . . a Hamlet . . . a Lady Macbeth. My God, Hedda is *trapped!* Hedda is *desperate!* Who hasn't felt trapped and desperate in surroundings too small for them? She is a dashing personality in a social straitjacket! She is gathered together, when we meet her in that first scene, like a force . . . ready to strike. The very air of the theater should eddy with the waves of her tension as she coils tighter and tighter . . . until she explodes! And the explosions have *waves.* They mount and mount and then recoil on her to strike *her* down. But, at the same time, you see—and this is what makes the part such a demanding one—we have to feel . . . we have to feel that when she points that pistol at herself and fires offstage, she is not only vindicating herself by flinging an unanswerable challenge at all the people in the world who have failed to live up to her ideals, she is also *freeing* herself."

Julian and I exchanged a look. Isn't she magnificent? we said, without words, to each other. We were also saying: It's a good thing she has us to understand and love her.

Later, when I played Hedda, I was to remember Ursula's passionate diatribe on the way she should be portrayed. I also recalled how Ursula had looked, at the steering wheel, flinging out those phrases as though she had an inexhaustible spring of eloquence to draw on, her face shining with haughty exuberance at her own performance as she sped her captive audience along that dark road.

I have often wondered if Julian recalled her words about Hedda's final vindication on the night he sat down at the piano and played his sister's favorite Chopin scherzo for the last time.

IX.

"Justin, your face is a mile long," said Ursula as we sat on the stone terrace overlooking the fields one Thursday afternoon in the middle of August. "What is going on in that head of yours?"

I had wanted her to ask that. I had purposely made my face a little longer than necessary so that she would be sure to notice and ask. Yet now that she *had* asked, I wasn't sure what to say, or even certain that I could express it. "It" was nothing definite, but rather a swarm of uncertainties, an oblique sense of sadness and impending loss. When I had not found her in the pond or in the hut—"The Finishing School," as we now called it—I had swallowed my pride and ridden to their house. Luckily I had found her outside, in her garden, picking vegetables. Just as I approached, she had hurled a monstrous-size squash down into the meadow. Her back was to me, but I had the feeling she knew I was there and had executed her flamboyant gesture entirely for my benefit. Then I had wondered if her not being at the pond was for my benefit as well: to test me, sort of; to see if I wanted to see her badly enough to come to the house, even though I knew (and she knew I knew) Thursday was Julian's busiest teaching day and I would not dare to ring the doorbell. Maybe her not being at The Finishing School—like the squash-throwing gesture, like the time she hid from me in the pond and I imagined her drowned—was to teach me never to expect the predictable where she was concerned.

"Nothing stays the same," I replied bitterly, staring out at the masses of spiky purple loosestrife that had sprung up all over the meadow surrounding the terrace: they were beautiful wildflowers, but their appearance meant that summer was almost over. The rich clusters of scarlet bee balm, which had been like flames licking the edges of the terrace in July, now drooped in their exploded glory, revealing blasted brown centers. High in the branches of a tree, a katydid chirred. When my grandfather heard the first katydid, he always said: "Well, Justin, six weeks till the first frost." I had never liked winter as much as summer, but I liked to hear him say that because he said it every year. It was comforting to know you could count on some things staying the same from year to year. Only, they didn't.

"What do you mean by 'nothing'?" Ursula coaxed.

"I mean everything. Everything *changes*." As I uttered the words, their proofs assailed my senses on every side: up at their house, Julian's four o'clock student had finally mastered the difficult passage of the "Moonlight Sonata" I had heard her butchering in previous lessons; down in the field that now belonged to the Cristianas was a brand-new fence separating their land from DeVane land (I had watched it come into being, seen them unloading the posts from the truck, heard the pounding of the sledgehammer through the summer days: I had concluded that the reason why Ed Cristiana had never followed up on his movie invitation was that he fell exhausted into bed every evening and dreamed of hammering rails into posts); and yet it seemed that only yesterday Ursula and I had sat on this very terrace and watched Mr. Cristiana pace the unfenced boundaries of his new land on Gentleman Johnny, while Julian had gone inside to express his fury through the "Mephisto Waltz." Even the light on the mountains had changed. I remembered the afternoon I had first seen those mountains, when I had followed the hay-wagon road into the fields in search of the music, and there they had been suddenly, different from any mountains I had seen before: low-lying, austere, old-looking, their subtle, purplish-blue ascent culminating dramatically in the sharp ledge marked by the mysterious tower. They had seemed a hopeful vista to me as I stood there in the soft spring light, fresh green grasses waving all around me, only minutes before I met Ursula for the first time. Now the axis of earth had shifted toward winter and the light on the mountains was sharper, less dreamy and diffuse.

"Of *course* everything changes," said Ursula. "If it didn't, we'd have stasis. You wouldn't want everything to just stop, would you? We'd be sitting here like those poor people in Pompeii that were found hundreds of years later, frozen in lava in the act of doing whatever they were doing at the time the volcano hit. But what *particular* thing has changed that gives you that woebegone look?"

"Well, for one thing, the summer's almost over. Soon I'll be back in school."

"You don't impress me as someone who hates school. With your curious mind, you should be looking forward to what you'll learn next."

"It's not *like* that!" I said impatiently. "Can't you remember school? Most of it is just boring: what crops grow in what countries—that sort of thing."

"I don't remember much about lessons in our school. But, as I told you, it was a one-room school. The dynamics are different in a one-room school. One is more aware of what's going on around one." She laughed. "The thing I remember best, just at this moment, is how Abel Cristiana and I used to beat up the Democrats. This was a rigid little enclave of die-hard Republicans—still is, to some extent—and we had been raised to believe that Democrats were a pitiable sect of sloppy, misguided heretics. There were two little boys, I remember, that we terrorized. We would make them *buy* their way out of a beating by giving us the cookies out of their lunch, and—once"—she closed her eyes and snorted with laughter—"Abel made each of them eat a bite of a grasshopper sandwich. We had found a dead grasshopper on the way to school and I forfeited part of my cheese sandwich so we could substitute the grasshopper. Ugh! I can still see how it looked covered with mayonnaise. Children are beasts. Probably more so when they grow up in the country." She laced her hands on her lap and looked very smug at the thought of the beast she had been. All her sympathies for my melancholy state had vanished during the telling of this story. I thought it was a nasty story. Every time she and "Abel" got together, in these stories, they were always torturing or teasing others: like the time they had both pretended to be drowned at the bottom of the pond and had scared little Julian. No wonder he hated Abel Cristiana. Killing his pet raccoon, and all this cruel teasing. I hated Abel Cristiana a little myself; not so much the red-faced, paunchy farmer who had driven me home and told me how he had saved the German horses, but this gleefully destructive childhood chum of Ursula's, whom she remembered with smug smiles and snorts of laughter. What if I had been a child in that one-room school? *I* was a Democrat, or my family was. Probably Ursula and "Abel" would have ganged up on me, made me eat some foul thing in my sandwich: a grasshopper, a worm, *a snake!* Ursula, if she had met me when she was fourteen, would probably have scorned me as a sissy.

She must have read the disapproval on my face. She switched back into her adult personality and said in a superior tone, "Of course, *anything* can be made interesting if it's taught well. The whole secret of teaching is to capture the student's imagination. When I taught French at that girls' school in New York during the war, I saw immediately we were going to get nowhere with the textbook: *'Which is the way to the train station?' 'Has the postman been already?'* I remembered all too well how I had taught myself French, painstakingly, with records and textbooks, during those years when I was nursing Father, only to get to France and realize I had no words for many of the situations I found myself in, or for things I most wanted to say. I told my class this. *'Most of you will go to France after this war is over,'* I told them, throwing the textbook into the wastebasket beside my desk, *'and I am going to prepare you for the kinds of experiences I was fortunate enough to have, but was not prepared for, in* terms of expressing myself.' Then I drew up a little scenario for them, resembling my own, in which they would find themselves staying with distant relatives, with illustrious ancestors in common—this won over a girl from New Orleans, named Lisa Thibodeaux, at once, because she *had* such relatives—and perhaps there would be a young man, an attractive young man with whom it would be easy to fall in love, and quite tempting to marry, even if one had higher ambitions in mind; and then we set about creating the kinds of dialogues that might arise out of these circumstances. What fun we had! *Nobody* missed my class! One day, another teacher, who had seen my class's slavish attention through the glass-paneled door, asked me, 'What are you *teaching* them in there?' I said, 'I am teaching them to conduct their affairs in French.' I'm sure she thought I meant the business type of affair, she was that dull, unsuspecting sort."

"Did you tell your class about you and Marius in the moonlit ruins?" I asked, unable to keep the surliness out of my voice. Ursula was at her worst today, her most cruel. Here I was feeling blue because the summer would soon be over, and she knew very well why that made me sad: it would be harder to see her; I would have to make formal calls on her, because when it got cold she would no longer be down at the hut. Yet here she was, surely knowing it if she could read my face as she said she could, telling me about all these other girls who meant nothing, to whom she had told the same stories she told me.

"Oh, I'm sure I alluded to the *romance* of it," she replied carefully. "After all, that was my stratagem, wasn't it? To hook their imaginations on romance, which their daydreams were full of, anyway. But of course I didn't dwell on the erotic aspect. One doesn't discuss that except with special, close friends." She was trying to placate me now, but I didn't believe her. "Anyway," she concluded with an airy defensiveness, "the point of my story was merely to illustrate that I believe any subject can be made interesting by the right teacher. I am sure that there is some teacher in this world right now who can make the subject of *crops* absolutely fascinating. By rights, he should be teaching in the Clove school system, with all its farm children. But he's probably at Princeton, or the University of Bologna . . . someplace like that."

I was silent. She was going to have to woo me better than that.

After a minute she asked in a teasing voice, "Do you know what we've forgotten, Justin?"

"No," I said. "What?"

"We were going to go to the mountain."

"What mountain?" I was not going to make it easy for her.

"The one up there, silly," she said, pointing across the fields. "Here you are, already memorizing the crops of India, when we have another full month of glorious weather. One day next week we should make our pilgrimage to the old hotel and the tower. We'll stand on top of that tower and I'll point out this house to you. I'll make a picnic lunch—leave it all to me. Would you like that?"

"I'd like it if you would," I said.

"I'd love it. We'll leave here about ten, get to New Paltz around ten-thirty. I know a wonderful trail that will take us about an hour to hike. It leads right into the hotel. We can picnic and relax a bit, and then we'll climb to the tower. I haven't been up there in ages." She smiled her special smile, and I decided to forgive her for her earlier behavior.

Up on the road a car door slammed. The car drove away.

"That was Jill Van Kleek," said Ursula. "The last of the brats departed for another day. Let me see, for supper I am going to have fresh corn, sliced tomatoes and green peppers, and fried eggplant. A vegetarian supper. Too much meat makes one's spirit heavy. The Buddhists have the right idea."

No sooner had she won me over than she was abandoning me again. I got up to go because I wanted to stay so much. I wanted to stay and eat the corn and the tomatoes and the eggplant, sitting between them like their child in the ghostly dining room. I wanted to be Julian, adored and cared for and catered to by the sister who was now devoting her life to my triumphant comeback. I wanted to be Ursula, wrapped securely in the duties of the destiny I had accepted, with my own household to command. I ached at my powerlessness, I chafed at my subordinate role in everyone's life. It would be years before I could sit back in a chair on my own territory and consult my taste and then declare with perfect authority: "This evening for supper I am going to have . . ."

From the open windows of the house came a little tune on the piano. At first, because of the precise and spritely way it was played, I thought it was something by Bach. But after the opening bars, I realized it was "Dixie." After a few more bars, as it gathered chords and then switched tempo and assumed a whole new mood, I realized I was being treated to a medley of great composers' renditions of my Southern anthem. I was charmed. Ursula was surprised at the beginning, too, but as soon as she understood what her brother was playing, she smiled broadly and assumed a sort of benign guardian-spirit possessiveness over the proceedings, as if she herself had been the instigator of them. "He must have looked out and seen us down here," she said to me, as thundering, Beethoven-like chords for "Look away, look away" rolled down the slope of the lawn. "Since he was a boy, Julie has cultivated the irresistible trick of 'summoning' people by playing their special music. Even Father would drop what he was doing when Julie played the overture from *Tannhäuser*, and I am a pushover for the Chopin 'Scherzo in B-Flat Minor.' But I haven't heard him do this for anyone besides me in years. It would be unthinkable if you didn't come in for a moment after he has paid you this great compliment. You have time, don't you?"

I had time. We ate at six-thirty, and I knew exactly how long it took me to ride each way.

Julian was still tinkling "A-way, a-way, a-way down *South* in Dixie" in Debussy's style when we reached the living room. Smiling shyly at me, he finished his performance by playing more and more softly until his fingers moving over the keyboard made only the ghost of a melody.

I wasn't sure what to say. At school back in Fredericksburg we had been taught there were some performances after which it was wrong to clap because it spoiled the mood. This might qualify as one of those times, so I simply smiled back at him in a way that I hoped would show I felt honored.

Ursula put her arm around my shoulders and told him, "We are feeling a bit low today. End of summer, everything changes, nothing lasts. . . . Oh God, Julie, do you remember being young? It hurt so much, but it was so damned exhilarating! I think I'm jealous of this child for feeling the things I know she's feeling so intensely!"

Julian, still seated at the piano, looked up at me with his soft, muted brown eyes that never flashed or pierced or probed as his sister's did. An understanding seemed to pass between us. I felt that he could read my heart not out of perceptive curiosity but out of a gentle, companionable sympathy. He knew how I felt about coming here. He knew why the thought of summer ending made me sad. He knew how I felt about this woman who stood next to me, holding me in her circle of power.

He played a few strange bars on the piano, dissonant yet compelling. "There's a wonderful poem about . . . these things," he said. "I once set it to music so that an old f-friend and teacher could sing it. It's one of Rilke's *Sonnets to Orpheus*. I'm not sure I did it justice, but the sounds went with . . . what the w-words made me feel."

"It's a haunting piece," said Ursula. "You must play it for Justin."

"I'd love it if you would," I told him.

Ursula and I sat down on the sofa and Julian played the music he had written. His eyes were almost closed, and he touched the keys with a slight restraint; he looked as though he had sent himself into some other realm and had to be careful not to be swallowed up by it. The music was not melodic; it was more like a series of phrases struck off with a plangent, eerie insistence. Several times Julian hummed aloud, or emitted abrupt, guttural sounds as he played. The whole thing sent shivers through me: the weird, often dissonant notes; the way he looked; the intent, solicitous way Ursula looked at him. The atmosphere in the room was thick with some history they were living in, as he played this music.

"Ah, it needs the words," said Ursula, as soon as he had lifted his fingers from the keys. She jumped up from the sofa and went to the piano. "Here, let me try, Julie, I want Justin to have the full force of it. Justin, you won't understand the words, they're in German, but you'll feel their expression. I'll explain what the poem says later. And the other thing you've got to keep in mind is that this piece was written for a lieder singer with a very deep baritone voice, a bass baritone, it's called. So you'll have to imagine that."

She stood behind her brother as he played the piece again, and sang in German, in a deep, throbbing voice, much lower pitched than her usual one. With her bold posture, her hand laid lightly on Julian's shoulder, singing in a man's voice, in the harsh foreign tongue, she might have been a man. She had slipped into one more transformation, escaped from me into a language I could not understand a word of. I was afraid to take my eyes off her; if I did, she might turn into something else, completely unrecognizable, and I would lose her forever. She was too much for me and she knew it: I saw it in the triumphant way she looked at me while she sang. And Julian, too, seemed mesmerized, as if someone else besides his sister had silently entered the room and laid a hand on his shoulder as he played.

She is right, I thought. I *am* feeling everything so intensely that it hurts. But what am I to *do* with all these feelings?

She was also right about the envy an older person feels when remembering (or confronting in a young person) the taut drama of youth, strung with all its erotic and spiritual demands, demands that are frequently inseparable from one another. Now that I am close to Ursula's age, I can look back on that afternoon and envy that girl on the sofa, all a-vibrant with the strange music and the sight of the pair before her, afraid she is going to lose this magical woman during one of her transformations, yet *knowing that this fear of loss is part of the magic.* From where I sat, I could look through the open window and see the tower on the mountain, where she had said we would go next week. But what if it rained on the day she wanted to go? Oh, young Justin, what would I say to you if I could penetrate the time barrier and mur-

mur in your ear? I am so much more certain of myself than you were; I am probably happier, as the world defines happiness. Yet you draw me, you awaken me, as I watch you sitting there, surrounded by your treasures of so many intense desires and fears. Exult in your riches—though of course you won't—because the day will come when you will look back enviously on your longings. The day will come when you understand what Rilke was saying in that sonnet which Julian set to music: that the act of longing for something will always be more intense than the requiting of it.

Which is what Ursula said to me, in her own words, after they had finished the song, and Julian, looking faraway in thought, had excused himself and gone upstairs. She came back and sat beside me on the sofa. "The reason that song is so haunting," she said, "is that it's about a special kind of love. It's a love that can never be satisfied. It's more like"—she leaned her head back against the sofa and contemplated the low ceiling with its old beams—"it's more like a *yearning*. The person in the song is really addressing a powerful and constant state of yearning more than he is any real lover. It's the state of this yearning that torments him, yet he also loves his torment. He *needs* it. Because he understands that being able to feel this yearning so exquisitely is his secret strength." She reached over casually and put her hand on top of mine. "Do you understand that?"

I could barely nod. I was so full of the things she was describing.

"That is one of the best compositions Julian ever wrote," she said, removing her hand as easily as she had bestowed it. "That is the power of the artist, you see. If you are an artist, you learn how to trap the yearning and put it where you want it, put it where it goes. That's the secret all true artists come to know."

Is that, then, what I am trying to do in reviving you, Ursula? Trying to steal back some of the ardor you aroused in me and put it to use in my art?

♩   ♩

"Oh, there you are, Justin," said my mother, who was setting the kitchen table for supper. The job that was mine. "We were starting to worry."

"Yes," said Aunt Mona, "I was just about ready to give Ursula DeVane a ring and ask if you were over there and tell her to send you home." Since Ursula's visit to our front hall, on the night of *Hedda Gabler*, my aunt had stopped teasing me about my "grand friend," and begun speaking of Ursula as if she were her own friend. She always used the whole name, pronouncing it with relish and a certain pride. Aunt Mona had been won over by Ursula completely that night. "Why, she's not so stuck up as I thought" had been her verdict. She had even gone so far as to say that if Julian DeVane hadn't been such a fool at the recital, she and Ursula DeVane might have become "good pals" by this time.

"Oh, were you over with Miss DeVane again?" asked my mother with that innocent vagueness she affected when she preferred something not to be so even though she knew it was. She, to my disappointment, had not been won over by Ursula, though I could not exactly figure out why, and couldn't bring myself to ask. The only comment I had heard her make to Aunt Mona, during one of Aunt Mona's revisional bursts of approval for Julian DeVane's sister, was that "she seemed very outgoing."

"I was riding on Old Clove and she happened to be in the garden," I said. "Then *he* saw me through the window and played 'Dixie,' sort of in my honor, so I had to go in and thank him—"

"That child-hater played *'Dixie'* in your *honor?"* Aunt Mona snorted, waggling her wavy crest.

"He doesn't hate children," I felt I must say. As far as I had been able to determine, the only person he hated was Abel Cristiana. But I could see it displeased my aunt to hear this; she was not ready to revise her opinion of *him*. "Besides," I said, walking the fence and hating myself for my cowardice, "maybe he doesn't consider me a child." I lifted the lid on a large steaming pot. "Oh, corn!" At least I would be eating one of the same things they would be eating for supper. "Are there any tomatoes?"

"There are a couple in the refrigerator, if you want to slice them," said my aunt. "And when you thanked him, what did he say?"

I took a knife from the counter and began slicing the tomatoes carefully onto a plate. I had hoped she would not pursue the topic further. "Well, he played another piece. It was this poem he had set to music." I had forgotten the poet's name, and anyway I didn't want to mention that it was in German. I remembered what Mott had thought about Julian DeVane's staying in Argentina too long during the war, when everybody knew Argentina sympathized with the Germans. "And then she and I discussed the poem. What it meant and all that."

"Sounds very educational," said Aunt Mona. "I would have enjoyed that kind of afternoon myself. You know, if he hadn't behaved so abominably to Beck, she and I might have found a lot to talk about. I don't pretend to be as well traveled or as cultured as she is, but I would be a ready listener. And I might have been able to give *her* a few tips, as well. On decorating, for instance. I really think she liked my house, and I could have suggested—in a tactful way, of course—some ideas to perk up that old house of theirs."

Now would be the opportune time to tell them about our proposed picnic on the mountain, I was thinking all during my aunt's fanciful picture of her might-have-been friendship with Ursula. Ursula had said we could go next Tuesday if the weather was nice, and it would follow naturally out of the topic right now if I could announce casually that "Ursula DeVane" had asked me to go up to the mountain where there was this historic old hotel and we would have a very educational expedition. I could get the whole thing over, in the presence of my mother, who I was sure would allow me to go even though she was not as enthusiastic about my friend as my aunt was. But I hesitated, and then my mother changed the subject, and then Jem appeared for supper, and then Becky, and the opportunity was lost.

"Pass the butter for the corn."

" '*Please* pass the butter for the corn,' Beck."

"Oh, *you* want the butter for the corn?"

"Beck, that's not funny. I want you to be a lady. I may not

have had much when I was growing up, but my aunt did teach me manners."

"Please—pass—the—butter—for—the—corn," intoned Becky, rolling her eyes toward the ceiling. Her mother pushed the plastic butter container across the table. *"Thank—you,"* intoned Becky like a robot. As she proceeded to slather butter on her corn, she shot me a smirk.

"What do you think's happened to that little boy who lost both his parents on the *Andrea Doria*?" Jem asked.

"His aunt and uncle have taken him, darling," said our mother. "Don't you remember? We read it in the newspaper. He and his three younger brothers will be raised by the aunt and uncle."

"Does that still make him an orphan? Or are orphans just children who have to go live in an orphanage, like Mott did, when their parents die?"

He's still an orphan," said my mother. "Anybody who's lost both parents is an orphan."

"Then *you're* an orphan," Becky said to my mother. "Both your parents are dead."

"Well, technically, yes, I suppose I am. But the term is usually reserved for children."

"I was a real orphan," said Aunt Mona, warming to the subject, "and so was your father, Jem. My brother, Rivers, and I lost our parents when we were very young, much younger than the boy on the *Andrea Doria*. My mother and father were out one evening delivering life-insurance policies from door to door, or sticking them in people's mailboxes, because it saved on postage, you see. My father had just started himself this little insurance business. And as they were pulling back onto the road after putting a policy in a mailbox, a farmer in a truck came along in the dusk and hit them head on."

"Did they die instantly, like the parents on the *Andrea Doria*?" Jem wanted to know.

"Well ..." I saw Aunt Mona and my mother exchange a look. "Pretty *much* instantly. Our mother lived a few days, but she didn't know anything. And then our aunt came down to Georgia and got us, and took us back to Virginia to live with her."

"Will the boy be much *poorer* now?" asked Jem.

"Oh no, all those people are very rich," said Aunt Mona. "After all, the boy's parents had the deluxe suite on the ship. That was the part that was hit. If they had been traveling third class, they might still be alive today."

Becky took a ferocious bite of corn and narrowed her eyes at her mother.

After supper, I dawdled about, putting off the moment when I must tell my mother about going to the mountain with Ursula, a task I knew would grow harder the longer I put it off. If I told her tonight, however much she reserved her approval of Ursula, at least she couldn't say I hadn't informed her of my plans ahead of time. I helped Aunt Mona load the dishwasher. I wandered out into the warm evening and climbed part of the way up the hill to the old, abandoned farmhouse, where, to my disgust, I saw children playing. I turned away and started down again, stopping to watch the sky. The clouds still had bright sun on them, as did the tops of the trees; but the grass was already wet with dew and there were lights on in the houses. It got dark much earlier now than it had a month ago. Soon it would be dark by suppertime. Then the darkness would steal away more and more of the afternoon. When I got home from school, there would hardly be time to hop on my bike and ride up Old Clove Road and back before dark. And even if I did, it would be too cold for anybody to be waiting in the hut by the pond. The Finishing School would be closed.

When I finally got around to going to my mother's room, I was not happy to find Becky there, making herself at home on the bed, while my mother sat in front of the typewriter, halfheartedly pecking at a typing lesson. She looked amused and slightly embarrassed over something, and Becky looked very proprietary and pleased with herself, her long legs stretched out the length of the bed, her arms folded Indian-style across her flat bosom. They looked very intimate, the two of them. What could they have been talking about?

"Where's Jem?" I asked, standing haughtily in the doorway.

"He's watching television with Aunt Mona," said my mother. "Come in and sit down, darling. I was getting so bored with my typing."

Becky grudgingly removed her legs from the lower half of the bed so I could sit there. I crossed the room and sat down in a chair. I wanted my mother alone but was too proud to say so. So far, during my friendship with Ursula, I had honored Aunt Mona's injunction not to "open old wounds" by discussing the DeVanes in Becky's presence, although Becky surely knew I went there often. But what could I do if she planted herself in my mother's room?

"I only came to ask if it was all right if I went on a picnic next Tuesday," I said, suddenly afraid I might not be allowed to go.

"Next Tuesday?" asked my mother. "I don't see why not. Is it with—?" She hesitated, also aware of Aunt Mona's concern over Becky's "wound."

"Ursula DeVane," I said clearly, watching my cousin, who did not even blink. "She's going to take me to that old hotel on the mountain, the one Aunt Mona told us about when we first came up here; you know, it's real old. We're going to go up there and look around and hike and take a picnic."

"Well, let me know what you want to take, and I'll buy it when we go to the supermarket on Saturday."

"Oh no, she's making the lunch. You don't have to do anything."

"Oh," said my mother. She sighed. "Well, I hope the weather is nice on Tuesday."

"So do I."

Nobody said anything else. My mother frowned over the typing exercise book and tapped a few keys. Becky eyed me covertly from under the fringe of her bangs. I wanted to get up and go, but I wanted to drive Becky out first. More and more, lately, she hung around my mother, had a little crush on her; was always asking her familiar questions, yet never using her name; was always trying to wheedle praise and compliments from her.

Then Becky stuck out her legs full-length again and wiggled her toes. "I *still* think you ought to write to him," she announced to my mother, in a feisty voice.

"Write to who?" I asked.

My mother blushed.

"Craven Ravenel," said Becky.

I knew my mother had told Becky all about meeting the Ravenels at the theater in New York. I had considered it unnecessary, myself, but understood that it was my mother's kind way of including Becky—who, after all, had been treated to the famous dance-card story—in our outing. But this detestable familiarity on Becky's part was too much. I wondered how my mother could permit it. Obviously they had been discussing Craven Ravenel when I came in, and Becky wanted me to know it.

"There is no reason to write," my mother told Becky firmly. To me, almost apologetically, she explained, "Becky has been letting her imagination run a little wild."

"But he wanted you to write," persisted the obdurate Becky. "He gave you his *card*, didn't he?"

"That was just politeness, Becky. Any gentleman would have done the same. I had just told him of your uncle's death and he felt sorry for me. *Any* kind old friend would have said, 'If I can ever help out, let me know.' Which is what the card meant. But I don't need any help. Why"—she patted the IBM typewriter—"before this year is out, I may even have a job."

"I *still* think you ought to write," said Becky. "Maybe his wife will get sick and die, you never can tell. Then he could marry you."

"Becky, I really can't let you talk like this. It's disrespectful to the memory of your uncle Rivers. I don't *want* to marry anybody. And . . . I think this conversation has gone far enough."

Becky shrugged and raised her eyebrows. She looked intently down at her toes. My mother's face was an interesting study, for she had not been able to keep out of it her old, nonmotherly delight in wicked remarks; but the quick flush of naughtiness had been replaced at once with an exaggerated frown, meant to instill respect and bring the proceedings back within the bounds of propriety. I remembered this "double look" of hers from our former life: my father, especially when he was in those dangerously high spirits, late in the evening, would often say things that you could see tickled my mother's fancy even though they offended her ideals of propriety.

After a moment, Becky, affecting lassitude and boredom, said in her high, toneless little voice, "I think I'll go up and see what's on TV."

My mother and I were left alone. There was an unusual awkwardness between us. I identified something in this room that hadn't been here before: a nostalgic, exotic scent. My mother was wearing perfume again: her old perfume. I started to say something about it, but couldn't decide whether she would be pleased or not. Who had she been wearing it for—*Becky?*

"Will you . . . will you be glad when school starts?" she at last asked, looking at me thoughtfully.

"Oh, I guess. It'll be nice meeting some more people my own age." I knew, with a daughter's true instinct, that this was what she wanted to hear.

"I suppose you'll see your friend Miss DeVane less often," mused my mother, "when you get caught up in school life again."

If only she knew how my heart ached at that thought. But I kept my feelings out of my face and answered like a good, simple girl: "Well, I won't neglect her *totally.* Joan Dibble, either. After all, they've been my two best friends this summer."

My mother gave me an odd little smile.

I prayed for it not to rain on Tuesday. Tuesday dawned bright and clear and cool, perfect for our plans. (Nine years later, I would pray for sunshine on my wedding day. The sun shone; there was not a cloud. It seldom occurs to us to pray that the consequences of such days will be equally bright, as long as we can have what we want on those particular days.)

Ursula came at ten to pick me up. Once more she stood in our hallway and dazzled my aunt and elicited reserved pleasantries from my mother. She wore a khaki shirt and pants and heavy brown boots, which made her look quite different from the way she had looked in her flamenco-dancer clothes. After we drove off in the old green station wagon, she said, "Your mother is a cordial woman, but I puzzle her. I don't think she likes me very much."

"It's not that," I said. "It's more like she's afraid *I* like you too much."

"She probably thinks I'm Sapphic," said Ursula, shifting into high gear and shooting down a country road whose ditches teemed with blue, purple, yellow, and white wildflowers.

"You're what?"

"Sapphic. After the sixth-century B.C. Greek poetess Sappho. She loved women the way most women love men. I'm not built that way myself, but I suppose I lay myself open to suspicion—never been married, live with my brother, oh, I know the kinds of things people imagine! I have had some experience with that kind of thing, though. A young girl tried to *devour* me at that school where I taught French in New York. It got unpleasant at the end."

"How did she try to devour you?"

"Well, it started off with a harmless schoolgirl crush. I was used to that sort of thing, in teaching, becoming the object of a crush. It's not a bad thing, in itself. It's gratifying to know you can influence young lives: it keeps you up to the mark. And it's good for the girl, in that she outdoes herself to please you in your subject, and therefore learns more. But Kitty went too far. Oh, she was a very clever girl, Kitty was, used to getting everything she wanted from her father. Her mother had died when she was a little girl and she'd had nannies and then been sent to Swiss boarding schools until the war broke out. Then she came back to New York, which was her father's base of business—he was a diamond merchant—and entered our school. We got on immediately because she was more cosmopolitan than most of the other girls, having lived abroad so much, and there was a certain unconventional style about her that amused me. Also, she was by far the most fluent student in my class—having learned so much French at her Swiss schools—and she and I used to carry on these hilarious dialogues in class when we were constructing those romantic scenarios I told you about: you know, the ones to make the girls want to learn French." Ursula giggled. "I remember once she took the part of Marius DeVane, making his first overtures to his visiting American cousin. Of course, I didn't call him Marius—we named him Jean-Louis. Jean-Louis De Rossignol. *Rossignol* means 'nightingale' in French. What a success Jean-Louis De Rossignol was in that class! Oh God. But then Kitty's father invited me out to dinner, 'to discuss Kitty's problems.' We went to a very expensive restaurant, and he really put himself out to charm me. He was a suave, canny sort of man, good-looking in a swarthy, Levantine way. He started out by telling me how much Kitty thought of me. 'I'm very fond of her, too,' I said. Then he told me the disturbing circumstances of his wife's death: when Kitty was only a baby, he had taken his wife abroad with him on a business trip. While they were staying in a villa near a small coastal village in Spain, he and his wife had a horrible argument and his wife locked herself in the bathroom and swallowed a bottle of sleeping pills. It was a bid for sympathy, of course; he was supposed to knock down the door and sweep her off to the hospital. He knocked down the door and got her to the car, only to realize he had no idea where the nearest hospital was. He kept driving along this deserted road, hoping he was headed in the right direction, and then he had a flat tire! Well, you can imagine the rest of this story, can't you? He had to walk miles to the nearest house with a telephone, and when the ambulance finally got there she was already in a coma, and she never came out of it. It was a hair-raising story, and he told it well. Poor little Kitty, I thought; no wonder she is always hanging around, bringing me presents that are embarrassing to accept because they're too expensive for the kinds of presents girls should give teachers: she's *never* had a mother. At least I didn't lose mine until I was ten, and, in my case, I contributed to her departure, but poor Kitty. And I said something to the effect that the girl must have felt a huge *lack*, all these years. Which of course played right into his hands, that canny businessman. Over dessert, he proposed."

"You mean, he asked you to *marry* him?"

"Don't sound so incredulous, Justin. I'm not exactly a hopeless spinster. . . . I was even less of one then. I had barely turned thirty."

"I didn't mean—"

"I know you didn't, I was only teasing. *Anyway* . . ." And she waved my apology aside, eager to pursue this odd story that had risen up out of nowhere and come between us at the outset of this beautiful day, which was to have been for the two of us alone. I was caught up in the story and wanted to know what had happened, but I hated sharing the station wagon with the invisible spirit of the clever, cosmopolitan Kitty, whose "unconventional style" was so amusing, whose family disaster was so much more dramatic than mine. "Kitty had told her father she loved me and wanted me for a stepmother," Ursula went on. "And he put the whole thing to me frankly: nothing but his daughter's happiness would ever induce him to marry again. He said I was an attractive, cultured woman, and that was enough for him: it would be an honor for him to claim me as his wife before the world. As far as our private life went, he said, I could have my choice: I could simply accept and become his daughter's stepmother, and Kitty and I could live wherever we wanted; or, if I decided I wanted the full conjugal rights of marriage, he would be only too happy to oblige. Over crèmes de menthe I thanked him for the compliment, but explained I was not ready to marry, that my French fiancé had been killed in the war and it would be a long time indeed before I could think of marriage. And if I did marry, I said, it would be because I loved someone and didn't want to live without him and because he felt the same way. 'Oh,' he said then, 'if it's love you want, we can manage that, too.' He was obviously not accustomed to having his deals turned down. He said, now that he thought of it, he was beginning to fall in love with me already, and that if we went out to dinner a few more times, perhaps I would start to fall in love with him. 'It's certainly not what I had in mind when I came out this evening,' he said, giving me an unsavory wink, 'but I'm willing to broaden my offer. I'm not sure how happy it will make *Kitty* if we fall in love, but I'm willing to experiment.' It was at this point I realized there was something fishy about the entire evening, but I was naive in some ways, even though I was thirty years old, but it was not till I got back to my place that I understood the full extent of my naiveté. I told Kitty's father that I was exhausted and that I didn't think his plan could work under any circumstances, and he took me back to the brownstone next door to the school where I and several of the other teachers had little studio apartments. He kissed my hand and told me to call him if I changed my mind. 'Kitty won't let you off as easily as I did' were his last words.

"He was right. Kitty was waiting for me in my apartment. She had climbed up the fire escape and broken a windowpane to get in. When I turned on the light, there she was in my bed, without a stitch on. She smiled up at me mischievously and said, in French, 'You see, my darling, I fixed everything. Now we can be together forever and travel where we like and it will all be perfectly *comme il faut.*' She was *very* annoyed when I didn't follow the script she had been preparing for weeks in her head. I sat down and tried to reason with her. I realized that the schoolgirl crush had been something more. But I now learned that she had been this way for years, that her father knew it and found nothing wrong with it, as long as it made her happy, and that her father had assumed *I* was of the same persuasion and was entirely willing to marry his daughter's lover in order to give us *carte blanche.* She told me that I had given her every indication that I felt the same. I was flabbergasted! I protested, but to no avail. She presented me with evidence—or what *she* considered evidence. There was the day when I had looked at her a certain way, or touched her hand in such-and-such a way when we were performing our little French skit in class in which she played the part of Jean-Louis De Rossignol. I had blushed at her compliments, she said; I had accepted her gifts; and once I had answered a note of hers, which she said was a love note but I had thought was a joke: I had thought she was simply prolonging the 'Jean-Louis De Rossignol' courtship skit, and I had playfully responded. But—here she was, in my *bed.* And the more I tried to protest, or to reason with her, the more emotional she became.

She accused me of leading her on, of making her fall in love with me, and she threatened to scream and wake all the teachers and tell them I had lured her to my room and tried to seduce her if I didn't get into bed with her and hold her. The old Phaedra revenge on Hippolytus, you know."

I did not know what "the old Phaedra revenge on Hippolytus" was, but, just now, there were other things I wanted to know more. *"Did* you get into bed with her?"

"I compromised. I lay on top of the covers and spent most of the night holding her and stroking her head—as a mother would—and explaining to her why this thing could not be. Finally, around four a.m., I convinced her to climb quietly back down the fire escape and go to her room. But that wasn't the end of it, by any means. She pursued me the rest of that semester, alternating between dolefulness and aggressiveness. Thank God she transferred at the end of the year to another school. But one of the teachers later told me that Kitty had 'confided' to a number of people that she had 'spent a night' in my room, and however much I protested that nothing had happened, my reputation was never the same. Not that it was a matter of life and death: our headmistress was 'of the persuasion' herself, though she was positively puritanical when it came to safeguarding the innocence of our students. In her opinion, I imagine, I had made a foolish tactical error but had been wise enough not to repeat it. Now, if it had been another *teacher*, she would no doubt have blessed our union and welcomed us into the fold."

We were ascending a steep road now, the old station wagon laboring in low gear. At each new curve, more and more of the valley spread out below us. But the lovely view had been dimmed for me by the story of Kitty. It had raised all sorts of murky questions and speculations.

After we had driven in silence for a few minutes, Ursula said, "Justin, you look unhappy. You don't mean you've never heard of lesbians?"

Back in Fredericksburg there had been two dancing teachers, Miss Drake and Miss Culpepper, who lived together over their dance studio, and attended the Episcopal church every

Sunday, snuggling together to take communion at the rail. I had known, in that subliminal way that children know things, that these two women were "different": I sensed it in the way my grandmother always greeted them after church. She spoke to them almost tenderly, as though they were wounded or handicapped and she didn't want to show that she had noticed.

"I think I knew what they were, but nobody ever used the word," I said.

"Well, most people call them lesbians," said Ursula, adding, after a moment, in her schoolmistress tone, "after the Greek island of Lesbos, where Sappho lived and wrote her poems."

"We'll walk from here," she announced, parking the station wagon on the left side of the road. Below was a sweeping view of the valley, with the lumpish primordial shapes of the Catskills beyond. On the other side of the road was a steep, forested bank.

"But where's the hotel?" I asked.

"Oh, up the hill a bit. I thought we'd walk the old bridle path. That's the way we always got in when we were young. If you drive in at the hotel gate, you have to pay for a day pass. This way is free."

"Oh." Did she mean we were going to sneak in?

"Since you are young and strong, I'll let you carry the backpack with our lunch. It's Julie's Army backpack. All his old Army issue comes in very handy. See, today I'm not only wearing his fatigues, but I've also got on his marching boots." She stuck out a foot clownishly. "We're both size nine, isn't that fortunate?"

She spun me around and strapped the pack to my shoulders. Then we crossed the road and started climbing the bank. She went first, quite agile in the heavy boots, and kept offering me a hand when I lost my foothold in my sneakers.

The instances of physical contact between us had always been like special treats to me: I could count the times that she had put an arm around my shoulders, or laid a hand on top of mine, or corrected my posture by thwacking the side of her hand against my back. I had loved such moments, and, up until now, had found nothing wrong in hoarding them in my memory or hoping for more. But when she had strapped the pack to my back, giving me a brisk, affectionate pat on the rear when she was finished, and each time she now grabbed my hand to haul me up the slope, I realized my pleasure was no longer innocent. I still felt the specialness of her touch, and wanted it, but now I was afraid there was something wrong with me because I wanted it. Was I one of those women who loved other women? What would Ursula do if she discovered she had harbored *another* one all summer? I tried to imagine her describing me to some future friend: ". . . there was this young girl who moved here from Virginia, she was very sweet at first, and such a good little companion, such a good *listener*. My brother and I became quite fond of her. But it got unpleasant at the end. What she wanted was . . . not what I was able to give. I'm not built that way myself, though I suppose I lay myself open to suspicion. . . ."

I clambered up the last stretch of bank unaided, even though I stumbled twice and Ursula kept offering her hand. "All right, Miss Independent"—she laughed—"have it your own way."

We reached the bridle path, which wound alongside a sheer rock-faced bluff. As we began to walk, Ursula explained the history of these rocks, which were millions of years old, and the history of this mountain range. The outline of it, which we could see so well from her terrace, had been chiseled and polished, she said, into its present form by glaciers during the Ice Age. But my mind kept escaping back obsessively into what she would think of me if she were to decide I was not normal, and I was aware of losing the very details I should be storing up to relate to my mother and Aunt Mona as proof of an edifying day.

"What is your mother going to do with the rest of her life?" Ursula suddenly asked. "I mean, she can't go on being a widow forever and living with Mona Mott. She's still young. And quite attractive, too."

"She's teaching herself typing from a book. After Jem starts school in the fall, she's hoping she can get some kind of job in

Kingston. Maybe as somebody's secretary. Or at least as a receptionist."

"Hmm. That's very enterprising of her, but not her *style,* somehow."

"What do you think her style is?" I was curious to hear Ursula's "pronouncement" on my mother, even though it felt disloyal to want to.

"Oh, a sort of . . . *princesse éloignée.* She has this faraway, above-it-all aura about her. One gets the feeling she would never easily let herself be known to anybody. Of course, many people find this sort of remoteness fascinating. Men especially: 'the eternally mysterious female.' " Ursula's voice took on its melodic lilt of irony, but beneath that lilt I detected a fascination for this woman who did not quite like her. I could tell, from the energy with which she was pursuing her description of my mother, that Ursula found the subject interesting and perhaps envied my mother a little.

"My own mother had something of the *princesse éloignée* about her," Ursula went on, "but, in her case, it was affected. She pretended to be remote in order to cover up her deficiencies and insecurities. But your mother doesn't strike me as the affected type. On the contrary, she strikes me as someone who knows exactly who she is."

Here a difficult choice presented itself. We could pursue the topic of my mother and I could unburden myself of my conflicting thoughts on the matter while at the same time satisfying Ursula's obvious interest in what made her tick. Or I could take advantage of this opportunity to find out more about Ursula's mother: after all, she had brought up the subject twice already today. There might never be such a good opportunity again.

"What happened to your mother?" I asked Ursula. "I mean, if you don't mind my asking."

"Oh, I don't mind," replied Ursula a little too breezily, as if she had been waiting for my question. "I assumed you knew *something* by the very fact you never asked."

"Well . . . I . . ."

"The Cristiana children told you, probably. Any number of

people might have told your aunt. Everyone around Clove old enough to remember knows that my mother had to be institutionalized. It was no secret at the time. Our father informed the community when it was necessary to send her away. It was a comfortable private institution, of course, even though it was a strain on Father's finances. Several years later, she died in the same institution and Father informed the community of her death. He was a lawyer, he was privy to other families' secrets and sorrows, and he felt he owed others some accounting of our sorrow. He did not tell them all the *details*, of course. Nobody tells all the details, do they? Almost everyone lies a little. Some people lie a lot; they even lie to themselves. My father used to say it was a rare person who came to the office to seek his advice who could actually tell an accurate story of how his grievance came about. That's because most people run from what they can't understand—or don't want to understand. Lying is a way of running. My mother's madness was a lie: I believe that. I believe madness is often the show we put on when we haven't got what we wanted. Only, by the time you put yourself in the hands of the doctors, you've locked yourself into a part you have to keep on playing. At least until someone proposes another part for you. That's what happened to our mother. She lost her appetite one day and a doctor asked her if she was trying to starve herself. That gave her the inspiration: she stopped eating altogether, and, despite the doctors' efforts to feed her intravenously, she succeeded in starving herself to death. People around here never knew that part. Father withheld the details even from Julie, who was still only a little boy. Julie only found out from me much later, after he came back from the Army."

I thought of the languid woman in the old photograph in Julian's room. She hadn't looked happy in the picture. But to just *stop eating*, to starve yourself . . . "She must have been very unhappy," I said.

"In all my childhood, I don't remember her ever throwing back her head and really laughing. She was so afraid of life . . . so timid. She was socially insecure and terrified of doing something *gauche*. So, most of the time, she didn't do anything at all. She sat around looking distant and beautiful and hoped she would pass for what people around here expected from a DeVane. But she kept getting it wrong. There was the matter of her clothes, for instance: she made all her own clothes, sent off for the most exquisite fabrics from a store in New York, and then she would make herself the kinds of clothes that no one wore in the country. And she would go shopping for groceries in them. She would get all dolled up, even with a hat and *a veil*, to go to Twiggy's! People laughed at her. I remember them laughing, because I was with her. They would nudge each other and exchange glances, and then the most hypocritical of them would come up and say, 'Oh, Mrs. DeVane, you always turn yourself out so nicely.' It drove me wild! I was so ashamed, but I was furious at them, too!''

I looked over at Ursula, stomping along the path in her brother's sturdy boots. Her face, pink from exercise, was at the moment wearing an expression of baffled youth and rage, such as the young Ursula in the grocery store must have worn. I had the eerie sensation of being able to glimpse Ursula as she had looked all those years ago, angry and humiliated beside her mother.

"Why didn't somebody tell her about the clothes?" I asked. "Why didn't your father?"

"My father was like most men. He liked his wife to look nice, and the clothes made her happy. She *did* look nice, just terribly overdressed, and the clothes did make her . . . well, not happy, but contented. She loved sewing them and draping them on her body and turning this way and that way in the mirror. She wanted to dress me, too, but I wouldn't stand still for the fittings. I gave her a pretty awful time, poor woman. I can see it more objectively, now that I'm older. I'm older than she ever became. When she died she was ten years younger than I am right now. And I was to give her a worse time, still. *I* was the one who precipitated her madness. I drove her over the edge, you see." She stopped on the path and fixed me with the bright brown eyes. "Do you want to know *how?*" she demanded. She was looking at me as though she wasn't sure I could pass the test.

"Yes," I said. "I mean, if you want to tell me."

"I do want to tell you. I've thought about it for some time. I want you to be my judge. Because you aren't much older than I was when I precipitated our family tragedy. I want you to imagine yourself in my place and then tell me if you would have done the same thing . . . or if I am a monster."

"I'll . . . try," I said nervously.

"Good!" she replied. She stooped and vehemently broke off a long, leafy branch from a sapling. "I don't know where all these gnats have suddenly come from. A trail of them has started following us, have you noticed? Well, since you are the lunch-bearer, I shall be the gnat-fanner." We began to walk once more, she flamboyantly waving the branch before us, clearing a path through the gnats.

X.

"*O*nly one other person alive knows this story in its entirety, and that's Julie. I told him everything after he came back from the Army and was very demoralized and didn't want to live. Father and I had kept a lot of it from him because he was just a little boy when it happened, but now I thought it might make things better if he knew all of it. So even though it meant risking his love, I told him what I had learned about our mother and what I had done about it. There was the chance that he would blame me for her death, but I was lucky: he didn't blame me. He said he had known a lot more than we thought, and that, even though he was just a small boy, at the time he had sensed our mother was an unhappy woman, even before Karl came, and that Karl had only precipitated things; if it hadn't been Karl, it would have been something . . . or somebody . . . else before long. And having it all out in the open brought us closer than ever. He stopped speaking of wanting to die, and he let me lecture him about not wasting his talent: he started practicing again. He could even joke about it. 'We can't let Karl get away with killing two DeVanes,' he said. The only thing I ask of you is that you don't tell this to your mother or your aunt or anybody; and I wouldn't want Julie to know that you know. I don't want him upset in any way before his recital next year. I can't risk having the whole thing start over."

"I won't tell *anyone*."

"Dear Justin, you say that so earnestly. I love your earnestness. Don't ever lose it, though I suppose you'll have to lose some of it out of self-defense. Earnest people are so often teased. Oh God, where to begin this tale of woe? With the hut, I suppose. The hut by the pond that we have christened your 'Finishing School.' The last person to live in that hut—it had a roof then and was quite habitable in the warm months; after all, it had housed a miller and his wife, year-round, in my great-grandfather's time, when there was a mill there—the last person to live in that hut was a tutor of ours, a young German named Karl Klauss. He wasn't really a tutor, he was one of Father's benevolent causes. The poor boy had come over from Schleswig-Holstein to work for a great-uncle, but by the time he arrived the uncle had died and the bank had repossessed his mortgaged farm. Father acted as the bank's lawyer and felt sorry for Karl, who spoke little English and didn't have money for the passage back to Germany. Karl's hope had been to work for his great-uncle and earn enough to go back home and put himself through the Berlin Hochschule für Musik—he had a beautiful bass-baritone voice. When Father found out Karl was musical, he offered him the hut and his meals in return for giving us piano lessons. I was hopeless, right from the start—I'd rather have been outside playing than practicing—but it was Karl who discovered Julie had perfect pitch, and it was Karl who, I'm convinced, made Julie want to be a pianist. A child can have talent, you see, but if that child doesn't have the *desire*, he will never be a truly inspired musician. Father also got Karl a paying job playing the organ on Sunday at the Dutch Reformed Church in Kingston—you know, where we had that wretched recital and Julie got so caught up in memories that he acted unwisely and upset your cousin Becky. Father loved matching people up with jobs and benefactors. He was one of those old-time country lawyers who hardly ever collect a fee. He preferred the old influence-and-barter system: 'I'll draw up your will for you, and you send me a ham the next time you slaughter some pigs. . . .' 'I'll defend your son for writing that bad check, Doctor, because I know you'll take care of me if I ever get sick.' Father liked that way of doing business because it kept him in the center of things, it gave him a kind of patriarchal power in the community. That's why Julie and I are in our present predicament. Father lived off his capital, and whenever he got strapped he'd just sell off some timber or another piece of land. In my great-grandfather's time, all the land on the other side of the road belonged to the DeVanes, and all the fields between here and the Cristianas'. In those days, the Cristianas were barely hanging on, they had only about ten acres to farm. Now *we* have only ten acres and Abel has a hundred and fifty. How the mighty are fallen! And Julie and I can't very well pay our electricity bills with hams that were eaten thirty-five years ago. Though, I must say, the doctor in question never once sent a bill for caring for Father all during his last illness. And you saw how Twiggy wouldn't let me pay for the basil plants that day in the store. Twiggy is still paying off his debt to Father; Father saved Twiggy's farm once. However, much as I wish we could, we cannot exist on basil any more than we can on memories of our family's once-exalted position in Clove.

"So Karl came to live in the hut by the pond. It was in the spring of 1922. I was ten and Julie was six. Karl was twenty-two, the same age as the century. He was a sad, comical thing at first sight. Thin and angular as a scarecrow, with pale skin and red, red cheeks—cheeks like a painted doll's. And the way he ate! Ravenously, voraciously, keeping an eye on everything on his plate, as if he were scared some part of it would run away! He told us in his broken English that his family had almost starved during the fourteen–eighteen war, and that sometimes six people had to share one potato among them. And his poor English: it came out in clumsy, unmodulated blasts . . . like a bull in pain. And he would blush if you looked sideways at him: his long, pale face would turn red as his cheeks, all the way out to the tip of his long, beaklike nose. He seemed to me like a large, funny pet that Father had brought home to entertain us. But, from the first, Julie adored him. He thought of Karl as his personal possession because the two of them spent so much time together. Karl became a kind of baby-sitter. The two of them would go for long walks in the fields and Julie would teach Karl the names of things in English. Julie was the perfect little teacher—you know how children delight in repetition—and Karl felt less self-conscious trying out his new language in the presence of a child. And, in turn, Karl discovered Julie's talent and got him interested in playing the piano.

"In the evenings Karl would play and sing for the family. As soon as he began to perform, he shed his forlorn, comical aspect. He became a person in control, a *force*. He had a rich, doleful, slightly *sinister* bass-baritone voice that lent itself well to the songs he liked best, the romantic and melancholy songs of Schubert and Schumann and Brahms. There was one song, Schubert's 'Der Doppelgänger,' that he sang so well it made us shudder. It's a song about a man who is watching another man staring forlornly at the house where his beloved used to live, and then the watcher realizes that the other man is himself. When Karl got to this part of the song, Julie would cringe and moan in a little ecstasy of terror, and burrow up against our mother, who would smile and burrow back against Julie and pretend to be afraid also. And Father would arch his eyebrows to show he was pleased with the whole setup: this useful, talented young foreigner under his protection, entertaining our household. And as I watched Karl and listened to him sing, I became aware for the first time of the formidable power of art. I understood how art has the power to seduce us all—it can even turn the artist from a ridiculous, frightened person into a seducer.

"Our mother, after an initial revulsion at Karl's foreignness, became devoted to him. She was grateful to him for being so good to Julie, but, more than that, he gave her a purpose. Here at last was someone who felt more out of place than she did. She learned to cook his favorite German dishes and made shirts for him out of her soft, beautiful fabrics. Within no time, Karl began to fill out and look sleeker; he looked more like a man. And, blushing and bowing, he became her grateful knight. To him she was the exalted lady of the manor, the figure she had tried for so long to impersonate.

"It was no secret to anyone that my mother and I were at war. Our natures clashed. From as far back as I could remember, she had wanted me to be the kind of child I wasn't: a sweet, passive little girl, a dressmaker's mannequin. And even when I was very young, I had a sort of contempt for her. My father was amused by it; I think he had long since gotten over his infatuation for the young bride he had brought back from Albany, but he was too proud a man ever to admit making a mistake. He enjoyed telling people that I was such a thorough DeVane that he sometimes believed he had given birth to me out of his head, the way Zeus had produced Pallas Athene. My father and I were allies, and he defended me when my mother complained that I was a roughneck. My great-aunt Clothilde, who had married a Hasbrouck, had been a roughneck as a girl, he said. When he was a boy and she was an old woman, she told him stories about how she went off for days, fishing and camping out with her brothers, and once, in a fit of rage against some family discipline, she had run away on her horse, riding bareback in the pouring rain all the way to Alligerville, where an old uncle lived. I would calm down when I married, my father told my mother, adding somewhat proudly that it was in the nature of DeVane women to be headstrong and cheeky when they were young. Naturally, I overheard all this and became more headstrong and cheeky than ever: I felt it was my birthright to defy my mother now.

"Then, just after Karl came to us, some nuns opened a private school for girls in Kingston, and were accepting applications for the fall. My mother begged my father to send me. 'Think of the advantages,' she said. 'DeVanes don't go to Catholic schools, whatever the advantages,' he told her. 'We are descended from Huguenots, remember?' But now that she had this idea of a private school in her head, she couldn't let it go. As the summer wore on, she kept nagging him. I was a smart girl, she said, changing her tack, and it was a shame for a smart DeVane to be wasting her brains in that one-room school. She nagged until I heard Father say he would consider it. It was too late for this year, he said, but he would ask around about good boarding schools. I probably *should* have more mental stimulation, even though he would miss my wit and energy around the house.

"After that, she had her weapon. Whenever I disobeyed, or tore my clothes, or refused to stand still and let her braid my hair 'for neatness,' she would shake her head and say, 'I'll be *so* glad when it's time for you to go off to school, where they'll turn you into a lady.' She made it sound like some evil spell: I saw myself hobbled and imprisoned in airless clothes, forced to sit simpering in some institution's 'parlor,' sipping tea out of a fragile china cup with my little finger curled. I would lose all my wit and energy. I would have to leave this place, the place of my heritage. Even at the age of ten, I understood how certain places keep the spirit alive. I needed this place that was my home. It nourished me with some elixir, gave me confidence and strength. I still feel that. During those times when I was away, in France and England and New York, I knew I lacked a certain something this place could give me. Oh, I knew I could live without it—I would have had to, had I become a famous actress, traveling all over—but, at ten, I was terrified. My soul was forming. If I were sent away, I might lose something this place was carefully building into me. And I was terrified and in a rage, all at the same time. 'My mother is trying to separate me from my birthright,' I told Abel Cristiana, who was my friend and playmate. 'She is trying to kill the DeVane in me! She's jealous because she is not a real De-Vane.' Abel didn't have much love for my mother, either, because she thought he was a raggedy little 'yokel' and always looked offended when I brought him into the house. 'She is destroying me,' I said to Abel. 'She is trying to turn me into a weak thing like herself!' 'Maybe she will die,' Abel said, to comfort me. He had been my best friend since I was in second grade and he was in first and he had tried to bully me by aiming his slingshot at me; but I had outbullied him with sarcasm, and after that we joined forces and encouraged and protected each other's interests. 'Oh no, not die,' I told him—that was going too far— 'but I wish maybe she could contract tuberculosis, like Mrs. Johannsen did, and be sent away to a nice sanatorium. We could go and visit her and take her presents, and she could have her sewing machine there, but she wouldn't be able to ruin my life anymore!'

"Then one day, in midsummer, Abel came to me very excited. He said he had been waiting around in the woods by the pond earlier that afternoon while Julie was having his nap and I was reading in my room—Mother always made me rest after lunch, to 'digest.' Abel had been waiting for Karl to go off on the hike it was his custom to take in the afternoons; then Abel could splash around in the pond as noisily as he pleased. But Karl didn't come out of the hut, and Abel was about to give up and go home when he saw my mother enter the woods carrying a shirt. She knocked at the door of the hut, looked nervously around her, then went inside. Abel crept closer and looked through the window. He saw Karl, very red in the face, take off the shirt he was wearing. Then my mother put the other shirt on him. As she buttoned the shirt, she suddenly laid her head on his chest. Then they began kissing. 'She would be in lots of trouble if your father knew that,' Abel said.

"Now I had a weapon. But I was sick and disgusted. Our mother, with her air of being the grand lady, and Karl, who was living on my father's bounty, that comical foreigner, hardly more than a boy! Of course, our mother wasn't ancient, she was barely a decade older than Karl, but at the time it seemed ancient to me. Oh God, how strange it all is, the vagaries of fate. Now I'm *this* age and—" Ursula stopped walking and looked around her. Her expression was wide-eyed and disoriented. She looked down at the sapling branch she had been carrying for some time without waving: the gnats had gone away. She tossed the branch into the ferns that grew beside the bridle path. Then she gave me a challenging look, her eyes fierce, as if to ask: Are you still with me?

"Did you tell your father?" I asked, trying to keep my voice neutral. For the sake of the story, I wanted her to have told him: it would make it more dramatic. But I quailed for the foolish, unsuspecting mother, that nervous, unsmiling young woman in the old photograph. How defenseless and isolated she must have been amidst all that DeVane pride.

"I hadn't truly made up my mind," said Ursula, resuming our hiking pace, "but I thought I'd better see the evidence with my own eyes before I did anything." We were in deep woods now, the sun striking us intermittently through layers of leaves; all around was the smell of mossy earth and the horse-droppings we frequently encountered on the bridle path. "My father might not accept the story at second hand; and my mother—if I did decide simply to blackmail her by threatening to tell my father if she insisted on pursuing the boarding-school idea—might deny everything, saying that Abel was a dirty-minded little yokel. So I made up my mind to spy on her, to follow her the next time she went to the hut. Silly woman, she went the very next afternoon. I watched from my room as she left the house and cut across the fields. She must have thought she was safe: Father at work, her little boy asleep, her troublesome daughter reading in her room—I had pretended at lunch that I couldn't wait to get back to my book.

"I streaked out of the house and went the long way round, down Old Clove Road, cutting back via the old haywagon road and approaching the hut from the rear. This took more time, of course, than following her through the fields, but there was less chance she would see me. Nevertheless, I was afraid that by the time I arrived she would have finished kissing him and there would be nothing left for me to see.

"I needn't have worried. There was more to see than I had bargained for. When I looked through the window, they were on the floor, her skirts pushed up and crushed . . . those clothes she was so careful about! And there were his bony knees and elbows, sticking out from more angles than I had thought possible. Oh, it was horrible. I don't mean that I was innocent about sex . . . when you grow up in the country, you learn about those things early. But it was the shock of *those two,* and their clumsy, furtive coupling. They had put down the covers from his bed onto the floor and there was our mother writhing about with the penniless young foreigner my father was housing and feeding.

"I ran home the way I had come, sobbing. But, as I ran, I split into two parts. One part was a frightened, sobbing ten-year-old child who had lost her mother just as finally as if she had seen her killed. The other part was a cool, intelligent girl who plotted exactly what words she would use when she told her father what she had seen. But the strangest thing was that I loved my mother-who-had-been more than ever at the moment. I realized how safe and admirable, by comparison, that other mother had been. All her silly airs, her vanity and fastidiousness, her constant harping on my behavior, had been at least respectable. And, in a sense, she had helped make me as tough and independent as I was by giving me something constant to rebel against. But she was no longer constant. She was something else, some new thing entirely. The 'old' mother was gone and I felt it was my duty to warn our father before she brought shame and ridicule upon us, before she contaminated or hurt Julie, who was still a trusting, innocent child.

"That was how I reasoned. Does it sound extraordinary to you? Was it abnormal? Or couldn't it have been just the most normal reaction in the world? You see, she had *stopped being* the person I knew. She had become another woman. And I couldn't predict what this new woman might do. For all I knew, she might run away with Karl. They might even take Julie with them. I recalled that the question of my going to boarding school hadn't arisen until after Karl had come. Maybe she had been plotting to get me out of the house so it would be easier to carry on her liaison with Karl. Now that I'm older, I can see her side. She was lonely, without inner resources; my father was far too old for her. Karl became her playmate, her pet, her project. And then, one day, a spark ... perhaps when he was singing ... and the sexual possibilities flashed into being. Oh I know what *that* can be like! But I didn't know then. I was just ten years old, and what I had seen through the window of the hut seemed a threat to my whole existence. Children are the most conservative creatures, and I was fighting to preserve what I had.

"That night, I told my father. I went to him in that old part of the house we call 'the office,' where he often went after supper to work on his DeVane archives: to write letters to new DeVanes he had discovered, or to answer letters from other DeVane correspondents. I told him what I had seen, and I told him simply that it had 'frightened me.' I was careful not to pass judgment or condemn anybody: that was for him to do. He heard me out, his face perfectly composed except for a momentary quiver around the eyes. Then he said, 'You know, Sissie, DeVanes have lived in this valley for more than two hundred years and not once has anything dishonorable been brought against our name. I hope nothing ever will.' Then he told me he was going to put my love for him and my loyalty to the family to the test. The test was that I would not mention to anyone else what I had seen. I promised him. I was afraid to tell him that Abel had seen them kiss. But at least Abel hadn't seen what I had seen. How glad I was that I hadn't asked Abel to meet me at the pond for more spying; and how glad I was that Abel hadn't shown up on his own!

"My father told me that I must keep completely silent about the matter and act as though nothing had changed. 'You must treat your mother with respect,' he said. 'Only, don't be *too* good, or she will suspect something. Just be your usual rambunctious self, but show respect. I will take care of the rest.'

"Things went on as usual for several weeks. Mother continued to sneak off to the hut. I would watch her from my window, feeling as though I were watching an animal walking into a trap. I warned Abel away from the woods. I told him (copying Father's tactic with me) that the test of our friendship was going to be that he would never tell about the kiss. 'There are circumstances that I can't relate to anyone outside the family,' I said, 'but everything is going to be taken care of, if you don't go and spoil it by talking.' Abel swore he would never tell. He kept his promise for many years, until he was a grown man. Then he and Julie had a terrible argument one time, when Julie came home from Juilliard. Julie, who can be quite snobbish, insulted Abel's pride, and Abel got back by insulting our mother. I could have killed Abel, but Julie *had* gone too far. He had hurt Abel, and Abel had lashed out with his secret. Julie had hated Abel ever since Abel trapped his pet raccoon, but after that fight they never spoke again.

"Then one evening Father came home and listened to Julie play a new piece Karl had taught him, and then he told Karl he wanted a word with him alone. This is the showdown, I thought. But when Karl appeared at the supper table, he looked elated. His appetite was more voracious than ever, and he kept smiling to himself between bites. Then Father announced that he and some friends, who had been impressed with Karl's playing at the Dutch Reformed Church, had gotten together a 'little scholarship fund' that would allow Karl to go back to Germany and begin his studies in music at the Hochschule in Berlin. 'It would be selfish of us to keep you here longer for our own purposes,' Father told Karl. 'If you are going to be trained properly and have a career, now is the time to start. It's because we've become so fond of you that we must let you go.' Then he looked at our mother and said, 'Isn't that so, Ida?' And her expression was that of an animal caught in a trap.

"Things went quickly after that. Karl's passage was booked. He spent most of his time with Julie, who was heartbroken that his beloved teacher was going away. He told Julie that if he practiced hard, he would grow up to be a great pianist and that he, Karl, would be in the audience one night and come up afterward and shake hands. Karl wrote a whole notebook full of instructions, telling Julie how to play pieces he wouldn't be ready to learn for years.

"Only once after Father's announcement did I see our mother go to the hut. But she came back immediately and went to her room and cried and didn't come down for supper that night. I understood what had happened: Karl had sent her back. Unaware of the true cause of his 'scholarship,' he was not going to risk alienating Father now. He had thrown her over. After that, she spent her days in the sewing room, making clothes for Karl to take back with him to Berlin. Sometimes she would send a tragic glance across the room to him, but he seemed unaware; he was so wrapped up in his good fortune. To this day I don't know whether 'friends' helped pay for Karl's 'scholarship,' or whether it all came out of Father's pocket to save our family pride. The latter, I imagine.

"On his last evening with us, Karl played and sang. Of course, he concluded with 'Der Doppelgänger,' and I've always believed it was partly that song, and the look he briefly sent our mother as he sang it, that gave her the inspiration for her madness. The words are from a poem by Heine, the great German poet, and, roughly translated, they go something like this:

> *"Still is the night, the streets are all resting,*
> *In that house yonder lived my beloved;*
> *She has long ago left the town,*
> *But the house is still standing in the same place.*
> *I see there a man who stares at her window*
> *And wrings his hands with the power of pain.*
> *Horror besets me when I see his face,*
> *Because the moon shows me . . . my own!*

"I think that, in the weeks after Karl left, my mother came to identify herself with the woman in that song. She heard Karl's voice in her memory, and dwelt on that single look he had risked sending her on his last evening, and she came to believe that she was the woman who had gone away and that Karl would always love that woman, as the haunted man in the song did. The suggestive power of art is so strong that it can convince us of all kinds of things.

"Cold weather came and she retreated further and further into herself. She stayed in the sewing room most of every day, making clothes for Julie. We later found that she had made the clothes in sizes he would not need for years. She stopped going out, even to the store. Father brought the groceries home each evening. She continued to cook for us, but the meals weren't good and she often burned things. She grew careless about her dress, and Father had to remind her she had worn the same clothes for several days at a time. Once I went into the sewing room to ask her something. I must have come up behind her without her hearing. She turned and gave a shriek and brandished her scissors at me as if she were going to stab me. I ran for my room and bolted the door. Then she followed me and said she was sorry, that she had been miles away in her thoughts and that when I had come up on her like that she had mistaken me for someone who had broken into the house and she had been frightened.

"Then one day in November, when Julie and I got home from school, there was a distant cousin of ours, Mrs. Hasbrouck, who sometimes sat with us when our parents went out. Mrs. Hasbrouck told us that she would be staying with us for a few days while our father settled our mother in a place where she was going to have a rest. Our mother never came home again. Father took us to visit her several times, but she was getting progressively worse, sinking into her madness, and something unpleasant always happened. Once she started screaming, 'Get her away from me, that devil,' when she saw me, and, the last time we ever went, she told Julie he was only pretending to be her son, that her true son had gone away. 'He went back to Germany to study,' she told Julie. Poor Julie tried to reason with her. He pointed to the clothes he was wearing. 'When you made them for me, they were too big, but look, now I can fit into them.' She went into a violent rage and tried to tear the clothes off him. That was the last time we ever saw her. Julie stopped speaking about her, after that. But he would often talk about Karl. 'I wonder what Karl is doing now?' he would ask. When he learned a new piece from his music teacher in Kingston, he would say, 'I wish Karl could hear me play this.' And when we went to the Dutch Reformed Church in Kingston, he would ask us, 'Do you remember when Karl was up there, playing that organ?'

"But what I want to know, Justin, is what you would have done if you had been in my place. Would you have done what I did, or do you think I was a monster? You must be honest. If you're not, you know, I can read it on your face."

She had caught me unprepared. I was still deep in the land of her troubling story. I had almost forgotten I existed. "I'm not sure," I said, after a moment. "I mean, I just don't know what I would have done." After another moment, I added, "But I can understand why you thought you had to do what you did."

She pounced. "Ah, you said 'thought you had to'! That means *you* don't think I had to!"

The goading note in her voice worried me: it was as though she *wanted* me to accuse her. I was disturbed by all the things I had heard, and also I felt trapped. This day which was supposed to be our outing had turned into an ordeal. I felt as though I dangled precariously on the cusp of my childhood and that the least wrong move, the least wrong thought, would send me tumbling prematurely into the uncertain abyss of adulthood, where morals, backed up by experience, could never be simple again. Ursula's story of Kitty had already made me wonder whether I would grow up to be a normal woman. Her tale about her unfortunate mother raised troubling questions—more, perhaps, than she was aware of. Did she, for instance, approve today of the way her father had handled things? Did she believe he had been a good man? Had she and her mother *always* been at war? Surely there had been some good moments, some times of affection between mother and daughter. And all that talk about "the De-Vanes," their specialness, their superiority: did she still subscribe to that, as she still believed that the "spirit" of the DeVane place provided her with an "elixir" to be found nowhere else in the world? And if she did believe this so strongly, could it not be the reason why she had never been able to break away and become the actress she had wanted to be? Or was it that after *failing* to become that actress, she had justified her retreat by convincing herself that she had to get back to the elixir that was her birthright?

Her story had made me question her adult perspective more than ever before, and yet, somehow, by telling it to me she had implicated me in it: it bound me to her even as it raised serious doubts about her character. I felt, in a strange way, *motherly* toward her, as if it were my duty to shield her from the consequences of her skewed vision. And this meant shielding her from my own doubts about her. She had made me older on this walk, and I fought down a surge of resentment. Wasn't I supposed to be the petted child on this picnic day, and she the responsible adult? Would this bridle path that we were taking so as not to have to pay at the gate never end? The perspiration trickled down my back, beneath Julian's Army pack that contained our lunch. Would we ever eat it? The woods were thick and close around us: we had met not one soul in the time we had been walking, and there wasn't the least sign of a hotel. Yet I knew I was not being fair. I had wanted for a long time to hear about the mysterious, mad mother; only, while I had waited, I had constructed a different story, something vaguely sad, or even tragic, but not so morally ambivalent and with so many disturbing loose ends.

"Poor child," said Ursula then, with her uncanny insight into my feelings (or, as she claimed, my face), "I have overloaded you."

"No you haven't. I was just . . . thinking. I was trying to think out how I would have acted. It's just that it's so difficult. I mean, I didn't know your mother, and so I keep picturing mine. And I don't think mine would have . . . I mean, I'm not saying she's better than yours, but . . . well, her circumstances were different."

"Of course they were," she replied coldly. "Everyone's circumstances are different from everyone else's. I'm not asking you what your mother would have done. I'm asking about betrayal. Would you have betrayed your own mother, whatever the 'circumstances'?" She was being unreasonable, I thought, because she was disappointed in me. Yet she had managed to regain control over me by showing her disappointment.

"I *might* have," I ventured miserably, as if saying such a thing was equal to doing it. "If I had felt as threatened as you did. But I would have felt guilty about it, probably for the rest of my life."

"I do!" cried Ursula passionately. "I do feel guilty! The older I grow, the more that woman haunts me. This summer her ghost has been breathing down my neck. There are certain parallels, you see, which I can't go into, but it is as if she were determined to make me feel what she felt, and to suffer what she suffered. You are part of it, too. . . ."

"I am? How?"

"Well, you are like my daughter, a dream daughter I might have had. And I look at you and talk to you and read your face, and it would be, oh God, so painful if you ever betrayed me. So now I can see it from the other side. Except that I truly believe I love you more than my mother ever loved me. I respect and admire you. I wouldn't want to change you, as she wanted to change me."

"Thank you." Overcome by the suddenness and extravagance of her declaration, I tried to hide my feelings by shifting the subject slightly. "Whatever happened to that Karl?" I asked. "Did you ever hear from him anymore?"

"Did we ever hear from him anymore?" she repeated with arch mysteriousness. "Ah, Justin, do you remember how I told you our family history was as convoluted as a Greek drama? Well, Sophocles himself couldn't have plotted this one any better: Karl *came back* for Julie."

"Came back?"

"Yes, he came back. Just like a bad penny. And Julie went off with him and spoiled his own career. Karl showed up at Julie's Carnegie Hall recital. Yes, that's right, my brother's brilliant night, crowning all those years and years of studying and practicing and all our scrimping and saving so Julie could have his chance. And he was brilliant that night, he played like a god. And there were eleven hundred people in the audience. I credit myself for that: I organized that recital within an inch of its life. I spent more than two thousand dollars, hired the best recital manager in town, had beautiful fliers printed, with Julie's picture, and I made Julie compile a list of every person he had met while at Juilliard, every old dowager at whose brownstone or Sutton Place apartment he had played chamber music, and I sent these fliers to them all, some with personal notes. I went around the city of New York myself, posting the fliers in every allowable space I could find—and some not allowable! I put them in hotel lobbies, apartment buildings, everywhere! And we got eleven hundred people. That's no mean achievement. I'm talking about Carnegie *Hall*, not Little Carnegie, where most Juilliard graduates give their recitals. I was determined Julie was going to make a splash and he did. He had never looked so beautiful or played so well. Only, as fate would have it—our peculiar convoluted fate—Karl Klauss was winding up a tour of lieder singing in this country and was stopping off in New York, looking for some way to keep from going back to Germany—they were just about to start the war, you know—and he comes down to breakfast with his accompanist one morning at their hotel, and what do you think he sees? A flier announcing the recital of Julian De-

Vane. A flier I myself had put up, because it was a hotel popular with musicians.

"So Karl came to Julie's recital and went backstage afterward. Julie was overwhelmed. When he finally understood who this big German was—Karl had filled out quite a bit, to put it kindly—he kept repeating, 'You came. You actually came. You *said* you would, all those many years ago, and you actually came!' He hung on to Karl's sleeve and made him stand there beside him while people came up to congratulate him on his performance. And to each one of them he said, 'This is my first teacher, Karl Klauss, and without him I wouldn't be here tonight!' And Karl, I must say, caught on to his role at once and played it to the hilt. He told everyone who would listen how he had discovered Julie's perfect pitch, and how, when he himself had won a 'scholarship' to the Hochschule and had to return to Germany, he had left instructions behind for Julie in a notebook. Instructions I happen to know that Julie's teacher in Kingston never used; she told Father they were full of affectations meant to cover up a lack of solid technique.

"After the recital, I had a small reception back at Julie's apartment. Karl came and drank champagne and ate at least fifty hors d'oeuvres, and I heard him telling anyone who would listen how, when he was a child, he and his family had shared a single potato among the six of them. But Julie was simply mesmerized. He stayed at the side of his old teacher, hanging on to every word Karl uttered in his booming voice. And when Karl made a toast to 'your dear parents, who took me in when I had nothing, and whose generosity set me on my life's course,' my brother actually wept. It was just too much for him, this dramatic reappearance of the man who had been his last connection to the time when he had both his parents. Now, even Father was gone; he died the year before Julie's recital.

"I thought that Karl had blossomed into a bombastic old phony. If he had felt that grateful to my parents, why had he never—except for one thank-you letter, shortly after he left our house—gotten in touch with us again? Yet I understood the pull Karl exerted on Julie. He was a poignant link with Julie's childhood; he was vitally connected with Julie's music. And—I have to confess it—I was glad of his timely appearance, even though I didn't think he had changed for the better. I was sailing for France on the *Normandie* in a month's time, and I had been worrying that Julie would miss me and there would be no one to encourage him in his music. And when Karl came to see us a day or so later and announced that he had sent his accompanist back to Germany without him and that he was going to apply for a permit to stay in America and work, I thought it sounded like a good idea when Julie asked him to share the apartment in New York. I thought Karl would be paying half the rent. I later learned that Karl paid for very little during his years with my brother.

"And when Julie wrote to me in France, when I was staying with the DeVanes and was all involved with Marius, that he had been on tour with Karl, accompanying him in some singing engagements, I still didn't see any real cause for concern. And then, just as I was about to leave for England, Julie wrote a rather sad letter, saying that Karl had been denied his permit because the immigration office didn't think that he would be able to support himself singing lieder with the increasing anti-German feeling in America, and so Karl had signed on with an impresario who was taking him on tour to South America for the winter. Julie mentioned that he was helping Karl with his passage money, as he was low on funds, and I thought: Well, Karl Klauss has set sail twice out of the family's pocketbook, but we have seen the last of him now. And I went on to London to enroll at the Royal Academy of Dramatic Art. I had waited so long to begin my own life, and I felt I had every right to start now. I had nursed Father for almost six years, when other girls my age were going to college and getting married; I had done everything in my power to launch my brother's career. And I probably didn't read Julie's letters as closely as I should have, during the next year. I should have read between the lines, but I didn't. He wrote about the engagements he was getting, which weren't the kind I had expected him to take. He was playing mostly with chamber groups, in private homes, or in small halls. I wrote him that he should get after his manager and tell him he wanted bookings with orchestras—

that was the way he was going to make his name. But Julie wrote back that he liked chamber music, he liked being part of a group, that it was less lonely. Julie is not very aggressive, you see. He can provide the art, but he needs someone behind him to advertise him and push him out into the world.

"Then the Germans started bombing London, and, at about the same time, Julie wrote to tell me that Karl wanted him to come to South America. Karl said there was plenty of work for the two of them because concert life down there was booming, especially in Argentina, and Karl's impresario had put together an irresistible program: Julie would accompany Karl in his lieder singing, but would have at least two solos of his own for each appearance. 'If you were still here, I might try to stay and make a go of it in New York,' Julie wrote me, 'but you have to pursue your own career now, and, to be honest, I miss Karl.' I cabled Julie back at once: 'Returning soonest. Wait for me.' Well, it took me more than a month to get out of England. It would have taken a lot longer if I hadn't had the idea of offering myself to something called The American Committee as an escort for children who were being evacuated to the Americas. The woman organizing things liked me, and I found myself in charge of fifteen children, sailing across the Atlantic in the middle of a convoy. I hadn't heard again from Julie, but I felt that he would wait for me; he had always done what I had asked him before. I felt full of power and purpose. I was going to get Julie back on the track, and then I would perhaps enroll in another acting school in New York. Everything still seemed possible. I kept my fifteen children beautifully occupied the whole way: we played charades and had spelling bees, and I made the children act out scenes from their lives as a way of getting acquainted. It worked wonderfully. That was when I realized I was a good teacher, that I might be able to support myself teaching while I went on with my acting lessons.

"But when I got to Julie's apartment, I found out he'd been gone for weeks. He'd left for Buenos Aires without waiting for me. I didn't see him again until after the war. He stayed on in South America, concertizing with Karl, until Karl found another accompanist who happened to be a rich young woman who wanted to marry him. The impresario told Karl they would make an even more irresistible team than Karl and Julie had made. So Karl more or less told Julie, *'Auf Wiedersehen.* It's been fun, but you're in the way now.' Julie was heartbroken; he also happened to be broke. He went to the American Embassy and offered himself as a soldier—we had entered the war the year before—and they paid his way back to basic training in Texas. He hoped he would be sent overseas and killed. He didn't want to live. But when they found out about his talent and his training, well . . . you know that story . . . he spent the rest of the war playing 'Happy Birthday' at the Officers' Club and accompanying the chaplain on Sunday. He stuck it out, but when he was demobilized he fell apart. I quit my job at the girls' school and brought him home to Clove. I resolved that I would devote all my energy toward saving him. I let him talk about Karl, and in turn I told him the whole story of what had happened in 1922. I nagged and shamed him into wanting to live. 'I was going to play Saint Joan, in front of George Bernard Shaw,' I said, 'but I threw it all up to come home and save you from ruining your career. And now you say you want to die. If you die, what will I have to live for? My sacrifice will have been pointless. Whereas, if you live and fulfill your potential as an artist . . . if you make our name famous . . . I will feel it has all been worth it.' My strategy worked. He stopped talking of death and began playing again. He took on one student, an extremely promising boy, who has since gone on to Juilliard himself—he was the same boy Julie called into the church during that recital, just before it was Becky's turn to play her piece; that boy did a lot toward restoring Julie's faith in music and in himself. And then IBM opened a plant in Kingston, and before we knew it we had enough children—even when we were being picky—to keep the wolf from the door. Now, unless something really unfair happens, I intend to reverse the family fate and see Julie on the concert stage again, where he belongs."

"That song he played for us that day," I said. "The one you sang the words to in German? He said he wrote it for an old friend and teacher. That was for Karl, wasn't it?"

"Yes. But, Justin, that is the redemptive power of art. It can make something haunting and beautiful out of something that, in real life, was painful and degrading. Julie wrote that song to win back Karl, when he sensed Karl was abandoning him for the woman. Karl never sang the song, though he kept promising to do it at their next concert. Then there was no 'next concert.' Yet, there is the song. *It* exists. It will exist after Karl is gone, and perhaps after all of us are gone. But if Julie's career finally takes off, the way I am hoping it will, he'll be able to make his own programs, and one day—maybe you will be there to hear it—some splendid bass baritone will come out on the stage and stand next to the piano and sing that song while Julie plays it. Then we *and* art will have triumphed!"

When at last we emerged from the woods, and the rambling wooden hotel with its towers and gables and porches rose up before us across the dark blue lake surrounded by white cliffs, the scene seemed to me simply a continuation of the world into which Ursula had drawn me. As we followed the path around the lake toward this Old World landscape, it was as though my own life, with its still-to-be articulated themes and concerns, hovered like an unborn shape in this storybook atmosphere fraught with so much history. Ursula had switched moods, in that masterful way she had, and was relating to me in a blithe, ironic manner how this place had started off as a mountaintop tavern whose proprietor had chained drunks to the trees until they sobered up, and how two Quaker brothers, inspired by the romantic cliffs and the grand, sweeping views, had bought the land from him and built this mountain house modeled after a European resort—but with the difference that guests could drink no alcohol in the public rooms, or dance, or play cards. "Father used to entertain his political friends up here a lot before he married. They'd drink whiskey and play cards in their rooms, and then, on Sunday morning, they'd go down to the parlor and join all the other bleary-eyed guests who had been drinking and playing cards in *their* rooms, and everybody would participate in a nice church service. Father used to say that the reason the hotel was so popular was that it completely embraced the divided American soul."

But I was not so acrobatic in my mood-shifting. I was still caught up in her terrible family story and all its implications. All I could think of as we walked along together was: *She has to make it all right. She just has to. Nothing must prevent her from saving him. If anything happened to prevent it, her life would be meaningless.* And I wanted to cry for this vision of a defeated, wasted Ursula. I walked beside her with a knot in my throat, while her voice gathered wit and music as she elaborated on her concept of the Divided American Soul, pious on the outside, demonic within. *I love her,* I thought. *No matter what she has done, she is the most interesting person I have ever known.* And at that moment I would rather have been inside with her and her wrongness than separated from her and judging her.

"We'll take a quick look around inside the hotel before our lunch," she said, leading the way up to the long porch, where people, many of them old, sat in large oak rocking chairs, gazing out at the lake. We crossed the porch and went inside, and she showed me old-fashioned rooms and then a vast parlor, with a giant fireplace and oak beams and chandeliers, and lots of quaint wicker furniture. Even the sunshine pouring through the French windows seemed old-fashioned. "Oh God," she said with a sigh. "I haven't been in this room since I was a young woman. Father brought us up here to dinner to celebrate Julie's going off to Juilliard. That was in nineteen thirty-*five."* She did a strange sort of dance turn on the carpet, and I remember feeling embarrassed, hoping that nobody would come into this room and see her, in her rumpled Army fatigues and her brother's thick boots, dancing around like that. Then she stopped in her tracks and looked at me critically: "You'd better take advantage of the bathroom before we go off into the wilds again," she said.

"I don't need to." I wanted to punish her for treating me like a child.

"Very well, suit yourself. *I* need to. Be right back." And off she went, leaving me alone in the parlor, whose wicker rocking chairs seemed to stir faintly with ghostly sitters. I went to one of the windows and looked out at people on a putting green. Their clothes were modern. I could not decide whether I was glad or sorry for this reminder of present-day reality. I felt tired and hungry and vaguely apprehensive, and realized I should have gone with Ursula to the bathroom.

When she came back, she raised her eyebrows at me challengingly and gave me an impish, knowing smile. "Sure you won't reconsider?" She knew that I needed to. "Go down that hall," she said, taking me by the shoulders and aiming me in the proper direction. "It's the third door on the right."

My reflection in the bathroom mirror came as a shock. I was so real, so visible, so young, It was almost an affront to these surroundings, to the spell of the past Ursula had woven around us, that I should be so solid. Yet there I was, bending over the sink to wash my hands. That was my face, miraculously unlined, dewy with perspiration. Those were my long, brown arms and bony shoulders and my small breasts, about which I still felt ambivalent, sticking out beneath my blouse, which had been pulled askew by the backpack Ursula had strapped to me. I still had my whole life before me. *I* hadn't yet done anything I would regret for the rest of my life. And it seemed perfectly possible to me, as I stood there, relieved and pleased by my fresh, unmarked image, that with resolution and a little prudent foresight—and from learning from the example of people like Ursula—I could get through life without ever committing any act that would haunt me later.

"You know," said Ursula, "I had a *memento mori* while you were in the bathroom, but it turned out to be rather wonderful."

We had climbed the pathway halfway to the tower and stopped to eat our lunch in one of the little summerhouses built along the cliff. From where I sat, I saw the hotel stretched out below us, against a backdrop of distant valleys and mountains. I tried not to look through the cracks in the floor of the summerhouse, poised as it was above a steep ravine.

"I'm not sure I know what—"

"It's a reminder of your mortality. From the Latin: 'Remember you must die.' I was standing in the lobby, waiting for you, when this old man and his nurse came in from the porch. I suppose I must have stared, something I don't usually do, but he was so very old and white and frail, he was practically transparent with age, and I was impressed by the sheer phenomenon of someone that ancient, standing perfectly erect beside his nurse, who was carrying a folded blanket. Their backs were to me while they waited for the elevator, but then, all of a sudden, he turned around and looked me straight in the eye. His eyes were very smoky, the way old people's get, but there was a force in them. And I knew he was thinking: One day you will be this old, and one day not long after that you will die, but it's not as horrifying as you think. It was as if he were trying to tell me: 'You are much more afraid of death and age than I am.' And I *smiled* at him. The smile just came out all by itself. He acknowledged it with a slight bow, and then their elevator came." She passed me the canteen of red wine with one of her knowing, "mysterious" looks. She was obviously expecting me to "get" something from this anecdote.

I washed down a bite of ham sandwich with the wine and watched a swimmer breaststroking intrepidly across the dark blue lake, too far below for me to tell whether it was a man or a woman. "And it was wonderful?" I repeated her word, not wanting to admit I didn't understand why.

"Yes. It put things in perspective. It made me see ... well, I have known it all along, but I tend to forget. Death is not the enemy; *age* is not the enemy. These things are inevitable, they happen to everybody. But what we *ought* to fear is the kind of death that happens in life. It can happen at any time. You're going along, and then, at some point, you congeal. You know, like jelly. You're not fluid anymore. You solidify at a certain point and from then on your life is doomed to be a repetition of what you have done before. *That's* the enemy. There are two kinds of people walking around on this earth. One kind, you can tell just by looking at them at what point they congealed into their final selves. It might be a very *nice* self, but you know you can expect no more surprises from it. Whereas, the other kind keep moving, changing. With these people, you can never say, 'X stops here,' or, 'Now I know all there is to know about Y.' And that's the kind of person I hope I shall be always." She reclaimed the canteen of wine and took an enthusiastic swig.

I said, "But ... if they're always changing and moving, couldn't that mean they are just unstable?"

"Ah no, far from it. They are *fluid*. They keep moving forward and making new trysts with life, and the motion of it keeps them young. In my opinion, they are the only people who are still alive." Then she cocked her head to one side and narrowed her eyes at me and said with a mischievous lilt, "You must be constantly on your guard, Justin, against congealing. Don't be lulled by your youth. Though middle age is the traditional danger point, I suspect that many a fourteen-year-old has congealed during the long history of this world."

I took my second sandwich out of waxed paper and bit into it. It was very good. Just rich, ripe tomato from her garden, with something sprinkled on it: a mixture of sugar and salt and something else ... little pieces of basil. I remembered the day in the store when I had seen her sauntering toward me with that little box of basil plants balanced on her fingertips. "How will I know if it starts to happen to me?" I asked.

"Well, if you wake up one morning and think: Another day to get through, that might be a danger signal. Though not necessarily. Everyone has dreary interims. You just have to distinguish between a dreary interim and the onset of jellification. However, if you catch yourself becoming complacent, I'd say that was a bad sign. Or repeatedly choosing the old, familiar routine rather than rousing yourself and striking out for new territory, whether it's mental or emotional, or actually going somewhere new. Father used to tell how our ancestors, the Sires DeVeine, roused themselves every spring when the snows melted, and left their cozy stronghold and rode down the Jura Pass looking for a new challenge. Sometimes it would be a Crusade, or other times it might be just terrorizing the locals, but the point was they knew they had to keep moving. And that's why there are still so many of us. When it really came time to move, after Louis the

Fourteenth revoked the Edict of Nantes, our Huguenot ancestors had moving in their blood and were able to go to Germany, and later to America—to this very spot"—and she waved her hand in a proprietary way over the surrounding mountains and valleys. She took another hefty swig from the canteen and looked extremely pleased with herself, so much so that I fell under her confident spell once more. I guess she saw it in my face—as she said she saw everything—for she magnanimously passed me the canteen as though offering me her own rare potion against ordinariness and congealment. "If you ever feel it coming," she said, "you must do something quickly. The best antidote I have found is to yearn for something. As long as you yearn, you can't congeal: there is a forward motion to yearning."

As I drank, she leaned forward and looked at me as if she were burning to confide another secret. But then she stopped herself. I think I know now what she was about to tell me. If I had been older, she might have blurted it out then and there, and we would have sat on, in our summerhouse over the ravine, tenderly mauling her confession in an amicable, winy way until we had extracted its choicest juices and, by doing so, strengthened our bond of womanhood. But, just on the verge of telling, she must have decided that I was, after all, still a child. She must have thought: No, it's one thing to tell about my mother, but this other thing would be too much. Or maybe she just thought she had told enough for one day.

What if she had gone on and told me? Would things have turned out better? Or would her confession only have delayed the inevitable tragedy and kept me from being the agent of it?

We packed up the canteen and our folded picnic papers, "like good citizens," as Ursula said, and she insisted that I strap the backpack to her for the rest of this outing. "I don't want to be accused of violating the child-labor laws," she joked. "As it is, I could probably be cited for corrupting a minor by giving you Beaujolais out of a canteen. But you did say your grandparents served you wine at the table."

Then we climbed the remainder of the cliffside path to the tower we had come to see: the focus of this excursion; the intriguing landmark that had looked down upon the site of our friendship all these summer days.

I was disappointed in the tower. It had looked more mysterious from afar, when it had been a lonely, dark shape against the sky. Up close, its stones were sleek and yellow, and a metal plate attested unromantically that it had been built as recently as 1923. Also, we were not alone. While we had been climbing the cliffside path, a horse-drawn wagon full of hotel guests had been making its way up the winding carriage road, and so we found ourselves climbing to the tower with a dozen or so noisy strangers whose mundane remarks echoed harshly up and down the circular metal stairwell.

On the observation deck, Ursula had to spin me around, because I had been looking in the wrong direction, confusing (and preferring) the sunny valley of New Paltz with that of Clove. "No," she said, "we're over there," and pointed to a cluster of farms and fields and woods that lay to the northeast in a remoter, bluish haze. "Do you see that metal roof with the sun flashing on it . . . see, that tiny square of silver? Well, that's Abel Cristiana's tin roof. Then you follow the line of those fields to the right until you come to the dark wedge of pines. The pond is in there, and our 'Finishing School.' Then if you continue on, you'll see a clump of trees. Those are the trees that surround our house." As she said "our house," she gave my shoulders a light squeeze, as if to say: It's your house, too. After a moment, she added wistfully, "It's different from the way I remembered it. I mean the landscape really is different. The last time I was up here, there was more open field, there were so many more *farms*. But that was a long time ago. Seeing the way this view has changed makes me realize just how long."

I caught the underlying sadness in her voice, although I couldn't see her face; she was still standing behind me, her hands resting lightly on my shoulders. For the second time that day, I felt close to tears for her sake.

As we started back down the cliffside path, the sadness

gathered in me until it became overtaken by some other emotion—more like superstition, or fear. Ursula strode ahead, saying
she couldn't wait to get away from the noisy tourists. As I
watched her figure in Julian's soldier clothes and boots and
backpack hurrying down the path, her hair floating in a lively
mass around her head, I worked myself up into a superstition
that if I allowed her to disappear from my sight I would lose her
forever. I knew I didn't mean I would lose Ursula the woman,
who had been in the world a long time before I had been, who
had done many things I might not know about or understand; I
meant the Ursula I had been bewitched by and had believed in
all summer.

And then I stopped dead still in my tracks and purposely let
her disappear from sight around the next curve.

I began to cry. I considered waiting right where I was until
she should miss me and turn around and come back for me.
Would I revoke the spell if I summoned her back into sight the
same way I had cast her out of it? But even as I asked myself that,
I was slowly walking down the path again.

She was waiting for me at the next turn. When she saw I was
crying, she wanted to know if I had fallen and hurt myself.

I wept all the harder at her innocent question, and at her
look of increasing concern. "I think . . . I think I'm just tired," I
sobbed.

There was another one of those little summerhouses just
ahead of us on the path, and she led me to it and made me rest.
She sat down beside me and looked anxiously into my face. "I
should be killed," she proclaimed, "for walking you half to death
and talking you half to death and getting you drunk in the bargain. Why don't you just push me over the edge of this summerhouse and be rid of me?"

"I don't *want* to be rid of you," I protested, and burst into
fresh tears.

"Well, of course you don't," she said, the humor returning
to her voice. "But all the same I'm a brute."

"No you're not."

"Yes I am."

"No you're *not!*"

"Have it your own way, then," she said, smiling. She put an arm around me and I nestled on her breast like a weary child. With her other hand she began smoothing my hair away from my face in a soft, regular motion until my sobs subsided. I noticed that the mountain ranges, on a level with us at this height, were spinning slightly. Maybe I *was* drunk. But her steady caress was wonderfully soothing.

Then an old couple passed our summerhouse on the way to the tower. They carried walking sticks and wore funny baggy walking shorts and matching brown shoes with tassels that flapped. There was something touchingly comical about their alikeness. They nodded pleasantly to us, and Ursula called hello. After they had disappeared around the curve of the path, she said in her low, amused voice, "They thought we were mother and daughter. I could tell from the way they looked at us. They thought you were tired and bored with walking, and I was giving you a little pep talk before we went on. It was a nice feeling, having them think you belonged to me."

The sun flashed on the spinning mountains. I closed my eyes in a kind of swoon. "I do belong to you," I said. Even as I said it, I knew it wasn't completely true, but I wanted it to be true. I wanted things to be as simple as they had been before we had climbed the mountain, before we had driven up here today. If only we could stay up here together now, and not go down to the world again, I might be able to make it all true.

"Oh child, child," murmured Ursula, resting her chin on the top of my head. Positioned as we were, I couldn't possibly have seen her face, but now I am fairly sure that her eyes were not closed, like mine. I see them restlessly scanning the valley below us, squinting through the blue haze to pick out a certain winking rooftop, or a beloved clump of trees. She had given a sustained, disturbing, and captivating performance to her audience of one, and was pleased with the results. But now she was anxious, perhaps impatient, to get back down the mountain and attend to other performances.

XI.

After Tuesday's picnic, I made a resolution to stay away from Ursula for at least one week. I had always spaced my visits far enough apart so she wouldn't get tired of me. Normally, after two or three days had gone by, I would feel it was okay to go again. I would have stayed away long enough for her to start wondering what I had been doing; and I would have given myself enough time to absorb all the feelings and sort out all the questions that each visit with her invariably stirred up. But after the day on the mountain, I felt almost invaded by Ursula. I felt overwhelmed by the things she had told me. They forced me not only to reassess her but to ask troubling questions about myself. I needed time to reestablish where my personality stopped and hers began. So, after she had taken me back to Lucas Meadows on Tuesday, I told myself: "You are not going over there until *next* Tuesday."

I wasn't the least bit tempted on Wednesday and Thursday. I enjoyed the luxury of thinking I had begun to tire of her. On one of those days I lay stretched out on a chaise beside Joan Dibble's pool, too lazy even to swim. I helped Joan speculate as to why she had not yet received an answer to her letter to Rex Harrison. "They usually write right back," she said. "They don't always write their own letters, but they make their secretaries do it right away. It's good public relations."

"Maybe he writes his own letters and that's why it takes longer," I said. "Or maybe he's run out of photos of himself and has to wait for a fresh supply so he can include one with his letter." The backs of my legs still ached from Tuesday's long hike. We had walked more than five miles, Ursula had said. My eyes were closed against the bright August sun, but I knew Joan, round and relaxed as a friendly Buddha, was surveying me complacently from her chair under the umbrella while I sunned myself on her chaise. Any time now, Mrs. Dibble would bring out a tray of cakes and sandwiches. In this companionable and undemanding atmosphere, I allowed selected playbacks from Tuesday to sift through my mind at the same time I was listening and talking to Joan. "You are like my dream daughter," Ursula had said. "I truly believe I love you more than my mother ever loved me. . . . It would be, oh God, so painful if you ever betrayed me."

"I think Rex Harrison is such a popular actor," I told Joan, "that he doesn't have to worry about public relations. But he struck me as a real nice man and I'm sure you'll hear. Maybe it'll even be in his own writing."

"That would be worth waiting for," said Joan.

Every evening I went up to the empty farmhouse on the hill behind Lucas Meadows. It had become the refuge for my mental life. In Aunt Mona's house, I was tugged back and forth between the demands and restraints of family life; at Ursula's, my imagination was in service to whatever she required of it at the moment; and even though I could relax at Joan's, I was aware that I left the difficult parts of myself behind when I went over to bask in her hospitality.

I had made a practice of frowning so fiercely whenever I met young children playing around the old farmhouse in the evenings that they now left as soon as they saw me coming up the hill. The place had become mine at sunset, and I would sit on the back steps, facing away from our development, and watch the sky change, and go over my life's concerns: not in chronological order, but letting one thing lead to another, and that thing in turn suggest something else. I thought of my mother and Ursula and Ursula's mother; I thought of my grandfather writing down figures in a notebook while I carefully measured the dimensions of the window in a slave cabin and called out the measurements to him; I thought of people's deaths, and of poor Julian writing that song for Karl and Karl never singing it, and Julian wanting to die. I thought of Kitty, lying without a stitch on in Ursula's bed, smiling up at her surprised teacher and saying in French, "You see, my darling, I fixed everything." I put myself in Kitty's place, in Ursula's bed, and then wondered if the strange feeling that resulted meant I would never marry, and that one day I might snuggle up against another woman and have people like my grandmother speak carefully to me because I was different but could not help being what I was. Did I love Ursula? Was I "in love" with her? Was there a difference? Was there some wise, detached person I could ask and who would tell me without judging me? If so, where was that person? Then I suddenly had the urge to go to ask Ursula. Just hop on my bicycle and ride over there and say, "I had to see you for a minute. I want you to tell me honestly, just as an impartial observer would, whether you think I care for you in an abnormal way. If you think I do, I won't bother you anymore, but, you see, I need to know the truth for myself." What would she say? Would she laugh? Would she be disgusted? Would she make me sit down and put her arm around me and stroke my head and say, "Child, child"? I would want her to do the last, of course, but would she, after I had asked her such a thing? The impulse to go to see what she would do—to put myself out of this misery of suspense—became almost overpowering. Then I remembered it was not even Friday yet. And besides, I had never ridden over to her in the evening. I might interrupt their supper. Then she would think I was something even worse than abnormal; she would think I was getting to be a nuisance.

On Saturday, just before lunchtime, I bicycled down to Terwiliger's Store and prowled the aisles, pretending that my mother had sent me for something and I had forgotten what it was. I loitered in front of the soup shelf until old Mr. Terwiliger's beady eyes practically accused me of planning to steal the minute his back was turned. Here by the soup shelf in May she had surprised me, sauntering forward with the basil. But that had been because I wasn't expecting it; things didn't happen like that when you lay in wait for them.

I bought Jem a box of Animal Crackers to appease Mr. Terwiliger, and a Tootsie Pop each for myself and Becky. I chose purple for Becky, her favorite, and was leaving the store feeling let down but virtuous when a truck drove up with two men in it. The ruddy-faced driver, in denim shirt and jeans and cowboy boots, jumped out so lithely that it took me a second to realize it was not a young man but Mr. Cristiana. "Hello there," he said to me pleasantly, heading into the store. Ed was in the truck. "Hi," I said, going over to his window. "How's the fence-building? It's almost finished, isn't it?"

"Yeah, and it's a good thing," he said. "Look what happened to me last night." He opened the door of the truck and stuck out a foot with a cast on it.

"You broke your foot!"

"Ankle," he said. "But the foot's fractured, too," he added importantly. "The doctor said I was lucky to get off as light as I did."

"What happened?"

"Oh, Turk went crazy and tried to kick his way out of his stall. Dad was off taking one of his after-supper walks and nobody could find him. So I had to go over and talk to Turk. I rubbed him down some, and he got calmer, but then, when I tried to leave the stall, he shouldered me into a corner and kicked hell out of me."

"Were you scared?"

"No, I was just mad at myself for getting into that corner. It's one of his favorite tricks and I should've known better."

"I would have been mad at *him*."

"Oh, Turk can't really help himself. He's driven by his hormones, Dad says. All stallions are." He said this proudly, as though it were a good thing to be driven by your hormones and go around kicking people.

"Well, I sure hope it heals soon." I was trying to decide whether Ed had grown more manly-looking over the summer, or if it was just his deep tan from working outdoors and his interesting injury.

"Oh, it'll heal, but not in time for football training. I'll have to sit on the bench this fall."

"That's too bad," I said, trying to think of some upbeat consolation to finish with. But nothing came to mind. Why was it so hard to talk to a simple country boy outside a grocery store, when I had spent hours in the company of a sophisticated woman like Ursula? "Well," I said, drifting backward toward my bike, "they're expecting me at home." I was eager to put an end to this awkward exchange, yet I felt I had failed in the use of my female charms.

"We never did go to that movie," he blurted out. "Are you doing anything tonight?"

"Not really," I said.

"I could pick you up around quarter to seven, if you want. I'll have to get somebody to drive us." He stuck out his injured foot again, as if that, and not the fact that he was under sixteen, was now the reason for needing a driver.

"That'll be fine," I said. "See you then."

As I rode away on my bike, I had the feeling that he was just as relieved as I that our conversation was over. Well, at least we wouldn't have to talk in the movies. Nevertheless, I rode home elated with my victory. It was the outward aspect of it that pleased me most: I was being taken on a date by a boy, and that was a sign to all the world that I was a normal girl and wanted what normal girls want.

"I remember my first date," said Aunt Mona. "It was a catastrophe. As we were walking out to the car, I felt something funny happen to the ruffle around the bottom of my skirt. When I got in the car and had a chance to examine things, I saw that my aunt had only *basted* the ruffle to the skirt and then forgotten to stitch it on the machine. I knew I was sunk if we got out of the car and walked even a few steps: my ruffle would fall off and I'd be humiliated. So I told my date, 'You know, what I really feel like doing is just driving around some. I'm so tired I don't even want to get out of the car.' He gave me a funny look, but then he said okay and we drove out into the country, and I was just congratulating myself on how smart I'd been, when he pulls into this dirt road beside a lake and starts to maul me. 'Hey, what do you think you're doing?' I said, and pushed him away. His name was Bobby Mayfield—they called him Rapid Robert at school, but I thought it had something to do with sports. 'I thought that's what you wanted,' he says, not in a very nice tone. 'I thought that's what you meant when you said you didn't want to get out of the car.' And then we had a fight and he drove me home without a word, and he must have told all his friends, beause it was a long time before anybody asked me out again. What's that old saying, 'For want of a shoe, the horse was lost'? Well, for want of a hem, my reputation was lost. Of course, my poor aunt did her best. She was overworked with all her clients, and had taken time to run up a skirt for me in time for my date. But I've often wondered where I might be today if she had remembered to stitch in that ruffle."

"Married to Rapid Robert?" suggested Becky with a sneer. "Then you'd have to let him maul you all he wanted." She stuck out her tongue and twirled her purple Tootsie Pop around and around against the insolent pointy tip.

"What are you going to wear?" my mother asked me.

"Not a skirt with a ruffle on it," shrieked Jem, cackling hilariously at his joke.

"He's here!" called Aunt Mona, stationed downstairs at her picture window. "He's coming up the front walk on crutches!"

I was dressed and sitting on the edge of my bed, waiting for my cue. The rows of milkmaids smiled at me from the curtains and dust ruffles: they approved of what I was doing tonight. The doorbell chimed; the door opened; the feminine voices of my mother and my aunt spun a welcoming net around Ed's monosyllabic replies. "Justin!" Aunt Mona called coyly. "Someone down here to see you!"

I walked slowly beside Ed, swinging along on his crutches, to the car, where Mrs. Cristiana, now large in her pregnancy, waited behind the steering wheel. Ed opened the back door for me, then went around and got in on the other side next to me. Although his mother had given me a friendly smile, it would have made it less awkward if she had bantered, like Mrs. Dibble, about her role as chauffeur as she drove us silently into the small village of Clove and stopped in front of the movie house. But Mrs. Cristiana either had other matters on her mind or was not one for making small talk.

I don't remember the movie at all, though a look into "My Personal Life" shows me that I carefully recorded it under "This Year's Movie Record." It was *The Eddie Duchin Story*, with Tyrone Power and Kim Novak. Ed Christiana's name is printed in capital letters in the "Went With" column, and I had drawn up an extra column, on my own initiative, where I "rated" each movie with an E, G, F, S, or B, for Excellent, Good, Fair, Stinks, or Best of the Year. *The Eddie Duchin Story* got a G, which may have meant that I really thought it was good, or that I thought it deserved at least a "good" rating because it was my first movie with a boy.

It's not surprising that I don't remember a single scene from the movie, because I was encased, the whole time we spent in the dark theater, in an impenetrable cocoon of self-consciousness. What was Ed Cristiana thinking of me? Would he try to hold my hand? Should I let him if he tried? Would I be his girlfriend at school this year? Would that be advantageous to the impression I would make on others at the school? Would it please Ursula to know that I was "going with" the son of her favorite childhood companion? I decided that, on the whole, it would be a good thing. I ticked off his assets: he was tall; my aunt and mother would be pleased; he already liked me, so I wouldn't have to work to "get" him; and it might amuse Ursula: we could talk about it, and she would tease me a little, but at the same time we would both know I enjoyed her company the most. And also, it would reassure her that I was not going to give her the kind of trouble Kitty had. In every sense, it would be good for my status and self-esteem.

About halfway through the movie, Ed reached over resolutely and laced his fingers through mine. Then he guided our entwined hands to his knee and rested them there gingerly, as if they comprised a sort of clenched beast that needed to be restrained. We sat balancing the beast until our palms sweated and—if my arm was any indication—the blood drained from our respective arms. I suppose I would have become his girlfriend if what happened two nights later had not happened. Of course, after it happened, he avoided me. I don't blame him. If I had been in his place, I would have avoided me too.

We found Mrs. Cristiana waiting for us in the lobby afterward, instead of outside in the car. She told us, slightly embarrassed, that she had been about to drive home and then had changed her mind and decided to stay and watch the movie herself. As she made her confession, she looked incongruously girlish despite her huge stomach and shapeless maternity smock.

"But won't Dad be worried that you didn't go home?" Ed wanted to know.

"I called him from the pay phone in the drugstore," she said. "But he wasn't back from his evening walk. So I told Ann to tell him." She gazed thoughtfully into space for a moment, then added, "I hope you two don't think I was spying on you. I didn't even see where you sat. But it has done me good to get out of the house."

Mott felt it was his duty to take us to church on Sundays, since Aunt Mona had stopped going. "Now that I'm a working girl, I owe myself one lazy morning a week, and Sunday is it," she said. "Besides, Mott, now that we're separated, it won't hurt you with IBM that your wife doesn't go to church. I have nothing against religion, but as far back as I can remember, church has seemed to me more of a social thing than a religious thing. People don't go to church to worship the Lord; they go to see who else is there and what they're wearing. I don't think the Lord minds one bit if I take my cup of coffee back to bed on Sunday morning and lie there thanking Him for a day of rest. It's the one morning in the week I don't have to get up and put on high heels and stockings."

So every Sunday Mott and Becky would drive back to Clove from his houseboat in Kingston, and then drive Mother and Jem and me all the way back to Kingston, to the Episcopal church there, since there wasn't one in Clove. Mott was a Methodist, having been raised in a Methodist orphanage, but he said the Episcopal church would suit him just as well. The most important thing, he said, was for us to have something we had known back home. I think Mott was the only one who enjoyed these Sunday mornings when he would proudly accompany us all to St. John's. We took up a whole pew, the five of us. I was afraid everyone would think Mott was my father and he was married to my mother and we were their children; people probably did think that. During the service, Jem would fidget; Becky would sigh loudly and roll her eyes every time she had to stand up or kneel for the responses; my mother and I shared a hymnal and I could hear how she sang in a faraway, off-key voice. I knew and she knew that she was not an avid churchgoer. In our family, church had been my grandmother's province. My grandfather had been an agnostic; my father had liked to sleep late on Sundays, and my mother often stayed in bed with him while my grandmother and I went off to church. I missed my grandmother beside me. She had sung in a sure, clear voice, enunciating the words firmly, as though she believed every one of them equally. I missed her perfume—a subtle scent that reminded me of many small flowers not everyone would know the name of—and I missed the elegant little crosses she made with her thumbnail on her forehead and chest after the Gospel had been read. Nobody did that in this church. As I knelt between Mother and Becky in this building of dark gray stone where we knew nobody, and listened to the congregation muttering the General Confession in rough, clipped accents, I could scarcely believe I was hearing the same words. "The remembrance of them is grievous unto us; the burden of them is intolerable": with her rich, soft-consonanted voice, my grandmother had made them sound like a very old poem that still had its magic in it. I realized that, for me, my grandmother *had* been church.

During the sermon, I daydreamed. Almost all my mental images concerned Ursula's tales of the past, things Ursula had said, or might say in the future, to me, things I had saved up to tell Ursula, and possible interpretations she might invest them with. When the sermon was over and the congregation's voices swelled into the final hymn, I was listening to music I had never heard: I was hearing Karl sing "Der Doppelgänger" in his sinister bass baritone, and imagining the entire DeVane family—whose lives would be changed by this person—succumbing to the power of Art.

She is the most interesting person in my life, I thought, as we filed out of church and Becky tugged at Mott's jacket and said, "Well, *after* we take them home, can we go out to eat?" Even her old memories are more interesting than anything that has happened to me, or anything that is likely to happen to me in this place, I thought, and asked myself what harm there would be in riding over to the pond this afternoon. *She* did not know about my silly resolution to wait a whole week. Why had I made such a resolution anyway? It seemed pointless. It even seemed heartless. Why, maybe she thought I was tired of her. Maybe she was feeling hurt by my neglect.

It was after lunch, and I was loading the dishwasher. Mother and Aunt Mona sat with the Help Wanted section of the Kingston *Freeman* spread open before them on the kitchen table.

"Here's one," said my mother. " 'Saleslady. Paid vacation and hospitalization. Schumann's, North Front Street.' "

"Louise, you wouldn't be able to stand Schumann's. Their clothes are sleazy."

"I wouldn't have to wear their clothes, would I? It would just be a job. And they might hire me."

"Louise, your attitude is wrong. You're too humble. Of course they would hire you. But the job's not good enough for you."

"Mona, dear, *I'm* not very good. I've been practicing my typing faithfully and look at the mistakes I still make. Nobody in their right mind would hire me to type their letters."

"Well, what else have we got?"

"Here's a possibility. 'Excellent opportunity for intelligent woman with pleasant voice for part-time telephone survey work from your own home.' Except I was hoping for something full-time. But doing it at home would be good for Jem. Then I could be here when he gets out of school."

"You don't need to be, Louise. Beck and Jimbo will ride the same bus home from elementary school. We've already gone over that. You just worry about finding the right job for yourself."

" 'Middle-aged woman, to keep house for lady living alone. Hours flexible.' I wonder if I qualify for 'middle-aged'?"

"Are you just trying to make me mad, Louise? You? Cleaning somebody's house?"

"Well, if it's an honest living and it pays well . . . If I were alone in the world, I wouldn't mind being somebody's live-in housekeeper. I'd take care of their house and they'd take care of me."

"That's just ridiculous, Louise. That's just irresponsible. I can't understand your attitude. I can't understand a person not wanting to be in charge of her own life."

My mother smiled ruefully.

"Shall I turn on the dishwasher," I asked, "or will it be too noisy?"

"Oh, turn it on, Justin," Aunt Mona said. "We're getting noplace fast over here."

"I think I'll go for a bike ride," I said.

"I was wondering when you were going to remember your friend Ursula DeVane," said my know-it-all aunt. "Or maybe you want to see someone else on Old Clove Road today. A certain gentleman on crutches who just might be sitting on the porch."

"I do not," I said, angrily turning on the dishwasher.

"Come and kiss me," said my mother as I started off in a huff. Her hand lingered on my hair after we had kissed. I saw from the way she glanced at me that she believed Ed Cristiana had displaced Ursula in my affections and that was why I had snapped at Aunt Mona: for guessing the truth. Although I was glad she was relieved of one of her worries, her mistake made me feel lonelier than ever.

There was no one sitting on the Cristiana porch. There was no one at the pond, either.

But it was still early. It was not even two. After my disappointment at not finding her there, I reasoned that this was the earliest I had ever come. I sat down on the crumbling doorstep of The Finishing School to wait. From my position I would be able to see where she would emerge from the pines. "Hi," I'd say. "Boy, are you still sore from Tuesday's hike?" "Well, hello there, Miss Independent," she'd say, quickening her stride, "I was beginning to think you were angry at me." "Why should I be angry at you?" "Ah, why indeed! For walking you like a soldier. For getting you drunk and making you cry. For telling you all those terrible stories about my family." "No," I'd say, "it's just that I've been kind of busy. I had to go spend some time with my friend Joan, and then last night I went to the movies with Ed Cristiana."

Time passed. It was so quiet I could hear the whish of the wind in the tops of the pines and the tiny drones of insects around the pond. Periodically, a katydid would dominate everything with its insistent announcement that winter was coming. School began next week. Where was she?

I got up to stretch my legs and walked around the pond. I imagined that I had brought my bathing suit and that I changed into it and went for a swim and she found me in the pond. Or maybe I would even dive under and hold my breath and scare her, as she had done to me that time. But I knew I was too cowardly to go into that pond.

I went inside the hut and walked around, picturing how it must have looked when the roof was whole and there was furniture in it. Karl's bed. Yet they had done it on the floor, she said, "her skirts pushed up and crushed . . . those clothes she was so careful about! And there were his bony knees and elbows, sticking out from more angles than I had thought possible. . . . They had put down the covers from his bed onto the floor."

To have more room, I supposed. His bed was probably too narrow. A "tutor's" bed. When the father had that bed moved in, he naturally assumed only the tutor would want to lie in it.

Ursula's blanket—or, rather, Julian's old Army blanket—was folded, palletlike, in the corner of the hut, just as it had been when I first surprised her lying on it, trying to read her book. That corner of the hut had been in sunshine when I first crossed its threshold, but now it was in shadow. "There I was, trying to reread Proust," she had said when she was thanking me, ironically, for my dramatic entry into her day, "but he is all wrong for this year. I have reached a time in my life when I need to be refreshed by the unexpected."

Had I, then, fulfilled my role for the summer as her "unexpected"? Maybe by now there was nothing unexpected left about me. Maybe I was a known quantity to her, and she was no longer "refreshed" by me. She knew when I was likely to come to the hut, and what I would say when I came; she also knew when I was likely to stay away. Probably she had driven away from Lucas Meadows on Tuesday afternoon, after our hike, smiling to herself and thinking: Poor Justin. I really overdid things today. I'll bet anything she is resolving right this minute to stay away from me for a whole week. She'll almost make it, too. She won't break down until . . . let's see . . . next Sunday afternoon.

She still did not come. The act of waiting, in such circumstances, contains a built-in paranoia that only intensifies as the frustration is prolonged. Of course she isn't coming, I thought, pacing around inside the hut, whose walls emanated an ancient smell of dampness and decay; she knows I'm down here, but there's nothing more she needs from me. She even knows my answer to the question she had been dying to ask me. "What I want to know, Justin," she had said, "is what you would have done if you had been in my place. Would you have done what I did, or do you think I was a monster?"

And what a pussyfooting answer I had given! "I'm not sure," I had hedged. "I don't know what I would have done. But I can understand why you thought you had to do what you did."

Even that had been a lie. I didn't understand. Maybe if I had risked saying, "I don't understand, but I want to, I want to, more than anything," she would be down here now. She was a woman of risks, she approved of risk-taking. And maybe she *wanted* me to judge her sternly. She would have respected me for it, and found me more interesting. But I had not said what I really felt, because I was afraid I would lose her. And now I probably *had* lost her. She thought of me as a predictable, polite little coward, not worth leaving the house for. No wonder she didn't feel it worthwhile to walk to the pond to see if I was there. Old same-as-ever, pussyfooting Justin.

Why hadn't I said, "No, I have to tell you the truth, Ursula. I would not have done what you did. I might have hoped somebody *else* would find her out and bring her to her senses, but I would not have betrayed my own mother even if she had murdered somebody. Because she's my mother, and I couldn't respect myself if I did a thing like that."

I looked down at the Army blanket, folded into its pallet shape, and forced myself to imagine my mother rolling around on it, with her legs around a stranger. Nausea crept into my chest. I remembered the sound of my mother's passion-cry, coming from behind the closed door of their bedroom in Fredericksburg, the afternoon of my birthday a year ago. The nausea rising into my throat, I snatched my father from his rightful place and put a stranger in the bed beside her and replayed the sound of her cry. If I had looked through the keyhole and seen this other man, who had, say, sneaked in through the window while my father was downstairs reading a book, would I have gone down and told my father?

"No," I croaked aloud in the empty hut.

Suddenly I didn't want to be here anymore. The hut was changed now that I knew its history, and I didn't like the things I thought here, or the way they made me feel. Ghosts were not just Halloween things in sheets; ghosts were real; ghosts lingered in the air when people had done things. The ghosts of their deeds lingered with them. How could *she*, especially, bear to come down here and lie on that blanket and read and think in the very place where she had seen what she had seen, and then done what she had done about it? How could she call such a place her refuge? And how could she make a joke of it, even on my behalf, by calling it a "Finishing School," when a whole family, and one person's *life*, really had been finished by it?

I couldn't wait to get out of the hut, out of the woods. I tripped on a root and almost fell, I was hurrying so fast. I was afraid she *would* come now, and I didn't want to see her, feeling the way I felt. My initial instinct to wait a whole week had been right, I told myself, running toward my bike. I had not yet assimilated all she had told me. I rode back down the haywagon path to Old Clove Road feeling I'd had a narrow escape. If she had come, she might have read things in my face that would have hurt her and then have made her hate me. Because people had to hate those who hurt them: it was self-preservation.

The strangest thing was that I still could love her. And, in some ways, I loved her more than ever. I felt, as I pedaled grimly uphill, that I would like to suffer or endure some great sacrifice on her behalf. It would be my payment to her for not being able to believe in her as I had wanted to. If I could suffer for her sake, I might be relieved of some of the pain I felt at losing her as my ideal.

At the top of the hill, where the land leveled off at the Cristiana farm, I was met by a new sight: Mr. Cristiana, whip in hand, was riding the stallion around the ring. Somehow, I had never imagined Turk with a rider on his back, and it was a letdown to see that proud, dangerous force trotting in a circle on a tight rein, lifting his feet obediently to the rhythm imposed by the man rising and falling in the saddle. Mr. Cristiana saw me pass and waved, and I waved back.

All beautiful, dangerous idols fall, I thought, if you keep your eye on them long enough.

On Monday morning, I woke out of a deep sleep, knowing that something was wrong. In the first place, I never woke up this early. My mother was indulgent about letting me sleep as late as I wanted in summer, and sometimes I did not make it down to breakfast until ten o'clock. It was usually the light that finally woke me, streaming through the cotton fabric of my milkmaid curtains and shaming me into getting up. But today it was a noise unlike any I had ever heard before: a brutal, repetitive, metallic impact, followed by a creaking, splintering sound.

I lay there, staring groggily up at Ursula's poster of the *Normandie*, which I had taped on the wall facing my bed. From my position, it was as if I were in the ocean and the prow of the great ship were bearing down on me. What could such a terrible noise be? And what was it doing here in our development? We'll tell Mott and he'll complain to IBM and IBM will give somebody hell, was my first reaction. Then I heard Jem's shrill shriek and his feet pounding up the stairs. He burst into my room. "They're smashing the house in!"

"What?" For a second, I thought he meant ours. But that couldn't be. The sound was not close enough for that.

"The old farmhouse up on the hill! There's this big old yellow bulldozer smashing it in! The front porch is already gone, I saw them do it!"

"Oh *no!* We've got to stop them!" I was already out of bed, fumbling in my closet for something to put on. "Run down and tell Mother to phone Mott at IBM and have him send somebody over to stop them!" Purple spots danced in front of my eyes, I had leapt up so violently from bed. "*Hurry,* Jem! Don't just stand there."

Jem raced downstairs and I heard him cry, "Call Mott!"

Shaking with outrage, I pulled on my underpants and shorts. There was no time for the stupid bra. Still buttoning my shirt, I ran to Aunt Mona's bedroom, which had a view of the hill and the farmhouse. Just as I looked out the window, the yellow monster rammed its powerful blade into the front of the house. Jem was right, the porch was already gone—the front steps with it; now, at this latest blow, the whole front of the house shuddered and lurched forward. "Stop it!" I shrieked out of the window. But the man at the controls went on butting the trembling house with his machine.

I ran downstairs, half-crazy. Even if Mott was starting out right now, it might be too late when he reached Lucas Meadows. But it was worth a try. Maybe the house could be salvaged.

I stopped, appalled, at the entrance to the kitchen. There sat Becky, being served like a queen by my mother, who was setting a stack of hot buckwheat cakes in front of her. Nobody looked the least bit upset.

"Where's Jem?" I demanded loudly.

My mother raised her eyebrows at my tone. "He's gone back up the hill to watch them tear down that old house." She reached across the table and handed Becky the syrup, which she could perfectly well have reached herself.

"You mean nobody has called Mott?" I said threateningly.

"What's this about calling Eric?" said my mother. "He's at work, he won't want to be disturbed. Justin, what's wrong with you? You aren't even dressed properly—"

"They're tearing down the house," I screamed, "and you don't even care! And even if you did care, you have no power! You can't do anything! At least Mott works for a powerful organization. He can make them stop. I'm going to call him—"

"Justin, you are *not* going to call Eric Mott. Get control of yourself. That old house has been condemned. Eric was one of the people who kept after the village to get it condemned. It wasn't safe for children to play around."

She spoke of it already in the past. Outside, the sickening clanking, crushing, splintering noise went on. I knew it was already too late.

Becky, seeing that I was about to break down, stopped dousing her pancakes with syrup and watched me with interest.

"You mean you *knew* Mott was trying to get them to tear down the house," I said, "and you didn't even *tell* me?"

"Justin, I don't understand why you are so upset about that old house. I know you go up there by yourself sometimes, but—"

Becky looked down long enough to cut a neat wedge of buckwheat cakes—her favorite breakfast, which Mother made for her frequently—with her knife and fork. She checked to see that the slabs of butter were securely inside, then poured a bit more syrup on the wedge and guided the dripping morsel to her mouth. Chewing with obvious pleasure, she resumed watching me. Even if I had been about to cry, that impudent little gaze would have dried my tears at their source.

"You don't understand," I said to my mother, wanting to hurt her as much as I could, "because you don't understand *me*. I may be your daughter, but I've come to the sad conclusion that you don't understand the way my mind works or what is important to me. You just aren't capable of it."

I watched long enough to see her whiten at the lips. Then I left the kitchen. I went back upstairs to my room and lay down on the bed and listened to the destruction of my sanctuary. As the morning grew brighter and hotter, the quality of the noise changed. I knew it was because there was less resistance each time the big machine lurched forward with its destroying blade. I knew that by now the house as I had known it existed only in my memory.

On the other side of my closed curtains, I saw the clear blue outline of the little bottle Ursula had sent me for my birthday. On that morning, I had awakened full of longing for the old life in Fredericksburg; now I would have accepted the earlier part of this summer, when Ursula DeVane still shone from the distance as my unblemished heroine, and the old farmhouse stood securely on the hill—a silent and trusted repository for my daydreams and meditations on life. I considered getting up and parting the curtains, banishing the milkmaids into shadowy folds, so the bottle could "assert its blueness," as Ursula had put it in her letter; but the present hopelessness of "Raspberry Ice" suited my mood better. When my mother found me lying in its muddy, mauve gloom, she would realize just how depressed I was and would be sufficiently worried to overlook the harsh things I had said.

She was a long time in coming upstairs, and when she did I could see that she had not forgotten my words. She did not come over to the bed and kiss me and stroke my head. Standing formally in the doorway, she simply said she was about to take Jem shopping for school things in Kingston and asked if I would like to go along.

"No, thank you," I said.

"It might improve your outlook on life to get out in the sunshine and look at some fall clothes. Becky is coming. We'll probably stay in Kingston for lunch."

"Fine, you all go on," I said, thinking of the good time they would have without me. "If I get hungry, I'll fix myself a sandwich."

She continued to stand there, in her formal way, looking at me as if I were a problem to be solved, rather than a flesh-and-blood daughter. "I don't know . . ." she began, "I think I'd feel better if you came along. I feel uneasy leaving you here by yourself, in the mood you're in."

"If you think I have to go, then of course I have to go," I said, raising myself up with a sigh, though I was relieved that I would not have to stay here by myself.

"Yes, I do think so," she said coolly. "Soon you'll be an adult, and then you can do whatever you please. But, for a few more years, I'm afraid you're going to have to please me."

"At this rate, I probably won't make it to adulthood," I said tragically.

"Just what is that supposed to mean?"

"Everything is being taken away." I began to cry. "By the time I'm grown up, there'll be nothing worth living for."

Whether it was my tears, or my words, she came in and sat down on the corner of my bed. She looked at me gravely, but did not touch me.

"I may not be capable of understanding the way your mind works," she said slowly, "but I will tell you how it looks to me from where I sit. You haven't had a bad summer. In fact, you've had a pretty good summer. You've had places to go and things to keep your mind busy. You've had Joan, whom you say you like, and Joan's nice pool to swim in; you've had the interest of Miss DeVane, who has interested you, too. You are always animated when you come back from a visit with her; my guess is, you have had at least one person this summer who understands how your mind works—"

"I didn't really mean—"

"No, let me finish. The other night, you went out with a boy you seem to like, and in another week you'll start back to school, where there'll be more new friends and new things to learn, and, who knows, maybe even more people who are capable of understanding how your mind works. And underlying all this—I know it seems trivial to you—is a house to come home to, and food put on the table for you, and people who care what happens to you, and love you, and want you to have the luxury—yes, the luxury—of making sense of the world in small, safe doses until you have built up a character strong enough to last you the rest of your life. You have a home, and you have me in it, whatever my failings. So, forgive me if I don't see that 'everything is being taken away' from you, though it may look that way this morning."

"I'm sorry for what I said downstairs. It was just that they were tearing down the house, which was my important place, and there you were, spoiling Becky with her buckwheat cakes. I just wanted to hurt you, that was all."

"Well, you did a pretty good job." Then she relented and kissed me. "Now get dressed properly and let's see if we can't find something nice in Kingston for you to wear back to school."

"She was the most wonderful woman I had ever met," Rebecca Mott, counselor and psychologist to precocious criminals, would tell me years afterward, across the table in a vegetarian restaurant of her choosing. "After you came to live with us, and I saw how wonderful she was, I used to fantasize that she had had an affair with my father while your father was still overseas. I had her meet my father when he was on leave after sinking that Japanese sub, and they conceived me. Your father was off in Europe and never even knew. She went back to you and your grandparents in that snobby house in Virginia, and nobody knew anything. She wore a tight corset to keep them from knowing. Then, just when she started to get big, she went off to another town by herself and had me. And my father wanted to marry her, but she wouldn't, she said it would hurt too many people. So he met my mother and told her, 'I will marry you on the condition that you agree to raise this baby as our own and never tell a soul.'

"And then when your father was killed in that car accident, and your grandparents were dead, and there was nothing to stay in Fredericksburg anymore for, your mother said to herself, 'Now there is nothing to stop me from being with my other daughter.' And she called my father and said, 'I want to be with Becky. You'll have to find a way.' So my father moved to the houseboat and separated from my mother so my real mother could come and live in our house. I carried that fantasy around in my head for years . . . years after you three had moved out of our house and gone back to the South. I kept that fantasy alive even when I was old enough to realize that the dates would have made it impossible. There was no physical way I could be your mother's child.

"But you I could never understand. With a beautiful, kind mother like that, you preferred to spend time with that ugly, crazy woman over on Old Clove Road. I'll never understand that. But I was glad you were out of the way. It was so much better when you weren't around. I remember that day when she took us all to Kingston to buy clothes for school. I tried on this royal-blue sweater and she said, 'Oh, Becky, you look so pretty in that sweater, I am going to buy it for you myself.' And then we went to that cafeteria for lunch and I remember I had chicken à la king—it was one of the best meals I ever ate, even though I don't care for meat anymore—and the whole day would have been perfect, except for you moping around. What was the matter with you? All you did was sigh and mutter under your breath about 'when are we going home?' I remember wishing you would get run over by a car. I told my analyst about that. She said it was a natural reaction. I didn't mind Jem. He could be a nuisance, but he was okay. Except I was jealous of him getting to have all those naps with her."

"I wanted to get back to Lucas Meadows that day," I tell my cousin, "because I wanted there to be time to ride my bicycle over to Old Clove Road and see that crazy woman. I can't agree with you that she was ugly. I loved the way she looked, probably just as much as you loved the way my mother looked. I needed to see her because I was upset about that old farmhouse's being bulldozed. I used to sit up there almost every evening, and it had come to be a sort of extension of myself. And I felt she would understand this in a way my mother couldn't. But, as it turned out, we got back from Kingston too late for me to go over there before supper. And then after supper I decided to go anyway. Oh God, how I wish I hadn't."

"Oh. Was that the famous evening?"

"That was the famous evening."

My cousin, whose looks haven't changed much since she was a pert-faced girl, flicks her flat gray gaze at me. "You still feel guilty about it?"

"Of course I do. I always will."

"You ought to try analysis."

"Oh, I'll probably just stick with my guilt. I work a lot of things out in my acting. Maybe that's why I hold on to my little storehouse of pain. Every so often I come across a real treasure in there that I can use in my acting."

My cousin shrugs. "Suit yourself." She looks at her watch. "Well, I've got to get back to the real world."

She never came to see me once, the whole seventeen months I was in that play. She didn't apologize or make excuses. Once, during the run, when we were having lunch like this, she flicked her eyes at me and said tonelessly, "Everyone's talking about that play you're in; that must make you feel good." It was the nearest she had come to acknowledging my success, and I felt absurdly grateful for even that tidbit. Yet she's got a reputation for being a wizard with those murderous kids everyone else has given up on. Something in her connects to them and they respond. My cousin still interests me more than I interest her, and that, I suppose, is why I persist in asking her out to lunch and enduring her slights. I always have to invite her; but she always accepts. One day, I keep telling myself, I am going to crack the code of Becky. Some days I feel closer to success than others.

It gets dark earlier at the end of August, but for those who eat at the family hour, there is a good-size portion of light left between supper and dark. Children can play for another hour outdoors; it is still safe to ride a bicycle; a man or a woman so inclined can go out alone for a walk and return home before the sky has lost its final translucence and people start to wonder where they are.

After supper I made myself go up the hill to survey what was left of my old sanctuary. I went slowly, my head down, in case anybody was watching me from our house. I was acting my sorrow a little, just as someone in mourning feels she has to put on an outward show of sorrow even though her grief really is sincere. After we had come back from Kingston, I had heard Mother and Aunt Mona speaking, in low voices, about my being "upset." I had stood on the stairs outside the kitchen and eavesdropped as my mother told my aunt how I had rushed down and wanted to call Mott and ask him to stop the destruction. I thought it was loyal of my mother not to tell Aunt Mona the other thing I had said. (Now I realize that she was far too hurt by it to want to repeat it. The fact is, she still hasn't completely forgiven me, because, every few years or so, when we are talking, she will slip in that old, deadly phrase: "Of course I probably don't understand the way your mind works, but . . .")

"I'll phone Mott later, and maybe he can explain to her why it had to come down," I heard Aunt Mona say.

Some children from the development were wandering

around on the hill, gaping at the interesting heap of rubble that, only this morning, had been a house. A toilet stuck up incongruously from the piles of splintered boards. That fallen tower of bricks had been the chimney. The children parted warily, and somewhat respectfully, to make room for me, as though I were the owner of the house and had come back, after an absence, to find it devastated. They watched curiously as I walked, deliberately grave, around the boundaries of the old farmhouse. It had seemed to take up so much more space when it was standing. Tomorrow, Aunt Mona had said, the men would come back and load the lumber into trucks. "It's good, strong, seasoned wood," she had said. "Some builder will be tickled to death to buy it." If it was such good, strong wood, then why did the house have to come down?

Jem joined me, still out of breath from running up the hill. "You're not going to cry, are you?" he demanded.

"Of course not," I said, addressing myself to the rest of the junior audience as well as to him. "I just think it's a shame, that's all. They could at least have taken away the toilet. It's like leaving someone's underpants on top of their casket."

One of the children snickered.

It was impossible to say a real good-bye to the place with all these children milling around. Jem, who now played with a couple of them, jumped up on a board that had fallen on top of a brick, and walked it, seesaw-fashion. Several others followed suit, one small girl falling off. Dumb Mott, I thought; the house is far more dangerous as a heap of rubble than it was standing there minding its own business. And I had actually wanted to phone him to save the place!

I turned and started back down toward the development. Dreariness filled me like a lethal injection. The sky was still bright. The sun still shone on the tops of the trees, though the ground was already in shadow. Yet there was nothing to look forward to, nothing to forestall my return to ordinary family life, to the inevitable drawing of my bedroom curtains, when the milkmaids would flounce once more around me, flashing their pert, uniform smiles.

"Wait, Justin!" Jem caught up with me. He took my hand.

"What are you going to do now?" The disconsolateness in his voice betrayed that the end-of-day malaise had hit him, too.

Suddenly I knew what I was going to do. And nobody was going to stop me. To make certain of it, I wasn't going to ask permission.

I didn't say anything until we were in the garage, where I kept my bike. Then I said, "Jem, I need to be alone for a while. Will you please tell Mother I've gone for a ride and not to worry; I'll be back before dark."

I swung up on the bike and was off down the driveway before he could answer.

"I wasn't going to see you until tomorrow. I made this silly rule that I wouldn't see you for a whole week. The reason was, I had to think about what you told me, I had to decide how I felt, all on my own, without you watching my face. At first, I'll admit, it seemed strange that anybody could do that to their mother. But things happened today that—well, I won't say I would betray my mother in the exact same way you did, but I see now that she can't understand me the way you do. And I did hurt her today. You and I are two of a kind: we both hurt our mothers.

"I think I have more in common with you than anybody else. You said I was like your dream daughter. Well, I've decided I want to be your friend for life and your mystical daughter.

"Don't worry, I'm not going to turn into another Kitty. I'm just not built that way. In fact, just this past Saturday night, I had a date with Ed Cristiana. But that doesn't change the way I feel about you. You're something different in my life; you're unique. Nothing can ever change the way I feel about you. I've put it to the test this week. You're not perfect, but who is? This week I've learned that when you really love someone—and I don't mean in the Kitty way—you come to accept everything about them, all the moments in their history that have made them into just what they are. And I can accept everything in your past, because it has made you *you*. . . ."

⊐   ⊐

All I wanted to do was to ride to her house, see her alone, and tell her that. Then ride off again, leaving her surprised and moved and flattered. Fifteen minutes there, five minutes for the declaration (its brevity would impress her and make the event more ceremonious), then fifteen minutes back. There was a whole hour before dark. I wanted her to know, and it seemed urgent that she know tonight. Then I could carry the security of her knowing back to Lucas Meadows with me. It would be like a pledge between us, a profound moment in which we sealed our bond of alikeness and swore to be true to it. She would enter into the spirit of my declaration. She loved things like that; she loved drama and courting Fate. She would rise to the occasion, I was positive, even though her mouth would twitch with the beginnings of the irrepressible smile: the smile that told me I was young and she knew more than I did but nevertheless she found me charming.

And then, carrying our solidarity inside me, I could ride home, say an affectionate goodnight to my mother, thank her for the skirt and the fleece-lined jacket she had bought me in Kingston that day, and go up to my room and face "Raspberry Ice" and the milkmaids with impunity. Henceforth I would render unto biological motherhood its filial dues and affections, but my secret pact with Ursula would have vaccinated me against losing touch with my best, my imaginative self.

As I whizzed past the Cristiana farm, I caught sight of Ed's little brother carrying a pail of something across the stableyard to the barn. He didn't see me, and I was glad. I didn't want to break the intensity of my purpose by having to call hello.

I flew down the hill and over the wooden bridge and past the haywagon road. She wouldn't be at the hut now, not this late. The only thing I was really worried about was that I would catch them in the middle of eating. I shrank at the image of one of them coming to the front door, wiping his or her lips on a napkin. "Oh! Justin? What a surprise. We're still having supper, but do come in." How embarrassing that would be . . . but I decided I had to risk it. My declaration must be made tonight; I had become superstitiously urgent about it now: it must be made before nightfall, it must be made before Tuesday, the "allowable" day on which I could see her again. I had to see her now, to prove to myself that I accepted her with all her strangenesses and faults.

The DeVane house, with its austere black shutters and ancient gray stones half buried in limestone mortar, looked lonely and forbidding. In contrast, the road in front was just now a generous, curving swath of orange-gold, reflecting the late-afternoon sun. I laid down my bike and, feeling nervous but fated, walked up to their porch and knocked firmly on the door.

Julian DeVane opened it. "Why, hello." He was obviously surprised to see me. He was carrying a long-stemmed glass of red wine.

"Oh God," I said. "I interrupted your supper."

"N-no, we ate early. We had s-sardines on toast. It was our f-favorite meal when we were little." He smiled wryly, inviting me to approve of their childish indulgence. "Won't you come in?"

"Is Ursula busy?"

"She's gone for a walk. I was just s-sitting here drinking wine."

"Oh." I tried not to let my disappointment show. "Well, I wanted to tell her something, but I guess it can wait."

"C-come in, anyway. She'll be back. This time of day is so m-melancholy, don't you think?" He gave me a wistful look, his head cocked to one side. There was a disheveled air about him I hadn't seen before. I realized that he was probably a little drunk.

"Well, okay," I said, "but I really can't stay long." I went in and he closed the door softly behind us. "They'll worry if I'm not home before dark. How long do you think Ursula will be?"

"It varies. S-sometimes she g-goes in one direction, s-sometimes in another. You know Sissie. She's p-predictably unpredictable. Will you join me in a glass of w-wine?"

"No, thanks. I'd better not drink and drive."

It took him a minute to respond to my joke, but then he uttered a soft, appreciative laugh. Swaying slightly, he led the way to the chintz sofa, where, from the looks of things, he had staked himself out for a sunset hour of lugubrious drinking. A stack of library books and a vase of pink and white phlox had been pushed to one side of the table to make room for a rotund half gallon of Chianti. I sat down on the edge of the sofa, in the corner next to the books; he sank down with a sigh and topped off his glass with more wine. "Wh-where have you been all week?" he asked. "We m-missed you."

"Oh, I had all these social obligations. And then buying clothes for school—all that stuff." Outside the window, the sky grew fiery-brilliant behind the darkening mountains and the tower as the sun began its descent. I was thinking I would have to make a few minutes of polite conversation before I could leave. Then maybe I could still find Ursula, meet her as she was returning from her walk.

"Will you be gl-glad when school starts?"

"In some ways I will. In others I won't." I waited for him to pick up on the last part, which meant I would miss his sister.

"Ah," he said ambiguously, nodding.

We both stared shyly out the window at the sun slipping down toward the ridge of the mountains.

To break the silence, I said, "I guess you've been practicing a lot?"

"Practicing?"

"For your recital next year. Your comeback," I reminded him.

"Oh," he said. He tilted his glass and swirled the red wine around. "There's still p-plenty of time for that," he said, meditating on the little whirlpool. Then he took a sip of wine and swallowed it very slowly. "You know, anyone with the m-money can hire a hall and give a recital," he said. "A 'c-comeback' is another matter. Especially if you haven't been anywhere to c-come back to."

I didn't know what to say. I looked down at my tanned knees, aligned like two upside-down shields. How it would hurt Ursula to hear him talk like that!

"Ursula has great faith in you," I said. "And . . . well, I'm not any musical expert, but when you play, something happens inside me. I think that's important, the way your playing makes other people feel."

It sounded incredibly naive, even though I was sincere.

He put down his wineglass and contemplated me with his oblique, in-turned brown eyes, so much softer and less demanding than his sister's sharp, pouncy, penetrating ones. "You are a lovely girl," he said. "My sister cares for you a great deal. You've been g-good for her."

"I don't know about good, but I care for her a lot, too."

"That's obvious," he replied with a gentle smile. He looked down at his hands and flexed his fingers. "I haven't c-cared for many people, but I've grown quite f-fond of you, too."

"Well, thank you."

We both looked away, and there was another shy pause.

Then he said, "I have a s-selfish reason for hoping you'll st-stay in our lives."

I couldn't imagine what he was going to say next. Influenced by the tenuous, dreamlike quality of my being here like this at this hour, and his being in this wine-loosed, melancholy mood, I was seized by the fantastic notion that Julian DeVane might be going to propose marriage to me—when I "came of age," or something. It might be that he really loved me, or it might be more in the spirit that Kitty's father had proposed marriage to Ursula: because he wanted to please his daughter. But Ursula was not Kitty, I reminded myself. Nevertheless, in the space of those few silent seconds, I imagined myself into a bizarre but strangely contented future, in which, by making myself Julian's child-bride, I would have gained Ursula as a sister forever.

"You have?" I asked him, with indrawn breath.

"Yes. S-so that after I disappoint her, she will have s-someone else to transfer her ambitions to." He picked up his glass and drank deeply, as if the wine were medicine. "Sissie n-needs that."

I have had several decades in which to consider the other ways I might have responded to him. And I have the rest of my life to play with alternate endings to that scene. A playwright with a penchant for the less sensational denouement might simply have had the girl, who was sympathetic and perceptive for her age, tell the depressed musician, "You know what *I* really need right now, at this sad, sunset hour? A little of that solace my grandfather used to call 'J. Sanity Bach.'" And to oblige his young guest, the musician would pull himself out of the seductive suction of his down-spiraling reverie and go to the piano, and prop up the lid, and take out the music for *The Well-Tempered Clavier*, or maybe the *Goldberg Variations*, and, as the light dimmed slowly on the set, he would play himself and the girl back into the rational, balanced universe of that artist whose life and work seem so blessedly immune from the petty snares and torments of this world. And, soon after that, the humorless, overprotective uncle, summoned by the aunt to console the girl, and sent by the mother to find the girl (who had not returned from her bicycle ride before dusk), would knock at the door and provide comic relief, unctuously refusing a glass of wine from his sanguine host, and judiciously shepherding the girl off the set.

Soon after their exit, the sister would return from her walk. Teasing her brother for sitting morbidly in the dark, she would turn on the lamps. (In a way that indicated symbolically that she was the light of his life?)

"Justin came by," he would say.

"Justin! At this time of evening?" (The sister looks startled, not very pleased.)

"She wanted you. But she ch-cheered me up."

"I'm glad. But what on earth made her want to wander around here at *this* hour?" (The look of alarm and displeasure remains on the sister's face, but the brother doesn't see it.)

"S-something she had to t-tell you. Then her uncle showed up, l-looking highly suspicious of me, and made her go home. You d-didn't see them when you were coming back from your walk, I take it?"

"No. Tonight I decided to cut across the fields."

"Dear old Sissie. You have to have your v-variations."

(The sister goes to the window and gazes out intently at the blooming night. Her back is to her brother, her profile to the audience. One hand goes to her throat and remains there, long enough to indicate her awareness of a crisis narrowly averted by sheer good luck.)

"Ah, me," she would say, recovering her light and amused tone. "The urgencies of the young."

And her secret, as well as her brother's bout with despair, would be kept under wraps a while longer. Long enough, perhaps, to turn the action into another mode of drama in the next act: a more contemporary mode in which all the characters are permitted to survive the last act because their creator has endowed them with enough blissful ignorance, or cynicism, to avoid any fatal confrontations with the really unspeakable betrayal, the unthinkable compromise, the ultimate shattered ideal that would destroy an old-fashioned "hero," obsessed with notions of destiny and honor.

But I am not a playwright, neither in the ironic nor in the tragic mode.

I was not even an actress then. I was a fourteen-year-old girl who liked to think of herself as sympathetic and perceptive for her age, but who was beginning to be repulsed and a little scared by the overwhelming reality that pervaded the twilit room where Julian DeVane and I sat. That reality was acknowledged failure—tantamount to damnation in the eyes of the young. I felt sorry for Julian DeVane, of course, and even sorrier for Ursula, who I knew had invested too deeply in him to be able to "transfer her ambitions" to someone else. But the atmosphere of the room was becoming so oppressive I could not bear it. Now I could smell the sour wine on his breath. I thought I sniffed faintly the toast from their supper, and it made me depressed, no longer envious, to think of all their years of suppers together, abetting each other's childhood fantasies about the destinies they were entitled to.

I wanted to get out of there, into what little light was left, before I was infected by Julian DeVane's pervasive despair.

"I'd better be running along," I said. "If I'm not back before dark, my mother will worry. I'm not supposed to ride at night, because I don't have a light on my bike."

Julian put down his glass and walked me to the door. "I'm afraid I haven't been very good c-company, but you were sweet to listen," he said.

I was cheered up by all the light still left outdoors. It had been much darker inside the house. He remained in the doorway, watching me to my bike. With the long-stemmed glass in his hand, his languid figure leaning against the doorframe, he looked like a model posing as a decadent aristocrat.

I felt I should say something encouraging before I rode away with all my youth and hopes. "You just wait!" I called to him. "When you play that Chopin scherzo at the end, you're going to bring down the house!"

He smiled, then, and raised his glass to me.

I've never been able to relive this next part fully. I mean, I can remember—all too well—what happened, and how things looked and sounded, but I have absolutely no memory of what I was feeling or why I did anything I did.

I'm still able to recall everything about starting home, down Old Clove Road. I was hoping against hope that I might still meet Ursula on the road, returning from her walk, and that I could stop and tell her what I had come to tell her. And then ride off romantically into the last light, leaving her touched and bemused.

By the time I cycled past the haywagon road, where I had so often turned in on my way to the pond, on days when I *knew* she would be waiting for me, I had accepted the probability that I was not going to see her tonight. The road from here on bordered Cristiana land, and it was unlikely, with all that bad feeling between her brother and Mr. Cristiana, that she would go strolling in the direction of their house. She had undoubtedly walked in the opposite direction, and that was why I hadn't seen her.

I braced myself for the effort of the steep hill ahead. Then one more possibility occurred to me. She might have cut through the fields and stopped at the hut. Maybe to have a swim. That was the kind of thing she might do: swim naked at dusk . . . fearlessly! . . . smiling to herself as she splashed and floated among all those invisible pond creatures, the thought of which made me writhe with squeamishness.

I circled and went back to the haywagon road and jolted down its bumpy terrain until I reached the place where I always dismounted, and I pulled my bike into the trees so nobody could see it from the road and be tempted to steal it. From there I went along on foot, as always, into the little pine forest, toward the pond.

I can remember the silky feel of the pine needles carpeting my approach. And how, when I entered the woods, the darkness of them came on as suddenly as if a canopy had been lowered over me. Yet I could look up and still see light sky. I saw what I thought were two birds, darting in and out of the light in a skittish, abnormal pattern; then I realized they weren't birds, but bats out hunting for insects.

I remember the uncanny, buoyant certainty that flooded me, as the dim gray shape of the hut came into sight through the trees. Of course she's there, I remember thinking. I bet you anything she's there.

Then the "cinema" memory takes over. My senses continue on with me, but not my feelings, thoughts, or motivations. I am like an observer at the movies, positioned by the camera behind the eyes of the girl. I can "see things from her angle," but I have no access to her mysterious inner workings.

When, exactly, was it that I heard their voices? It seems as though I heard them while I was still far enough off to retreat with no one the wiser. I could have gone home and licked my wounds, and contemplated her treachery, and no one would have been hurt but me.

But maybe I didn't think of it as treachery yet. Maybe I wanted to be sure, before I condemned her. At any rate, I continued stealthily on to the hut. I held in my breath so they wouldn't hear me. I was careful to approach on the hut's "blind" side, where there was no window.

There was never any attempt to sneak up and "spy" through the empty window socket in the other side: as Abel Cristiana had spied on Ursula's mother and seen her kissing the German; as Ursula had witnessed the furtive coupling of the tutor and the "lady of the house."

Even if I had tried, I doubt that I could have seen much. The woods were already too dark.

I slid down on my haunches, bracing my back against the rough stones of the windowless wall of the hut, on the eastern side.

I could hear them talking. Their voices were too low for me to make out what they were saying. It was mostly her voice, anyway. The caressing, ironic voice of the old *raconteuse*, weaving her magic around someone else.

Intermittently, there came a low, gruff reply. Once, a short, harsh laugh.

The light drained out of the sky. I must have known it was getting late. I mean, I registered it with my senses, but did I think about them, over in Lucas Meadows, growing concerned about me? Didn't it occur to me that someone would come looking for me? What was I transfixed by, as I crouched there, hugging my knees? Was it numbing sorrow? Or stubborn revenge?

I knew from the leisurely exchange going on behind the walls that they had already done what they had come to do. Or did I know it? Maybe I still held out hope that they were only in there to talk.

I don't remember.

My neck was getting stiff from craning it forward so as to try to catch words as their voices floated out of the open doorway and around the thick wall to me. Once I thought I heard my name, but I couldn't be sure.

The reflection of the sky was slowly swallowed up by the darkness of the pond. Legions of little pond frogs sang their hearts out.

I sat on. Doggedly.

Then I saw a flashlight dancing jerkily along. It came from the direction of the DeVane house, closer and closer through the trees on the other side of the pond. I heard two men's voices. A polite, hesitant one. A sterner, businesslike one.

". . . n-not now, I don't think," said the first. I heard the stutter clearly, amplified by the pond.

Then: "Justin?"

The call of Mott, piercing the stillness, ringing across the pond. Not really expecting an answer; just covering all the possibilities.

Dead silence inside the hut.

Why didn't I just sit tight and wait for them to go away? If no one answered, surely they would have.

Or did Mott start shining the flashlight all over the place, in the pond, in ever-widening arcs toward the hut, and, rather than have him illumine something unbearable to his companion, I offered myself as a decoy.

I'd like to *think* that was my motive.

But in that case, why didn't I simply get up, call out, "Coming!" and go straight over to them. "Sorry," I could have said, "I just lost track of the time," and meanwhile I would be leading them away again, back through the trees and across the field, and up to the DeVane house, and on to Mott's car, waiting in front. Then when we were driving off, and Julian was safely and ignorantly back in the house, I could have said, "Oh, Mott, my bike. I left it down the haywagon road. But I don't think anybody will steal it. Mother can drive me over to pick it up first thing tomorrow morning."

That would have been the sensible thing to do. Everything might still have been saved.

But I didn't do that. Instead, I leapt up with a cry ("harrowing," Ursula would describe it to me in our final interview), and raced headlong to the pond and threw myself in.

I remember the sensation of hitting the water. Like a mean, cold slap in the face and chest. My clothes and shoes filled in-

stantly with pond water, dragging me down in a frightening, unexpected counterforce, just as I was surfacing. I went under
again.

As I struggled once more to the surface, I saw Mott tearing
off his shoes. But before he had time to take the plunge, I was hit
broadside by another body, which started grappling with me,
trying to get her arm around my neck. *She wants to drown me* was
the first thought I can remember. I struggled, swallowed water,
fought. "Be still, you silly child!" she cried, maneuvering herself
around me and treading water.

Then I realized she was trying to *rescue* me.

"But I can sw—" I choked, and then my mouth was brushed
by a small, cold, resilient object that I subsequently realized was
one of her breasts.

"Help me, for God's sake!" she cried, fastening her elbow
around my neck in a lifesaving vise.

Then I went limp, humiliated beyond resistance, and let her
tow me to the edge of the pond.

As soon as we reached the bank, I freed myself. I could hear
her breathing raggedly—the heroic "rescuer"—as she climbed
out behind me.

Mott was standing by, already holding out his jacket to me.

A barechested, barefooted Abel Cristiana also waited at the
bank. When Ursula struggled up the bank, he came forward and
wrapped the Army blanket from the hut around her naked body.
His stomach hung out over his belt, but he at least had had time
to put on his pants.

As the horsebreeder wrapped Ursula in the blanket, I saw
her look beseechingly toward her brother. Julian DeVane turned
his face away.

("I assumed you couldn't swim," Ursula told me in our last
interview, in my aunt's living room. "I thought you were trying
to drown yourself. . . ."

"Of course I can swim. I told you. I've been swimming
practically all my life. Don't you remember me telling you that?"

"Yes, but I thought you might have been lying. To save face."

"Not everyone is a liar," I replied cruelly.)

Mott put his jacket around me. "I'm sorry about this," he said to Mr. Cristiana. The horsebreeder nodded, stony-faced, and led Ursula away to the cabin, presumably to dress.

Then the three of us were walking back through the woods and across the field: Julian, Mott, and I. Mott, holding me carefully around the shoulders, as though I might escape, aimed the beam of his flashlight for our feet to follow. It was difficult for me to walk, with the water squishing in my shoes. The two men did not speak until Mott said, "I'm going to get her right home and have her mother put her into a hot tub." As though he were my father.

"That's a good idea," replied Julian.

He accompanied us all the way to Mott's car. I noticed that he was trembling, but I couldn't bring myself to look at his face. I couldn't bring myself to say "I'm sorry" or even "Good night." But I remember the gentle pressure of his fingers on my arm, just before I got into Mott's car. "It will be all right," he said softly, almost as if he were comforting himself as well as me. "Everything will be m-much better in the m-morning."

XII.

It was morning, but there was nothing good on the side of waking up: I knew that, even in a semiconscious state. The phone jangled, was picked up on the first ring. My mother's voice, one floor below, spoke quietly, confidentially, to someone. Then I must have slept again. "She's got to know," a voice said. "Know *what?*" I demanded; but no sound came out, so I figured I must still be asleep.

Finally I opened my eyes. Becky was peering at me from the doorway.

"What do you think you're doing?" I asked.

She shrugged. "She wondered if you were awake yet," she said in her bland little voice. She was scrutinizing me in a strange way, as if I had broken out with some disease but didn't know it yet. "I'd better go tell her you are," she added, giving me a final, interested once-over before she turned and ran downstairs.

My mother came in. She, too, had the air of entering a sick-room. She felt my forehead with the back of her hand. "You don't *seem* feverish," she said, sitting down on the edge of my bed. "Do you feel feverish?"

"No, ma'am. Just sleepy."

"You've slept fourteen hours. You went right to sleep after your bath. It's noon now."

"Is it?" I was surprised, but made no attempt to get up.

"Are you hungry? Becky and Jem are having grilled-cheese sandwiches downstairs."

"No, thank you. I think maybe I'll just lie here a little longer."

"Justin, would you like to tell me what happened last night?"

"Didn't Mott tell you? He's the one who came poking around. Nothing would have happened if he'd stayed home and minded his own business."

"I sent him to look for you, Justin. He'd come over from Kingston especially on your behalf."

"On *my* behalf?"

"Mona called him. Because you felt so bad about the house being torn down. We thought maybe he could explain why it was necessary. You wanted to call him yourself yesterday morning."

Yesterday morning. Had all this happened only since yesterday morning?

"What did Mott tell you happened last night?"

"That he went to the DeVanes' house to ask if they had seen you, since he couldn't find you anywhere on the road. Julian De-Vane told him you had been there visiting with him and might have gone looking for his sister at the pond. He said you often met her there. He offered to show Eric the quickest way, across the fields. And, just as they got there, you ran out from the woods behind the hut and . . . jumped in." Her eyes sought mine. I knew she wanted to ask *"Why?"* but thought it wiser to wait until I offered the information. But *I* didn't know why. Only that I regretted it bitterly, and yet was already constructing justifications for the act so that I would not be disgusted with myself beyond endurance.

"Did Mott tell you about them?" I asked, making my voice hard.

"Yes, he . . . last night he thought there was a chance of . . . well, saving some innocent people pain. Eric is a kind man, Justin, you should give him credit for that much. After you had gone to bed, we did discuss the chances of keeping their secret, at least until Mrs. Cristiana has had her baby . . . maybe even longer. Eric said he believed you could be counted on to . . . keep your own counsel. But now I'm afraid things are too complicated for that. . . . I'm afraid it is all going to come out. Oh darling, I wish I could shield you from this, but I can't. . . ."

"Shield me from *what?*" The look on her face was enough to make me sit up in bed.

My mother took me in her arms. "Ursula DeVane phoned Eric this morning. To ask if he would be willing to appear before the coroner—they always try to establish evidence of a motive, even when it's— Oh, Justin, that poor woman's brother hanged himself last night."

Late that afternoon, Mott brought home my bike, lashed to his luggage rack. I watched from a window as he methodically unwound each piece of rope, lifted the bike tenderly to the sidewalk, propped it on its kickstand, then coiled up the ropes and returned them to the kit of useful items that he kept in the trunk of his car. He wheeled the bike up our cement driveway and into the garage. Although I could not see him there, I could imagine his self-satisfaction as he completed the safe return of one more cherished item to its proper home.

Then he came in, and accepted Aunt Mona's offer of a cup of coffee. He had taken off early from work, he told us, and stopped by the coroner's, as Ursula had asked him to do. Every member of the household, wanting to hear more, followed him to the kitchen.

"She really wanted you to tell *all?*" asked Aunt Mona, sliding a meaningful look toward Jem, who had been told that Mr. DeVane had died, but not how, and nothing about the "all" Aunt Mona was alluding to. As for my cousin Becky, I judged from her complacently knowing demeanor that she had been told as much as my mother knew; from up in my room, I had heard them buzzing away, after Jem had gone outside to play.

"I questioned that, myself," said Mott, sipping his coffee

importantly. "I phoned her back, just before I left work this afternoon. I said, 'You're sure, now, that you want me to go through with this?' And she said yes—she sounded very calm—she said she'd already told the whole story just as it happened. She said she knew it wasn't going to be as easy on her this way, or on certain other people—"

"I should say *not!*" interrupted Aunt Mona caustically.

"—but she said she felt she owed it to her brother's memory," Mott went on. "She said it was better for people to know he had done it in anger—she used a French phrase—than to think he had given up on life. Apparently there'd been bad blood between him and the other party for a long time."

"Did he die of bad blood?" Jem asked Mott.

"Not exactly, son," said Mott, rumpling Jem's hair, "but I would say it definitely contributed."

"There was no question of—" my mother began hesitantly. "I mean, at the coroner's, nobody said anything about Justin's having to be involved."

"No question at all," said Mott firmly. "I explained the circumstances, and he agreed that there was absolutely no point in upsetting the child further."

Becky flicked her eyes at me—to see my reaction at being called "the child," I suppose. But, although I knew that my behavior over the past twenty-four hours had earned me an indulgent demotion in the eyes of protective adults, I was not sorry to have the mask of "child" to hide behind while I dealt with my own disturbing thoughts.

"I'm so relieved," said my mother to Mott.

"I ought to go and see her," said Aunt Mona. "I ought to take something over there. A casserole? After all, he was Beck's piano teacher; and she was so friendly to me when she came to pick up Justin. Or maybe a cake would be more suitable. Louise, help me; you know the etiquette of these things."

"I don't know about 'etiquette,'" said my mother, "but I *have* had some recent experience in these matters. Speaking from the receiver's end, I think a person is more grateful for something solid and simple you can pick at, to keep up your strength—but without feeling you're pampering yourself with a whole meal. Cakes are more for the company that comes."

"I phoned Bill Van Kleek this morning, after I heard," said Mott. "His daughter took music from DeVane. Mrs. Van Kleek said she was going to take over a tray of cold cuts."

"I wonder about fried chicken," said my aunt. "But she might not like it our Southern way."

A distant smile lit my mother's face. "When my mother died, this woman in her garden club had her maid fry up the most delicious-looking chicken. And after the funeral guests had all gone home, we were sitting down to eat it—just the family—and I had to take a phone call, and when I came back I burst into tears. Rivers jumped up from the table and put his arms around me and said, 'You've worn yourself out with all this grief and company, Louise,' and took me away to bed. But the real reason I was crying was that, when I came back from that long telephone call, I saw that Rivers was eating the last drumstick, and no one had saved one for me. Of course I couldn't tell him that. Now I'm so glad I didn't, and I'm even gladder Rivers had that drumstick."

"I think maybe a casserole's wisest," said Aunt Mona.

Julian's funeral was held on Wednesday. As Wednesday was also the first day of school, there was no serious question of my going. If I had wanted to go, I think my mother would have let me; but I didn't want to. And yet I thought about the funeral all during the school day. I didn't want to think about it, but I kept seeing images. I saw the church: the same Dutch Reformed Church where the young Karl, fresh from Germany, had played the organ, and where Becky had been humiliated during her recital; I remembered how Ursula had told me Julian had been haunted by that church, distracted by its memories to the point of bad judgment: how he had thought it would *inspire* the children when he called in his old pupil from the street just before Becky was supposed to get up and play "Für Elise."

And now that gentle, stuttering, melancholy man was dead.

One more person in my life was dead. But he was the first one I had known who had wanted to die.

He had hanged himself from one of those ancient meat hooks upstairs in the oldest part of their house, the part they called "the office." Using his belt for a rope, he had stood on a chair until he was ready, and then kicked it away. Had his last thought been: This will punish her for betraying me? Or: Now I don't have to go through with my comeback? I thought it might have been a combination of both: her act's having given the final push to a decision already brooded upon for years. But nobody had asked for my testimony. "The child" had been upset enough. And what did it matter anyway? It wouldn't bring him back. *She* was the one who was left to suffer. Let *her* choose his motive and broadcast it to the world, even if, as she had told Mott, "it wasn't going to be as easy on her this way, or on certain other people."

Her story—the one she told to Mott and the coroner, and which filtered down to me through my mother and my aunt— was that, after the fiasco, when I was led away in my wet clothes, she and Abel Cristiana had remained for a while at the hut, discussing what they ought to do. Abel thought perhaps he would have a man-to-man word with Mott, and she would talk to "the girl," and perhaps they could prevent it from spreading all over the village and hurting Abel's family. Neither of them believed Julian would say anything; he would simply rage inwardly and perhaps "punish" Ursula with silences and looks of disgust; she knew he would never disgrace the family name by telling anyone.

Then Abel had gone home, and she had sat for a while longer on the threshold of the hut, fully dressed now and wrapped in the blanket because it was chilly, but unwilling just yet to go back up to the house and face her brother's acrimony. And then, like a miracle, she heard what she thought was her reprieve. Coming across the field and through the trees, carried upon the stillness of the night air, were the unmistakable notes of her favorite piece, the Chopin scherzo. She took it to mean he had forgiven her, was signaling: *Let things go on as we planned.* She was overcome with gratitude and relief as she listened to the music. When it was over, she sat just a little longer, smiling to herself with embarrassment, thinking of what she was going to say: after all, what she had done was not *that* awful; and she *was* proud that she'd had the courage to run out naked like that, when she believed the girl was drowning.

She walked back to the house across the fields, thinking that maybe they would open a bottle of wine and talk the whole thing through—as they had talked through so many things in the past.

He was not in the living room waiting for her, as she had expected. She called to him and there was no answer. She saw the empty half gallon of Chianti on the table and concluded that he had gone upstairs and passed out, after playing the music. She went up to his bedroom, but when she turned on the light, she saw that the bed was empty.

Then she thought he must have gone outside, perhaps down to the terrace, where they often sat together after dark, sipping wine and making plans. But he was not on the terrace. Had he gone back to the pond to look for her? But even in the dark, it was unlikely that she would have missed him. She called out, called his name across the field.

Could he have *driven* off? She hurried up the slope and around to the old barn, which they now used for a garage. No, the station wagon was still there.

Then she looked up and saw that the light was on in "the office." On the field side, as she was coming home, she would not have been able to see it, because on that side of the wall was only the old "mow" door, sealed now.

What was he doing in "the office"? Her first thought was: Maybe he's looking through the file folder I've been keeping for his recital, going through the flier samples and the estimates from the recital managers—his way of showing me that bygones are really bygones and he's more interested in getting on with what matters.

But then why didn't he answer me when I called out? When he heard me come upstairs to his room, why didn't he call through the door of "the office" and say, "Sissie, I'm in here"?

When she found him, she first tried to hold him up, relieve the pressure. She climbed on the chair he had kicked away and tried with all her strength to support his hanging body with her one-armed embrace, while with her free hand she worked to loosen the belt buckle. Then she abandoned that futile, exhausting method and ran to the sewing room in search of the sharp scissors.

She managed to cut him down, and slapped his cheeks, and put her mouth down on his and breathed and breathed.

She told Mott she thought she had felt something, at one point: a breath? a quiver? She couldn't be sure. Just a hint, the barest promise of life.

She called the rescue squad, who arrived remarkably fast; but it was simply too late.

Aunt Mona and my mother and Mott went to the funeral. The church was "respectably full," Aunt Mona said. All the parents of Julian's pupils were there, and IBM had sent an impressive casket spray. The talented young musician in tennis clothes who had ruined Becky's recital was there in a dark suit to play the organ. He played beautifully, although he broke down once. The pallbearers were Mr. Terwiliger from the store and five male members of the Huguenot Society, all of whom, Aunt Mona said Mrs. Van Kleek had told her, were direct descendants of the first patentees of New Paltz.

"She asked about you," my mother said, that evening.

I looked up from my homework, which I was trying to make last as long as possible. I was doing it in Aunt Mona's living room, a neutral place I had gravitated to since Tuesday. I had been in this room hardly at all since we came here last spring, and so it was antiseptic when it came to memories and associations. *She* had stood in its doorway and flashed her eyes mirthfully on the prize seafoam-green carpet crisscrossed with its plastic runners, but she had not come in, she had not sat down. It was not her kind of room, and that made it easier for me to be in it, rather than upstairs in my room, where the air was still thick with my former feelings. Or downstairs, for that matter, in my mother's perfume-scented quarters, where Becky lounged at her convenience. I would be welcomed down there, by my mother, at least, with solicitude ("the child" had had a shock), but I hung back in self-conscious reluctance from the scene I knew I was destined sooner or later to play there: the Prodigal Daughter returning, chastened, to her true mother.

"She wanted to know how you were," my mother went on. "She asked if you had suffered any ill effects."

"And what did you say?" Was that cold, guarded little voice mine?

"I said you were young and strong and going to be just fine. I thought it was kind of her to be so concerned, when she must be going through the most unimaginable . . . I mean, I thought I had the copyright on sorrow, but I wouldn't change places with that woman for anything on earth."

"Neither would I," I said with more feeling.

"She also said to tell you she hoped you would come and see her. 'When she's ready' was how she put it."

I stared down at the colored picture on the first page of my civics textbook: a view of the Washington Monument and cherry trees in blossom.

"I'm not ready yet," I said.

"That's completely up to you."

Giving me the new, solicitous look, my mother wavered in the doorway. Her tact was such that she would not cross into my antiseptic territory and with tearful hugs force acknowledgments . . . confessions. She would wait; she knew how to wait. That was what her look eloquently said. Then she went back to her own territory, where Becky was no doubt sprawled with her homework and Jem was still giving off hyperactive sparks from his first day of school.

Be cold. Be guarded. Be polite. Think of it this way: last spring you came here—were dragged here—against your will. There was nothing here. Nothing except school and a roof over your head. The past gone. The future, years ahead; too far ahead to think about. And then you met this person, and this person interested you and made the summer fly by. And now you're back where you started. School. A roof over your head. The future, someday. Look at it that way.

Outwardly I was cold, guarded, polite, dutiful—above all, dutiful. Duty is a wonderful time-filler; it makes you feel useful, it makes you like yourself; it keeps unpleasant thoughts at bay. I remembered my grandmother, when she came home from the hospital after her operation: how she got out her yarns and started embroidering pillows and Christmas tree ornaments, even though Christmas was almost a year away. "In case I'm not feeling all that good, later," she had said. And she had been right to do her Christmas embroidery early.

I studied. I went for bike rides around the development with Jem. I helped Jem with his reading and his lettering. I set the table. Loaded the dishwasher. Ran Aunt Mona's vacuum cleaner over the seafoam-green rug, first carefully lifting all the plastic strips. I heard them muttering about me and my "shock." Aunt Mona, entering into the spirit of my dutifulness, suggested we do a "fall cleaning." One Saturday afternoon, we took down curtains, ran them in loads through the washer, dried them on "Fluff," then ironed them in relays and hung them again. "You know," I said, "I've been thinking. I really would like to paint my room. I mean, I like the color you painted it for me last spring, but now I'd kind of like a change." Aunt Mona was beside herself with enthusiasm; her earrings quivered ecstatically as we discussed possible colors.

How easy it was to deceive people.

But at moments when my guard was down, just before falling asleep, for instance, I would see pictures. Sometimes I felt she was sending these pictures to me. I saw her eating supper alone in that gloomy kitchen; saw her dusting his room, stopping to look at certain photographs; saw her deciding not to dust "the office" yet; saw her sitting on the old chintz sofa, her feet up, looking out the window at the mountains and the tower. Staring at the piano, with its keys covered; remembering certain music. I would feel a surge of pity, and be glad I could feel it. Wouldn't I be a monster if I couldn't?

But the great fascination with her was gone. Evaporated. And with it, the "love" I had believed would last forever. I could *remember* feeling it, but that was in the past. It was as though she had died, too. ("You see, she had *stopped being* the person I knew. She had become another woman.") She had said that about her mother, the way she had felt about her mother after spying on her in the hut. I was aware, even then, at fourteen, of the ironies and parallels between Ursula's trauma and mine. I had repeated her history; I had visited upon the adult Ursula her own childish betrayal. Yet I also felt betrayed. I felt . . . somehow . . . *used* by Ursula, made to perform by her as the catalyst-figure in her tragedy. She had led me on with her charms; she had sown her seeds of suggestion; she had done everything but give me cues! She had been a witch, I decided, able to make me perform in her story, robbing me of the chance to be the heroine of my own story. But I was no longer bewitched. I felt sorrow and guilt about Julian, but, I convinced myself, it would have happened sooner or later, probably. I remembered how he had been talking, the night of his death. And hadn't she told me how he had wanted to die after Karl had gone out of his life? I did, truly, feel pity for her, for the wasted existence she was now doomed to, in that house filled with its terrible history. (With the romantic blindness of the young, it never occurred to me that she could leave the house, go somewhere else and start over. Something in me didn't even want it.) But the pity I felt for her left me free. I was glad not to be obsessed by her anymore. Glad not to be always wondering what she was doing, wondering if I felt "too much" for her: I felt like someone who had come in close contact with a fatal illness and survived—though others had not been so lucky. I hoped to get on with my own life, even if there were not many exciting prospects in this village. I frankly hoped to avoid meeting her.

Aunt Mona and I became buddies. She would join me in the living room, put her feet up, and watch her programs, the sound turned low, while I did my homework.

"You don't have to keep it that low," I said one evening.

"I don't want to disturb your concentration."

"You won't. I don't mind the sound."

"Well, if you're sure, maybe I will turn it up just a little."

We drifted into a pattern. I would do some homework, watch the programs at the same time, and then we would talk during the commercials. My homework wasn't very demanding. I envied Joan Dibble her small private school in Kingston They were studying the Etruscans, a mysterious, artistic race of people in Italy who never got anywhere; but Joan said her teacher was going to prove they were better than the Romans. That kind of learning seemed more interesting than Checks and Balances, which I had already learned about last year in Fredericksburg.

"I know Louise is pleased with herself for being a working girl," said my aunt during a commercial, "but I think she's being exploited."

My mother had answered an ad in the paper, and now worked from ten to three on weekdays in a boutique that a lady named Barbara Feldman ran out of her own home. Mott had found her a secondhand car she could afford, so she no longer had to depend on Aunt Mona for transportation. Dr. Feldman was a dentist, and Barbara Feldman had told my mother that even if they didn't make a profit it was all right, because her husband could claim "Barbara's Boutique" as a tax write-off.

"She seems happy," I told Aunt Mona. "I mean, she soaks her feet when she comes home, but I don't think she feels exploited."

"I didn't say she feels exploited, I said *I* think she's being exploited. I know the ways of the world better than Louise, because I've been out fighting in it longer. Where else could that woman have found someone who would take that insulting pittance of a wage, *and* unpack all the stock, *and* dress the window, *and* stand on her feet all day, *and* model the clothes? I think it's an insult to someone of Louise's background."

"But she said she enjoys the modeling. And she likes talking to the women. And the thing she likes most of all is that she can get home about the same time Jem does."

"I suppose so," Aunt Mona conceded. "But if it were me, I

wouldn't put up with it. I just thank my stars I passed my real-estate boards. Now, look out, world, this gal is going to make some money."

"What will you do with it?"

"Oh, travel a little. See the world. Go claim my share of adventure and romance. I could hardly ask Mott to pay for *that*, now, could I? Though the dear soul probably would if I asked him."

"What about Becky?"

"Oh, I'll wait until Beck goes to college. That gives me eight years to make my fortune. I've got it all planned. In eight years I'll only be thirty-nine. I know that seems ancient to you, but there'll still be plenty of kick left in this old gal. I have a lot to make up for!"

In eight years, *she* would be fifty-two. ("You are turning into a woman," she had said, "and I . . . I am turning into an old woman." "*You* won't be old at fifty," I had protested. "Ah, Justin, it's such an experience just to watch your face. . . . But you mustn't fret or be outraged; it's the law of the world: as one generation comes up, the other goes down. Children bury their parents, and protégées grow wings and take off blithely from the nests of their aging mentors.")

One evening during a commercial, Aunt Mona said, "Well, guess what I heard through the grapevine today."

"What?"

"That Adelaide Cristiana has forgiven her husband. No reproaches, no recriminations, complete amnesty. The subject never to be mentioned between them again. On the condition that he never see her again."

"That seems fair, I guess."

"Yes, it's probably the best all around. She's got the new baby now. That makes five kids. You can hardly walk away from a wife and five kids, not to mention all that livestock. Not even for Cleopatra. The town wouldn't be big enough to hold the two of you if you did."

"What was the new baby?"

"You mean you don't know? You mean Ed didn't tell you?"

"Are you kidding? He hardly speaks to me. When he and Ann get on the bus every morning, they can hardly bring themselves to look at me."

"Oh, you poor child! Why didn't I think—!" She shook her plumage violently at her own stupidity; her earrings went into frenzies. "They know you were there—they connect you . . . but you mustn't think they hate you, or anything like that. Put yourself in their place. Wouldn't you feel hardly able to look at someone who had been there when—?"

"I've already done that. I don't blame them. I'd behave the same way myself."

"You're a doll, Justin. I told Louise there was no need to worry about you. I'm a close observer of people, and I knew from the beginning you were a smart, sensible girl. You're feeling lonely and shaken, but, my goodness, that's normal. You were with them so *much* this summer!"

(". . . I said, 'Louise, I've known Justin going on two months now, I'm a close observer of people, and in my opinion she's a smart, sensible girl. She's been brought up to tell right from wrong. Now, for some reason, she's taken a shine to Ursula DeVane, and Ursula DeVane seems to have taken a shine to her. I think we can trust Justin to get what she can out of knowing this woman, who is a cultured person, whatever airs she puts on—and leave the rest alone.' ")

"Well, it was a boy, the new baby," Aunt Mona went on, even though the program had started up again, and it was *I Love Lucy*, one of her favorites. "I guess they're glad; you can always use another boy around a farm. But, you know, your mother and I were discussing it again the other night, and we both agreed the whole thing could have been hushed up a lot more. If only she hadn't told the coroner everything, and played on Mott's sense of honesty to tell the coroner. There was no need for the whole thing to be all over town. What good did it do? I mean, it couldn't help the poor brother, he was already out of his misery. Why did she have to dramatize everything to the hilt? I told Louise it was almost as though she *wanted* to paint herself as the scarlet woman."

I had had similar thoughts myself.

I made new friends at school. Although I cherished the image of myself as a deep and solitary creature by nature ("You gave me the impression you were just a lonely waif, all by yourself in an alien land," *she* had said), I was a sociable person by upbringing. My grandfather had taught me to be curious about the lives of others; my grandmother had instructed me in the art of conversing with people in their own language, and had reminded me frequently that listening is also an art. And I had long recognized in myself—I am still not comfortable with the knowledge—that I had an enormous need to be liked. This caused me to invest considerable energy and imagination into "putting myself over" as a likable person—as I would later learn to project images of different characters to an audience.

The ninth-grade math teacher, who was also the football coach, nicknamed me "Dixie" on the first day of school because of my accent, and the name caught on. I was surprised to find, as the weeks went by, that I didn't resent it. On the contrary, it made everything easier. It gave me a new persona—a quick-smiling, fluent one, to whom shyness and brooding were anathema—and provided many more people with access to me. "Hi, Dixie," the captain of the football team called out as we passed each other. "Oh, hi there," I called back, not at all shy or worried about what he was thinking of me: it was "Dixie" I was playing, Dixie with her quick (if shallower) smile, and a whole set of mannerisms that made the day flash by with a minimum of self-consciousness and doubt. And she became "popular," more than the low-key Fredericksburg Justin had been among her old cronies. There I had been one of a group. Here I was something singular, exotic. The magnolia surrounded by cornfields. But such a "friendly" magnolia! A magnolia who "really cared about people" and "had an interested word for everybody." Being Dixie made it far less embarrassing when I passed Ed or Ann in the halls or saw them on the school bus twice a day. *"Hi!"* Dixie would say, with not a bit of memory resonating in her chipper tone. "Hi, there," more pertly, as the crystal of her "popularity" hardened around her like a multifaceted shield. She was not hurt by their coldness as much as I would have been. And before I left the village, I am sure *they* saw me more as "Dixie" than as the girl who, last May, had pretended she could ride, the obsessed and lonely girl who had pedaled past their house one too many times for the good of the family, the girl whose hand Ed had held as if it were a creature that might escape. Or the girl who remembered what she had seen at the pond.

The milkmaids approved of Dixie. And Dixie did not see why Justin had felt so threatened by the milkmaids. They were only an old-fashioned pattern printed on a fabric.

I did repaint the walls of my room, but it took two coats. Dour, muddy, threatening old "Raspberry Ice" wasn't going to be glossed over with a lighter color as easily as Justin had let Dixie cover up for her at school.

Late one afternoon, when Becky was practicing her ballet again in her room, and Aunt Mona was still at work, and my mother was soaking her feet downstairs after a modeling session with the Hadassah ladies, I removed the blue bottle and the crumpled poster of the *Normandie* from my closet and carried them down to the garage and put them under some other garbage in the can.

"What did you just throw away?" demanded Jem, coming up on me suddenly.

"Nothing worth keeping," I said, "just some old decorations from before I painted my room."

"Oh," he said, losing interest.

In the mornings, I sat on the right side of the school bus. In the afternoons, coming home, on the left side.

Just the opposite from last spring, when the view I could hardly wait for was the one of their house.

The trees changed color. From the window of the bus, I watched the flamboyant death scene of summer. The sumac glowed scarlet; the willows turned chartreuse, then straw-colored; the clusters of purple asters that grew by the side of the road hung on, stalwart and colorful as ever, even after the first frost.

Sometimes I forgot, and sat on the wrong side of the bus, the side closer to their house, and one October day I realized I had done this only when I happened to look out the window and saw her raking leaves. Her hair was tied back with the kerchief she had worn when I had seen her cutting lilacs last spring. She was thinner, I thought, but she raked with a conscious vigor and pride. The way you would rake if you expected to be observed and commented upon by people passing on the road.

The knowledge of her went straight through me. I might as well have been inside her body, holding myself in that valiant way, playing my part, knowing the village would observe me and say, "I saw her out raking leaves today. She looked thin, and still sad, of course, but, all the same, she had that pride."

For a moment, I *was* her. And the realization that this could still happen, that I could still understand her and feel her from the inside like this, was unwelcome to me.

One day in early November, Becky and I were making a cake after school. Or rather, I was making the cake, from a Pillsbury's Devil's Food Cake Mix, and Becky was standing by to scrape the bowl when the time came.

The front doorbell rang.

"Get that, would you, Becky? Mother's resting."

Becky groaned and rolled her eyes, but she went. She came back, carrying an empty casserole dish, and looking as if she knew something compromising about me.

"Who was it?"

"*Shh.* She's still here. She wants to see you."

Becky never used people's names. But I knew, from the way she arched her eyebrows, whom she meant.

"Why did you have to tell her I was here?" I whispered. "Now I'll never get this cake made." Yet I felt a strange excitement. Now I would have to face her. What would it be like?

What would I feel? "Don't you dare sneak any of this while I'm gone," I told Becky.

She was standing in Aunt Mona's living room, with her back to me, looking out of the picture window at the street, where several children, including Jem, were riding their bicycles. She wore a dark blue suit I had never seen before, with a skirt that was too long for the fashion now, and dark stockings, and those shoes with the thick heels and high vamps, also from another decade, that she had worn the night she came to pick me up for *Hedda Gabler*. Her hands were clasped behind her, and her head was held high: just as the leading actress might pose, with her back to the audience, looking out of a window, as the curtain goes up.

"Hi," I said from the doorway, in my cheerful, shallow "Dixie" voice.

She spun around, an expectant smile already prepared for me, and, as she did so, the heel of her shoe caught briefly on one of Aunt Mona's plastic runners. She looked down to see what the impediment had been, and when she raised her face again, the old mirth was tugging at her mouth. Her dark, mischievous eyes sought mine, inviting me to share the joke.

I smiled, but only politely. Letting her understand that my allegiances were now to the people of this house, however bourgeois their practices might appear to outsiders.

She caught my meaning at once. The irrepressible smile was repressed. Then she took me in with a sweeping glance that half convinced me she was reading the complete text of my thoughts about her since that night at the pond.

"Justin, how are you?" she asked at last, in her low, compelling voice.

"I'm fine, thank you." I walked across a plastic runner and sat down on the sofa. "Won't you sit down for a minute?"

"Why, *thank* you." There was a touch of irony now, the tone of an adult humoring a child who is trying to play grown-up. She sat down beside me on the sofa. Underneath the suit she wore a black pullover sweater and a white blouse underneath. Her hair had grown longer, and she had clipped it back with pins, just below her ears. She looked very schoolmarmish, very much in control. The new hairstyle was neater, but made her look more severe. Then I remembered that day in her room, when she had been brushing her hair in the mirror and had told me that she and Julie cut each other's hair. Now she no longer had him to cut her hair. That was also the day that she told me: "To know you is to love the way you look." How I had treasured those words!

Something in me softened. "Look," I said, "I'm really sorry about . . . well, everything."

She reached over and took my hand. "I know," she said quietly. "I know you are. I am, too. It's been awful, but I've survived. I've survived it. Today I just"—she bit her lip, looked as though she were going to cry—"well, I thought I would come and see how you were. I used the excuse of returning your aunt's casserole dish, but it was you I was hoping to see. . . ." She raised her head proudly, struggling with emotions. "When you didn't come to see me, I thought perhaps you had been hurt by all this. Or that maybe *I* had damaged you. I wanted to see for myself that you were all right."

"I'm fine," I said. "Nobody has damaged me."

"Are you sure?" She was beseeching me with her eyes. I knew she was asking more than if I had been damaged. She was asking whether I was still her friend; whether we were going to resume what we had. ("I have a s-selfish reason for hoping you'll st-stay in our lives," he had told me on the night of his death. "S-so that after I disappoint her, she will have s-someone else to transfer her ambitions to. Sissie n-needs that.") I began to have the most terrible fear that out of pity I might pledge myself to something, might promise to go back to her and let her mold my life.

"Honestly, I'm all right," I said, removing my hand from her grasp, pretending I needed it to smooth back my hair. "I'm *fine*. I really am. It's just that I've been busy with school. I just haven't had the time to come over."

Even I could hear the falseness.

"I see," she said, curling her lips in a dry little smile.

We both sat without speaking.

Then she took a deep breath and said, "There is something I would like to explain to you. About Abel . . ."

"I don't want to—" I put my hands to my ears.

"Please. I know you don't feel the same about me anymore, Justin, but I'm not as bad as you think. It was no . . . it was not just a cheap affair. Or even a sudden, thoughtless thing. It has a history. It goes back a long time. Abel once wanted to marry me. We were much younger then, and we were . . . we were already lovers. He was very much in love with me, but I knew Father would never hear of it, and I . . . well, I loved him, too, but I had larger ambitions for myself than just becoming Mrs. Cristiana. But, all the same, I couldn't break with him; there was something irresistible about him. Then Julie found out about it. He was home from Juilliard one weekend, and Abel came over, and they had the most terrible argument. You remember, I told you that they had fought? Well, it was over me. Julie told Abel that it would be a comedown for his sister to marry someone like Abel, and Abel's pride was hurt. So he did something much worse to Julie than beating him up: he told Julie about our mother and Karl. They never spoke again. Abel and I stopped seeing each other, and soon after that he married Adelaide. I thought it would end there. But it didn't. Don't judge too harshly . . . it might happen to you someday. You might find yourself magnetized by someone . . . and not necessarily the most suitable someone. When Julie and I came back here to live after the war, I saw Abel again and knew there was still something between us, but I fought it. My life was devoted to my brother now, and I wanted to keep it that way. I thought I could just . . . smolder in my unrequited passion and nobody, including Abel, need ever know. And I managed, I managed superbly for nine years! Then we had to sell off some land last year, and I had to do the negotiating, because Julie doesn't . . . didn't . . . speak to Abel. One afternoon we met at the hut—Abel wanted to buy the hut and the pond, too. We started talking about it, and I told him I didn't think I could let it go, it was too much a part of me, and then we just . . . well, it was as if someone had thrown a very tiny little match on a pile of dry kindling that had been *longing* to burst into flames." Her hands spread and lifted, describing the inevitable flames. Her cheeks were flushed with her story. Her eyes triumphantly sought mine, expecting me to reward her confession with my understanding.

But I didn't want to understand. I had not known "Abel" when he was young, and there was nothing in the man I knew to convince me he was "irresistible."

And, more than that, this new story of hers contradicted an old story I had liked better.

"I thought you said Marius DeVane was your first love."

For a second she looked as if she couldn't quite remember who "Marius DeVane" was. Then she answered with that breezy nonchalance people adopt when they decide to brazen their way out of a tight spot. "Marius *was* my first love, of course, in the sense that it was all magic and foreign and romantic. . . . God, it was so romantic, up there among our ancestors' ruins . . . and also he was acceptable. Even Julie would have approved of that marriage. That was what I meant when I said he was my first love. But I'm sure I never said he was my first lover."

No, but you said, "The erotic aspect was just . . . well!" and your face flushed exactly the way it did when you were talking about going up in flames with Abel. Were you, by any chance, thinking of Abel when you were entertaining a gullible girl with your story of Marius, last summer?

I said, "Well, that was the impression I got."

Now I just wished she would go.

In that uncanny way of hers, she read my thought. "Ah, Justin, I'm sorry we should end like this. I *have* hurt you, I see that, now. And you aren't going to let me get close enough for it to happen again. Nevertheless, before I go, I do wish you would tell me one thing."

I waited.

"Did you really want to drown when you threw yourself into the pond that night? Was it that bad, discovering Abel and me?"

"To *drown?* What made you think I wanted to drown?"

Her eyes were probing mine. "For the same reason Julie

wanted to die. To punish me. For disappointing him. You did utter that harrowing cry before you hit the water, and I thought . . . I mean, you *never* went in the pond. I assumed you couldn't swim. I thought you were trying to drown yourself . . . because of me."

Oh God, I wanted to scream, *you think you're the center of the universe!*

I said, as calmly as I could, "Of course I can swim. I told you. I've been swimming practically all my life. Don't you remember me telling you that?"

"Yes, but I thought you might have been lying. To save face."

"Not everyone is a liar," I said.

I saw her flinch. But she covered up admirably. She didn't want me to see how much I had hurt her.

"Well, then, my rescue mission was rather wasted, wasn't it?" she said with a little lilt of sarcasm. She squared her shoulders and lifted her chin, and this gesture recalled the old Ursula to me, the Ursula who had always been able to put me on the defensive after I had dared to criticize her. I remembered how it had been to love her.

"I don't know why I jumped in," I said, fighting the impulse to grab at her sleeve, to plead with her to forgive me for that heartless reply. "I still don't understand it. I just sort of . . . went crazy and had to do something. But I didn't want to *drown* myself."

As she stood up to go, she smiled down at me. It was a new kind of smile, not one that emphasized all the ways in which we were alike, but one that acknowledged all the ways in which we were different—and not necessarily to my advantage, either.

"Well, that's one thing off my conscience, anyway," she said.

I walked her to the door. Once, she gave an infinitesimal tilt toward me, and I stopped, thinking she might be going to kiss me; I was going to let her. But I was mistaken. Her eyes were formal, almost hard, when we said good-bye.

That winter, my mother received a flat brown parcel in the mail. It was from Craven Ravenel in Columbia, South Carolina. It turned out to be an old brown photograph, eight by ten, backed by cardboard, and wrapped carefully in lots of newspaper to safeguard its trip through the postal system. My mother scrutinized the picture, puzzled, then uttered a happy exclamation. There was a letter from the sender. He had been designing an addition for an old cottage on Pawleys Island for a client, and had happened to see this photograph, along with some others, on a wall of the cottage. He told his client he recognized the woman and the girl in that picture and thought the girl, who was grown up and widowed now, might like to see that picture. The client made him a present of it.

"That's my mother," my mother said, "and that's her father and his old friend, who was the Lieutenant Governor of South Carolina at the time. And that little blond girl, looking bored, is me. I remember that summer at Pawleys. I was ten. It was the last summer my grandfather was alive. We all went out on this deep-sea fishing boat, and before we left, the captain took our picture. Then we got out in the ocean and I was sick over the rail, but everybody was real sportsmanlike and pretended not to notice, and after that I was all right again. I even caught a big fish. My grandfather had to help me pull it in, though."

"You were exactly my age in that picture," said Becky, studying the face of the girl religiously.

"Charlotte would send her regards if she were here," Craven Ravenel *wrote. "She liked you so much when we met at* My Fair Lady. *But she's on a little junket abroad just now. We are separated, but very amicably. The girls visit back and forth between us. How are your two? I wish that you would write to me and let me know how you are."*

When my mother married Craven, after their long-distance courtship, conducted almost entirely by correspondence, we went to live in Columbia, and in the years that followed I became good friends with Charlotte. I liked her better than her daughters—although they were kind to their stepsister; they both seemed to feel it necessary to compensate for their mother's outspokenness by being as conventional as possible. In a way, Charlotte was like Aunt Mona. They were both women who had gotten married early and then sometime later had decided they had a lot to make up for and couldn't do it and remain the wives their husbands had married. Aunt Mona was trying to make up for not having had advantages in early life. Charlotte was trying to make up for having had too many advantages. They both did well. Aunt Mona made money, and traveled, and eventually bought a charming villa in Provence, where her twenty-years-younger French lover paints his Cézanne-like landscapes and awaits her with his affections and gourmet cooking whenever she can tear herself away from the real-estate business. I have been to stay with them several times, and they are amazingly compatible. He has very good taste in old furniture, and she has given him a free hand in the decoration of the villa. There are no seafoam-green carpets or plastic runners there. Charlotte took a law degree and went in for Legal Aid and liberal politics—to the chagrin of her ex-debutante friends. Although she recently lost in her second try for Congress, she gave her conservative opponent some sleepless nights, and she says she shall continue to "wave her red flag," as she puts it, "in the faces of all those ossified old bulls I can't believe I grew up with."

"You were wearing a red dress the first time I saw you, in the lobby of that theater," I told her on a recent visit. We were sitting on the porch of her farmhouse outside Columbia, sipping vodka tonics; she had been drawing me out in that effortless way she has, making me tell her all kinds of things about my life. "You were a bit formidable."

"Oh, that was my lucky day," she drawled in her merry contralto. "The day Craven discovered his true love was free, and could let me off the hook."

"It couldn't have been *that* simple, Charlotte."

"Honey, I'm not saying it was. Craven admired me quite a lot. He still does. But our personalities were miles apart. I knew after a year of marriage that we probably wouldn't make it to our Golden Anniversary. Craven would be so happy, you know, if he woke up one morning and it was a hundred and fifty years ago. Louise wouldn't be too upset about it, either; especially not if Craven was there. Whereas I would feel *really* inconvenienced if such a nightmare occurred. But Craven and I tried; we worked real hard on our marriage. When we ran into you all at *My Fair Lady*, we had been trying to have ourselves the proverbial second honeymoon, but we were discovering it was just not going to work. Lord, were we *kind* to each other on that trip! What a godsend it was for Craven when Louise just *appeared*, like that; it was exactly the thing he needed to help me convince him to give up on us and let me go off and 'do my own thing,' as the young say now. And things have worked out pretty well for all of us, don't you agree? Your mother and Craven will certainly celebrate their Golden, as surely as they live; and Craven couldn't think more of Jem if he were his own son. And my girls are as proud of you as if you were their blood sister. And look at how my granddaughter Suzie drove up from Randolph-Macon to see you in that play, even though she and her friend could only get standing room. You are Suzie's *idol*. You'll make it easier for her to get out, if she ever needs to."

Yes, Charlotte, things have worked out pretty well for all of *us*.

Maybe it's because things have worked out for me that I have the courage and the desire to go back to those days in Clove. ("It wasn't such a bad time," my mother was to say of it later. "I remember it as a sort of . . . pioneer period in my life. Despite sadness and uncertainty, it was . . . I don't know . . . somehow exciting. Do you remember my job? The only job I ever had? I still remember how proud I was the day Barbara Feldman gave me a raise. Her husband was so pleased with us for not making a profit that year, and he could write the whole thing off on his income tax.")

Maybe it's because I'm more confident of my own powers now, not so afraid of losing myself, of being molded by other people's needs of me, of being overwhelmed by them, that I can live in those strange, green days again and willingly be that girl.

It sends a lusty surge of renewal through me to recall how completely I was able to be charmed and possessed by that woman. Such possessions are rare now. I mean by another person. The only thing that I can rely on to possess me continually with that degree of ardor is my work. Most of the time I consider this a victory. Sometimes, however, it makes me a little sad.

So, here I am, in the middle of my own life, almost the same age she was then. And it has taken me this long to understand that I lose nothing by acknowledging her influence on me. I can ride back and forth on that yellow school bus now, and stare steadily at the windows of that house, eager for clues that will tell me how she is going on. Fall turns to winter; the lamp is already on in the living room as the bus hurries through the afternoon dusk. Then, I was afraid of imagining in too much detail what she might be thinking or feeling or remembering in that house.

Now, my thoughts go forward to meet hers. I know something of life's betrayals and stupidities myself; I know the ashy taste of not living up to some part of your dream. I even know the necessity for making constant adjustments to your life story, so you can go on living in it. She and I would have much to talk about now.

But I also know something else that I didn't know then. As long as you can go on creating new roles for yourself, you are not vanquished. I believe there is quite a good chance that Ursula DeVane, if she is alive today, does not consider herself vanquished.

Now I can say it, despite all that happened: I am glad I knew her. I only wish that she could say the same of me.

THE FINISHING SCHOOL

A Reader's Guide

GAIL GODWIN

A Conversation with
Gail Godwin

Rob Neufeld is the book reviewer for the Asheville Citizen-Times *and director of the program "Together We Read" in North Carolina. At present, he is editing volume one of Gail Godwin's diaries.*

Rob Neufeld: One of the most distinctive features of your writing is that you keep adding layer after layer of history and attitude to your characters and yet somehow manage to maintain the drama. Is this layering a method of yours?

Gail Godwin: The characters and the places have to be as real as possible. I have to know what the characters are seeing and thinking. I end up developing much more than I use, and sometimes I include passages that I later have to take out. When I started *The Finishing School*, I had gotten stuck in the opening on the story of how Justin's grandmother had met her husband. My mother said to me, "I think you need to get back to the drama."

RN: *The Finishing School* is just a little over three hundred pages. That's a nice length for a novel, don't you think?

GG: I wish I could make the novel I'm working on now that length because I love that length. *Father Melancholy's Daughter* was over four hundred pages, but it didn't feel like it. With my Christina stories [autobiographically based stories that have contributed toward *Evenings at Five* and other pieces], I'm building one large work that I'm calling *The Passion of Christina*.

RN: *The Finishing School*, along with *Father Melancholy's Daughter*, are two of the most cohesive yet complex novels I've ever read. There are many great novels that aren't so much of one piece. They have hinges that show. How do you make a long novel that has the continuity of a short tale?

GG: I have been pulling out big chunks of the novel that I'm working on presently—*Queen of the Underworld*—in order to reposition them or break them up into absorbable pieces. My goal in this novel is to sustain three months of the heroine's experience, seeing how her mind works—with no foreshadowing allowed. I want the reader to be there with her. I don't want any sidetracks to slow down the journey, which is very much of-the-moment. Sometimes, I am amazed at how much I discard from my drafts—months of work, including long forays into flashbacks. I ask myself, What is the trajectory I want? Can I put the information across without what Kurt Vonnegut used to call my "sandbagging flashbacks"?

RN: Could you talk a little more about the process by which you maintain continuity?

GG: I make diagrams of my novels with a ruler. I turn a page sideways and write the name of my novel on top. Then, I take a ruler and draw vertical lines to make ten divisions and a horizontal line to make twenty for the number of chapters. I start planning what happens where. If I have a character offstage for too long, I know I have to bring him or her back. I've done this with every novel I've written since *The Perfectionists*. It takes me two, three, or fours years to complete a novel. Over that period, you tend to lose track of things, so you have to keep refreshing yourself. I also write myself blue papers (after the kind of paper I'd once used in my typewriter). They're sermons or pep talks to myself: "Well, Gail, you think you're stuck. Why? You have a party with thirty Cuban exiles at it. What are they doing? You just have to get to the party and start anywhere—with the food, anything." Writing *The Finishing School*, I knew how many chapters it would become because I made notes of which scenes would go where. Since Justin hangs on to Ursula's every word, I knew I could have Ursula dole out her life story in bits anytime anything suggested something.

RN: Are discarded parts the seeds for other novels and stories?

GG: The one I just threw out was based on something that happened to me at St. Genevieve's [school]. It was about trying to talk with Cubans. I was sorry to lose it. It was twenty pages long. Then I thought, This would make another good Christina story.

RN: In the beginning of *The Finishing School*, Justin reveals that Ursula DeVane has "claimed a permanent place in the theater of my unconscious." Theater is an important concept for you. Madelyn Farley, a key character in *Father Melancholy's Daughter*, is a theater designer. Justin Stokes becomes a stage actress. In what ways does the theater of the unconscious resemble theater?

GG: There is a finite stage in the theater of the unconscious. There is a finite number of actors—not fifty, but only five or ten. The story crystallizes into figures of necessity. The drama must be riveting, and the setting has to be a place where you'd want to live for a few hours. Then, there are certain sets that you return to again and again in your imaginative theater, like recurrent dreams. I have Asheville sets. One is St. Mary's [Episcopal Church]. One is St. Genevieve's. They don't represent themselves. They represent points of growth. They stand for attitudes and challenges. You can learn so much from dreams.

[After a couple of moments of silence over the phone]

GG: My cat is vocalizing.

RN: Is that *the* cat [who becomes a protective spirit in *Evenings at Five*]?

GG: That's the cat. I named him Bud in *Evenings at Five* after my friend, a Jungian analyst. The cat's real name is Ambrose.

RN: There's so much fun in the world, isn't there?

GG: I know it!

RN: Later, I'll want to talk about your sense of humor. Now, let's talk about your sense of realism—particularly, how you represent what goes on in people's minds. Aren't people's thoughts at any moment a big mishmash?

GG: Not so much a mishmash. The actual process of thinking has a tempo of its own. It moves very quickly. Try tracing back your present thought to the thoughts that had initially led you to it. At first, you think you've gone through some astonishing non sequiturs, but I believe you'll usually find that they are all ordered in some way. One thing leads to another and you discover patterns. Everyone has his or her very own cloaking pattern. This kind of pattern—which is like storytelling—may involve a tempo, a costume, purposeful omissions, and intuitive progressions. The subconscious is your ally in coming up with fictions.

RN: Ursula DeVane says that her mother haunts her. Is a person's mind a scary thing?

GG: A person's mind is full of ghosts, and the main ghosts have real resonance and real power. They have vibrato. Think of how much you'd know about a person if you knew the main ghosts that haunted him or her.

RN: What kind of an adventure is it to create a character and go into his or her mind? Do you see that as an adventure?

GG: That more than anything else is what keeps me wanting to write—to get to understand the mind of anyone. José Ortega y Gasset calls it transmigration into other souls—seeing a situation from the other's point of view, or trying to. Barbarians don't do it very much. It's hopping into someone else's being and living another life.

RN: On your Web site, under "tips for writers," you suggest that a person write a story first in the style of Ernest Hemingway and then Anton Chekhov. What would it mean to write a story in the style of Gail Godwin? You seem particularly interested in the idea of transmigration. Justin "becomes" Ursula and "becomes" her fourteen-year-old self. Empathy is important to other characters as well. Justin's grandfather "becomes" the slaves.

GG: And the snake!

RN: That's a good trick! At any rate, do you acknowledge that kind of empathy as one of the distinctive features of your work?

GG: Yes. In the novel on which I am now working, *Queen of the Underworld*, the heroine is a young newspaper reporter in Miami, and she's staying in a hotel with Cuban exiles. One of the exiles had been an owner of a sugar plantation, but now he's at the front desk. He doesn't speak much English. It's interesting to notice how being an exile changes the way one moves. Your whole posture changes when you don't speak the language. The reporter then imagines herself in another country as an exile. It's an exercise in empathy for her.

RN: How do you go about becoming someone else?

GG: I usually start with visualization. I see other people—what they're wearing, what their gestures are—going onto a train, going into a restaurant. They're coming in thinking what, I wonder. With Aunt Mona, my first thought was, What kind of person would be the opposite of the kind whom Justin has been raised to admire—someone who is not reserved, who talks all the time about starting with nothing? Then I ask, What would she be like? How would she move, how would she furnish her house? It occurred to me that that character would be Justin's aunt, and Justin would have to go live with her—with a person who would not have been admired in certain circles in Virginia. Then, I had to visualize Aunt Mona—her birdlike qualities, her earrings. At a house I'd visited once, I had seen plastic paths laid down so you wouldn't have to walk on the rug. I thought it was bizarre and touching at the same time because it said, "I'm not used to having things that are expensive." Eventually, I start hitting the levels where I become the person. For example, I see Mona's sterling qualities. She's a fighter and wants to better herself. She's quite generous and warmhearted.

RN: That's a good acting method. Are you an actress?

GG: Robert [the late composer Robert Starer, Gail's companion for many years] told me I was.

RN: At one point Justin says about Becky, "One day . . . I am going to crack the code of Becky." Is Becky's story waiting to be told?

GG: Becky's, no. But there is a certain kind of character who has fascinated me throughout my life—a quiet, inscrutable person who appears to have who-knows-what going on inside. I met a model of this Becky when she was three—and now she's thirty-two. I can see how she's doing.

RN: At the end of The Finishing School, you suggest that having multiple personalities—or at least acknowledging them—is the secret to sanity. Going through transformations and acknowledging multiple personalities makes Justin whole.

GG: Yes, I agree. Justin does keep transforming. Being able to acknowledge having many personalities goes against the picture people have of themselves. The trouble with the phrase "multiple personalities" is that people think of cheap movies. You know, the doctor helps someone get rid of all the personalities except one, and that one survives, and then the person is healthy. We need another phrase. I like to say internal cast of characters.

RN: Can Justin accept the fact that one of her personalities—or internal characters—is a monster and still be okay?

GG: If Justin can recognize that then she'll be able to put it in its place. We all have monsters. Justin's monster is the ability to close down when she feels herself threatened or being turned into something against her will.

RN: Let's talk about how you set the stage for your stories. In The Finishing School, you have a kind of score. Chopin's Scherzo in B-flat minor and Franz Schubert's "Der Doppelgänger" play important parts. How did these pieces come to you?

GG: The most important piece is the one that Julian plays as an all-clear signal. I heard Robert play that, and it's diabolic. It summons trouble. Also, it's very hard to play. Above the sound of gathering force, there's a cascade of relief. I chose it intuitively.

RN: Would you be opposed to the book's being published with a soundtrack?

GG: It should be. My late editor, Alan Williams, when he called me to talk about *The Finishing School*, played the Scherzo and then came on to talk. Music can express many things that words cannot. Do you know the story "The Jolly Corner" by Henry James? A man comes back to New York and haunts his family's town house in order to confront the ghost of who he would have been if he had stayed. James's description of the climactic moment—the meeting of the two—doesn't work. The ghost comes downstairs and he's missing two fingers, which is supposed to represent that he had become a powerful business mogul. Music could have made it work better. For an eerie effect, you could tune violins up one whole tone, for instance.

RN: How have you collaborated with Robert on musical compositions?

GG: We created twelve works together, including operas. *Magdalen at the Tomb* and *Anna Margarita's Will* can be heard through links on my Web site, www.gailgodwin.com.

RN: Transformation is an important theme in your work, and it's an agonizing process for characters. Why is it so hard for people to realize who they're supposed to be?

GG: That's what my new book is about, transformation. The other key word—the heroine's key word in the book—is usurpation. She has gone through her life resisting usurpation. Other people and forces in her life have been trying to usurp her for their own reasons.

RN: Is that what Ursula was doing with Justin?

GG: Yes. Justin was the perfect blank page. Ursula was the most powerful person in her life when she was fourteen. Justin was almost completely drowned in Ursula's personality until she knowingly drowned, in a sense, in that pond. Even then, you could say that Justin has been controlled by Ursula because she was repeating Ursula's betrayal of her mother.

RN: You mark characters' passages with epiphanies. Do you like that term, "epiphany"?

GG: The term was drummed into me at graduate school. It belongs to James Joyce. "Shock of recognition" is good, but we need to come up with our own term. The quickening moment—I like that. It has to do with the speeding up of the story, as well as bringing things to life. The quickening moment for Justin—when everything comes together and comes to a head—is when she dives into that pond. She is, among other things, asserting her ability to swim. She is also trying to protect Ursula from being discovered with her lover.

RN: Just before Justin goes off and instigates the story's big event, she witnesses the demolition of her subdivision's old farmhouse. This leads to her getting angry at her mother for her indifference about this, and that leads to her running off to see the DeVanes. The fall of the farmhouse makes the plot work, but is it also symbolic?

GG: The farmhouse represents the place where Justin could be herself, where she could escape the conformity of her new home. It reminded her of her old home. She had a great need for it. When children who were playing around the farmhouse saw Justin coming, they left the place to her. They recognized a need in her that was so strong, it scared them. It spooked them. The farmhouse is a kind of symbol, but with a good symbol, you never can get to the bottom of it.

RN: There is a lot of humor in your books. Aunt Mona is a hilarious character.

GG: I had one person come up to me once and ask me why I was humorless. I'm not. I'm glad you mention the humor. There are levels of humor, and mine tend to lie in the subtler ranges rather than slapstick. Aunt Mona's funniness comes from her holding on to certain beliefs and habits with great tenacity, so there's a strength to her weakness. You see her asserting herself over and over again in predictable ways. You look forward to her comment, for instance, that things would have turned out differently for her if she had had others' advantages. And the contrast between her own terrible decorating style and her image of herself as someone who can give decorating advice is comical.

RN: That's right. When Mona warms up to Ursula because of Ursula's cultural knowledge, she suggests that she and Ursula might become good friends, and that she might give Ursula some decorating tips. It's very funny.

GG: In the end, though, Aunt Mona is redeemed from being primarily comic. There's a seriousness in that.

RN: People look at your fiction and see that, for instance, the mother characters in the stories are all very different. Yet, they keep wondering about the autobiographical content. How did *The Finishing School* come to light for you?

GG: It came out of Robert's and my experience of living in a 250-year-old Dutch farmhouse when we first lived together in 1973. We were not only thrilled by it, but spooked by it. That whole landscape was waiting to be put into a book. For a long time, I had had the idea of an older sister living with her brother in an old house, and a young woman would get involved. At first, my idea for the story had been melodramatic. The girl would be pregnant and the brother and sister would take her in because they wanted a child. They would have researched bee stings in order to figure out how to get rid of the girl. The other thing that inspired me was hearing Robert play the piano. You could hear him playing in the house when you were on the terrace. I once discussed with Robert the possibility of composing a piece for eleven cellos so that we could hear weird music coming out of the house.

RN: How did you come up with some of the characters' names? Jem is the name of the boy in *To Kill a Mockingbird,* and "Cristiana" suggests Christ, which contrasts with Abel Cristiana's personality.

GG: Jem's short for Jeremy. It's a good Southern name. I have a feeling that the name Jem had floated into my subconscious from *To Kill a Mockingbird.* Perhaps I was trying to give a little homage. Cristiana is a real big name around here—a Huguenot name—and I love it.

RN: Does the cover of the 1999 paperback edition of *The Finishing School* accurately portray the hut and pond scenario? How does it compare to this one?

GG: This new cover is even better. For the previous edition, I had sent a photo of Mohonk for the artist to use. There was no hut in the photo—that was added. This new cover is simply gorgeous, truly strange. You see a window of a hut and you look through it. You then see a vast expanse of field, and you realize that you're not looking out from the inside of the hut, but you're looking in from the outside as if into a vision of a vaster life. It relates to putting yourself in another person's place.

READING GROUP QUESTIONS AND
TOPICS FOR DISCUSSION

1. *The Finishing School* begins, "Last night I dreamed of Ursula De-Vane," which is reminiscent of the beginning of Daphne du Maurier's novel *Rebecca*: "Last night I dreamed of Manderley." Is a dream a good starting point for a story? Imagine one of your own dreams. How would you develop it? How does Godwin proceed? (I count nine different tacks she takes in the first six pages before preparing herself for the mantra "Fourteen. Be fourteen again.")

2. On page 3, the narrator admits, "I won't hire a detective to go in search of a real seventy-year old woman . . . But I will attend to what her image, playing its role in last night's dream, came to tell me." She then refers to the theater of her unconscious, "where each figure—based wholly or in part on some real person—has its function." This is a good time to consider Godwin's cast of characters, chosen for their special roles and symbolic weight. Can you imagine any characters with whom Justin might have engaged but whom Godwin weeded out? Are there any characters she included whom she could have left out?

3. When Aunt Mona dives to pick up a piece of food that Jem, Justin's brother, had dropped at dinner, Justin gives her mother a look to distinguish "Our Way of Life" from "Theirs." You can gain insight into the way of life represented in a novel's universe by asking yourself what the book or its characters have to say about a variety of key topics: religion, politics, the arts and literature, mass media, social class, race, gender, aging, the natural world, human nature, sex, current events, community, crime and punishment, etc.

4. Adolescents do not write many great novels, so we have to trust adults to create adolescent states of mind retrospectively. How accurately does Godwin do it? What aspects of adolescence would an accurate portrait include? How is Justin the same as and different from other adolescents? Review Justin's awareness of and involvement with sexuality, starting with the Cristiana poltroon farm. How many other adolescents are there in the novel (include the young Ursula!), and how do they fill out the picture?

5. When Justin receives her grandmother's pearl necklace, initiating her into womanhood, she muses, "There was a lonely, mysterious side of myself I was just beginning to know, a side neither masculine nor feminine but quivering with intimations of mental and spiritual things." Does the focus on sex stunt other developmental needs in teenagers?

6. There are some good passages for studying the nature of Justin's confusion. On page 79, you read that Justin goes up to the old farmhouse and paints an Ursula-like figure whom she then consults as an oracle. Upon returning home and being swallowed by circumstances there, her painted figure begins to look like one of the mindless milkmaids on her wallpaper—her newly forming self, she thinks. Can a person see his or her fate? How clearly does Justin do so?

7. Also, look at page 99. Justin senses the magic of her visit to the DeVanes draining from her as Aunt Mona defends her. How many people are fighting for Justin's allegiance? Who is Justin if she is not any of the people others think she is? On page 105, Justin thinks she might be a monster manipulating others in order to get her mother to move back to Virginia. Could she be a monster? Where does her goodness lie? This is a question that the grown-up Justin asks on page 106 as she looks back at her fourteen-year-old self. Why does she say, at this point, that she needs to go back and claim the girl she had been?

8. Make a list of the music cited in the novel, get the recordings, and play them. How do they affect your experience of reading and remembering the novel, if at all?

9. Satire lovers, how much satire can you take? How much satire is there in *The Finishing School*? Does it serve its role well? Would you want more? If there were more, how would that change the novel? Can you think of a novel that has a lot more satire in it? What is that novel missing that *The Finishing School* has. Look at the first instance of satire in *The Finishing School*, on pages 23 through 35. (Also, see other satiric passages on pages 146, 200–201, 213–16, 265, and 269–70.) No-

tice how Godwin introduces Aunt Mona's household—with a seemingly banal conversation that, nonetheless, introduces a lot of information and thematic notes.

10. We know that when Godwin introduces a subplot or anecdote, it has a double edge. For example, late in the book, Ursula makes Justin question the admirability of her grandfather's statement about his wife—"the only woman . . . who would behave exactly the same way if nobody were looking." Note the subplots in the novel and puzzle over their double meaning. You can start with the story of how Justin's mother had eloped (pages 32–33).

11. If you were to write a story in the manner of Gail Godwin, what would be the features you would include? In the preceding interview, Godwin says that one of her major motivations for writing is to understand what goes on in others' minds. In what ways is empathy an active attribute of Godwin's characters as well as of herself as narrator?

12. How do characters who are good at empathy fare and how do ones who are not? Look at Aunt Mona and the wallpaper and curtains she puts in Justin's room as an act of empathy. Look at Justin's mother and judge whether she is indeed to be condemned for not knowing her daughter's mind. Look at Ursula and her uses of empathy. Rate characters on their levels of empathy. See if you agree with your fellow readers.

13. In representing characters' states of mind, Godwin does not stick to linear narrative. How would you represent a character's mental activity? (Try tracking your own.) Find a passage in which Godwin uses flashbacks, reflections, wishes, and actions to dramatize a character. Do you find this exciting? Pleasing? If you take out everything but the drama, with what do you end up, greater or lesser suspense?

14. Justin moves from a Virginia town to an upstate New York one. Godwin lives in New York State, but grew up in the South. Is she a Southern writer? Does her writing have Southern qualities, or does she represent the South in her work? (See page 65.)

15. How would you interpret the dream about the magician and the grass-overgrown house on page 43?

16. Look at a passage of dialogue—pages 53 through 56, for instance. What are the dynamics? Godwin lets you examine how people jockey for position through their conversation, no matter how light it is. How do they do so in this passage? Justin's mother tells the story

about Justin's experience at a riding stable. The owner advises Justin to let the horse know who's boss, and Justin replies, "Oh, he already knows, sir." As with horses, so with people, no?

17. Somehow, you're going to have to deal with the character of Abel Cristiana. Try to remember as many things as you can about him. Is he a bully? (See page 205.) Why is Ursula attracted to him? What do you make of his World War II experiences (page 66)?

18. Godwin says that she keeps track of her characters so that no major character ends up sitting offstage too long. After a while, a character has to assert him- or herself. When and how does Justin's mother assert herself? Does she assert herself enough? See Chapter IV, for instance.

19. Would you call *The Finishing School* a symbolic novel? For instance, there are the birthday presents Justin gets—the blue bottle (from Ursula) and her grandmother's pearl necklace (from her mother). These are intentionally symbolic items. What about dream symbolism? Finally, what about the symbolism of actual things, such as the demolished farmhouse and the murky pond? Don't be literary, be real. Does symbolism have an effect on people's lives?

20. What's the deal with Ursula's first lover, the European with the same family name? Does the DeVane family have a condition, inflicted by history? What does Justin mean, on page 198, when she says that dining with the DeVanes was like "being abducted into a community of ghosts"? How does this aspect of the story compare to Edgar Allan Poe's "Fall of the House of Usher"?

21. Mr. Mott, as a character, comes to life late in the book. Did you dismiss him as an uninteresting character at first? Do you believe that any character—or person—can make an interesting subject for a story? What might be interesting about Joan Dibble?

22. Chapter VII is a good chapter to look at to see how Godwin uses foreshadowing (see pages 166 and 171). Grown-up Justin returns to the scene of the "crime" and gives hints about things to come. Why does Godwin leave the big revelation until the end—for just dramatic reasons? Is it so terrible that Justin can't admit it? What might be the parts that Justin can't bring herself to admit?

23. Have you ever known a brilliantly manipulative person? What techniques did he or she use? Does Ursula use those tricks? Can you be attracted to such a person and hold your own?

24. Writing experts say that the most important element in a story is voice, and that the most important element in voice is authority. You've got to believe and trust your main speaker. But what if there is more than one main speaker? Do any voices compete with Justin's for authority? What other voices made an impression on you in *The Finishing School*? Ursula takes over the first-person voice for a good portion of Chapters IX and X. How would it be if she had narrated the novel? Where do you think she ended up?

25. Do you agree with Ursula's need for perpetual youth and her motto, "As long as you yearn, you can't congeal"?

26. On page 245, Ursula confesses to Justin that her mother haunts her and she feels condemned to relive her mother's life. Is this a common condition, being haunted and falling into a fateful pattern? Can you see it in yourself? Does *The Finishing School* give us warnings about what may happen to us, or models on how people break away from such influences?

27. Does Godwin draw special significance from the double meaning of the word "finishing" in "the finishing school"?

28. Starting on page 289, when Justin considers how she might have responded differently than she did to Julian's despairing talk, do you see any paths for her other than the one that the plot (fate?) requires?

ERIC RASMUSSEN

Gail Godwin is the three-time National Book Award nominee and bestselling author of eleven critically acclaimed novels, including *A Mother and Two Daughters, Violet Clay, Father Melancholy's Daughter,* and *Evensong.* She has received a Guggenheim Fellowship, a National Endowment for the Arts grant for both fiction and libretto writing, and the Award in Literature from the American Academy and Institute of Arts and Letters. She has written libretti for ten musical works with the composer Robert Starer. Currently she is writing her twelfth novel, *Queen of the Underworld.*

Visit her Web site at www.gailgodwin.com.

"[A] tender story of a relationship that defies the grave."
—*The New York Times Book Review*

EVENINGS AT FIVE
A novel and five stories
by GAIL GODWIN

Every evening at five o'clock, Christina and Rudy began the ritual commonly known as Happy Hour, sharing drinks along with a love of language and music (she is an author, he a composer, after all), a delight in intense conversation, a fascination with popes, and nearly thirty years of life together. Now, seven months after Rudy's unexpected death, Christina reflects on their vibrant bond—with all its quirks, habits, and unguarded moments—as well as her passionate sorrow and her attempts to reposition herself and her new place in the very real world they shared.

Published by Ballantine Books
Now available in paperback wherever books are sold

The Guide's inside, so it's perfect for your reading group.
www.BallantineBooks.com/BRC